THE LEGEND OF
BAHIRJI-NAIK

A good spy is known by his successes. A better spy is known by his failures. But of the best spy, nothing is known at all. Anon

A spy should be a cook, a spreader of bed, water servant, hump-backed person, a dwarf, a pigmy, the dumb, the deaf, the idiot, the blind artisans such as actors, dancers, singers, players on musical instruments, a buffoon and a bard. Kautilya, *Arthashastra*

THE LEGEND OF
BAHIRJI-NAIK

RAIDERS OF SURAT

BOOK I

SHREYAS BHAVE

Leadstart

ISBN: 978-81-948043-8-3

Graphics and Cover design: Kitsune
Horsemen illustration & maps: TejoOo - Sheshagaoni Tejoguna
Layout: Kshitij Dhawale, Leadstart
Printing: Thomson Press

Published in India 2022 by **Leadstart**
A Division of One Point Six Technologies Pvt Ltd
Unit 25/26, Building A/1, Wadala (East)
Mumbai 400 037, Maharashtra, INDIA
T + 91 96 99933000 **E** info@leadstartcorp.com
W www.leadstartcorp.com

To Priyanka Kawale

About the Author

SHREYAS BHAVE, an Electrical Engineer from VNIT Nagpur, is one of India's youngest experts on railway electrification. He also administers an entrepreneurial YouTube channel at 'Our First Million'. Possessed of an abiding love for history, Shreyas was first inspired to take on the challenge of writing a fictionalized account based on historical record supplemented by the rich folklore that surrounded the legendary figure of *Asoka*. The trilogy was released to widespread acclaim and has been acquired for screen. His book *Prisoner Of Yakutsk*, a modern day thriller based on the mystery surrounding the disappearance of Netaji Subhash Bose, was published in 2019. The present book is the first in the trilogy based on the thrilling adventures of Chhatrapati Shivaji's intelligence duo, Bahirji-Naik (see Author's Note).

Apart from writing, Shreyas enjoys song-writing, composing music, sketching and watercolour painting. He plays the guitar and enjoys hiking up to the many hill forts of Maharashtra, replete with their hoary history and ghosts from the past.

Other books by Shreyas Bhave
Prince Of Patliputra
Storm From Taxila
Nemesis Of Kalinga
Prisoner Of Yakutsk

Contents

Author's Note

HAVING WRITTEN ABOUT THE ANCIENT MAURYAN EMPIRE in the *Asoka Trilogy*, the large question confronting me was how to choose the next historical tale to take on. Various characters, long gone, suddenly raised their heads from my years of book reading and events imagined, vying for attention and seeking a voice to tell their tales. The din was deafening. I had, however, set down a few rules regarding the kind of historical fiction I wanted to write, which inevitably made the selection even trickier.

The first rule was that the central figure had to be relevant in the minds of people today. It had to be a well-known figure from history/mythology. At the same time, there needed to be adequate blank spots into which I could weave my story. There is little author delight in writing about a character/event that is so minutely documented that one ends up writing a historical report instead of a fictional tale. Little did I know that the idea for my next book, which ticked all these boxes, lay hidden in one of my favourite and most admired figures of Maratha history.

There have been few rulers in the composite story of our world who have had as exciting a life as the Maratha ruler, Chhatrapati Shivaji Maharaj. There have been many books written on his life, such as *Shivaji: His Life and Times* by Gajanan Mehendale, and *Shivaji, The Grand Rebel* by Dennis Kincaid. In my own mother tongue, Marathi, there are treasure troves filled with gems such as *Raja Shiv Chhatrapati* by Babasaheb Purandare, to *Shakakarte Shivray* by Vijay Deshmukh. Every Marathi child grows up listening to the adventures of this great ruler and there is little doubt that the desire to write about him lay nestled in my mind from when I was a little boy.

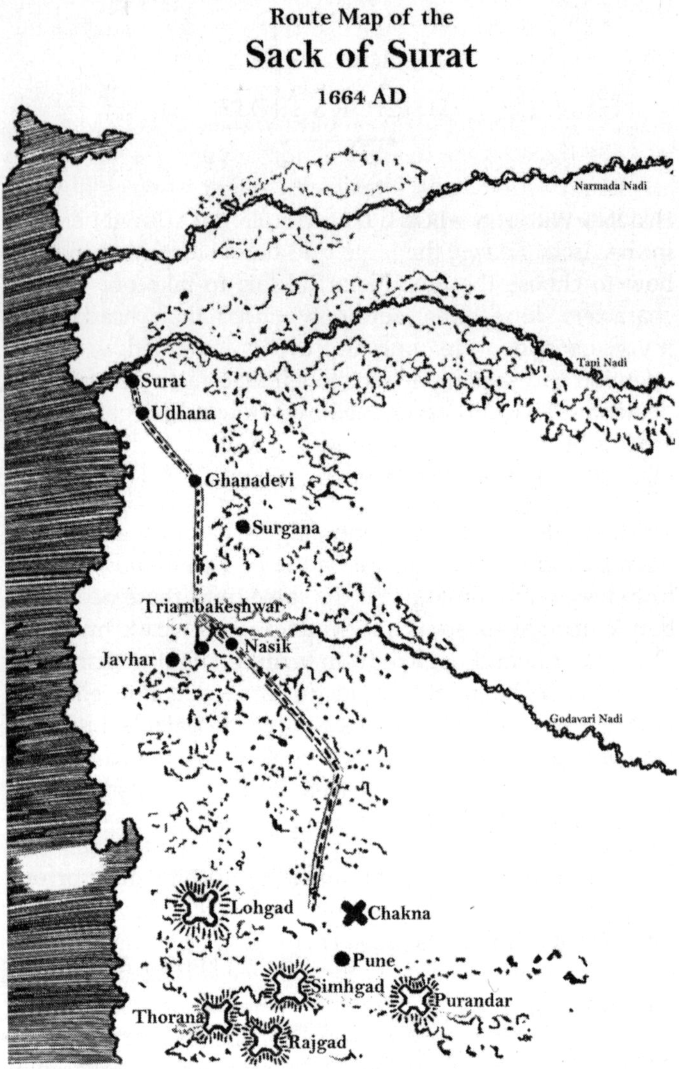

ROUTE TAKEN TO SURAT BY THE MARATHA FORCES

However, the history of the Maratha Swarajya is quite recent, having occurred in the 17th Century. Writing about modern history creates certain problems as it is firmly rooted in text books and contemporary accounts, and the liberties that can be taken by a fiction author are harder to find. Knowing that many books had already been written about Shivaji Maharaj, and one more by me would not add anything significant to an already laden shelf, I realized I ought to write about a character through whom I could explore the same period - the rise of the Marathas.

There are no historical accounts about the mysterious figure of Bahirji Naik. No records of him exist anywhere. It is as though he never existed at all. What is also surprising is that this lacuna exists at a time when record-keeping was an accepted way of life. Even letters written by Shivaji Maharaj in his own hand are available in museums and at his family estates. But Bahirji's existence is as ephemeral as the winter mists in the Sahyadris. However, we do know he existed, from the hundreds of stories told about him in the oral bard tradition. No boy who knows of Shivaji Maharaj, does not also know the name of Bahirji, the *Guptachar* (Intelligence Chief/Spy) of the first Maratha kingdom. So, zeroing in on Bahirji Naik was my way of not only bringing this tantalizing person to life, but also explaining the great events in the life of Shivaji Maharaj.

There are four main events in the life of Shivaji Maharaj which legend claims Bahirji Naik played an important role in. The first was the Siege of Panhala Fort in 1660, when Raje escaped an iron-grip encirclement by the massive Adilshahi forces sent to force his surrender.

The second was the Battle of Umberkhind in 1661, when a very small Maratha contingent defeated a large Mughal force in a narrow mountain pass in the Sahyadris. The third was the raid on the Mughal economic stronghold of Surat, in 1664 - one of the greatest surgical strikes ever pulled off in history. And the fourth was Raje's famous escape from Aurangzeb's court in Agra, in 1666.

I decided to begin my trilogy about this famous Guptachar with the raid of Surat, and then covering the other events in the subsequent books of the trilogy.

Just as Bombay is a character in many Bollywood movies, I wanted to give the same position to the city of Surat, in this book. It really was the Bombay of those times, when the Bombay of today still did not yet exist. I perused many books to understand how the city ate, drank and breathed during the period of the story. One of the books without which this one could not have been possible, is a treasure in the Archaeological Library of India, titled *Surat in the Seventeenth Century* by Balkrishna Govind Gokhale. A shorter, invaluable research paper I reviewed was 'Trade History of Surat' by Sagufta Parveen. Other valuable resources were the documents left by the English, among them a diary titled, *English factories in Surat* by Charles Fawcett. All these early recordists helped me set the stage.

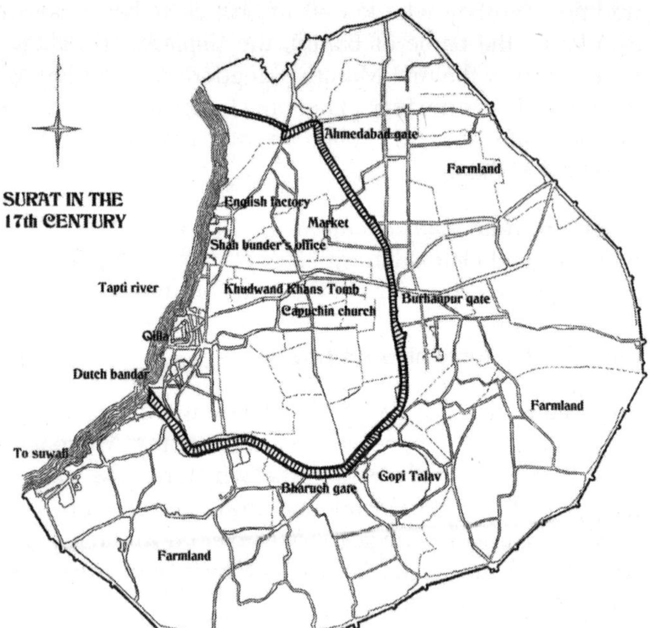

The locations in Surat which I have used in this book, are in fact, places that existed at the time of Shivaji, and still exist to this day. You can visit them in the 21st Century and imagine how the Marathas must have felt walking the same streets in 1664. From the banyan tree near the famous Gopi Talav, to the Maqbara of Khawaja Sulemani aka Khudwand Khan (erstwhile founder of the city), I have tried to maintain authenticity in descriptions.

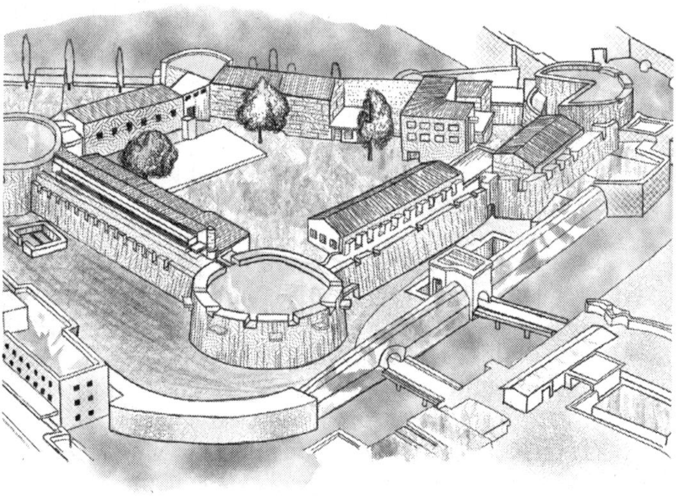

SURAT FORT

Surat Qilla is described exactly as it was in those times, its original architecture preserved even today. A sketch of it has been provided for the reader's clearer understanding. I wrote these chapters after visiting the fort.

Of the other locations in the story outside Surat, Rajgad Fort is one that is close to my heart as I have visited it on several occasions in pilgrimage, from my childhood. The sprawling *machis*, the Balekilla, and Padmavati Lake, described in the story, are all real.

With the stage set, we come to the characters of the tale.

One of the unique things about my portrayal of the famed Guptachar is that I early on decided to split the famous persona into two people. When I began writing, I realized that I had the creative liberty to create this split since no proof of Bahirji having lived actually existed. So if I was writing a story about a historically non-existent character, thereby breathing life into him, I could as well make him two persons rather than one. Also, the events and exploits of Bahirji, retold orally, tell of how he could be in two places at once, and had mastery of numerous arts. This made me realize that the character of Bahirji, as described in legend, had been bestowed with almost superhuman qualities and abilities. To bring some credibility to the character, I thought of splitting him into two people with complimentary qualities as well as human failings, making them more real and believable. Thus I ventured forth where historians fear to tread, creating the twin characters of Bahirji Bandal and Sadashiv Naik, the duo known as Bahirji-Naik.

Another important character is Shivaji Maharaj himself. There is ample evidence to prove that until his coronation in 1674, the 'Maharaj' suffix to his name was not used. People fondly called him Shivaji Raje, and this is the style I have used. The English spelt his name as *Sevagee* in their documents, so I have used the same in the mouths of the English characters in the book, to conserve authenticity. The Mughals often demeaned him by calling him 'Siva' or 'Siva, the Mountain Rat', and so do the Mughal characters in the book.

Any book on Surat would be incomplete without the Merchant Prince Virji Vora. This illustrious man, one of the most successful merchants of the time, went by many names and backstories. There have been doubts regarding his religion as well as his names. Documents refer to him variously as 'Bahirji Bohra', a Bohra Musalmaan, to 'Virji Vora' a Swetambara Jain. I have taken the same view of Vora and his lineage as Gokhale did in his book, *Surat in the Seventeenth Century,* in which he dedicates an entire chapter to Vora. The deals Vora made with the British and how he pressurized other merchants for commercial gain, is historically mentioned in many sources. It is through these accounts that we know that before the British became masters of the subcontinent, men like Virji Vora lorded over them.

The talk of the British presence brings us to the character of George Oxenden, one of the men who rose to fame in the first Surat raid. His stalwart defense of English property during the raid won him praise back home, as well as tariff concessions from Agra. However, Oxenden was known to be a shrewd Englishman and was certainly neck deep in Surti politics when the raid took place. It would be foolish to imagine the Marathas let him go without touching him.

Now we come to the actual sack of the city. Many aspects of how it was carried out are historical. The four-day span is also historically accurate. The events are as described in the records. However, the way in which those events are brought about is fictional. As is my literary wont, I wished to keep the historical facts of the event while weaving my magic fabric in the spaces between them.

The creative liberties I have taken need to be mentioned at this juncture. As an author, these liberties were necessary to complete some character arcs, but I made sure I could support such liberties with effective arguments. By all accounts, Inayat Khan's son did not die during the raid but was in the fort for the entire duration. There is mention of an incident after the raid, when he kills a farmer who throws a ball of mud at his father's entourage. The storyline of the gold bullion was an interesting plot element inserted by me into the story. There have been accounts of huge amounts of such treasure being discovered during the raid, the origins of which remain known. And, it is said, there is nothing more attractive to a writer of fiction than the word 'unknown.'

Also, there is no proof that Haji Kasim died in the raid, but again, nowhere it is mentioned that he did not. There are several opinions about whether ships were brought to Surat by the Marathas. One group suggests there were no ships and the spoils of the raid were carried away entirely on horseback. Another group says there were indeed ships, which sailed through the Suwali river mouth, and some of the loot, especially the gold bullion, was loaded onto these crafts. I have woven the narrative of my story to satisfy both these schools of thought.

The rampant corruption in the Mughal Empire, especially in the person of Inayat Khan, is evident in his cowardly action of hiding in the fort while the Marathas looted his town. He later faced strict action in Agra for his unmanly behavior. But his corruption was largely unchecked till the disaster of the raid. By showing the happenings in Surat in parallel to the actions of the Guptachars, I wished to stress how corrupt the Mughal cities were at the time and how different was the Maratha Swarajya that Raje Shivaji was trying to build, in comparison.

There are many streams of thought regarding the period of the Maratha Swarajya. People have strong opinions about how the events occurred, and the personalities involved. Without bias, I have coloured each character as I saw him, from whatever historical references I could obtain. For example, contemporary accounts say that Netoji Palkar constantly challenged Shivaji's decisions, and that Anthony Smith was an untrustworthy bastard of a man. But given the sensitivity attached to various opinions, I hasten to mention that all the personalities in the book can be considered fragments of my own imagination, with an equal possibility they were nothing like what I have shown, or were in fact exactly so.

The characters of Shashidhwaj, Vichitra, Samsher Ali, Hatim, Muhabbat Khan, and Fatima, are fictional. However, the other characters who support them, like Inayat Khan, Moropunt, Netoji Palkar, and Prataprao Gurjar, Nanaji Deshmukh, George Oxenden, Anthony Smith, Virji Vora, Haji Kasim and Haji Sayyid Beg, are all actual figures from history.

As one book ends, another begins. After the end of this book we are ready to move towards the attack of Jaysingh on the Swarajya, which paves the way for Raje's visit to Agra, where we see the character of Shashidhwaj come of age as a Maratha Guptachar. The Surat mission was a covert operation entailing direct action by the main men, but in Books II and III, the reader learns more about how the Guptachar organization functioned. There are also pending origin stories about how Bahirji and Naik came into Raje's fold, which are explored in the next books, as are the stories of the Siege of Panhala, and the epic Battle of Umberkhind.

Finally, I have tried to put forward how these four great events in Shivaji's life occurred, and how he built strong systems like his Guptachar network, which enabled him to lay the foundations of a kingdom that survived his untimely demise and went on to topple the seat of Mughal power, when Bajirao I captured Delhi. And as history has shown countless times in the past, before every Bajirao there was a Shivaji to lay the groundwork. And behind every Shivaji there were countless Bahirjis and Naiks.

CHRONOLOGY OF EVENTS DESCRIBED IN THIS BOOK

I. April 1663: Raid on Shaistekhan

II. 6th January 1664: The Maratha army reaches Surat

III. 10th January 1664: The Maratha army leaves Surat

Cast of Characters In Chronological Order

SHASHIDHWAJ: A simple, orphaned cowherd, whose only life is grazing the local *zamindar*'s cattle in the hills near his village, until he meets two illustrious people on the slopes of the Katraj Hills. Thereafter, his life spins into a series of adventures and intrigues. But can young Shashidhwaj take all that life throws at him? Can he make the tough decisions required of him? Or are his youth and innocence his undoing?

BAHIRJI BANDAL: Generally supposed to be Raje Shivaji's *Pramukh Guptachar* (Head of Intelligence). Origins unknown. Current location unknown.

SADASHIV NAIK: Thought to be Raja Shivaji's *Pramukh Guptachar*. Origins unknown. Current location unknown.

SAMSHER ALI: An upstart bandit roaming the streets of Surat, looking for easy game; open to any gainful challenge. A man of rich lineage, he has fallen on hard times. What happens when he meets the mysterious Master, who holds the key to his past, but will only part with it if Ali is prepared to make a great sacrifice?

THE MASTER: A mysterious man in a black cloak and iron mask, whose influence is evident in every dark niche of Surat's underbelly. What does Ali have that he desires?

RAJE SHIVAJI: An upstart Maratha Chieftain with ambitions as high as the sky and a mind as sharp as the edge of his *Bhavani* sword. But, following constant attacks by Mughal *Sardars* on his *subhas* and *parganas*, his meagre

Swarajya is in shambles, and his companions begin to lose faith. Will Shivaji rise again from these depredations to assert his dominance, or will the hand of fate erase his name from the pages of history?

NANAJI DESHMUKH: Shivaji's former Chief Guptachar, who also served Shivaji's father, Shahaji Raje. Now an old but much experienced man, he spends his days on Rajgad Fort, teaching youngsters sword fighting and archery. But is this his true vocation or merely a cover for something entirely different?

MOROPUNT PINGLE: Chief Advisor to Shivaji, he is an astute Brahmin with a sharp tongue and quick wit. Has performed the *Vakil*'s role for his Raje countless times. But now, in these dark times, with enemies growing all around them, will he remain loyal, or reconsider his position and allegiance?

HAJI SAYYID BEG: A rich merchant of Surat, he has a large house beside the English Factory, near the river. All seems to be going well for this Mughal trader as he enters his fiftieth year. But is turbulence about to rock his placid, prosperous world?

VIRJI VORA: With long flowing white hair and deep lines across his forehead, he is undisputedly the most powerful merchant in Surat. He believes that not a leaf falls from a tree in Surat without his knowledge. But what business does he have with Surat's devious Qilladar? What role does Vora play in the internal politics of this crooked city? And how does he deal with the situation when the whole sky comes crashing down?

HAJI KASIM: A young, upcoming trader in Surat, and Vora's main rival, with whom he competes for monopoly of the English and Dutch trade. He is known for his fascination with foreign wines and dancing girls. Word on the street has it that he deals not only in exotic goods, but exotic flesh. Will his sins come to haunt him when chaos descends on Surat? Can he win or will he be yet another victim in his devious rival's path?

INAYAT KHAN: Subhedar of Surat, appointed by *sanad* from Agra, under the seal of Diwan-i-Ala, he is a man more interested in safeguarding his own future and riches than serving the Mughal Empire. Will his schemes lead him to astounding wealth, or merely his downfall?

MUHABBAT KHAN: Firstborn son of Inayat Khan, appointed *Qilladar* of Surat through strings pulled and hands greased in Agra by his father, he performs the dirty deeds on his father's behalf. Involved in everything from smuggling to making their enemies disappear, he is about to pull off the biggest deal of all for his father. Will he succeed, or drag his father down with him as he falls?

SIR GEORGE OXENDEN: Born in Kent, he was the First Governor of the Bombay Presidency, and is now the President and Chief Director of all English affairs in Surat. He supervises all English factory holdings in northern India, and from Ceylon to the Red Sea, reporting directly to the Directors of the East India Company. He is a new arrival in Surat and has just begun to establish his influence. He is as tenacious as an English bulldog. But when the strong winds blow, can he hold his ground, or will he be uprooted in the ensuing chaos?

ANTHONY SMITH: A Scottish Highlander by birth, he is tall and broad shouldered. He is Oxenden's right hand man in Surat, for both official and unofficial business. But will he prove to be the rock Oxenden requires in order to survive in a sea of treachery?

NETOJI PALKAR: He is called Prati-Shivaji by the common folk because of his marked similarity to Raje. The recent mishaps in the Swarajya have served to raise doubts in his mind regarding his master's ability to succeed. Will he attempt to take over, or will the charisma of Shivaji make him bend the knee once again?

PRATAPRAO GURJAR: A nobleman from Bhosare, near Satara, he serves Raje without question. A loyalist, he speaks with his sword and thinks with his heart.

FATHER AMBROSE: Chief of the Friars Minor Capuchin in Surat, he is a missionary with a personal mission. But is the mission that dwells in his heart spreading the word of God, or accumulating the gold of man?

MOHANDAS PAREKH: A *baniya* dealer for Dutch tradesmen, he has established a firm foothold for Dutch trade in Surat, and is a persistent thorn in the sides of both Oxenden and Vora. A man with Dutch friends and dangerous enemies.

FATIMA: An orphaned dancing girl of foreign origin, serving in the house of the rich merchant Haji Kasim, no one knows her real name. Because of her yellow skin and narrow brown eyes, people claim she hails from the lands of Yunnan. Word on the street is that, though barely of age, she is more than a dancer in Kasim's household. What happens when she meets Shashidhwaj and sees a spark of goodness in a city as bent as the butcher's hook? Can love endure the storm?

Prologue

CITY OF SURAT,
SECOND NIGHT OF THE SACK

From his precarious perch, Ali could feel the city burn. The blazing flames that engulfed the low buildings reached up beyond the rooftops and lit up the night sky. Ali's fingers curled tighter around the rope he clung to. *I am hanging against a stone wall with nothing but a rope to hold me!* As the realization of sudden death dawned on him, his heart began to thump in his chest. His eyes suddenly seemed to lose focus and the scene they gazed upon spiralled into his mind, spinning around like a flaming dervish. Ali tried to swallow but his throat felt parched, his mouth dry of moisture. He breathed in hard but all he took in was smoke; all he tasted was fear.

'Careful, Rayiyas! It's a long fall,' the man below him cautioned as Ali prepared to climb up the wall, the rope clutched between his hands. Heaving strongly, he managed to hoist himself onto the tiled roof, landing on his chest, his legs dangling. He crawled forward, clutching at the tiles that rattled at his frantic touch. At his side, the rope became taut again as the man behind him began to pull himself up. Ali rose carefully to his knees on the sloped roof from which the chimney rose behind him, and stretched down his hand towards the next climber.

Hatim, the man who grabbed his hand and struggled up awkwardly, looked relieved to have found solid footing on the roof. Panting, he leaned against the chimney and watched as Ali helped the other men climb up, one by one.

'Just one alley away now, Rayiyas,' he finally said, addressing Ali with the ancient term for 'Master', as the last of the dozen men appeared on the roof.

Ali retreated from the ledge, wiping the sweat dripping into his eyes like stinging drops of bitter lemon, from his forehead. He nodded at Hatim's words, then turned to gaze down at the dark street below. How he longed to cover this last stretch to their target walking erect. Alas, it was impossible. There were raiding Marathas everywhere in the city tonight.

'Do you think anyone saw us?' Hatim whispered, watching Ali scan the alleys carefully.

'If they did, we'll soon know.'

The other soldiers around them adjusted the scabbards on their backs, dislodged by the arduous climb. The lanes below appeared unearthly and still, the cackle of the encroaching flames swallowing every other sound like some primeval beast.

Ali watched one of his men pull up the rope that snaked limply to the ground. When the knotted end of it appeared, Ali freed the other end from the chimney to which it had been anchored with a hook, and quickly coiled it again, feeling the weight of the hook as he took hold of the looped coil in one hand. Turning, he looked towards the main street, where the fire raged with the greatest ferocity, spreading from house to house on both sides, like an onrushing river of flame. Ali sighed as his gaze fell upon the three untouched houses that separated their destination from the onrushing flames. The church spire towered high above them, with the bell tower below.

'We don't have much time,' Hatim urged, his voice hoarse with worry. The men lined up behind him, ready to move on.

Ali paid no heed. Grasping the rope just below the metallic hook, he took aim. Ignoring the irritated grunts from Hatim by his side, he took his time and then, with a swing of his hand, threw the rope, feeling every muscle in his shoulders begin to burn as if on fire, as the hook snaked through the flaming night. It collided with its intended destination with a crash they could not hear because of the roaring fire. The hook broke into the bell enclosure and locked on the metallic grating. The bowl of the bell moved from the impact and a mournful toll filled the air.

Ali handed the rope to Hatim. 'We go one by one,' he told his men, his voice hard and decisive.

Hatim quickly secured the rope, wrapping it around the chimney several times. When he was done, he looked up, hot and sweaty from the effort.

Ali took hold of the rope first, looking ahead towards the church. The spire was a lurid red against the dark sky; the buildings ablaze around it; the flames leaping towards it like the fangs of a dozen serpents. Clenching his jaw, Ali lifted his legs till his ankles were crossed over the rope and he hung from it like a trussed animal over a fire. He felt every muscle in his body protest as he moved forward, one fist over the other. His heart hammered in his chest as he moved beyond the safety of the roof and found himself hanging precariously over the dark alley below. He did not look down, keeping his eyes on the brick wall of the church, which drew closer with each pull forward.

Halfway, the rope suddenly moved. Ali looked up quickly and saw the hook on the grating move and slip. His body became taut, expecting to be hurtled downwards. But his luck held one more time, for the hook caught again in the outer grating. Ali clung to the oscillating rope for dear life.

When the rope finally stopped moving, Ali moved forward again. *Allah smile upon me,* he prayed as he neared the brick wall. *Grant me success in my task this night.* When the bell tower railing was but an arm's length away, he lunged forward with hand outstretched and caught hold of it. He hung on for a moment, drawing a shaky breath, before climbing up and collapsing onto the cold stone floor of the bell tower. It felt soothing amid the heat all around. But he rose quickly, knowing time was running out. He pulled on the rope hard, testing it, but the hook did not move. It rested securely on the iron grating like it was meant to be there. Ali smiled as he stared at it. I *too, was born to be here tonight,* he thought. All his life Allah had prepared him for this moment.

Ali looked back across the dark alley over which he had made his perilous crossing, and signalled. He watched intently as the next man swung onto the rope, hanging below it with clutching hands and crossed feet. Ali drew his sword and moved away from the bell towards the wrought iron staircase. The steep steps spiraled down to the church below. His heart beat quickly with each step. *May all this effort not be in vain,* he prayed.

At the bottom of the stairs, he found himself in a small gallery above the altar. As his eyes adjusted to the dim light, his vision began to clear. Ali closed his eyes, suddenly hesitant to come upon the moment of reckoning with undue haste, for what he would now see in front of him would decide whether all his effort to reach this place had been in vain, or if he had been rewarded for his faith. Ali took a deep breath and opened his eyes. As he peered over the low railing and gazed downward into the church, he saw row upon row of barrels where there should have been pews. There were barrels to the left, barrels to the right. All he could see was barrels receding into the darkness.

As Ali heard a thump above him, signalling the next man had arrived, he smiled. All his hard work had been rewarded. Allah had indeed blessed him. Now all he had to do was escape the city, taking what he had wanted from the start.

SURAT FORT, SECOND NIGHT OF THE SACK

The city burned bright, lighting up the dark starry sky. The flames leapt as high as the spires of the Capuchin Church, devouring the nearby brick buildings like an angry Fire God unleashing his fury on the earth. The same fire burned in the eyes of Virji Vora, as the yellow light danced on the contours of his freckled face. He stood as still as a rock on the ramparts of the fort, gazing towards the horrendous spectacle.

'You shouldn't be standing here, Shethji,' a voice said from behind him, moving towards him through the narrow corridor that travelled along the battlements of the fort. 'One stray enemy arrow landing here would render futile all the mahmudis you paid my esteemed father, to ensure your safety here tonight.'

Vora did not need to turn to know who spoke. Only one person in all Surat possessed that deep, arrogant voice. Despite all the troubles that had befallen him in the last few days, Muhabbat Khan, Qilladar of Surat, had not learnt humility.

'No, we should not be standing here,' Vora agreed. 'We should be out in the streets, teaching those dacoits a lesson. Even an old fool like me.'

'Anger does not become the wrinkles on your face.' Muhabbat Khan strode forward and placed both his heavy arms on the battlements. He stood over six foot tall and his chest and head were clearly visible above the battlements. His rough beard flowed down over his chest, and his face was shadowed in the darkness above the flickering flares of the *mashaals* fastened to the outer walls.

'No, anger does not become me,' Vora agreed, glancing briefly at the man beside him. 'Nor does inaction become your masculine attire, Qilladar.'

Muhabbat Khan did not reply. Standing there on the ramparts, watching Surat burn, both knew there was more at stake that night than mere masculinity. His face was reflected in the flickering light as he stood upright again, twisting his moustache. 'Look around us,' he said grimly. 'There is no way out. *Ganim* surrounds us. Look at the burning city. How in God's name are we to do anything?'

Vora stared at the burning city. Flames stretched as far as the eye could see. Amid the crackling and hissing came distant screams and falling masonry. He wondered bleakly if some of those sounds came from his own house in the fashionable district, where the wealthiest merchants had their lavish residences. He knew they were now in a race against time. Whatever had to be done, had to be done without delay.

'What we need is a distraction,' he said, hands on hips.

'What distraction is big enough to allow us to put our plan into motion amidst all this?' Muhabbat Khan laughed, looking up at the smoky skies.

Vora glanced at the upturned arrogant face with its outthrust jaw and flowing beard. Desperate times called for desperate measures, he thought. The outlines of a plan had begun to form in his mind some time ago. Now, standing on these battlements, it came full circle. He wondered if he could kill two birds with one stone this time too, just as he had done all his life.

'Do you have something to discuss or did you call me out here just to stare at this horrible mess?' Muhabbat Khan asked gloomily.

Vora stood up straight and cleared his throat. 'As I said, we need a distraction. And what better way to create one than to strike right at the heart of the enemy?'

'I would land that strike myself if there was a way to do it,' Muhabbat Khan rumbled, his fingers curling into fists.

Vora stared at the man before him. Of all Muhabbat Khan's vices, cowardice was not one. He had a brash courage that would serve to fulfil what he had in mind. So the time had come to put his money on one more gamble, he thought. If he succeeded, he would be rewarded, and if he failed, there would be rewards again, but of a different kind. Vora smiled, realizing once again why he was the most successful merchant in Surat.

'You leave the strike to me.' Vora's eyes glittered coldly as he spoke. 'You put on your armour.'

ROOFTOPS BY THE RIVER, SECOND NIGHT OF THE SACK

Shashidhwaj leaned forward from his position on the rooftop and strained his eyes into the darkness to observe the scene unfolding before him. The man he was observing was standing just across the road, on the ground. He was pacing about, visibly anxious. As the glimmering light fell upon the man's face, Shashidhwaj's heart skipped a beat. There was something eerie about the man. He was covered from head to feet in a black cloak, his hands encased in black leather gloves that shone in the meagre light.

A light breeze blew back the man's hood, revealing his head. Shashidhwaj almost swore aloud. A black metallic mask covered the man's face, leaving only small slits for his eyes and nose. He did not pull on the hood again but walked anxiously to the side of the road, having caught sight of something. Shashidhwaj turned to see what the man had seen. His gaze rested on a group of men walking along the river, armed to the teeth with swords and spears, guarding two carriages pulled by horses, in their midst. As the light of the lamps fell over the carriages, Shashidhwaj saw they were filled with wooden barrels.

That was all he needed to see. Turning to the men with him, he said urgently, 'Find Bahirji! Tell him to bring his group here immediately. We have found the gold!'

CHAPTER ONE

KATRAJ

NINE MONTHS BEFORE

The young lad drew the back of his hand over his forehead to wipe away the sweat beaded there. With an involuntary grunt, he grabbed hold of the rough edges of the thick rope. The ox before him mooed loudly, shaking his large head. Shashidhwaj tightened his hold, refusing to let the ox's movements tear the rope out of his hands. He pulled strongly against the struggling animal and then circled the rope once more around the curved horns atop its head, tightening the rope into a knot.

The ox calmed as Shashidhwaj let go of the rope, which was now tightly coiled around both horns and secured with a knot. Shashidhwaj patted the animal on its forehead fondly, admiring his own dexterous handiwork. He moved away to pick up some hay. The ox mooed expectantly, and as the boy dropped it before the animal, lowered its horns with the rope tied to them, and began to nibble on the fragrant heap. Wet saliva dripped from the animal's mouth onto Shashidhwaj's hands.

'That's the last one ain't it?' a voice called from behind.

Shashidhwaj turned, wiping his hands on his vest. 'Aye, the last, and twenty before that,' he said as he walked amongst the cattle, checking that the rope around each animal's horns was fast, secured with knots.

'Good, good…' The man who had asked let out a puff of smoke as he withdrew his lips from around a clay *chillum*, blackened by long use. 'Twenty-one will do.'

Shashidhwaj rubbed his palms against each other, trying to rub off the encrusted mud. 'My pay?' he asked, looking up.

The man laughed as he banged his chillum softly against the high rock on which he sat perched. 'You'll get your pay when all this is over.'

'And when will that be?' Shashidhwaj rubbed his palms against his trousers, trying to clean them. The rope had left a strange stickiness on his palms that refused to come off.

The man with the chillum laughed again. 'Soon lad, soon. Patience is a virtue not favoured by the young, eh?'

The rubbing had no effect. Shashidhwaj's palms were still sticky. He spit on them and rubbed them against each other, hoping the moisture would help, but to no avail.

'Have you not heard that saying?' another voice now said. 'Patience is the greatest virtue of a spy.' It came from a man squatting beside a horse at the edge of the steep hill on which they stood.

Shashidhwaj gave up on his palms and walked over to where the man squatted. From this vantage point, even in the scanty light of dusk, he could see the valley spread out below.

'Spies, are we?' he murmured, glancing at the man beside the horse.

An amused chuckle was the only response. It was the man with the chillum, still perched on his rock, who replied, '*We* are spies, not *you*. Not yet.'

Wiping the sweat from his face, Shashidhwaj squatted down beside the man with the horse. 'Oh yeah? What kind of spies brag to every stranger they meet about their occupation?' he scoffed, laughing. 'It must be a first.'

'Not to everyone.' The man with the chillum took another puff. 'Only to cowherds.'

'He has a soft spot for cowherds,' the man by the horse explained, grinning. 'Seeing how he was a cowherd himself once.'

'But none of this explains when I will get paid.' Shashidhwaj banged a fist on the ground.

'Wanna leave early lad, and miss the fireworks?' The man with the horse pointed towards the rocks which lined the hill top. A lone lantern glowed in a circle of its own light, casting the rocks beyond into shadow.

'Just want to leave in one piece,' Shashidhwaj said, cracking his knuckles.

'You shall. That I promise.' The man with the chillum inspected his pipe and cursed. 'This dammed stuff doesn't even burn properly,' he complained. Getting down from his perch, he went towards the lantern.

Shashidhwaj turned to the man beside him. 'He says I'll leave unscathed, yet you do not tell me what it is you are planning to do.'

The man grinned, showing a flash of white teeth. 'First rule of a spy, boy: Never tell everything to any one person, and any one thing to every person.'

The man with the chillum had lit it again from the flame of the lamp and now took a long drag. The sudden sound of his coughing filled the air for a moment.

'You desire strange things, lad,' he said, blowing out the smoke. 'You say you want to leave, but you want to know what we will do with the cows. You do realize that both your wishes cannot be fulfilled together, do you not?'

The man by the horse chortled in delight. 'Yeah, you cannot

expect us to let you go till we tell you what we are going to do with your animals, and that we cannot do till we have done it, right?'

Shashidhwaj considered these words with closed eyes. Recent events unrolled in a flash before him. He had come upon these two strange men that afternoon, while tending his herd of cattle on the grassy slopes not a mile away. The sun had been bright and he had been resting in the shade of a cool *jamun* tree when the two had turned up out of nowhere on their horses. They were dressed in simple peasant clothing, their heads covered by a strange kind of turban. Swords in scabbards hung at their waists. As they dismounted, Shashidhwaj saw that one of them was taller and more muscular than the other, but they both had moustaches that drooped over thin-lipped mouths.

For a while they had ignored him, sitting down in the shade of a tree and eating their *shidoris* silently. It was only when evening came and he rose to gather the cattle to head back, that the men had stopped him and offered a generous amount of coin to buy the herd from him. They had offered him even more coin if he would help them prepare the cows for some strange ritual.

'But they are not my cows!' he had protested. 'They belong to the *zamindar*.'

But the two men had been as stubborn as rocks. 'Well then, give the coin to the zamindar,' the tall one had suggested. He was the one now squatting by the horse, looking at him with probing eyes.

'So what's it going to be, lad?' he asked.

Shashidhwaj recalled the strenuous labour it had taken to tie the strange rope the men had provided, around the cows' horns. On the spur of the moment, he decided that all that hard work would scarcely be worth the coin if he did not know what it had all been for. 'I will stay,' he said, scratching his chin, on which the first signs of a wispy beard had barely emerged.

'Brave lad. I like you already.' The man with the chillum smiled and emptied his pipe onto the ground, carefully grinding the debris into the earth with his foot. Then he put the pipe into the satchel he carried slung across his body.

'Like I said,' the tall man by the horse chuckled, 'he is fond of cowherds.'

'So what do we do now?' Shashidhwaj asked, sudden excitement making his eyes shine.

The entire evening had been filled with an air of mystery as the two men made themselves comfortable. 'We are spies and this is a covert operation,' they had declared. After that they had asked him probing questions about himself, his family, his village, the zamindar whose cows he was tending; all without revealing a nugget of information about themselves. When they learned he was an orphan, lived in the village below, and grazed the zamindar's cattle in return for food and a sack of hay in the barn to sleep on, they had looked at each other and laughed strangely.

'I don't know why I'm even listening to you!' Shashidhwaj had protested as he uncoiled the long rope they had asked him to tie around the horns of his cattle.

'For coin, my lad, for coin,' the tall man had replied without opening his eyes as he lay in the cool shade of the tree which was Shashidhwaj's favourite spot.

The same tall man now looked at him, very much awake. 'We are waiting, boy,' he said in a calm voice.

'Waiting for the dark,' the man who had been smoking the chillum earlier added. He had a slim build and was shorter than his companion.

Shashidhwaj stared up at the cloudy expanse of sky. 'Won't have to wait much longer then,' he said with a grin. The glowing ball of the sun had disappeared, leaving the edges of the clouds stained with crimson. Darkness was falling quickly.

The shorter man inspected the rope tied around one of the cow's horns. The animal mooed as he traced his fingers around the rope. He nodded, satisfied. 'You have done a good job, boy. Nice and tight, just as we asked.'

'I hope the coin is shiny and clunky just like you promised,' Shashidhwaj retorted with a smile.

The man merely picked up the lantern from the rock and walked over to where the other two were squatting.

'It's getting cold,' Shashidhwaj said. 'Why don't we light a fire?'

'Oh we will, my friend!' the tall man laughed. 'We are certainly going to light a fire.'

'Just not yet,' the other added, dropping a hand on Shashidhwaj's shoulder and gripping it hard.

Shashidhwaj squirmed, trying to free himself from the painful grip. 'So are you going to tell me what you are going to do?' he asked.

'No,' the man chuckled, letting go. 'We are going to show you.'

'And we'll give you a few hints in the meantime,' the tall one said. 'See if you can figure it out for yourself.'

'I can do that,' Shashidhwaj said with airy certainty.

The shorter one put the lantern down on the ground in front of them and bent to shield it from sudden gusts.

'Where to begin?' the tall man murmured thoughtfully.

'Why not begin with what is happening now?' his companion suggested with a wink.

Shashidhwaj was surprised to see the tall man sigh and hoist himself up, having squatted in the same place for over three hours.

'Look there, boy!' he said, pointing. 'What do you see?'

Shashidhwaj got to his feet too, and followed the outstretched finger. They were standing on the cliff, gazing eastwards into the valley. It was almost dark, with no moon, only the stars overhead. Shashidhwaj took a step forward in the direction of the pointing finger. But he did not need to. He already knew what was in the valley. The man could be pointing at only one thing.

Pune. The city of four thousand; the jewel of Marathwada. The city that was currently occupied by the enemy from the North - the Mughals - the Moslem Sultans of Delhi. Faint lights glittered where the city was. Other lights along its boundaries marked the massive occupation camp of the Mughal General, Shaistekhan. It was no secret. Everyone in the region knew this.

But as they stood looking at the lights glimmering in the dark, the truth suddenly hit Shashidhwaj. 'You are Raje's men, aren't you?' he said, looking his companion in the eye. They had to be. Shashidhwaj wondered why he had failed to notice the light orange colour of their strange turbans before.

The occupation of Pune by Shaistekhan's forces had been a great insult to the newly minted Swarajya of the local Chieftain, whom the people fondly called Shivaji Raje. The adults in Shashidhwaj's village avidly discussed Raje and his actions, but always in whispers. He himself had gleaned enough to know that Pune had once been Raje's seat of governance, and when Raje had declared his lands to be an independent kingdom, all sorts of enemies had converged upon him. The army of the Mughal Governor Shaistekhan, had been one of the most recent. He took his orders directly from the Mughal Badshah Alamgir in Agra. His sole aim was to capture Siva the Mountain Rat, and drag him North in chains.

The shorter, leaner man smiled. 'We are just his spies, lad,' he said. 'But his men are in Pune tonight.'

'But Pune is occupied by Shaistekhan!'

The taller man chuckled again, as if at a private joke. 'And that is why we are necessary. We are the ones who ensure that Shaistekhan does not know Raje is in Pune.'

'He is in Pune!' Shashidhwaj almost shouted.

'That is a nice way of keeping it a secret,' the shorter man reprimanded, throwing a quick look around to make sure none had heard the outburst.

'Oh let the boy shout,' the tall one said, amused. 'In some time everyone alive will know Raje is in Pune.'

'What is he doing in Pune?' Shashidhwaj asked, his eyes round as dung pats.

'He is going to sneak into the Khan's camp in the dark of night and kill him,' the tall man said calmly.

'Isn't that a spy's work?' Shashidhwaj asked, his nose wrinkled in thought.

'No.' The shorter man picked up the lantern. 'This is a spy's work.' He held the lantern up as high as his arm would stretch.

The taller man, taking a sash from around his waist, moved it in front of the lantern, covering and exposing the flame in quick succession.

'What are you doing?' Shashidhwaj asked, surprised by this strange behaviour.

'We are sending a message.'

The light from the lantern shimmered over the ground as the sky grew darker. The crimson edges of the clouds had disappeared and the stars now shone silver above them. The taller man played with the lantern, touching the hot glass with a finger and then pulling away quickly.

'Now what?' Shashidhwaj asked.

'Now we wait.'

'For what?'

'For someone to send us back a signal.'

'It has begun to dawn on you now, hasn't it boy?' the slender man remarked.

Shashidhwaj looked at his hands again. The stickiness was still there, as if etched into the lines of his palms. 'The rope will burn, will it not?' he asked, looking up.

'Indeed, it will. We are counting on it.'

'A thick paste of camphor and lac has been dried on the rope,' the man added. 'It should burn like wildfire, but ten times brighter.'

'The cows?' Shashidhwaj's heart skipped a beat. 'They'll burn too?'

'No they will not.' The tall man patted him on the shoulder and once again Shashidhwaj winced at the weight of the hand. 'The cows will start to run as soon as we light the fire. The flames will spread behind them. We are counting on them to run.'

Shashidhwaj looked at the herd of twenty-one cattle, grazing placidly, their horns tied together with the long rope. His mind contemplated the sight of them running together, a line of fire behind them. 'They'll look like a marching cavalry force,' he said at once.

The tall man laughed. 'You catch on fast, boy.'

'The cows will run down the hill, because it will give them speed,' the shorter man explained. 'And the faster they go, the more the flames will spread away from them. The guards on the wall will see them as a raiding party, headed straight for the walls of the city.

'But the fire will go out by the time the cows reach the wall.' The tall man scratched his beard. 'We have prepared the rope keeping that in mind. The soldiers who run out of the city walls to intercept the threat will be confused at finding nothing but bunch of grazing cows.'

'And you can search for them tomorrow by the city walls,' the shorter one told Shashidhwaj.

'You can give the bag of coins we give you to the zamindar. Tell him how we took the cows. That way, you will be richer by about twenty cows, minus one or two that may have strayed,' the taller one suggested, chuckling deep in his throat. 'A nice deal, won't you say?'

'The cows are meant to distract the Khan's men?' Shashidhwaj asked, gazing at the lights of the city in the distance. 'So Raje can slip in?' There had been no reply received to their signal yet.

The tall man nodded. 'Right on all counts boy, except one. Raje and his men are already in. The cows are to help them slip out.'

Another gust of cool air blew over them and Shashidhwaj felt goosebumps rise on his body. 'What if the Khan's men catch us?' he asked.

'The Khan's men are Mughals. I daresay they won't even be able to catch those cows till the night is over,' the tall man replied dourly.

'A spy should not underestimate his enemies,' Shashidhwaj observed piously.

The tall man grinned. 'A spy should not estimate anything,' he replied. 'A spy must *know*.'

Shashidhwaj opened his mouth to speak but suddenly the shorter man waved a hand, motioning him into silence. Picking up the lantern, he pointed it at the city. 'That's our signal,' he said softly.

Shashidhwaj turned to look. A few *kos* beyond the dim lights of the city, a bright dot was blinking. Another lantern message!

The tall man bent and picked up the sash he he had used earlier and wrapped it around his waist with quick motions. 'It is time,' he said.

'Indeed it is.' The shorter man raised the lantern and repeated the motion of covering and exposing the flame in rapid succession, using his hand. In response, the bright light blinked again. 'Round up the cows!' he said.

The tall man took the reins of his horse. The animal whimpered at the sudden motion after hours of lethargy. The man mounted and watched as his companion retreated from the rocks and walked towards him and handed over the lantern.

Shashidhwaj had run for one end of the rope and was now pulling on it. The cows tied to it, began to moo in protest. The man on the ground ran to the other end of the rope and pulled also. The cows, joined by the rope, began to move forward. The ones sitting rose to their feet.

'We will have to light both ends at once,' the man on the horse observed as Shashidhwaj slapped the cows on their rumps, turning them towards the gentler slope that led down to the city. He kneed his horse and it trotted forward towards the cows.

He waved the lantern at Shashidhwaj, who took it from him and watched as the man at the other end of the rope picked up a stick of wood and lit it. The surroundings sprang to life in the light. The animals seemed to find comfort in the sudden warmth and huddled together.

'On my count,' the man on the horse said in a voice from which all amusement had flown.

The other man took position to the extreme right with his burning fire stick. Shashidhwaj could feel his heart thudding in his chest as he took up his own position with the lantern, to the extreme left. The cows mooed, familiar with his smell. The end of the rope tied to their horns dangled to the ground.

'Take hold of the rope!' the man on the horse instructed, his gaze on the city below, as if waiting for another signal.

Shashidhwaj picked up the rope quickly, the heat of the lantern singing his other hand as he waited with bated breath for what was to come.

'Now!' the hoarse shout tore through the air.

Shashidhwaj wasted no time in flipping open the glass of the lantern and setting the end of the rope on fire. On the far side, he could see the shorter man setting alight his end of the rope as well. The rope in its entirety lit up in a single blaze, upheld as if by some invisible force. He heard the frantic moos of the animals and the rope that bound them began to slip out of his hands.

'Let go!' the man on the horse shouted over the crackling of the flaming rope.

Shashidhwaj heard him but his hand seemed frozen around the rope, unable to let go. He felt his heels dig into the soil as the animals began to move forward frantically. Then, in a flash of light, the taut rope in his hand gave way and he was hurled back, the lantern flung to one side. Looking up, he saw that the man on the horse, sword in hand, had slashed the rope.

The two men watched intently, and Shashidhwaj in amazement, as the line of cattle rushed forth, flames leaping behind them as they ran downhill. When they had covered some distance, their forms dissolved into the darkness and all they could see was fire, just like…

'A marching army,' the man on the horse chortled.

'Here, boy.' The other man threw a pouch at Shashidhwaj, who caught it mid-air. It was heavy and jingled with coin.

'It was fortunate meeting you, boy.' The man bowed with exaggerated courtesy before mounting his own horse, which had stood all this while under a tree, nibbling at the grass. 'If I were you, I'd run back to your village and hide where none can find you!'

Shashidhwaj nodded, watching the two men prepare to gallop after the cows, brandishing their naked swords. 'At least tell me your names!' he called after them as their horses began to move.

The two men looked back in unison. They pulled up, bringing their mounts to a prancing halt, swords still in hand. The tall man gave his now familiar rumbling laugh, showing his teeth. 'Should we tell him our real names or just our aliases?' he asked his companion.

'You know my rule,' the other shrugged. 'I don't lie to cowherds.'

'In that case,' the first man said, bowing slightly as he sat atop his horse, 'I am the humble Bahirji Bandal. *Pramukh Guptachar* of Raje Shivaji and his Swarajya.'

'And I am one Sadashiv Naik, also *Pramukh Guptachar*, the one who keeps this fool in check,' the other man said, pointing with his sword at his companion.

Without another word, they turned their animals and sped after the now faraway light of the cattle. Shashidhwaj watched the pair ride away till they too, were lost in the darkness. What had they said their names were? He tried to remember as he turned and set off along the dirt track that wound down the hill, back to his village. Suddenly he remembered. As he ran, he repeated the names lest he forget. They were quite simple really. Bahirji and...Naik. Bahirji-Naik.

As he sprinted towards his village that night, little did he know how important those two names were to become in his life.

Chapter Two

Road To Suwali

EIGHT MONTHS BEFORE

Samsher Ali's fingers curled around the tree branch and his nails clawed into the rough bark as the wind blew strongly against his body. The leaves around him rustled violently and his clothes clung taut to his frame. The wind had also dried up the perspiration that had beaded his forehead. He closed his eyes and breathed in the smell of the sea. When the gusty wind fell, he loosened his fingers and leaned back against the trunk again. The branch he was crouching on creaked under his weight.

'Are you alright, Rayiyas?' The voice came from below, from the cluster of bushes under the tree.

'Shush!' Ali reproved sternly. It was very dark, but his sharp eyes could just make out where the line of the road met the sky covered with stars.

'Do you see them?' The voice from below was a hoarse whisper.

Ali sighed, looking down angrily. In one swift motion he stood up and jumped off the branch, landing on the ground on all fours like a cat. He rose quickly and brushed the dirt off his hands before turning his angry gaze towards the one who had spoken. The dark bushes moved and faces appeared.

'Do you not understand what *shush* means, Hatim?' Ali's whisper was as sharp as his sword pointing at the chest of the man who stood at the very front of the group.

'I apologize, Rayiyas,' Hatim whispered in a low-voiced response, unsure whether to speak or not.

'Oh never mind.' Ali turned his sword and with a strong arc of his hand, sank the tip into the ground. The blade stood embedded in the middle of the road as Ali retreated, satisfied with what he had done. 'They are on the road. I saw them from the tree, leaving the lights of Suwali docks some time ago. They will be upon us at any moment.'

'Ready, men?' Hatim looked to both sides as the men around him brought up their spears and fell into position, covered once more by the vegetation around them.

Ali's free hand caressed his beard as he listened to the muted sounds and footsteps, the twist of knees as the soldiers crouched. He knew the question was not whether he and his men were ready, but whether his targets were.

The breeze rose again, bringing with it the sound of hooves and wheels rolling over the rutted road. Ali knew he was ready. He had prepared for this moment for nearly a fortnight. He had chosen the spot himself, having scouted the entire stretch of road that travelled from Suwali to the city, not once or twice, but five times. This heightened curve in the road where a peepal tree stood, was the best spot for an ambush. It was exactly halfway along the route, where neither the lights of the docks nor the glow of the city could be seen. The only light in the surrounding darkness of the night came from the single lantern on the side of the carriage, jigging up and down with every rotation of the wheels. The curving climb of the road meant the carriage would remain hidden from their sight until it was directly in front of them. According to Ali's plan, it also meant the men in the carriage would not see them till the very last moment. Ali folded his arms and stood alone in the centre of the road, waiting.

They heard the huffing of the horses as they made the climb. The dim glow turned into bright yellow light as the carriage climbed higher. When the light finally fell upon his face, Ali moved back two steps, his hand deftly moving to the wooden handle of the flintlock pistol at his side. The horses neighed as the coachman pulled abruptly on the reins, having spotted the sparkling gold handle of the sword embedded in the middle of the road. The carriage stopped not five paces from it. The yellow lantern light fell on Ali's chest and the ring on the finger curled around the trigger of the pistol.

In the same light Ali saw the white-knuckled hands of the carriage driver as he pulled on the reins. Alarmed, the man shouted something in a foreign language Ali knew well, but he did not care to register the meaning of the shouted words. His heart was racing in his chest, waiting to see who would answer the man's frantic call. To his delight, the doors on both sides of the carriage opened and two figures jumped out. Just two men.

'What is the meaning of this?' The loud voice belonged to the man on the right, who came forward, a pistol pointed straight ahead, the light falling upon him. 'Show yourself!'

From the left, the other man too, entered the circle of illumination, his face below his red hat as white as the driver's hands.

'Greetings, Parekh Shethji!' Ali kept his hand on his pistol as he walked into the light.

'Samsher Ali? What in God's name is the meaning of this?' The man with the flintlock looked surprised, but did not lower his pistol an inch.

'It is perhaps I who should be asking you that question.' Ali smiled as he removed his finger from the trigger and folded his arms, still holding the primed gun.

'Why are you blocking our path in the dead of night?' the man called Parekh asked.

Ali caught the tinge of fear in the voice and felt like smiling, but no hint of emotion showed on his face. 'The path you have embarked on can only lead to one place,' he said. Ali spat on the ground and calmly closed his eyes. His eyelids shone in the light. He remembered the words that had been spoken to him a few nights ago: *Those who steal from me must die.*

'Will you get out of the way or do I have to blow you away?' Parekh bellowed angrily.

Ali opened his eyes, blinded for a moment. 'I wouldn't do that if I were you,' he said, and coughed.

For a moment he thought Parekh had not grasped what was happening behind him, since his eyes and ears were focused on Ali. But the Dutchman at Parekh's side was alert enough, and spoke hurriedly, noticing the dozen shadows that had appeared from the bushes, men carrying long spears.

'You are surrounded,' Ali declared lazily as he watched Hatim climb up the back of the carriage and point his weapon at the driver. The others raised their spears, pointing at their targets. 'I would advise you to lower your weapon. Sure, you could blow me away, but I would be worried about the number of holes my men would make in your body before you bled to death."

Parekh's shoulders slumped as he spotted the men. He lowered his weapon. When he spoke again, though the words were the same, Ali knew their meaning had changed dramatically

'What is the meaning of this, Ali? I have never done anything to you.'

'True, true.' Ali spun on his heel, away from the light. Over his shoulder he said, 'But the question is, have you never done anything to anyone else?'

In the stark silence that followed, Ali was sure he could hear the heightened breathing of his victims.

It was the Dutchman who finally spoke. 'It's about the cargo, isn't it?'

'Wise man,' Ali nodded as he turned. 'If only you had been as wise in knowing who to sell this cargo to.'

'What do you want?' Parekh raised his hands in the ageless gesture of surrender and walked forward a step. 'Whatever you want, we can discuss it.'

'Ah, no. Stop right there.' Ali pulled his sword out of the ground swiftly and pointed it at Parekh's chest.

Parekh turned pale, stunned by the sudden movement. He swallowed, trying to think what to say to this bandit.

From his position on the carriage, Hatim declared, 'The cargo is in order, Rayiyas.'

Ali nodded. 'Good. You may remove the driver, but keep the horses.'

Hatim's strong hands fell on the coachman's shoulders as he pulled the man off the wooden plank.

'No…aah…' The shout of protest from Parekh turned into a shriek of agony as Ali pushed the tip of his sword into Parekh's uplifted arm. The limb fell to his side as Ali pulled out his blade.

'Take what you want,' whispered his victim harshly. 'There is gold on the Dutchman. The pocket watch in my breast pocket is worth a hundred mahmudis.'

'Bribing me, are you?' Ali lowered his sword to the ground. 'On any other night I would have accepted your offer, Shethji. But not tonight.'

'But why?' Parekh pleaded, his voice trembling on the verge of tears.

'Because tonight I have been asked to send a message.'

A loud crack reverberated in the air, awakening the birds

in the trees and bringing the leaves to dancing life. The horses neighed loudly, rearing up into the air, rattling the carriage. The Dutchman took a moment to understand what had happened as he saw the vapour rising from Ali's outstretched pistol. Then, as realization hit him, he touched the side of his own face and neck, feeling the warm blood that had splattered him from the gunshot that had blown away Parekh's face. His terrified shriek echoed across the skies as the man behind him pierced him with his spear, the point emerging through his ribcage.

'Unshackle the horses; they will be useful to us. Then burn the cargo,' Ali ordered.

He watched as Hatim slashed the coachman's neck, then pushed his pistol back into its holder. Ali grabbed the reins of one of the horses, calming it with soothing words. Placing a foot in the stirrup, he mounted in one swift motion, even as Hatim cut the ties that harnessed the horses to the carriage.

'There is no need to clean up after ourselves this time, Hatim,' Ali declared as the horse bounded forward, jumping over Parekh's dead body, lying on the bloodstained ground. 'Just set fire to everything and run in the direction of Suwali. It will be easy to hide in the taverns there until the hubbub dies down.

'And where are you going?' Hatim yelled in surprise, reaching for the lantern in order to pour its fiery contents into the carriage.

Ali saw his own dark shadow stretching along the road. He turned for a moment to say, 'To Surat.'

'To Surat?' Hatim asked in surprise.

'Indeed.' Ali smiled. As he had said to Parekh, he had come to send a message. Now it was time to deliver the news in person to the man who had asked him to do so.

***

As night lingered over the city, Ali's horse trotted in through the Navasari Gate, located in the southern section of the city. Surat was commonly known as a city with three gates but no walls. Tall gates made of brick and stone stood at three points on the city's periphery. Where the fourth gate should have been, the mighty Surat Fort stood. Behind it flowed the backwaters, mixing with the Tapi River.

Ali passed between the stone pillars, his gaze moving over the napping guards, their heads resting against the great columns of the gate, holding onto spears for support. Ali spat in disgust. *Foolish men! A waste of the crown's money!* The guards did not wake as he passed.

The main street led straight to the main market area. But Ali was not going to the market. Along the way, where his detour lay, he pulled on the reins to slow his horse. Looking to his left, he caught sight of the small arched gate that led to a narrow alleyway. He turned his horse and bent his head to pass under the arch. The street urchins, who never seemed to sleep, scattered and hid behind the brick pillars as they saw him pass with his sword hanging at his side. Ali paid them no heed. He knew that even though he was alone, no one would dare attack him in this city. Even the lowest street criminal knew who he was and feared him well.

The narrow alley continued to turn and twist until he finally emerged onto the wide, tree-lined street by the river. The house he was looking for stood tall against the dark sky, rising up two floors. Ali halted his mount directly before the main entrance. Unlike the guards at the city gates, the guards here immediately straightened on his arrival. Ali looked at them disdainfully. They were in the service of a master who was destined for a fall.

'Haji Kasim!' Ali shouted, his voice ripping through the silence. 'Haji Kasim, come out from wherever you are!'

Up above, on the second floor, Ali saw the windows light up. He knew his quarry would not be asleep tonight, for important goods were being moved for him, and he would have lain awake in wait for news of their safe delivery. A door was flung open and a man walked out onto the balcony above, dressed in a white undershirt and *lungi*. He peered through the darkness till he recognized who summoned him thus boldly.

'Why do you call for me like a beggar in the street, Ali?' Haji Kasim demanded from above. 'Why not come into my humble abode and have some toddy?'

'I would if I could,' Ali shrugged. 'But tonight, you may prefer to offer me poison after you hear what I have to tell you.'

'Then speak.'

'Mohandas Parekh is dead.' Ali never liked to play around with words. 'The consignment he bought secretly from the Dutch has been seized.'

'And why would you think that would disturb me, street rat?'

'Because you wanted the consignment for yourself.' Ali responded from atop his horse, the reins lying loose in his hands. 'Parekh was just a middleman.'

'Right on all counts but one,' Kasim smiled. 'He was not *my* middleman.'

Ali was taken aback by this declaration, but his face did not betray his surprise. 'It is not unusual to disown a man who is dead,' he smirked.

'My offer of toddy still stands.' Kasim raised his arms in a welcoming gesture.

Ali nudged his horse, turning the animal back the way they had come. 'Another night perhaps, Mir Kasim,' he called back. 'Tonight I have another audience to attend.' So saying, he trotted off.

Behind him, Kasim watched as Ali disappeared around the corner. If what he had said was true, it meant that he, Kasim, had lost a considerable fortune that night. He banged his fist angrily on the railing, barely feeling the pain. This was a serious matter. Yet, Ali was just the medium. Kasim well knew whose was the mind behind this setback.

As he walked back into the house and closed the door behind him, Kasim knew he would remain awake for the rest of the night, as well as in the coming ones, plotting how to get even with the worst enemy he had ever had.

***

Ali's heart was beating hard in his chest as he arrived close to the open fields again, this time through the Burhanpur Gate in the eastern section of the city. He rode through the Avenue until he felt the coolness in the air as the trees thickened around the entrance to the Gopi Talav. This famous lake had been built a century before, and was the main water source for the city. The gardens and trees around it provided convenient cover for clandestine night meetings.

Ali found his quarry waiting by a large tree, holding a fire stick for light. The man had on a black, hooded cloak that covered his head, throwing his face into shadow. The cloak billowed in the wind and the flame of the torch he held flickered. As Ali neared, he saw the iron mask that covered the man's face, hiding what the cloak could not. Not even the eyes were visible behind the two dark deep slits in the metal.

'I believe you carry good news,' the man said in Farsi.

Ali stopped and bowed. 'Master, the task is done. Parekh will not be transporting Dutch consignments after tonight.'

'Good,' the man Ali called the Master, nodded. 'And the Dutch Officer with him?'

'Dead as well.'

'You have done exceptionally well, Rayiyas.'

'Master...' Ali hesitated, unsure whether to voice the question that filled his mind.

'Ask,' the voice behind the mask said.

'I came through the city on my way here,' Ali said. 'I passed the house of Haji Kasim.'

'And?' There was a sudden note of anticipation in the cloaked man's voice.

'Kasim said that Parekh did not work for him.'

'Why did you think Parekh worked for him?'

'The Dutch ships came to port three days ago. All their cargo was unloaded and bid for two days ago. Yet Parekh moved the cargo only tonight, which makes me think the Dutch have brought in something exclusively for someone. And since Parekh wanted to move it secretively, it must have been something illegal.'

'What of it?' the cloaked man shrugged.

'I saw the cargo when I took them down.' Ali fingered his belt. 'Coral. The boxes were filled to the brim with coral. At present, the license to trade in coral lies only with the Angrez traders, and coral is bought by only one merchant in the city, who used his influence with the Subhedar to deter others from dealing in it. Hence, he dictates the prices...'

'And was Haji Kasim at such loggerheads with this merchant that he would dare break the law to get his price?' The cloaked man crossed his arms across his chest, under his cloak. 'If you want to ask me a question, young Rayiyas, ask it directly. Do not hide behind veiled words.'

Ali took a deep breath and stared at the mask. 'Are you Virji Vora?' he asked. 'Is that why you tasked me with killing everyone with the carriage, disrupting the delivery?'

'If I wished to display to the world who I am, I wouldn't wear this cloak or mask,' the Master said simply.

Ali's fingers went to the hilt of his sword. He knew that in this darkness, all it would take to see the man's face was a flick from his blade. But he noticed the Master's hands had also dropped to his belt. Ali retreated, unsure what mysterious weapon the strange man possessed beneath his cloak. Unfastening the holster and gun he had used to kill Parekh, Ali placed it flat across both his extended arms. 'The weapon you gave me,' he said. 'It has served its purpose.'

The cloaked man raised a hand. Instead of flesh, his hand was covered by a leather glove. His fingers touched the barrel of the gun. 'You can keep it,' he said. 'Consider it a gift.' With his other hand he placed a pouch beside the gun. 'One hundred mahmudis, as agreed.'

'One more thing,' Ali said, judging the weight of the pouch as the cloaked man turned and lifted the reins of his horse. 'The last time we met, you told me that after I had completed this task for you, the wheels would be set in motion for greater things to come.'

'Indeed, young Rayiyas. Soon, I shall send word. Tidings will come which will make you immensely wealthy, just as your forefathers once were.'

The words echoed in Ali's head as he silently watched the man ride away towards the city. Above him, the stars still glittered. He sighed. The Master had been right in everything he had said till now. But what mattered was whether he would continue to be right in the coming days.

Chapter Three

Vora's Gambit

SEVEN MONTHS BEFORE

As the bells of the port tolled, George Oxenden's eyes opened with a start. As light filled his vision, the thudding of his heart in his ribcage became stronger. Gasping for air, he straightened with a jerk in his chair and looked around. The wooden swinging half-doors to his chamber were shut, which meant he had not been asleep for very long. The man he was waiting for had still not shown up.

A soft breeze blew in through the open window from the sea and ruffled his hair. Oxenden looked out at the water and yawned. His office was located on the coast, in the dockyard village four leagues from the city of Surat, called Swally Hole, because of the deep water which facilitated anchoring of the larger ships which carried the main cargo. Smaller ships could negotiate the river and travel right up to the small *bunders* upstream. But the bigger ships had no option but to dock here. Over the years, the English had built it into a fortified outpost, with their own loading bays and warehouses. Goods arrived here from faraway coasts and went into the warehouses for direct trade, or to the English factory in Surat, for the production of manufactured goods. The ships would then be filled with indigenous items and dispatched back to where they had come from, continuing the cycle of trade.

Cursing softly to himself, Oxenden looked down at the stack of papers on his desk. Brushing away the numerous bills of lading, stock sheets and applications, he searched for the quill he remembered holding before the sentry had left his chamber to call on his would be visitor. Finding it at last, he ruffled through the stack of papers to find the ones he had graciously put his signature upon before dozing off. When he came to the ones on which the signature was missing, he generously dipped the nib into the glass inkpot of indigo, and carefully scribbled his name: *Sir George Oxenden of Kent.* What a farce, he thought to himself as he signed the last of the papers.

If there was any pomp and show associated with his being a Knight, he had seen none of it here in Surat. Most of his days were spent signing papers, and his nights supervising the unloading of ships. He often wondered who the bastards were who navigated the damned ships, for they never seemed to make port during the day, and inevitably disappeared into the city to get vilely drunk once the ship docked. The ships always came as dusk fell, causing him to spend his nights standing on the banks of Swally Hole, supervising the Hindoostaṇi labourers unloading the cargo into the warehouse. The same routine had continued last night till dawn, and Oxenden had not dared vacate his position, considering the value of the cargo. The lack of sleep had caused him to doze off as he waited for his visitor to appear.

The wooden swing doors finally creaked open, revealing a tall, broad-shouldered Englishman, his white shirt splattered with blue all the way to where it merged with the waistband of his dark trousers. Streaks of blue also besmeared half his face.

Oxenden laughed at the sight, knowing well that if the man turned around, the sight of his backside would be even more entertaining. 'Where in the seven hells did you get that paint, my dear Smith?' he asked. 'I'm sure I ordered you to be in Swally Hole all morning.'

The man, one Anthony Smith, frowned. 'It pains me to tell you Sir, that the whole lot of indigo traders in Swally Hole this morning, present a similar appearance.'

Smith was one of the newest men to be positioned in Surat, just as Oxenden himself had been, and the two men had found themselves arrived in the city almost at the same time. Like him, Smith seemed to learn fast, displaying none of the lethargy that Englishmen often imbibed after an extended stay here. Oxenden had found Smith to be a dependable figure ever since he had assumed charge in Surat. He had become the go-to man for all important matters that Oxenden wanted overseen. And so he had sent Smith to the docks this morning to oversee the loading of the ship which he himself had emptied last night. Timely loading was necessary so the ship could be on its way, allowing the next one to come in to take its place. Given the lack of berthing space available at Swally Hole, only a few ships could dock at a time, so time was as prime as land out here.

'And what caused them to paint you in this fashion, my dear man?' Oxenden reached for an engraved wooden box lying on his desk and drew out a cigar. He used a small pair of gold scissors to chop off the end. Striking a match against the edge of his desk, he lit the cigar, puffing a few times before placing it between his incongruously sensuous lips.

'Because I told them not to load their indigo sacks in the hold, Sir,' Smith replied in exasperated tones as he collapsed into the chair opposite. 'May I?' he asked, hand poised above the cigar box. Oxenden nodded and Smith quickly drew out a fat cigar.

'And why on earth would you do that?' Oxenden enquired somewhat peevishly. 'Supervising the loading of the indigo was exactly why I asked you to be on the docks this morning,'

'That is what I have come to explain, Sir,' Smith said. His

polite manner and address bespoke the English gentlemen. 'First, they told me they could not barter the corals we had brought in, for the indigo. Then they asked for hard cash or a letter of credit, which I knew we could not produce. Even though I knew damn well that there was no point explaining all this to them, I tried to do so, resulting in this act of hooliganism by an over enthusiastic trader.'

'Bollocks!' The amused smile disappeared from Oxenden's face. 'How can they possibly refuse the barter? They wanted the corals.'

'One of the more restrained ones told me their coral stocks were overflowing and so they had no use for more.'

'Smith, I think that both of us know very well that the man was lying,' Oxenden growled. 'We personally visited the warehouses a week ago and there was certainly no coral in them!'

'Sir, that is exactly why, before coming to you with this painted face, I went there again, and found them to be, to my utter surprise, filled to the brim with coral!'

Oxenden sank back in his chair in thought, his jaw clenched. This was a most sinister occurrence, nothing like what he had hoped to hear this morning. He had more important matters to attend to. The visitor he was expecting was no doubt on his way, and he simply did not have the time to deal with this new trouble.

'This is horeshit, Smith,' Oxenden said angrily. 'I have to meet with the representative sent by Sir Abraham Shipman, who has come all the way from Bombay. There is the important issue of the Island of Bombay to be discussed. But now I have to deal with this.'

'If you ask me Sir, it has to be the Dutch,' Smith said diligently. 'They have been bringing coral illegally into the market for some time.'

Oxenden shook his head. 'No, all that stopped when their

local dealer, Parekh, was murdered. They decided coral was too bloody a product to bother with after that. We are the only remaining sellers of coral in the market.'

'But that does not explain how there is an excess of coral in the hands of all the traders in the local market,' Smith said, exhaling smoke from his cigar. 'This is our first shipment since the *farman* was issued.'

'The doctor merely gives the medicine, my man.' Oxenden's fingers massaged his chin. 'It must be the patient himself who administers the dose.'

Smith's eyebrows rose. 'You see another hand at work here, Sir?

'Not a hand, a head; a rather bulky one under an embroidered hat.' Oxenden slammed his fist on the table, causing the glass ink bottle to wobble and tip over, leaving a trail of ink which crept to the table's edge and then dripped onto the floor. He ignored it. With his other hand, he pressed the burning end of his cigar onto the desk, leaving a circular burn mark. He had begun to see the connections clearly now. For a long time they had but one buyer for the coral they brought into Surat from the Indonesian Islands. But this time that buyer had refused to purchase their coral. Unnerved by this sudden refusal, Oxenden had quickly orchestrated deals with the other merchants in town, bartering his coral for indigo, pleased at his quick thinking in a crisis. Now he realized that his self-congratulation had been premature.

'I do not know of any man the like of whom you speak,' Smith remarked.

'There is only one man who could have caused this to happen.' Cursing softly, Oxenden reached for the dumb waiter in the corner and picked up his bright red hat. He gazed at it for a moment, dusting it off before putting it on.

'And who would that be, Sir?' Smith asked curiously, helping his boss into his bright red coat.

'A name you will soon know only too well, 'Oxenden sighed. 'A name everyone who comes to Surat soon learns to recite like their daily prayers.' He pushed the doors open and went out, making his way out of the building to where his horse stood tethered. He would have to make the bumpy journey into the city to confront the said man, face to face.

***

Virji Vora stood on the wooden boardwalk that connected the small bunders along the Surat River, facing the backwaters. On the horizon, he could see the rooftops of Suwali, and the sloped roofs of the Angrez warehouses. He could just make out the line of labourers dragging heavy sacks to the carts. As he stood admiring the effect of his handiwork, he did not notice the distinguished Englishman standing behind him, a little distance away. Either that, or Vora was pleased to make him wait.

Oxenden stood there for some time, his fashionable walking cane in his hand, staring at the back of the embroidered white hat on his quarry's head. But the man showed no sign of acknowledging his presence, so finally, he cleared his throat to announce himself.

Vora turned quickly. The wisps of hair peeping from under his hat were stone grey, but the man himself appeared to be in the prime of health. Seeing who called to him, the light of interest died in his eyes. 'Oh, it is you,' he muttered desultorily.

'I wonder how the indigo traders in the city suddenly find themselves with an excess of coral?' Oxenden asked, looking Vora in the eye.

'I am just a merchant, but such things do happen when someone offloads a large quantity into the market at a very cheap rate.' Vora smiled, showing his yellowed teeth.

'And who could that be but our exclusive buyer, who suddenly developed cold feet and told us he could not buy our corals after our ship had already made port?'

'In my defense, I did tell you that you could sell this lot to any trader in the city who was interested, with my blessings,' Vora retorted.

'But no one was!' Oxenden banged his walking stick on the sidewalk, making the wooden floorboards rattle.

'And how is that my fault?'

'You were the one who offloaded the coral in the markets at the last moment.' Oxenden pointed a finger at Vora's chest. 'It had to be you. No one else had the quantities, nor the gumption, to do something like that.'

'As a free trader I can do anything I want.' Vora turned away and spat on the ground.

The action caused the blood to rush to Oxenden's head. 'I thought we had a deal,' he snapped, tapping his cane on the wooden floorboards to emphasize his words.

'Did we?' Vora leaned back against the cast iron railings that separated the boardwalk from the water. 'I am an old man. Perhaps you can remind me of the terms.'

'You permitted us to sell our coral to other merchants this time, instead of exclusively to you,' Oxenden reminded Vora. 'You signed a contract to this effect.'

'Oh did I?' Vora replied musingly. 'Now what would you say if I were to tell you that being the forgetful man I am, I decided to change the terms?'

'Damn you!' Oxenden spun away towards the sea, his face flushed with anger. Taking a few deep breaths, he slowly turned back, his eyes hard. 'The Dutch were right about you. You are a man without honour.'

'If such was your opinion of my character, why did you offer me terms?' Vora asked, unabashed. 'You could have made the coral deal with any other merchant, but you came to me.'

'Parekh asked me to give you a chance.' Oxenden looked away towards the horizon. What Parekh had actually told him during a casual meeting was that none other than Vora had the cash or goods to match the value of the corals. What Parekh had carefully omitted to mention was that Vora was a devious creature.

'Well, Parekh is dead,' Vora said, his eyes dreamy.

'Is that a threat?' Oxenden asked angrily, lifting his cane and holding it against his rotund abdomen.

'Make of it what you will,' Vora replied in the same calm voice he had used from the start.

'Damn you man!' Oxenden muttered. 'You can't change the terms of a deal just like that.'

'Oh but I can, and I just did.'

'I have these Waivers of Rights.' Oxenden reached into his folder and held up a bunch of papers. 'Signed and delivered under your seal.'

Vora shook his head. 'You are still new here,' he said, shrugging his shoulders.

'Not so new that I do not understand what these documents mean.'

'You are free to make a complaint to the Subhedar,' Vora replied negligently. 'But you will find it to be a tedious and time consuming process. Your ships need to sail now. And they cannot do so without being loaded. Be practical my friend.'

'Are you holding me to ransom?' Oxenden asked.

Vora shrugged. 'Only if I need to.'

'I am the President and Chief Director of the English East India Company in Surat, as well as their factories in the northern India, and from Ceylon to the Red Sea. If I choose to, I can directly approach the Imperial Court in Agra and make an official complaint against you.'

'If that is so, why are you here and not on your way to Agra already?' Vora asked, his brows lifted.

Oxenden sighed, knowing he was beaten.

'Ah, because your ships need to sail,' Vora said unctuously. 'And if they do not, your masters back home will be displeased with you for creating a major loss. Perhaps they would even remove you as President. And all this could happen before you even reach Agra to lodge that complaint, you know. I'm told the wait time at court is a scandal.'

'What do you want?' Oxenden asked, irritated with this jousting. If the wretched man was holding out for something, he would have little choice but to give it to him to get this nuisance over with.

Vora smiled. 'You are learning to ask the right questions.'

Oxenden offered a gratuitous smile.

'I want your word, President,' Vora said. 'I can have your ships loaded before sunset with all the indigo in the world, if you give me your word.'

'Regarding what?' Oxenden asked cautiously. Owing Virji Vora a favour was akin to handing your last pawn to the Devil himself.

'There is a particular task that requires to be done.' Vora rubbed his chin thoughtfully. 'It is important and only a man like you can execute it.'

'What do you want done?'

Vora shook his head. 'Not me. Someone important.'

'I can't give my word without knowing what you ask,' Oxenden growled.

'And I cannot load your ships without knowing your

answer.' Vora folded his arms across his chest.

Oxenden sighed. He knew that if the ships were not loaded by nightfall, he would be unable to answer the inevitable questions that would be posed by the Company Directors in England.

'Very well,' he said. 'Have it your way.' Whatever is in my power, I will do.'

Vora smiled. 'Then listen closely, my friend,' he said, 'for this will take all your ability to execute smoothly.'

As Oxenden listened, the lines on his face changed curiously. He made a mental note to postpone his meeting with Abraham Shipman's representative. The unimportant matter of the barren Island of Bombay, and the foolish Portuguese garrison guarding it, could wait. What Vora was discussing was important. Far more important.

Chapter Four

The Boy Rebel

SEVEN MONTHS BEFORE

Shashidhwaj ran through the grass like a rabbit, his nimble feet more in the air than on the ground. The grass was thick and the overhanging branches low, but he used them to grab hold and propel himself forward. The men pursuing him were not so lucky, for they were on horseback.

'Come here you piece of shit!' one of the pursuers cursed as he thrust another branch out of his way.

Shashidhwaj did not stop. In fact, he would not have stopped even if he had hurt his legs or scratched his bare arms. It was on his not stopping that the success or failure of their plan depended.

'We will catch up with you, boy!' a second man shouted even as his horse whinnied as it stepped into the thorny underbrush. 'This forest does not stretch forever.'

Indeed, it did not. Shashidhwaj well knew that it ended exactly fifty steps ahead, where the tree-line opened into a vast open meadow. He had counted the steps twice, before he had whistled loudly to catch the attention of the guards. He already knew it would take him fifteen minutes to cross the forest and emerge into the meadow. That way, the guards chasing him would be far enough from the main road so that none would see or hear their cries. It was part of the plan.

"You better run with all your strength, boy, for we are coming to get you!' the first man shouted after the scampering figure.

Shashidhwaj clenched his teeth as he jumped over a rock, but kept up his pace. Ahead, between the trees, he could clearly see sunlight peeping through the dense foliage. He struggled to look up while keeping an eye on the path ahead at the same time, as he ran. The signal they had decided on was a whistle, but now he realized that it was hard to whistle while running for your life! If only he had practiced doing that on the two runs he had made before.

He broke out of the trees into the meadow with a leap and landed awkwardly on his feet. Behind him, he heard a loud crack as one of the guards slashed an obstructing tree branch with his sword. 'We got you now bastard…'

The man's words ended in a loud scream. Shashidhwaj heard a distinct twang, followed by the neighing of a horse, followed by another shout. He stopped and turned, catching his breath. The two horses rushed passed him, riderless. The sight that confronted him was marvellous.

One of the guards was strung up a tree by a rope that ran from his shoulder across his torso like a sack of open grain about to be tied up. He was struggling to free himself and not be strangled. The other guard had not been so lucky. One hand had caught in the rope and he hung there, arm outstretched, the entire weight of his body dangling from the knot around his forearm.

Shashidhwaj's gaze moved to where his two companions were tightly holding onto the ropes to maintain the cursing men's airborne positions. He heard the distant sound of hooves; the horses were still galloping away. He did not look around, knowing they would have by now disappeared into the forest. 'You did well, Vichitra,' he shouted, making his way forward.

The boy he referred to was still perched atop a tree, looking intently at his handiwork. On hearing Shashidhwaj's voice, he fastened the rope in his hand to the branch and jumped down in one smooth motion, landing on all fours.

'You bastard! Let us down at once!' The first guard grappled with the rope over his shoulder. 'You have made a huge mistake and will face severe punishment!'

Shashidhwaj signalled to Gouhar, the boy on the right, who still held the other rope. He released it and the guard fell to the ground with a scream, not getting even a moment to move his hands before Gouhar was upon him, holding him down with his powerful arms. On his knees, he worked on the belt around the Guard's waist, freeing the now soiled scabbard.

The other guard, still strung up, reached for his sword with his free hand. 'Now!' Shashidhwaj shouted to Vichitra.

They quickly loosened the rope tied to the branch and the second man thudded to the ground like a sack of potatoes, his hand still trying to pull out his sword.

As soon as the man's body rammed into the ground, Shashidhwaj, still holding the rope, yelled, 'Pull!' As the boys yanked with all their might, the man rose up again, surprised by the sudden movement. His hand, jarred by the momentum, came free of the knot and he flew through the air, landing once more on the ground, face down, the sword flying to one side.

Shashidhwaj let go of the rope and ran to secure the sword. Even as the man pressed his palms into the ground to get up, Shashidhwaj was on him, straddling his back while the man yelled curses.

'Still think you can get us?' Shashidhwaj asked the guard. Vichitra, using the same rope that had held the man, was hog-tying his hands and legs.

'You bastard!' The guard opened his mouth only to find it full of mud. He spat angrily. 'I thought you were just a bunch of thieves, but you are brigands!'

By now, Gouhar had freed the other guard's sword and was holding it up like a trophy.

'See, I told you, we don't need to buy swords when we can get them for free,' Shashidhwaj said, smiling at Vichitra, who had finished his task of tying up the guard, and rubbing the dirt from his hands, had got to his feet.

'Why do you want a weapon for, you piece of dung?' the tied guard growled.

In response, Shashidhwaj straddled the man and sat down on him with all the force he could muster. The guard screamed in pain.

'Well, we'd be rather sad brigands without swords, wouldn't we?' Shashidhwaj retorted, placing the naked sword across the back of the guard still pinned under him.

'You stole the zamindar's cattle,' the guard accused.

Vichitra came forward and placed a foot on the guard's tailbone.

'Speak carefully, fellow,' Shashidhwaj warned their victim. 'Presently, we hold your life on a string, like we held your body suspended a few moments ago.'

'You should be punished!' the guard retorted angrily.

'I am happy you show so much passion to punish us,' Shashidhwaj said. 'A less motivated man would not have chased me through such thick foliage.'

'I would have seen the ropes if I hadn't been so focused on you, damned rat!' the guard grunted.

'What are we to do with them?' Vichitra asked.

'Tie this one up.' Shashidhwaj got to his feet, picking up the sword.

The guard below him immediately attempted to move, but a strong kick was all that was needed to make him fall back on the ground.

'They just don't give up do they?' Vichitra laughed as he reached for the rope.

Shashidhwaj stared at the naked blade in his hand as Vichitra tied the hands of the guard behind his back. The blade sparkled in the sun. *My first sword!* he thought, as he observed the iron hilt blackened with sweat and dirt from constant holding. It was not as beautiful as he had imagined, but holding it gave him a strange thrill.

'This one's done,' Vichitra nodded, getting to his feet.

'Good.' Shashidhwaj reached for a heavy pouch hanging from the belt around his waist. Carefully, he drew out two copper coins and tossed them to Gouhar, who caught them with a delighted smile. 'You did well,' Shashidhwaj told him. 'Now make yourself scarce. These two will look for you for sure, but they don't know where you live and the Maval is a big place.'

The young boy looked at the coins in their hands and then at Shashidhwaj. He did not need to be told again. In a moment, he had turned and was running rapidly towards the meadow.

'We need to get out of here,' Shashidhwaj said to Vichitra, bending to pick up the scabbard which still lay on the ground. Slowly, he pushed the blade into it, careful not to damage the leather. Then he pushed the scabbard into his waistband. Vichitra, in the meantime, had helped himself to the guard's belt and helmet.

'The zamindar will find you, you bastards!' the guard behind Vichitra yelled, wetting himself in fear as he struggled to free himself.

The sight made Shashidhwaj laugh. 'Let the zamindar find you first,' he scoffed. 'Looks like you need some help to clean up.'

'He will come, and he will seek you out!'

'By the time he does, we will have disappeared.'

'You don't get me, lad,' the first guard scoffed. 'There are already men looking for you in the forest.'

The words made Shashidhwaj's heart skip a beat. These two had been easy game. They had been patrolling the Mukhya Rasta that led from the village to Pune. He had attracted their attention and they had pursued him as a thief. But who were these other men the guard spoke of?

'They will soon find you,' the second guard said. 'And then you will be dragged to the village square to answer to the Zamindar for his lost cows. And you will be hanged for what you have done to us.' He stopped, relishing the thought.

Shashidhwaj took a deep breath. If he was afraid, he did not show it. 'Let them search,' he said. 'It will just mean a supply of more free swords for us.'

'Those men are not just guards,' the first man taunted, his face still in the mud. 'And they *will* find you, mark my words.'

'We must go,' Vichitra urged.

Shashidhwaj nodded. They turned away, leaving the two guards behind them, at the edge of the trees.

'You are nothing but thieves and bandits!' the first guard yelled after them.

Shashidhwaj stopped in his tracks and spun around angrily. Vichitra tried to stop him, but Shashidhwaj was too quick. In a flash, he was right back by the cursing guard's side. As the man looked into the angry face above him, Shashidhwaj suddenly realized that what he saw in the guard's eyes was terror.

'What did you call me?' he demanded angrily, drawing the sword.

The guard opened his mouth but spoke no word. He simply stared, his eyes round as marbles, fright etched in every line of his face.

'Never call me a thief again!' Shashidhwaj held the sword by the blade. In one swift motion he raised the hilt and brought it down on the guard's helmet. Metal hit metal with a loud clang but the guard uttered no sound. He had been knocked out.

'Let that be a lesson to you,' Shashidhwaj muttered.

'We must go!' Vichitra urged urgently.

Shashidhwaj glanced at him and nodded. He sheathed the sword again. 'Let's go back to the hideout,' he suggested. 'If what the guard said is true, we don't have much time.'

The two lads began to run.

***

By the time they reached the hill in the middle of the forest, the sky had turned crimson and the sun had slipped from sight. Shashidhwaj stopped where the hillside fell steeply into a ravine, to take in the sight.

Vichitra was less eager to admire his surroundings. Instead, he sank down on the ground, panting. 'Damn, this sword is heavy,' he complained, unbuckling the belt.

Shashidhwaj had to agree. The clunky metal sabres were indeed pulling them back. They would have covered the distance to their hideout in half the time on any other day. They had kept wobbling as they ran. When Shashidhwaj had lifted it to carry on his shoulders, the leather scabbard chaffed his neck till the skin was raw. Finally, he left it in his waistband, as Vichitra had done.

'How will we fight the zamindar and his guards if we can't even walk a few miles with our swords, brother?' Vichitra groaned, lying supine and exhausted.

The question worried Shashidhwaj. He too let his sword fall

to the ground and felt instantly lighter. 'These belts are too large for us,' he said, observing the long leather strap usually worn from shoulder to hip across the chest. 'I think it would be easier if we cut them to make them shorter. Those oafs carried them around quite easily. It should not be so difficult for us.'

'Those oafs were twice our size,' Vichitra replied sourly. Picking up a stone, he took aim and threw it towards the red rimmed horizon. It hit a tree and rolled down the slope into the dark ravine.

'Their size didn't stop us from stealing their swords,' Shashidhwaj reminded his friend, hands on hips.

Vichitra said nothing, still catching his breath.

Shashidhwaj looked up at the flocks of birds in the sky, circling to rest in the trees. 'It's just a matter of time,' he said. 'Soon we will be as free as those birds, and all the people of the village with us. The rule of the tyrant Zamindar will end and we will liberate the villagers like Raje Shivaji did our people.'

Taking his eyes from the birds above, Vichitra dug his elbows into the ground and turned to look at his friend. Sometimes he just did not understand the fellow. 'Those birds fly in groups,' he observed. 'For now, there are only the two of us.'

'Two of us, and two of those.' Shashidhwaj pointed to their swords.

'All I can think of is that we still have to carry them down the slope,' moaned his friend.

Shashidhwaj laughed, pulling Vichitra to his feet. 'Let's go. It will soon be dark. We should get to the cave.'

Vichitra dusted off his clothes and lifted the sword belt again. He followed in Shashidhwaj's wake as they moved along the narrow trail that led down the rocky cliff. Shashidhwaj led the way, peering through the poor light. By the time they arrived at the bottom of the hill, it had turned dark.

'Finally here!' Shashidhwaj said as they arrived at the small dark opening of a cave.

'I'll get the fire going.' Vichitra dropped his sword thankfully and bent towards a stack of wooden sticks near the entrance. Shashidhwaj felt around for the flint stones they had left earlier. He passed them to Vichitra, who had by then piled up the sticks and filled the hollow centre with grass. He struck the stones and finally, after an attempt or two, got the fire going. He blew into it, then moved back on his haunches as smoke hit his eyes.

'Why don't you bring the wheat and water we collected yesterday,' Vichitra said from his place by the fire. 'I can make some *khichdi*.'

Shashidhwaj walked towards the entrance of the cave, the glow of the fire behind him. Suddenly, he stopped in his tracks. He backed away from the cave entrance slowly, one step at a time. Seeing this, Vichitra opened his mouth to enquire what he was doing but shut it immediately when he saw Shashidhwaj's taut finger fly to his lips.

'Shush…there is someone inside the cave,' he whispered.

'What! How is that possible?' Vichitra whispered back but shut up when he saw what Shashidhwaj was pointing towards. There were footprints on the ground.

'We must get out of here!' Shashidhwaj reached for the hilt of the sword he still wore at his waist. Despite his joy at acquiring it, he had secretly hoped he would not have to use it so soon. As he pulled Vichitra by the arm, away from the fire, he could feel his friend shaking. 'Be strong! Perhaps whoever is in there has not yet seen us,' Shashidhwaj whispered hopefully.

Mouth shut in mute horror, Vichitra merely nodded. As they turned, the air suddenly came alive with a swooshing sound and then the clang of metal hitting the stony ground. When Vichitra realized what had happened, he let out a cry. Shashidhwaj, who still held him by the arm, remained calm as he saw the arrow land quivering in the earth not a few paces from them.

'The man inside may not have heard you, but the one outside has,' a voice said from the shadow of the trees outside.

Though Shashidhwaj could not see into the pitch darkness, the voice sounded strangely familiar. He drew his sword slowly, the blade sparkling in the firelight. 'Come out and show yourself, whoever you are!' he said loudly. Now of all times, he could not be afraid.

The archer moved into the yellow light, revealing the bow in his left hand and another arrow in his right. But his face remained in shadow. Shashidhwaj tightened his grip on his sword, letting Vichitra's arm go. The lad scurried back to the fire and armed himself with a burning brand.

'I am not afraid of you,' Shashidhwaj said angrily to the figure outside. 'Come forth and fight.'

'You are making a mistake,' the voice said.

'It is *you* who is making a mistake,' Shashidhwaj retorted. 'Take one step forward and I will run you through with this sword.'

'You mean the sword that is twice your size?'

This time the voice came from behind him. Shashidhwaj felt a sudden weight on the blade. Before he could turn, he felt the sword fall out of his hands. He tried to hold on with all the strength in his wrists and fingers, but it escaped his grasp as if it had a life of its own. Enraged, he turned to physically attack the man behind him. The man extricated his sword and pushed him down onto the ground near the fire, at the feet of the terrified Vichitra, who stood frozen in his tracks.

Angrily, Shashidhwaj tried to rise and punch the metal breastplate of his attacker, but when he looked up, he froze. 'It's you!' The hoarse words somehow found their way out of his dry mouth.

'Or rather, it's us.' The other man propped up his bow and came forward to join his companion.

The firelight glimmered on their faces as Shashidhwaj looked from one to the other. Sure, the beards had grown longer, and the men were covered with dust, but there was no mistaking these two, whom he had met less than a few months ago on the slopes of Katraj.

'Are you here to hurt us?' Shashidhwaj asked carefully, knowing well what these men were capable of.

It was Bahirji who moved first. He reached for his pockets and drew out his chillum. He turned to the fire and squatted by the flames, lighting the pipe. 'Asks the boy who was threatening to kill me not a few moments ago,' he said casually.

'What are *you* doing here?' Shashidhwaj asked, staring at him blankly. Why were they in this desolate cave? It did not make any sense to him.

Vichitra stood staring at the strange men, still shocked by their sudden appearance.

Shashidhwaj nodded to him. 'These are the two men I told you about. The Guptachars.'

The look in Vichitra's eyes transformed from fright to ardent admiration. 'You mean the ones who gave you the coins which you never gave the zamindar?'

Shashidhwaj nodded, regretting having told this to Vichitra. 'Have you come for the coins?' he asked, trying not to stammer.

Standing by the fire, his tall figure casting a grotesque shadow into the cave, Naik shook his head. 'We care naught for the coins we give away, lad,' he said carelessly.

'But I did not give them to the zamindar sahib,' Shashidhwaj muttered, 'like my friend here just said.'

'I am more interested in what you did with the cattle,' Bahirji said, taking a drag at his chillum. 'How did you find them after what happened that night?'

Shashidhwaj sighed as he remembered the long morning he had spent tramping outside the walls of Pune, looking for the cows he had let loose the night before. 'It didn't take long,' he said. 'None were hurt. Found them right by the city walls.'

'What about the city guards?'

Shashidhwaj shrugged. 'The guards were a hindrance but some of the coins you gave me came in handy.'

'A few coins for twenty-one cows?' Naik laughed, 'A sharp trade, I must say.'

'Actually, I found only eighteen.' Shashidhwaj counted on his fingers. 'Don't know where the other three went.'

'So what did you do with the cows?' Bahirji asked, amused by the tale.

Shashidhwaj looked around, but there was nowhere to go. He was at the mercy of these two. 'I sold them,' he sighed. 'At the weekly fair at the Pune stables.'

Naik folded his arms. 'Did they go for as much coin as I gave you, or more?'

'More.'

'So I win the bet, Naik.' Bahirji spit into the fire, filling the air with the pungent smell of his chillum. 'I told you he would never give the coin to the zamindar, and that he would round up the cattle.'

Sighing in disgust, Naik reached for the pouch slung at his waist and drew out a gold coin. He tossed it towards the fire, where Bahirji deftly caught it in one hand.

'You look as gloomy as the zamindar when he told us the story,' Bahirji chuckled, observing his bright coin. It gleamed in the shimmering light.

'So the Zamindar sent you?' Shashidhwaj moved back a step. 'Are you the men his guards were talking about? The ones sent into the forest to catch us?'

'You already know we do not work for the zamindar, lad,' Bahirji said, getting to his feet and pocketing the coin. He looked pleased with himself.

'But then what are you doing here? Have you come for your share of the coins?' Shashidhwaj asked.

'The men with the swords usually do the asking, boy,' Naik said drily. 'So we ask, you answer. What are you doing here?'

Shashidhwaj took a deep breath. If he had walked into their trap, what was the point of lying? He decided to reveal the truth. 'I am raising a rebellion against the zamindar,' he said obstinately.

By the fire, Bahirji burst into laughter. Naik appeared amused too, but kept his composure. 'Why in the seven hells would you do that?' he asked. 'You had all that coin. Why would you not spend it or go to live in the town, or just move away and buy your own cows? There were a thousand things you could have done, yet you chose to come here to this smelly cave and tell us you are rebelling against the zamindar?'

'The zamindar is a tyrant.' Shashidhwaj said, holding his ground. 'He beats small children. He molests women and takes the wives of the village folk.' He clenched his jaw in anger. 'He is a bad man.'

'And what is it you intend to do? Fight him?' Naik looked from one young face to the other. 'Just the two of you?'

'Yes.' Shashidhwaj raised his chin stubbornly. 'We have coins now. It is just the start. Soon more will join us.'

'And where did you get those swords?' Bahirji asked, pointing. 'Really bad craftsmanship I see. You'll be lucky if you can hold them up in one piece.'

'Very noble dreams you have, boy,' Naik said, 'but I'm afraid we have to put a stop to them.' He whistled, and they heard the sound of hooves. The men's horses now stood outside in the darkness.

'No you won't!' Shashidhwaj moved fast as he slid across the ground and grabbed his sword with his right hand. When he stood upright again, he saw that Vichitra too, had drawn his blade, looking afraid but determined. Shashidhwaj's anxious gaze flickered from one to the other of the men, waiting to see how they would react.

Bahirji watched him for a few moments, then turned his chillum upside down and let the charred remains fall into the fire. 'You know what, the boy is right Naik,' he said. 'We have been to this village he speaks of, and what he says is true. They hate and fear the Zamindar and his guards. Eyes do not lie.'

Naik nodded. 'Indeed. Also, I didn't like that face. For sure the zamindar is an ugly bastard.'

'So are you two going to join me in my rebellion?' Shashidhwaj asked, not lowering his sword.

Bahirji burst into laughter. This time, even Naik could not help but smile a little. 'No, lad,' he said. 'Instead, you two boys are going to join us in ours.'

'Listen to me closely.' Bahirji was no longer laughing. His eyes glittered strangely as he looked at the boys. 'You live in the Swarajya now. It is a land of laws, unlike the Mughal realms outside. Here, bad men are punished, but they are punished by the law, not by sixteen-year-old rebels.'

Shashidhwaj looked at him unconvinced.

'True,' Naik nodded. 'Let me put it this way. Twenty years ago, a sixteen-year-old rebelled so that no other sixteen-year-old would have to rebel again.'

Shashidhwaj knew Naik spoke of Raje. He lowered his sword. Seeing him do so, Vichitra did the same. Naik quickly put out the fire, and they all went outside.

Taking hold of the reins of one of the horses, Bahirji pointed to Vichitra. 'That one is somewhat skittish, Naik,' he said. 'Why not take him to Javali with you? The jungle might toughen him up a little.'

'And this one has no lack of courage.' Shashidhwaj saw that Naik was pointing at him. 'Maybe someone needs to teach him to be afraid of certain things.'

'You know the best person for that job,' Bahirji laughed, mounting his horse. 'And you know where to find him. Old Nanaji Deshmukh would love to have a student under his iron grip again.' Bahirji looked down at Shashidhwaj. 'Perhaps he will finally stop treating *us* like recalcitrant pupils.'

'Come, lads!' Naik said in an authoritative tone. 'Get your things and mount up. 'We would love to sit by a warm fire, but we cannot waste any more time here now that our mission is complete.'

'And what mission was that?' Shashidhwaj asked, sheathing his sword.

'To find the boy who took our money and started a rebellion of his own,' Bahirji smiled. One of his teeth sparkled in the yellow light like gold.

Shashidhwaj saw the smile and wondered, was this really it? Was he to throw in his lot with the Guptachars now? He looked towards Vichitra, who was staring at him, bemused, and nodded reassuringly. 'I trust these men,' he said. 'Let's get our things and go with them.'

Vichitra finally smiled, letting out his breath in a long whoosh of relief.

'We ain't got all night!' Naik said loudly. 'I will count to ten. One, two…'

His voice dissolved into the air as both Shashidhwaj and Vichitra dashed back into the now dark cave. They were out again in a few moments, clasping their bundles and swords.

'Better say your good-byes,' Bahirji advised, as he took the small bundle of possessions from Shashidhwaj and helped him climb up behind him. 'It will be a while before you two see each other again.'

Shashidhwaj looked at Vichitra, perched behind Naik. The boys said nothing, merely nodding at each other, their faces grave.

'Where are they going?' Shashidhwaj asked Bahirji as the horses broke into a trot.

'The first rule of spies is to never to reveal where they are going.'

Naik looked back at them once and then kicked his horse into a gallop. Soon man and boy were lost in the darkness.

'So where are we going?' Shashidhwaj asked, peering over Bahirji's shoulder. He felt a sudden thrill thinking of the adventures to come.

'We are going to Rajgad, boy,' Bahirji said as the horse broke into a canter.

The wind brought the words back to Shashidhwaj like an echo. How sweet they sounded. *To Rajgad…*

Chapter Five

The Lion's Den

SIX MONTHS BEFORE

The afternoon heat in Surat was unbearable as usual. Oxenden hated being out at this time of day, especially in his long official wig and red officer's jacket with its pinstriped medals. He longed to shed these stifling accoutrements and wear something more loose-fitting. But he could not do that today, for the meeting he was to attend was of utmost importance.

As he crossed the moat that led to the Qilla, Oxenden observed the bastions on both sides with interest. They were round with battlements on top, and had a distinctly Saracen look. The walls were massive, with an elephant's girth. As he walked in through the gates, he was well aware that it was impossible to take the fort from land. It had been built to ensure that. Any attempt to take it had to be made from the sea.

From within the inner courtyard, the ramparts behind the battlements became visible. Oxenden silently counted the cannons mounted on them. They were a dozen facing in each direction. At the far end of the courtyard he could see the remaining two bastions, towering over the Subhedar's official residence. Then his gaze moved back to the open courtyard and he caught sight of the large bearded man standing there, staring at him. Oxenden walked up to him.

'Welcome,' said Muhabbat Khan, Qilladar of the fort, and the Subhedar's son. He sported a long moustache and unkempt beard. 'It has taken a while for the President of the Angrez to step foot in the Quila' he observed in a low, rumbling voice.

Oxenden took off his hat in greeting, but frowned at the words. 'In our country, it is considered polite to await an invitation from the host,' he said.

'And yet you visit our country without one,' Muhabbat Khan remarked, leading the way towards the main building. 'I hope Shethji Vora was clear on the etiquette to be followed for meetings with the Mughal Subhedar?'

Oxenden nodded, remembering the terse instructions Virji Vora had given him a short time ago. He was to remove his shoes before entering the chamber. Smoking was not permitted. He would not be offered any alcoholic beverage, nor should he carry such a gift for his host. Oxenden glanced at the bottle of dark honey that Smith, following behind, was carefully carrying in both hands.

'The Shethji knows both our cultures well. I am sure his instructions were correct,' Oxenden responded, none too pleased.

'Such knowledge has made him the most successful merchant in town.' Muhabbat Khan gave a hearty laugh. 'Take off your shoes here.'

Oxenden's brow beaded with sweat as he struggled to remove his leather boots while Muhabbat Khan slipped easily out of his *paydans*. Cursing silently, Oxenden bent and removed his boots one after the other. Immediately, a servant came forward with a pitcher of rosewater and a towel, so he could wash and dry his hands.

Smith did the same, placing the honey jar carefully on a ledge first and then picking it up again after the ablutions were done.

Oxenden looked for a place to hang his jacket but there was none, so he kept it on.

'Welcome to the abode of the Subhedar, my father,' Muhabbat Khan announced, ushering them in.

Oxenden walked in, Smith following like a silent shadow, relieved to be out of the sun at last. Large *pankhas* swung above them, their ropes pulled by servants.

'Through here.' Muhabbat Khan led the way down a narrow passageway that led to the main hall.

On entering, Oxenden smelled smoke but it was not the distinctive aroma of tobacco. It must be what the locals called opium, and the wealthy smoked with such delight, Oxenden thought.

Inayat Khan, the Mughal Subhedar, was seated on a low chair, close to the floor, his legs crossed. In his hand he held the embroidered pipe leading to the *hookah* by his side, propped up by bolsters on either side.

'I offer the Subhedar of the Mughals, my formal greetings,' Oxenden said stiffly, as Vora had instructed.

A smile appeared on Inayat Khan's face and he gestured for Oxenden to sit. 'Welcome,' he said. 'You are our most valued guest. What can I offer you? Some *sherbet* perhaps?'

'I am told your buttermilk is the best in Surat,' Oxenden replied politely, remembering Vora telling him that the drinks served here, other than simple buttermilk, would cause him discomfort later.

Oxenden watched Muhabbat Khan gesture to a servant, who hurried away to do his bidding. It took him a while to settle into the low chair offered him. He finally did so, wondering how on earth he was to rise again. Smith continued to stand in the shadows behind him.

Raising his hand, he indicated the ceramic pot Smith held. 'A gift, Subhedar' he said. 'A bottle of the finest honey from Egypt. A sample of one of the wares we send back home to our country from the East. Her Majesty, the Queen of England, is known to prefer this particular honey above all others.'

Smith immediately held out the pot of honey in both hands. A servant immediately came forward and took it from him, taking it to the Subhedar and bending low with it in his hands so his master could inspect the gift.

'Honey!' Inayat Khan laughed, his harsh featured face lightening into lines of amusement. 'You offer me honey?' He threw Muhabbat Khan a questioning look.

'I told the Shethji to speak to him,' his son said with a shrug, disassociating himself from the *faux pas*. Who but an Angrez would offer a Mughal honey?

Inayat Khan transferred his gaze to Oxenden.

It was Oxenden's turn to smile ingratiatingly. 'The Shethji told me how your religion preaches humility and simplicity,' he said. 'What better gift can there be than the purity of honey?'

Inayat Khan cleared his throat and waved a hand. The servant immediately backed away with the gift, disappearing from sight.

'I do not recall the name of your predecessor in Surat,' Inayat Khan said, 'but it appears that he did not fulfil his duty in instructing you about local customs before he left.'

Oxenden smiled, knowing he had deftly deflected the matter of the gift of honey. 'No, we did not have the opportunity to talk,' he now said, 'for the man was taken away in chains, charged with corruption.' He recalled the great scandal it had caused back home. The Directors of the East India Company had made a quick decision, based on Oxenden's reputation for incorruptible integrity, and sent him to Surat immediately. 'It appears that he misappropriated the ships' stores and sold them for gain. But he did write a letter to me in which he made it clear that to do business in Surat, we were obliged to pay the local government taxes.'

'Ah taxes,' Inayat Khan nodded sagely. 'But there are some things that defy the written word, don't you think?'

'So, do you pay your taxes?' Muhabbat Khan asked, having taken a seat beside his father.

Oxenden had not expected such directness. It was said that Mughal etiquette dictated skirting around a harsh subject delicately. But Surat was a commercial town, and perhaps the only language here was currency. Well, if this was how it was, so be it, Oxenden thought.

'The right question perhaps is, am I paying the right taxes?' he offered.

Inayat Khan burst into laughter, hookah smoke emerging from his mouth and nostrils. Beside him, Muhabbat Khan folded his arms. Apparently it was going to be a long session with this Angrez.

A servant came in with a tray on which sat three gleaming glasses filled with frothing buttermilk. He offered these to the three men. As he drank, Oxenden felt the coolness travel down his throat and closed his eyes for a moment.

'That is indeed the question,' agreed Muhabbat Khan, lowering his glass. 'Do you think you are? For six moons you have been the Angrez President in Surat, yet you have paid us nothing. You bring into our ports materials worth thousands of mahmudis, yet not one mahmudi finds its way to us.'

'But our Company has been paying taxes regularly for the privilege of trading here in Surat, directly to Agra.' Oxenden stressed the last three words.

'Then perhaps you should do business in Agra.' Muhabbat Khan stood up. 'And not here in Surat.'

'Relax, my son.' Inayat Khan reached out and touched his son's sleeve. Then he looked at Oxenden. 'The Mughal Empire is generous. The punishment for crimes of an economic nature is also economic. When a man has not paid his taxes for some time, we do not throw him in jail. All he has to do is pay a fine in addition to the unpaid taxes, and the thing is done. We understand such things.'

Oxenden folded his arms across his chest. 'The Shethji told me this' he said. 'What he did not tell me was what the fine would be.'

'Therein lies the catch.' Inayat Khan placed the hookah pipe aside and got to his feet. He walked over to the windows, his hands crossed behind his back. 'There will be no fine,' he finally said, turning. 'Instead, you will earn yourself a nice quick profit. Whether to share that profit with your Company, lies at your discretion.'

Oxenden took a deep breath. 'I'm listening,' he said.

'We have found ourselves in possession of a vast amount of mahmudis in the past few years.'

No doubt from all the taxes, Oxenden thought dourly.

'Now, normally we would use the mahmudis for whatever purpose we chose,' Inayat Khan continued, 'but in light of recent events, there have been some limitations placed on this.' He glanced at his son.

'There has been word that Agra is looking to declare such mahmudis illegal. There have been rumours that the Alamgir, blessed be his name, is soon to issue a *farman* from his holy seat in Agra, to change the mahmudi into another coin, a process the common folk call *sikkabandi*. People will be able to exchange their mahmudis for the new coin at Imperial Exchequers in every town. But it will be hard for men of our stature to officially show we have so much coin to exchange,' Muhabbat Khan explained speciously. 'Debating the legality of this matter is a task for clerics. But it does mean that both merchants and vendors will refrain from accepting mahmudis soon.'

'But what you speak of is the changing of an entire currency,' Oxenden said worriedly. 'It could disrupt the entire flow of trade for many months.'

'Agra doesn't give two figs about disruption of trade,' Muhabbat Khan said drily. 'Coins have been changed for far less. A few decades ago, the Emperor Shah Jahan banned an entire series of coins because he did not like the symbols upon them. This is a far more plausible reason.'

'But in case of such an action, you would find your years of…ah tax collection… rendered useless.'

'Thus the offer we are about to make you.' Inayat Khan sat down on his low seat again. 'Coins change when rulers come and go, but from time immemorial, there has been one currency that has never changed. Gold.'

The word brought clarity to Oxenden's mind. He now saw what was to come. 'We have not brought gold bullion to India for years,' he remarked musingly. 'Normally, bullion is brought in during the first few months of establishing trade with a country. As we have an abundance of the local currencies and established quality barter systems, there is no need for gold bullion.'

'Yes, that was how we got the idea,' Muhabbat Khan said. 'We checked the amount of gold you brought to Surat in the initial years. Your country is like a gold mine.'

'But our business in Surat has now matured,' Oxenden said hastily. 'There is no longer any gold bullion on any of our ships coming into these waters. All they carry these days are corals, glassware, and tobacco. Our trade situation here does not require any gold.'

'The situation here is known to you,' Muhabbat Khan suggested, 'but not to your masters back home.'

'You are the President of the Angrez in Surat, as well as all of Hindoostan, are you not?' Inayat Khan asked. 'I am sure your word carries immense weight. A letter from you about how your investigations have revealed large scale corruption among officials, leading to mistrust in the system and a reticence on the part of traders to deal in coin, will easily persuade them to send another shipment of bullion to re-establish such a lucrative trade.'

'And do not worry about the sikkabandi, for it will not affect you at all,' Muhabbat Khan said, waving his arms. 'Though there is no certainty it will really happen, we do not wish to take the risk, being the cautious men we are. And if it does happen, I am sure Agra will not ask foreign merchants like you to prove your source of mahmudis. They would just exchange them in the regular way. As you said, you have conscientiously paid your taxes.'

Oxenden sat on, deep in thought. This was getting interesting. If the father-son duo wished to be direct, he could be too. 'And suppose I bring the bullion into Surat,' he said. 'What would you pay me for it?'

Muhabbat Khan gestured and a young courtier came forward, carrying a scroll. He whispered something into Muhabbat Khan's ear. Muhabbat nodded and dismissed him. Then he looked up to face Oxenden. 'The prevailing rate is twenty-three mahmudis per *tola*,' he said. 'However, considering the special efforts you will have to make to bring it in, we can offer twenty-four mahmudis per tola.'

'Twenty-five and it's a deal,' Oxenden said, crossing his arms with an air of finality. An inveterate Bridge player, he knew he held the better hand in this game.

Father and son looked at each other. Neither face betrayed any emotion. Muhabbat Khan turned back to Oxenden. 'We agree,' he said.

The Englishman closed his eyes for a moment and then nodded. 'Also, there is the matter of security,' he said. 'I would not trust my men to unload such valuable cargo into our warehouses.'

Muhabbat Khan nodded. 'We can arrange security. I know a good man.'

'It is done then,' Oxenden said. 'What you are asking me to do will take some time, maybe a few months. But it is not impossible.'

'You do this and your fine will be cancelled,' Inayat Khan said.

'But remember this, *Firang*,' Muhabbat Khan said, suddenly ferocious, 'deceive us in any way and I will personally make sure that not a single one of your ships is able to load or unload in Suwali again.'

'The Shethji has already made sure of that,' Oxenden said, struggling to his feet. 'In my country, when gentlemen shake hands, the deal is sealed.' He removed his glove and extended his hand.

Muhabbat Khan gazed at it for a moment, then stretched out his own and shook hands.

Inayat Khan looked piously at the ceiling. 'The less I know about all this, the better,' he said. 'Regarding this matter, you will speak only to my son. The sooner it is done, the better.'

'Indeed, indeed,' Oxenden murmured. 'I will take my leave of you now.' He bowed slightly and walked out, Smith hurrying behind him.

When the Englishmen had departed, Inayat Khan turned to his son. 'Who do you have in mind to oversee the unloading and transfer of the gold?' he asked.

Muhabbat Khan gulped down the last of the buttermilk in his glass and put it down. 'Only the very best criminal scum this city possesses,' he mocked. 'The one who is always successful in whatever task he undertakes. The one they speak of in whispers in the inns. The one they call Rayiyas.'

Chapter Six
Atop Rajgad

FIVE MONTHS BEFORE

On Rajgad, the sun seemed to rise early. Either that or the gruelling training regimen had taught him to sleep less. When Shashidhwaj's lids rolled up, filling his eyes with light every morning, the first thing he was conscious of was his aching back. He wanted to keep lying on the comfortable mattress of hay, close his eyes and go back to sleep. Alas, life was not so easy!

The last few days had been a blur. From the hills of Katraj, atop Bahirji's horse, they had ridden through forested mountain passes, following Naik and Vichitra, and crossing a river. It was at the river that they had separated, Naik and Vichitra taking the path that led to Javali. Bahirji and he had continued on, and after a day of hard riding, the Sahyadri Hills had appeared against the skies. Bahirji had pointed to where they were heading, explaining that the hill used to be called Mountain of Murumbdev by the locals, but now that Raje had built his fort atop it, it was known as Rajgad.

In the dim light of dusk, Shashidhwaj strained his eyes to get a good look. 'All these hills look the same to me,' he complained.

'And the builders of Rajgad made pretty sure that they would,' Bahirji taunted as he prepared a small campfire.

As Shashidhwaj lay on his back on the hard ground that night, the starry skies and the constant chirping of crickets kept him awake. 'So what do you do as Raje's spy?' he asked finally, turning on his side.

'I'd be a bad spy if I told you.' Bahirji, tired from the long ride, was in no mood to indulge the boy.

'But do you fight enemies?' Shashidhwaj persisted. 'You infiltrate enemy camps? Kill the Mughals?'

The boy was like an irritating mosquito in his ear, Bahirji thought. 'We do whatever needs to be done,' he said sleepily.

'It must be so exciting!'

Even in the darkness, Shashidhwaj could feel Bahirji smile. 'Indeed it is,' he said.

'Aren't you ever afraid?'

'Of what, boy?'

'I don't know. Of getting hurt? Being caught? Dying?'

'And aren't you ever afraid of asking questions?'

'I wouldn't ask once I know the answers,' Shashidhwaj cajoled.

Bahirji just laughed and closed his eyes.

Shashidhwaj gave up and stared at the sky. Gazing at the numerous stars overhead, he never knew when sleep overcame him.

It was in the early morning light that he finally saw Rajgad Fort clearly. It appeared like a huge bird, with its black legs spread across the arms of the hill. The mound in the middle had fortifications on top.

Bahirji pointed, saying, 'That is where Raje lives.'

The steep cliffs were made of hard rock. The thought of Raje climbing to the top every day made Shashidhwaj shiver with excitement.

They rode along the dusty path that led to the bottom of the rocky hill on which the fort stood. Bahirji gestured to Shashidhwaj to get off the horse. The boy did so and then watched silently as Bahirji hitched the horse to a tree.

'We will have to walk from here,' he said.

The memory of that first day brought a smile to Shashidhwaj's face as he rolled off his hay bed. It seemed but yesterday that he had trudged up that hard climb to the fort. Since then, two moons had passed. Shashidhwaj stretched his arms lazily over his head. Suddenly, he heard the sound of approaching footsteps.

'How many times do I have to tell you that only boys who rise before the sun do something worthwhile in life?' Nanaji strode in, chiding. 'The sun is up, but you are not.'

'I'm awake,' Shashidhwaj protested. 'I was merely thinking.'

'Thinking about what, my head?'

Nanaji Deshmukh was his usual grumpy self in the morning. Shashidhwaj saw no point in arguing and jumped out of bed as fast as he could. He walked out of the hut and went towards the drum of water to splash his face.

Nanaji, standing like the figure of nemesis behind him, tossed him a *pancha*. 'Go have a bath and return on the double,' he yelled. 'I do not have all morning.'

Shashidhwaj did not need to be told twice. He slung the cloth over his shoulder and set off for the water tank, some distance away. Nanaji's hut was located on one of the *machis* of the fort, below a huge *jamun* tree. A fresh water lake had been created nearby, dug from the rocks, next to a temple dedicated to the Goddess Padmavati. So both the lake and the machi were known by the same name. The water from the lake was collected in small tanks a few feet away, where folks living on the machi could use it. Because of the ample space available on the machi, it was like a small village in itself, with numerous huts and a few stone buildings. It was here that most of the families of officials resided. The fort granaries were also located here.

As Shashidhwaj poured cold water over himself, shivering in the wind, he wondered what strange training Nanaji had planned for the day. He wiped himself dry with the pancha and set off back to the hut on the double. Nanaji was not known for his patience.

Every morning, Nanaji woke Shashidhwaj with a long series of irritated shouts and curses, grumbling about how the youth of today loved sleeping more than working. After he had finished his morning rant and gone into the yard to prepare for the day's training, Nanakku, his long-suffering wife, would quickly slide a *thali* to Shashidhwaj, containing a short repast. It tasted better than anything he had eaten back in his village. Today was no different, and Shashidhwaj ate the simple meal with relish.

Following his arrival on Rajgad, the first thing Nanaji taught Shashidhwaj was swordsmanship. Much to Shashidhwaj's discontent, his teacher was more concerned with how to hold the sword and how his grip was all wrong, than in allowing him to hack and slash at the cloth dummies in the yard. In fact, there was little hacking or slashing. Whenever he complained about this, Nanaji would tell him that hacking and slashing would come easily once he had perfected his grip and footwork. Shashidhwaj did not see how that would come about, but one look at Nanaji's stern face had taught him that silence was the better part of valour and it would be best to bend his mind to following instructions precisely.

Once that was done, they had moved to archery. Shashidhwaj hated holding the heavy bow and keeping the bowstring stretched as Nanaji moved around him with a stick. He felt the stinging strikes on his back and calves as Nanaji complained how he was not pulling the string using his back muscles, and how his legs were positioned wrong. Only when his shoulder muscles felt on fire from the strain of pulling the bowstring, would Nanaji, finally satisfied, ask him to let go of the arrow, the target being a tree. The arrow always found its mark. Shashidhwaj was convinced he could have done it just as well without undergoing the beatings from the stick.

These activities occupied the morning hours, when the sun was mild and it was pleasant outside. Once the sun turned into a scorching ball over their heads, they would move inside, and much to Shashidhwaj's dismay, Nanaji would teach him his letters. He had by now learned to read full sentences. It was writing that he struggled with. Nanaji would angrily comment on how bad his handwriting was. This would cause his hand to shake even more as he drew and redrew the letters. Nanaji also taught him other strange languages, instead of helping him make better use of the tongue he already spoke. He would always say that a spy had to know the language and script of the enemy better than his own.

The evening was reserved for horse riding. Shashidhwaj was delighted that finally here was something for which Nanaji could not follow him around with a stick. Nanaji's back hurt when he rode, hence all he could do was stand in one place and bark instructions and curses. Shashidhwaj was happy that the curses were few, for horse riding was something that came naturally to him. After the first few lessons by Nanaji, he could ride around the machi pretty well on his own.

However, once these usual skills had been covered, Nanaji's exercises became stranger and stranger day by day. And, on this day, when Shashidhwaj walked into the stable beside the hut, someone suddenly grabbed him from behind and he felt the tightness of a rope around his wrists. Nanaji pushed him and he lost his balance. Shashidhwaj grunted, spitting out dirt. He strained his head backwards to look at Nanaji, but the rope did not allow him to turn.

'Your task is to escape from this,' Nanaji said, standing

over him. He let the end of the rope fall to the ground and rubbed his hands in anticipation.

Shashidhwaj struggled with the rope that secured his hands behind his back. He clenched his teeth, trying to break free. Amused, Nanaji watched him struggle for a while. Then he laughed. This was such a rare occurence that Shashidhwaj stopped moving and turned to stare.

'Do you think you'll tear the rope apart with your arms, boy?' Nanaji asked.

'If only I was bigger and stronger.'

'One thing you should know, boy, ropes will always be stronger than your wrists, however big you become.'

Shashidhwaj tried to get to his feet, but Nanaji hit his stick on his legs and he fell back to the ground.

'The only way to defeat a rope is to find something stronger than the rope,' he said.

Shashidhwaj looked to where he was pointing - the iron gratings that held up the feedstock for the horses. He moved towards them, dreading another hit from Nanaji's stick. But it did not come, which meant he was moving in the right direction.

'Always remember that it is not sharpness that beaks the rope, but heat.' Nanaji took a length of the rope between his hands and tightened the portion between. He held it against the metal grating and rubbed. 'With more rubbing, the same heat can be created on a blunt rod that from a sharp blade.'

Shashidhwaj struggled to do the same with his hands tied behind his back. 'Nothing is happening,' he complained.

'Another lesson, boy,' Nanaji grunted. 'All good things in life take time.' He watched amused as Shashidhwaj kept rubbing against the iron rod, his teeth clenched.

'How much time will it take?' Shashidhwaj asked, stopping for breath.

'The first time I did it, it took me half a day.' A mischievous grin crossed Nanaji's lined face as he folded his arms across his chest. 'You get better at it, but it takes practice. That is what you have to do here, practice. So that when the enemy captures you like this, you are already good. Lunch will be served after you have freed yourself, boy,' he announced, walking out of the shed.

Shashidhwaj cursed under his breath as he returned to rubbing the rope binding his wrists, against the pipe. He remembered looking into Nanaji's glimmering brown eyes when Bahirji had first introduced him outside his hut on Padmavati machi.

'He looks so kind,' Shashidhwaj had commented, looking at the old man's slender frame.

'Do not labour under any such misapprehension, boy!' Bahirji had whispered to him. 'The man is a proper bastard. I'm sure you will be hating him the next time I see you.' Then, as Nanaji had approached within earshot, Bahirji had quickly bent to touch the venerable master's feet. Shashidhwaj had copied him without wasting a moment.

'He taught me all I know,' Bahirji had said after Nanaji had moved away. 'And let us hope he will teach you many things too, in the time you stay here.'

'But I can already wield a sword,' Shashidhwaj boasted. He had hoped to come to Rajgad and become a spy. He did not want to be schooled.

'Yes, we already saw how well you can wield it in the jungles of Katraj,' Bahirji laughed.

Nanaji returned, holding two empty coconut shells filled to the brim with buttermilk. He gave one to Shashidhwaj, and when Bahirji put forward his hands, Nanaji simply ignored him and began drinking the liquid himself. 'I trust you have given up your chillum by now,' he said.

Shashidhwaj suppressed a smile as he watched Bahirji trying

to discreetly ensure that the pipe at his belt was well hidden. 'Of course, Nanaji,' Bahirji said piously. 'Never again since we last met.'

Nanaji stared at him, his eyes as unmoving as the Sahyadri Hills. 'Ummm...' he muttered dryly. 'Wouldn't want you to be a bad influence on young boys like this one.'

'Oh, Naik provides good impressions for the both of us,' Bahirji said, looking around hopefully for some sign of Nanakku. But there was no buttermilk in his fate that day.

'Yes, good man Naik. I miss him,' Nanaji said between sips of buttermilk. 'I wonder why it was not he who brought this boy to me.'

'Naik has gone to Javali,' Bahirji told him. 'And perhaps you should appreciate the fact that it is I who come to see you, unlike your favorite student, Naik, who is always looking for some excuse to stay away.'

'Alas, it is so,' Nanaji commented dryly.

That night, when they slept under the open sky outside Nanaji's hut, on heaps of dried grass, Bahirji pointed out the constellations to Shashidhwaj. 'Do you see the group making the rectangle?' he asked. 'We call them the Saptarshi, after the seven great sages.'

'What were their names?' Shashidhwaj asked curiously.

'Their names do not matter,' Bahirji told him. 'What matters is that if you move your hand straight along the line of the final three stars, you come to the star folk call *Dhruva Tara*.'

'The star that never moves!' Shashidhwaj exclaimed. Even he knew about that one.

'And this star always points to the North. Remember that. Someday, in the deep forest, or in the desert, this knowledge can save your life.'

Shashidhwaj nodded. 'Are you leaving tomorrow?' he asked. He had heard Bahirji instruct the stable master to prepare another horse for him in the morning.

'I have work to do, boy,' Bahirji said from his grass bed. 'My days of lounging around like you are long over.'

Shashidhwaj felt a sudden lump in his throat. 'When will I see you again?' he asked.

Bahirji merely said, 'When it is time.'

Shashidhwaj turned on his side and looked at the Guptachar. 'Can I ask you something?'

'Haven't you been doing a lot of that already?'

The boy paid no heed to this. 'Why did you bring me here? Why me?' he asked, his voice taut.

Bahirji let out a sigh. 'Because I see something of myself in you, boy,' he said finally. 'I saw it on the hills of Katraj, when we first came upon you. And then I saw it again at your cave in the forest.'

'Were you a cowherd too?' Shashidhwaj asked.

'Something like that.'

'Did you also concoct a rebellion?'

'Oh, I did, though of a different kind.'

'Will you tell me about it?'

'Not tonight.' Bahirji put an arm over his eyes and prepared to sleep. Suddenly, he moved his arm and looked straight at Shashidhwaj. 'I want you to learn like a man who thirsts for water, everything that Nanaji teaches you,' he said, his voice hard. 'Not everyone gets to train under him. He is one of the best teachers in the art of spycraft and, in his prime, was Raje's Pramukh Guptachar. You have got this chance because I see potential in you. But know that if you slouch off, the chance will disappear as fast as it appeared.'

Shashidhwaj nodded seriously. This was like a dream come true for him. Ever since he had been of an age to understand, and seen the tyranny of the zamindar in his village, he had yearned to wield a sword and save his village folk from oppression, like a hero from the *Puranas*.

'I will learn everything,' he said. 'I promise that a day will come when I will beat you in all the arts of a Guptachar.'

Bahirji broke in a chuckle and closed his eyes again. 'Keep your enthusiasm for Nanaji, boy. Now sleep, for it will only happen in your dreams.'

Shashidhwaj had waited, hoping that Bahirji would speak again. But nothing more came from him and he was soon snoring like a horse. Shashidhwaj lay awake, staring at the sky, tracing the line Bahirji had just taught him, pointing North. Finally, sleep claimed him.

Little did he know then that it was the last undisturbed sleep he was to have for many a day. Every morning, at the first light of the sun, Nanaji would be standing at his bedside with a stick in one hand and a bucket of cold water in the other.

Shashidhwaj sighed now, remembering the night before Bahirji had left. Despite the burning pain, he continued to rub the rope against the iron pole, refusing to give in. Sweat ran down his face, trickling over his cheeks and dropping from his chin to the ground. Behind him, he could feel the rope giving way. It was just a matter of a little more... He clenched his teeth and rubbed. Suddenly, he felt his hands break free.

Nanaji walked in at this opportune moment and observed his movements with interest. He smiled. 'Less than half a day… Looks like Bahirji wasn't wrong after all.'

Shashidhwaj freed his hands and collapsed face down on the ground, panting. He could think of a thousand stinging replies but nothing came out of his mouth.

'Next time, try not to exhaust yourself,' Nanaji said

laconically. 'Ain't much use freeing yourself if you don't have the energy to escape afterwards.' He turned away.

'Can I eat now?' Shashidhwaj asked, still flat on the ground.

'Only after you show me the moves I taught you two weeks ago.'

Nanaji threw something at him. Shashidhwaj heard the thud of something heavy hitting the ground and quickly spun over. A naked sword lay beside him, waiting to be picked up. In an instant Shashidhwaj forgot all his weariness. He got to his feet, his fingers curling around the hilt of the weapon like an old familiar friend. He looked up and saw Nanaji facing him, sword in one hand, shield in the other. So it was going to be a real swordfight this time.

Shashidhwaj suddenly remembered Bahirji's smile as he had left Rajgad in the wee hours. Standing beside Nanaji, he had watched the Guptachar mount his horse in one fluid motion. His eyes glittering, Bahirji had said to Nanaji, 'I am never wrong about men. It is the Goddess' gift to me. The boy will make a great Guptachar. He has the will.'

'We will see,' Nanaji had responded.

'When will I go on missions like you?' Shashidhwaj had asked with the eager impatience of youth.

Bahirji had looked down from his horse and observed the young face thoughtfully. 'Maybe sooner than you think,' he had said with a smile.

'When?' Shashidhwaj had asked excitedly. He couldn't wait to set off on horseback, sword tied to his back.

'When you can beat Nanaji in a swordfight, you can come with us,' Bahirji had said. 'I see that you now have a little stubble,' he had laughed suddenly. 'Let it grow out. I daresay it will prove pretty useful.'

Then he was gone in a cloud of dust, leaving master and

student standing on the machi, gazing after him.

Now, as they faced each other, Shashidhwaj clenched his teeth and swung his sword with all his might. Bahirji's promise hung in the air like a third sword. *When you can beat Nanaji in a swordfight, you can come with us...* Nanaji was going to face a tough fight today, for Shashidhwaj could not wait to make Bahirji keep his promise. More than that, he could not wait to be one of them. A Guptachar!

Chapter Seven

A Bet in the Market

FOUR MONTHS EARLIER

Oxenden felt the moist heat envelop him as he and his two escorts walked into the market square in their dress uniforms. He was not sure whether the heat emanated from the skies or the thousands of people thronging the square. On most days, he avoided such places, or rode in the vehicles the local folk called *palkhi.* He would get into the wooden box, fixed with poles on either end, which his servants would then pick up to carry him forward. Today, however, he had no choice but to walk, for the main market of Surat during peak hours wasn't a place a palkhi, or even a horse, could venture.

Men rubbed shoulders with him at each step and Oxenden could not hear his own orders, barked to his men. Nor could he see Smith, a few paces ahead of him. He removed the cotton glove from his right hand and wiped the sweat from his brow. The stench was making his stomach roil. He wondered how much longer it would be before they could escape this hellhole. But Smith was nowhere to be seen. This annoyed Oxenden further, because how long they remained depended exactly on the time Smith took to locate their target.

Oxenden stopped by a wall and watched the two men with him look for Smith. His thoughts faded in the hubbub around them. From above, there were shouts as someone threw down a clay pot. Even as Oxenden moved aside reflexively, it broke into a thousand fragments at his feet. The men nearby began to laugh. Oxenden sighed. Where had he got stuck! This was worse than Piccadilly Circus on Guy Fawkes.

One of the men with him caught his attention and pointed. Oxenden followed his finger and saw Smith's hat on the other side of the market. Oxenden pulled his glove on again and pushed into the crowd. Making his way slowly, he emerged on the other side.

Smith was standing near a large stall at the corner. Coloured fabrics hung on bamboo supports and gaudy decorations festooned the poles. Oxenden nodded at Smith and stopped near the grand stall, where Virji Vora stood, admiring the fabrics on display.

'How do you like my new business venture, President?' he asked cheerfully.

Oxenden smirked. He would have preferred to conduct his business with Vora through proxies like Smith, but Vora's fragile ego was well known. If he had sent Smith when Vora had asked him to come personally, it would have been perceived as a slight. And now of all times, he needed the sly merchant. 'It does indeed look grand,' he commented dryly.

'But why so morose?' Vora asked. 'I thought you would be in a cheerful mood following your conversation with the Subhedar.'

'Indeed I was, until I was made to drag through this crowd.' Oxenden could feel the dryness in his throat. He craved a nice cup of tea back in Swally Hole. Instead, he was here in this stinking place, crushed nearly to death.

'I asked you here for a reason. To show you this.' Vora jerked his chin towards the stall. 'I wanted to give you a gift for listening to my wise counsel about the small matter the Subhedar needed attended to. And to show you how profitable it would be for you if we listen to each other.'

Oxenden observed the neatly decorated wares in the stall, and textiles of the finest weave, which the locals called *bafta*. It was fine cotton, dyed in red, blue and black.

'What is this gift?' he asked. 'If I remember correctly, we purchase tons of these fabrics for every ship load.'

Vora shook his head at the Englishman's simplicity. 'The best gift in the world is information,' he said. 'And what I am going to tell you now will save you a lot of money.'

'I'm listening.' Oxenden waited. The cloth was one of the most expensive items he regularly purchased from the Surat markets to send back to England, where it was much in demand with women of the ton, who fashioned it into the latest modes. Anything Vora told him to bring the price down would be valuable.

'I expect you have always tried to negotiate down the price of this cloth,' Vora said, lifting a layer and offering it to Oxenden, so he could feel the texture of the fabric. 'And have always failed in doing so.'

'You are right about that,' Oxenden agreed. The dealers in this kind of cloth never budged from their quoted prices, and his buyers were obliged to inevitably give in. 'The dealers claim the weavers sell it at a huge premium because it is a monopoly product. No one has been able to make cotton this good, not even the Chinese, hence the high prices.'

'But that will change now that I have entered the market,' Vora declared nonchalantly, putting the cloth and waving a hand in dramatic fashion. 'You see, the Chinese sell this bafta to Cambodians at twenty rials a *gaj*. Now, if our manufacturers can match the rate, a whole market would open up in Cambodia. But our artisans are set in their ways. They do not understand that they can make more money at a lower price, by increasing the market size. They prefer to cling to what they know - a limited market at a higher price.'

'Is this your gift, then?' Oxenden asked, brows uplifted 'Do you want me to buy from the Chinese? That would cost more, for our ships would have to sail around the Indian coast to Achin.'

Vora shook his head. 'I wouldn't call it a gift if it were not. What if I tell you that you could get the cloth at the same price as the Chinese, from me, here in Surat?' He smiled, pleased at his own ingenuity.

'I like the sound of your gift, but it sounds rather too good to be true.' Oxenden wiped his brow again, wishing the man would get to the point. It was far too hot for such fencing.

'You will not think so after I explain the rationale.' Vora dug into the rolls of cloth again and pulled one out. Unravelling it, he held it up to the sunlight. Light traversed through the fine cloth and fell in coloured rays on Oxenden's face. 'What do you think this cloth is made of?' Vora asked.

'Yarn,' Oxenden muttered, staring at the thousands of threads in the warp and weft that could be seen clearly against the light.'

'The weavers are foolish and want higher prices.' Vora folded the roll and dropped it back onto the pile. 'But they need yarn to produce it; without which they are just sitting ducks. Now, if someone was to buy all the yarn in the market and leave nothing for these weavers, they would find themselves in a precarious position indeed. All they have known their entire lives is weaving bafta. And if they cannot do that, there isn't anything else they can do.'

'So they will have to negotiate.' Oxenden had to agree that Vora's scheme was quite remarkable. Ruthless certainly, but remarkable. 'Everyone will choose less profit over no revenue.'

'And we shall have Gujarati bafta at Chinese prices,' Vora winked.

'So have you purchased all the yarn in Surat?' Oxenden

asked. It would be a strange thing to do, for Vora could not dispose of so much yarn without it getting into the hands of the local weavers. Then he understood. 'Oh, you want me to purchase it.'

'You are more intelligent than your predecessor, who was more avaricious than astute,' Vora remarked. 'No wonder he got caught by the higher-ups. So foolish, don't you think?'

'I can buy the yarn and sell it in England,' Oxenden mused. 'It will not fetch me a good profit, but it will not make a loss either. And the result would be that the next time our ships come to Surat, they will be able to buy a much cheaper bafta of the same quality.'

'Using loopholes in the market is how we make real money, President Oxenden,' Vora smiled. 'The day you purchase all my yarn and load it onto your ships, I can offer you a future contract bearing my signature and seal, for a lower price of bafta in future. With this scheme, you and I could be Kings of Surat's textile market.'

'Kings who would soon become beggars,' a loud voice declared from behind them.

Oxenden turned to see who it was. Vora did not have to. The smile on his face had already turned into a frown. A man stood gazing at them, a tall *Habshi* hat on his head. His long beard almost touched the belt he wore at his waist. He was dressed in an elaborate robe with a dark green border. Oxenden had never met the man, but from what he observed, and Vora's reaction, he did not need to be told that it was Haji Kasim who had graced them with his presence.

'The price of bafta will never reduce, not even with the weak strategy you have just proposed.' Kasim, casually chewing betle nut *paan*, looked from one to the other.

'Eavesdropping were you?' Vora scoffed, moving to stand beside Oxenden.

'Yes, and you should be glad, for I can save you from

getting into a huge loss.' Kasim spat the contents of his mouth onto the ground. Oxenden tried not to cringe in disgust but his nose wrinkled in distaste.

Vora shrugged, moving back a step. 'My scheme will work very well. You are simply jealous that you did not think of it first.'

Kasim placed a hand on his hip. 'Would you like to place a bet on your chances?' he suggested in a loud voice. 'A thousand mahmudis I will pay if the price of bafta goes down, as you say.'

The crowd around them suddenly fell silent as everyone stopped doing their daily business to listen to what these two famous merchants were arguing over. Even a fragment of information from the mouths of such merchants could mean a month's expenses recovered for lesser shop owners.

Vora looked at Kasim as if watching a monkey act in the street. 'You appear to have more mahmudis than you know what to do with,' he said. 'If you are so fond of giving them away, you should offer them to the holy fakirs who wander around Surat, instead of making a bet you well know you will lose. I, however, have limited money so I prefer to invest it in my business rather than on such frivolous bets.'

'I don't want your money, Vora.' Kasim said between his teeth. 'You are welcome to my money if you win. But if you lose, I just need your word.'

'About what?' Vora asked, intrigued despite himself.

'If I win, you will give me one of your servants. Any one of your choosing. And we shall call it square.'

Vora coughed. He looked around at the crowd, watching to see how he would respond.

'What's wrong?' Kasim mocked. 'Do you have limited servants as well?'

Vora lifted his chin. 'I agree. You will have one of my servants if you win, which I highly doubt. I think these are going to be the easiest mahmudis I have ever made.'

Kasim lifted an upturned palm. 'May the man Allah blesses, win,' he said. Turning, he walked away through the crowd.

With the stand-off over, people went back to their own tasks and the noise rose once more.

'Damn weasel!' Vora cursed, once Kasim was out of earshot.

'The two of you do not seem to be the best of friends,' Oxenden remarked as they walked away from Vora's stall.

'Haji Kasim is a friend to no man but himself.' Vora spit to his side. 'He has been acting like the damsel of the town ever since he strutted in.'

'You mean he is not from here?'

Vora shook his head. 'The bastard made his money in Bengal. He came to Surat a few years ago and has been a pain in my backside ever since.'

Oxenden looked at the bony face of the old merchant. 'I pity the man who comes anywhere near your backside,' he joked.

Vora flicked a hand, as if shooing away a fly. 'I offered him friendship at first,' he said. 'It is always wise to have friends rather than foes. It would have done me no good to have a rival. Alas, it appears Kasim prefers rivalry.'

'So why does he hate you?' Oxenden asked, amused.

Vora gave a laugh. 'One of his agents, whom you knew very well, was killed in the attack on the Dutch convoy,' he said. 'A man called Mohandas Parekh. With Parekh gone, many of Kasim's connections were gone as well. He thinks I was behind the attack.'

'Were you?' Oxenden asked, brows lifted.

'Why would I tell you even if I were, President?' Vora

smiled, shaking his head.

'Why did he ask for one of your servants? Seems rather odd since servants are aplenty.'

'Haji Kasim is as sly as a snake,' Vora said tersely. 'He knows that my servants conduct much of my business. He knows that even one of them would have a treasure trove of information about me and my work. And given the competition between us, he knows that even a few words about my work would be worth millions to him.'

'But why would your servant betray you by giving away information?' Oxenden asked.

'He would not if Kasim asked him like a gentleman,' Vora sighed. 'Unfortunately, he is not one. He would bribe the poor fellow. If he did not accept the bribe, he would be tortured. I have heard of strange contraptions kept in his house for such purposes. The poor servant, though loyal, would be forced to blurt forth whatever he knows.'

Oxenden shook his head, 'You Baniyas indulge in politics at a medieval level,' he remarked thoughtfully. 'I feel I am in ancient Rome. Simpletons like me are used to war. But you people have made Surat akin to the Senate of Ancient Rome, with your business intrigue.'

'I do not know this place you speak of, but I will tell you this, we have to fight to survive,' Vora replied. 'One wrong move and there are vultures out to get us.'

'So how do you propose to protect yourself in this bet?' Oxenden asked curiously.

'I won't have to, because the bastard will lose. I have been in the textile business for decades. If this young fool wants to dabble, let him. He will burn his fingers soon enough.' Vora gave a derisive snort as they stopped at the archway that marked the end of the market.

'We English are grateful for your generosity, as always,' Oxenden said, doffing his hat.

'And as long as you pay me back with the same generosity, we shall both prosper.' Vora showed his broken teeth in a flickering smile. Turning, he went back into the market and was soon lost in the crowd.

'What a sly old fox!' Smith, who was close behind, commented once Vora had departed.

'Aren't we all?' Oxenden mused as they made their way back to the stables to ride back to the comfort of Swally Hole, and a nice cup of tea.

Chapter Eight

Atop the Balekilla

FOUR MONTHS BEFORE

On Rajgad, the days seemed to stretch far into the night. The skies would be aglow until late, then suddenly darkness would fall. It was forbidden to visit Padmavati Lake at night, but Shashidhwaj still went, to pass the night hours. Most nights, he struggled to fall asleep. With his newfound skills, he found it an easy matter to sneak past the guards on duty by the lake. He was sure Nanaji knew of his nightly antics, but the old fox had chosen to ignore them, probably because he took pride in this display of his own teaching skills. So Shashidhwaj would sit beside the lake and stare at the reflection of the moon in the quiet waters. Sometimes, he would walk the long way to Suvela Machi in the west, where there was a hole in the cliff face, formed by years of high wind, and sit there, watching the stars, the wind in his face.

His days were spent training with Nanaji. They had moved beyond many of the initial subjects. Shashidhwaj noticed that what Nanaji was teaching him now, formed the basis of a Guptachar's methods. Nanaji had taught him how to sneak behind a man and take him down. He had shown him how to write secret letters with the juice of a lime, invisible to the naked eye, but emerging when placed near a flame. They trained from dawn to dark, stopping only for a meal at mid-day and again at sunset. Nanaji was secretly pleased to see how quickly the lad learned, but he kept his face stern and he was quick to curse.

In the meagre time he had to practice horse riding, Shashidhwaj visited other parts of the fort. He had discovered that the fort had three gates to reach the top. The one which he and Bahirji had taken on their climb, was the *Chor Darwaja*. It was a secret way into the fort, used mostly by the Guptachars. The other two were the *Pali Darwaja,* which the men of the army and Raje himself used, and the *Gunjavne Darwaja,* used by the common people.

On a couple of occasions, he had seen Raje himself, in the distance. Mounted on his horse, and with his high hat and long beard, he had appeared a remarkable figure, climbing the route to the Pali Darwaja with his entourage. Raje was usually out on campaigns, but when he arrived, the whole fort would take on a frenzied air. People would line up to see him, presenting reports and informing of orders executed, before he took off on yet another campaign.

In their lessons, Nanaji had explained to Shashidhwaj the structure of the Swarajya's army and administration, as well as that of the Guptachar organization, headed by the Pramukh Guptachar, a position Nanaji himself had held in the past, and was now jointly held by Bahirji and Naik. They reported directly to Raje, and took their orders from him. Under them were individual Guptachars, who in turn had had their own informants and assistants. When Shashidhwaj had asked where Raje had found Bahirji and Naik, Nanaji had merely smiled without answering.

In the packed days with Nanaji, that began at sunrise and went on till after dark, Shashidhwaj had not been able to descend to the fort itself and look about him. He made do with climbing the battlements around the Gunjavne Darwaja early in the morning, and staring down at the small houses and trees below. On one such excursion, he had caught sight of a familiar, cloaked man, climbing the dusty pathway to the Darwaja on his horse. Shashidhwaj's eyes lit up. In great excitement, he ran towards the black stone perch on the hillside, which the man would have to pass to reach the gate.

Sadashiv Naik's face was covered in dust from days of riding and it was hard to tell his moustache from his beard. But his head snapped up, and in one piercing glance, recognized the youngster waving at him. Shashidhwaj knew from gazing at his own reflection in Padmavati Lake that he now looked very different from the cowherd he had been. His body was lean and strong, and a growing beard covered his face.

'Back from another adventure are you?' Shashidhwaj asked, hands on hips, as Naik stopped his horse by the gate and jumped off.

'You can say that,' Naik nodded.

'Where's Bahirji?'

'Somewhere far away, being a pain in someone's ass.'

'At least, that way he's not a pain in yours,' Shashidhwaj chuckled irreverently.

'But now I have you to make up for that,' Naik retorted. He ruffled the lad's shoulder length hair playfully. 'Somebody looks all grown up now,' he commented. 'I hope Nanaji has been teaching you everything.'

'He has taught me so many things that I keep forgetting what is what,' Shashidhwaj joked as Naik crossed in through the gate.

Shashidhwaj took the reins from him and walked the horse to the stables. 'Feed him the finest hay,' he called to the Stable Master.

'I know who that horse belongs to,' the Stable Master rumbled, curling his moustache. 'I'm sure his owner would find out before I did if the animal was fed the wrong hay.'

Grinning at this sally, Shashidhwaj ran back to the machi.

Observing the delight on the youngster's face at seeing a familiar face, Nanaji cancelled further lessons and they spent the afternoon with Naik instead.

Shashidhwaj observed Naik's laden plate as Nanakku served them their mid-day meal. 'How come he gets to eat this full meal and you feed me scraps?' he complained.

'The benefits of working hard, while you sit on your ass here,' Naik laughed as he ate.

'Sit…huh! Nanaji makes me work all day. But I think I can beat you in a sword fight now.

'Can you lad?' Naik choked on his food, trying to hold back his laughter.

'Well…not in a sword fight maybe,' Shashidhwaj amended, getting real, 'but in a horse race perhaps.'

'Think twice before you challenge me to anything boy,' Naik cautioned lightly. 'Lose and I will make you brush and feed my horse for all the days I am here.'

'And what will you give me if I win?' Shashidhwaj, asked, his eyes steady on Naik's weather-beaten face.

'Anything you ask,' Naik replied expansively, pleased with the tasty food and his full stomach.

'I want to go on an adventure of my own,' Shashidhwaj said thoughtfully. Bahirji had said he could do so when he could beat Nanaji in a sword fight. He had already done that, not once but thrice, but Bahirji had not shown up.

'You know what, beat me and I will let you,' Naik agreed. 'But first I have an appointment to keep with Raje.'

'What! Raje is here?' Shashidhwaj said in surprise. Raje had left with his horsemen weeks ago and Shashidhwaj had not seen him return.

'He came back to Rajgad last night.' Naik finished his meal and drank down a mouthful of buttermilk with relish.

'You must have been fast asleep.'

'But how do you know?' Shashidhwaj asked curiously, knowing Naik had only just arrived.

'Boy, I am Pramukh Guptachar for a reason.' Naik smiled, finishing the buttermilk.

***

Naik was gone for the whole afternoon and the better part of the evening, so Shashidhwaj enjoyed an afternoon nap for the first time since he had arrived.

While his young protégé slept, Naik climbed the Balekilla, a mound at the centre of the fort, where Raje's quarters were located, and from where the entire fort could be viewed. When Naik finally returned, it was almost sunset.

'How about we have that horse race now?' he suggested, entering the hut.

Shashidhwaj jumped up in delight and rushed off to the stables to get the horses. When he returned, leading the animals, he found Naik and Nanaji in deep conversation. In the soft evening light, he stopped and listened.

'He came by the Pali Darwaja soon after you went up the Balekilla,' Nanaji was telling Naik. 'The guards had him wait because you were with Raje. Now that you are down, they will permit him to climb up.'

'He was in a camp near Nasik three days ago,' Naik said, staring intently in the direction of the Balekilla. 'I wonder if he followed me here? If he did, I have to admit I did not notice.'

'He knows you are up to something, Naik,' Nanaji cautioned. 'He will doubtless try and talk Raje out of it.'

'Let him try.' Naik twisted his moustache between thumb and forefinger. 'Raje is already convinced it is the right action to take.'

Shashidhwaj strained his eyes towards the path leading uphill to the Balekilla, and caught sight of a figure in the distance. He had on a soldier's helmet, and his armoured bodice shone in the saffron glow of the setting sun.

'Oh there you are!' Naik called, noticing Shashidhwaj with the horses. 'Now I wonder why you have brought three horses?'

'Oh Nanaji is going to ride with us,' Shashidhwaj replied, looking towards his tutor. 'What's a race without a referee?'

Nanaji seemed to be in an amiable mood for he agreed without hesitation. 'It would do me good to feel the wind in my face,' he said.

They raced from Nanaji's hut on Padmavati machi to the road that led to Sanjeevani machi in the east. The path was dotted with rocks, but it had become an everyday ride for Shashidhwaj, and he now maneuvered around them expertly, kicking his horse to pick up speed. Naik, however, appeared to be struggling, his mind elsewhere, as he rode along. When Shashidhwaj overtook him, halfway along, the youngster noticed him staring at the Balekilla.

By the time he reached Nanaji, who sat atop his horse under a tree on Sanjeevani machi, just where the Balekilla cliff started rising, marking the finish of the race, Naik was more than ten strides behind.

'I win!' Shashidhwaj shouted jubilantly as Naik finally pulled up beside him.

'It does indeed look that way.' Naik dismounted, a forced smile on his face.

'I taught you better than that, Sadashiv!' Nanaji heckled, laughing in delight at the rare sight of someone besting Naik.

'It appears you taught him better,' Naik said, joining in the laughter. But his eyes were soon pulled back to the Balekilla again, as if by some irresistable force.

'So now you have to let me have an adventure,' Shashidhwaj said. 'You promised.'

Nanaji glanced at Naik, to see how he would respond. Something seemed to be cooking in the Guptachar's mind.

The tall man turned his gaze back to the eager youngster. 'Unlike Bahirji, I keep my promises, boy. I will let you have your adventure,' he said.

Shashidhwaj grunted in excitement. 'So what will it be? Will I get to descend to the fort? Will I have to strike someone from behind? When do we go?'

Naik looked him in the eye. 'How about something that can be done here and now?'

'Like what?'

'Well, did you see the man climbing the path to the Balekilla?'

Shashidhwaj nodded, realizing what was coming.

'Well, how about I see you in action?' Naik suggested, pinching his beard. 'How about you sneak up the Balekilla and tell me what you see?'

'What!' Shashidhwaj stared at him.

'I am serious, boy.' Naik placed both his hands on Shashidhwaj's shoulders. 'I want to know what the man does, says, and hears atop the Balekilla. You wanted an adventure. It's like a match made in heaven.'

'What if I get caught?' Shashidhwaj asked, staring at the rocky cliff that went straight up.

'With that attitude, you definitely will.' Naik folded his arms and spit to one side.

'I guess if I climb up the cliff side, there won't be any guards,' Shashidhwaj mused thoughtfully.

'The less I know about this the better.' Nanaji waved and turned away.

'Oh come on, learn to have a little fun,' Naik mocked the old man, but Nanaji had already mounted his horse and was soon riding away. Shashidhwaj's eyes followed him till he was completely out of sight.

'So what do you say?' Naik asked, brows lifted.

Shashidhwaj shrugged. He studied the cliff carefully. To the untutored eye, it appeared to be a stark, vertical rockface. But he had done his share of climbing in the hills of Katraj, and Shashidhwaj knew what to look for.

'I can climb it,' he said, finally. 'But once it gets dark, I will not be able to get down.'

'The darkness will help you take the normal way back,' Naik told him. 'A spy should always take risks, but not so much that it results in his death.'

Shashidhwaj touched the rockface. It had cooled down in the mild evening sun. He placed a foot in a crevice and then glanced over his shoulder at Naik. 'Will you catch me if I fall?' he asked.

'And explain to everyone here why I had my new apprentice climbing the cliff to the Balekilla?' Naik laughed. 'No way in hell!'

'Hmmm....' Shashidhwaj grimaced, placing a hand on the rock. He stared straight up. The climb would not be easy he knew, but it did not seem intimidating either.

Once he began to climb, he saw nothing but the small cracks in the rocks to hold on to. His movements began to take on a rhythm. He would raise a hand and find a crack, grab onto it and then move his leg to where his hand had been earlier. He crabbed his way up the rockface.

Shashidhwaj did not know when he reached the top. But once his hand touched the grass tufts above, he pulled himself up and lay spread-eagled and still. The sky had turned dark blue and the sun had disappeared behind the clouds. Soon it would be dark.

Shashidhwaj turned on his stomach and took in the lay of the land. There was plenty of grass here, almost waist high, where he could hide if someone came. Beyond the grass he could see the roofs of buildings made of stone. This was the first time he had been on the Balekilla. He wondered where Raje lived. Raising himself to a crouched position, he moved silently through the grass. He could see the mashaals on the massive gate that led to the main area.

And it was in the light of these mashaals that he saw the figure he was looking for enter, now clearer than before. The man had a distinct military bearing. His frame was large and bulky, his moustache thick. When the guards at the gate saw him, they bowed respectfully and let him pass without question. Shashidhwaj moved through the grass, parallel to the man, keeping him in sight. He was walking towards one of the buildings on the far side, with walls of stone, and a thatch roof.

Shashidhwaj moved to the edge of the grass and stopped in his tracks. He saw a figure was walking out of the building, dressed in a white flowing tunic, tied with a belt around his waist. Raje. Shashidhwaj felt his heart skip a beat. It was the first time he was seeing his King at such close distance. Without his customary tall hat and hair tied behind his back, Raje's face appeared very different.

Shashidhwaj saw the armoured man stop. Raje narrowed his eyes to see who it was, then recognizing his visitor, exclaimed, 'Netoji!'

Nanaji's lessons on the hierarchy of the Swarajya flashed through Shashidhwaj's mind. Netoji Palkar was the *Sarnaubat* of the Maratha army, second-in-command to Raje himself. It was on his orders that the members of the *pay-dal* and *ghod-dal* moved.

Netoji bowed. 'You do not seem happy to see me, Raje.'

'I am happy, just surprised by your sudden appearance. Wecome, Netoji.' Raje spread his arms wide, walking forward to hug the man.

But Netoji remained where he was. 'You have not replied to my letters,' he said.

'Your words left me little to reply to,' Raje said, his arms falling to his sides.

'I put down honest questions, Raje,' Netoji persisted. 'Questions that many of my comrades also worry about, but cannot ask.'

'What you wrote were accusations.' Raje turned and started walking back.

Netoji moved forward to walk by his side. 'The *Mavlas* have not been paid wages for the third straight month,' he said. 'If that is not cause for worry, I do not know what is.'

'You wrote to blame me for the unpaid wages,' Raje said, without looking at his guest. 'I did not see cause to reply to such undignified language and baseless accusations. And from you Sarnaubat! From you? I did not expect it.'

'If you do not hear the concerns of the army from me, then from whom?' Netoji hurried to keep up with Raje. 'The men are losing faith, Raje. We may have mass desertion on our hands soon.'

'And are you losing faith too, Sarnaubat, along with them?' Raje asked coldly.

'I have always been loyal to you,' Netoji insisted. 'But you have to agree that had you listened to some of my advice, this day would not have come.'

'You wanted me to bend down before the Mughals and accept their demands!' Raje stopped in his tracks and spit on the ground. 'It is something I will never do.'

'We cannot afford to fight enemies on all sides, Raje.' Netoji stressed every word. 'In doing so, we were bound to empty our coffers quickly. It was only a question of today or tomorrow. And the day has now come.'

'The coffers are not yet empty.' Raje walked on. 'And I have succeeded in driving away the Mughal General Shaistekhan, whom you feared would lay waste to the Swarajya. I did not kill him, but I did chop off his fingers.'

'If the coffers are not empty, why do you not pay the army's wages?' Netoji lifted a hand to Raje's shoulder to stop him from hurrying on.

Raje came to a halt and pushed the hand away. 'Rations are going to the camps regularly, Netoji. The men have enough to eat and drink. They are not fighting on empty stomachs.'

'But the men need their wages too, to send home to their families.'

'And they will get them. Soon. But not today. Try to understand Sarnaubat, we cannot utilize the last funds left with us unless we have the opportunity to gain five times that in return. The men will understand.'

'Yes, and I have been trying to make them understand for months now.' Netoji crossed his arms. 'They understand what they signed up for. But I need to know how in the world you plan to fill our coffers again. Taxing the farmers won't do, for the rains have been scanty this year. If next summer the Mughals advance again, and we do not have coins by then, we are done.'

Raje's face was horrid as he turned to stare at Netoji. 'What disheartening talk from my own Sarnaubat!' His voice was loud and harsh. 'Tell me why exactly you are here Netoji, and I will tell you what you want to know. Then we can get this over with.'

'I have to know how you plan to get more funds,' Netoji said. 'I need to know I am not part of a Swarajya that is destined to fall before it has a chance to stand.'

Raje stared at him silently, saying nothing, his eyes glittering dangerously.

'I know that your favourite spies are up to something,' Netoji continued. 'One of them, Sadashiv Naik, visited me in my camp three days ago. He asked for data on the *ghod-dal* corps – how many horses we had, how many more we could obtain and train in the next few months... And he seemed vastly interested in how fast I could march my men. For research purposes, he said.'

'So you followed him here, Sarnaubat?' Raje asked, folding his arms across his chest. 'Without my summons?'

'I am your Sarnaubat, Raje,' Netoji replied. 'I can come to see you any time I need to. I know very well that those two Guptachars are up to something, and I want to know what. I have to be sure that it is not some foolhardy plan that will lead to us all to our doom.'

Raje stared at him silently. Bending forward, he whispered one word into Netoji's ear. It was spoken so softly that Shashidhwaj did not catch any trace of it. But it seemed to galvanise the Sarnaubat, for Netoji's eyes widened in surprise. His brows came together in a sudden frown.

'Those two Guptachars fill your head with rubbish,' he said loudly. 'And you allow them to do so.'

'You think we cannot do what they propose, Netoji?' Raje asked quietly.

'It is too risky,' Netoji stated firmly. 'For one, we don't have the funds for either back pay or advance salaries to the soldiers.'

'I will ask the men to ride with me without pay, and they will do it, no questions asked.'

'They did so when you raided Lal Mahal too,' Netoji reminded him. 'How many times do you expect them to do so? They have families.'

'Once the mission is fateh, the problem of unpaid salaries

will vanish."

'I propose something safer, something saner,' Netoji said. 'We could slowly raid the outskirts of Aurangabad perhaps. Or raid the supply convoys that go from there to Pune. They are bound to contain valuables.'

'And what would that fetch us, Netoji?' Raje asked, his manner changing from calm to agitation.

Netoji stared at the sky in the ensuing silence. 'What if you do as they plan, and fail?' he asked finally.

'I will not fail!'

'You gamble with the lives of your men.'

'They took that gamble themselves when they placed their lives in my hands,' Raje said, cupping his hands together. 'All this is a gamble. Look around you. Enemies to the East; enemies to the North; enemies to the South; bleeding us dry of our resources, but not of our faith.'

'Perhaps we could send an envoy to the Mughals. Just pretend to be friendly for a while till we can sort out this funding problem. Declare a truce till then.'

'Enough!' Raje spun on his heels. The movement made Netoji step back like a horse about to rear. Raje looked him directly in the eye. 'Do you not see all this?' He spread his arms wide and then upwards to the sky. 'This Swarajya. I did not build it just to give it away in a truce. Do you think the Mughals will give us a truce just like that? No, they will take our forts from us and render us toothless. Our future lies not in a truce, but in going on the offensive.'

Taut lines marked Netoji's face like a map. 'If this mission fails, it can destroy us.'

'Look around you, Sarnaubat!' Raje said sternly. 'We are already destroyed. It is just a matter of time. This mission is the only thing that can save us.'

Netoji stood still and took in a deep breath. 'If it was anyone but you,' he grunted, 'I swear, anyone but you, I would leave now and take all my men with me. But I still have faith in you, Raje. If you say it will work, I am willing to do my part.'

Raje placed a hand on Netoji's shoulder. 'Folk call you Prati Shivaji, because you look like me,' he said with a wide smile. 'But you do not think like me. Have faith in me, Sarnaubat. I shall not fail you. After we have made a success of this mission and saved the Swarajya, we shall meet again here, to make plans for the future. Till then, you must remain in Nasik and drill the men. Be prepared to march a long way.'

Netoji dipped his head. 'I will take your leave, Raje,' he said, bowing briefly.

Raje watched him go, then turned and went the other way towards one of the low buildings.

Shashidhwaj did not wait. He slipped through the grass towards the gate. He slipped past the guards, who were bowing to the departing Netoji. The Sarnaubat stopped to speak to them for a moment. When Netoji moved on, Shashidhwaj was already a hundred paces down the descending trail.

Racing down to Padmavati machi was easy. There were no guards on the pathway and Shashidhwaj wondered if he should have taken the same route up. It would certainly have been easier than climbing the rockface. At one point he almost tripped over a rock and was forced to decrease his pace. The trees on both sides of the pathway were abuzz with insects and the chirping of crickets. He longed for the heat of the campfire outside Nanaji's hut. However, such comfort was not to be his anytime soon.

Naik was waiting for him at the entrance to the machi. His face lit up when he saw the lad running towards him. 'Tell me that you heard every word,' he said at once to the out-of-breath Shashidhwaj.

'Not only did I hear everything, I saw…' Shashidhwaj

gasped out, his eyes agleam.

Naik let out a sigh. 'Recite it all to me just as it happened,' he instructed.

Shashidhwaj began his tale. When he finally finished, the expression on Naik's face was sombre.

'Are you sure no one saw you going up or coming down?' he asked.

'I am sure,' Shashidhwaj nodded. The guards at the gate had not even noticed him slipping out under cover of the bushes. Besides, why would they expect someone to leave stealthily when no one had entered but Netoji?

'And the man was still up there when you left?'

'His audience was over,' Shashidhwaj said. 'He must be on his way down.'

'You need to hide,' Naik said thoughtfully. He pointed to a small stone stairway that led down to a basement.

'But why?' Shashidhwaj protested, thinking of the warm campfire.

'I need to have a conversation with this man,' Naik said shortly. 'Now there are two ways that could happen. Either you hide like I tell you and listen, or I could tell you to sod off to Nanaji's hut. You tell me which it is to be.'

Shashidhwaj did not say a word. This was a Naik he had never seen before. Not the man with the humorous grin and casual jokes, but serious and fierce. Shashidhwaj went down the steps silently. Just where they ended, there was a small opening through which he could see to ground level. Shashidhwaj stared upwards.

The light from the mashaals soon revealed a lone figure tramping purposefully down the pathway. Netoji looked displeased. Lost in thought, his attention was not on the path. He did not see Naik standing in the shadows till he was right beside him.

Naik cleared his throat. 'Looks like someone needs to teach you respect, Netoji.'

Netoji stopped abruptly and turned his head, taking a moment to register the face in the dusk. When he did, he stood up straight and moved his shoulders to loosen them. 'Do words spoken on the Balekilla spread with the air then?' he asked.

Naik folded his arms. 'No, but you know we have eyes and ears everywhere.'

'So you're back again? From another of your *missions?*'

'Yes, but on orders, unlike you.'

'I am the Sarnaubat,' Netoji said with undue emphasis. 'I do not need orders to move in my own Swarajya.'

'There is a difference in not needing orders and not wanting them, Netoji,' Naik said softly.

Lines appeared on Netoji's face. 'Why are you here in my way, cowherd?' he asked loudly, jaw lifted pugnaciously. 'Let me be on my way, and you be on yours.'

Naik held his ground. 'On any other day I would have loved to do that, but not today, not after the scene you just made up there.'

'What of it?' Netoji shrugged dismissively. 'You never disagree with Raje?'

Naik laughed. 'Usually that moment never comes because Raje never disagrees with us.'

'That is because you fools tell him exactly what he wants to hear,' Netoji burst forth. 'Unlike me, who tells him the actual truth.'

'Truth which advises a truce?' Naik said, his voice hard as the rock beneath their feet.

Netoji was taken aback by Naik's exact knowledge of what

had been said on the Balekilla, but he quickly brushed it aside. His face set in a frown. 'I will not discuss covert matters of state with you in the middle of a road,' he said and began walking on

But Naik blocked his way, stopping him with one outstretched hand. 'It is hardly a covert matter because such a thing will never happen,' he said.

'What is it with you?' Netoji stamped his foot.

'No Netoji, the problem is with you. It is that you do not know your place.'

'Do you threaten me, lowborn?' Netoji's hand went to the hilt of his sword.

But Naik only smiled. He placed a hand on Netoji's shoulder. 'No, my friend. Rather, I offer you a discourse. Think of it like this. Our Swarajya is like a human body. It has arms, legs, and the organs of the human body. But if the organs forget their roles, would the body be able to function? Once you accept that Raje is the head of this body, and you are a mere arm, your frustrations will die.'

'Sometimes I wonder if Raje would forgive me if I were to pierce my sword through your guts,' Netoji said, looking Naik in the eye. 'The thought itches at me, you know.'

Naik laughed in his face. 'They say I'm a hard man to kill.'

'They haven't been trying too hard then.'

'Why nurture such deep hatred for us, Sarnaubat?' Naik asked with a flickering smile. 'We are on the same side after all.'

'Yes, but you people live in the shadows, while we actually risk our lives and shed blood in battle,' Netoji snapped. 'If I was Raje, I would know who to respect more.'

'Do you forget Umberkhind, Sarnaubat?' Naik asked, smiling grimly.

The question caused the colour to drain from Netoji's face. He opened his mouth to reply, but closed it immediately, knowing that he had nothing to say. He stood in silence till Naik moved out of his way.

'Have a safe journey back, Sarnaubat,' Naik nodded.

Netoji grunted, frustrated. Quickly, he walked off towards Padmavati Lake.

When he was out of earshot, Naik looked towards Shashidhwaj's hiding place. 'You can come out now,' he said in a low voice.

Shashidhwaj crept out from the basement. 'You are not afraid of anyone, are you?' he whispered, watching the tall figure of Netoji striding away from the machi. When the two men had stood face to face, Shashidhwaj had noticed that Netoji was even taller and bulkier than Naik.

'One of the greatest qualities of a spy is knowing who to be afraid of,' Naik's mouth twisted in a sardonic smile.

'What is Umberkhind?' Shashidhwaj asked, eyes still on the receding figure of Netoji.

'Umberkhind is that one thing that you do in your life, after which no one can challenge you again,' Naik muttered dreamily. 'All we have to really do in life is find our Umberkhind.'

Shashidhwaj nodded. Though the words made no sense to him, they sounded like the most profound words ever spoken to him. Then he suddenly remembered something else. 'Up there, Raje said you two have proposed a mission to him. What is it?'

Naik smiled, but did not answer. 'It is time you had your meal and went to bed, boy. Sleep while you can, for Nanaji will certainly not give you the day off tomorrow.'

Together, they walked towards Nanaji's hut.

That night, as Shashidhwaj lay flat on his hay bed, tired from all the riding, climbing and excitement of the day, he could hardly keep his eyes open. As he fought sleep, he heard a faint conversation from inside the hut.

'The boy is not ready,' Nanaji was saying. 'I still have a lot to teach him.'

'I think he is, and Raje agrees with me. Whatever he has left to know, he must learn in the field. Besides, being a young boy will prove better cover than any of our disguises.' Naik's voice appeared farther away than it actually was.

'When do you take him?' Nanaji's question was laced with concern.

'Bahirji will come in a few days,' Naik murmured in reply. 'I must go on and prepare the forward base. Meanwhile, teach him all you can.'

Nanaji nodded. 'He is a good lad.'

'He is, but now he needs to learn to be a good spy on the job.' Naik's voice was a harsh drone.

There was a prolonged silence. Shashidhwaj succumbed to sleep, dreaming of adventures on horseback.

CHAPTER NINE

THE PLAN

THREE MONTHS BEFORE

Ali knew he was late. He increased his pace without breaking into a run. It was night, and a man in a cloak, wearing a sword, running out of the gates of the city like a madman, would certainly have alerted the guards. But when he passed the archway, no one paid him any heed. The two guards were busy discussing the lack of rain that year. Ali realized that he could well have run out brandishing a sword and they would not have cared a fig.

The meeting spot was under the banyan tree by Gopi Talav. It was a secluded place, away from the main road. The message in Farsi, written on a torn piece of yellowed paper, had been brought by a street urchin. Ali cursed as he hurried on. Of all the men in the world, the Cloaked Master wasn't the one to keep waiting.

But when he neared the spot, he saw that the Master was not the only person there tonight. Even in the darkness he caught sight of two horses hitched to the fence that separated this stretch of the main road from the surrounding countryside. No doubt the men had walked from where the horses now stood. Ali stopped by the horses, observing them closely.

One was a prime stallion, with a decorated saddle. The other a mule, with a simple leather saddle.

When he turned away from the fence, the path became rougher. As he walked forward, the path grew ever narrower as the wild grass encroached onto it until the path was almost not existent. It was then that he caught sight of the big tree up ahead. Gopi Talav was just to the side, the cool night air blowing over it creating ripples on its surface. Two figures stood by the tree, waiting.

Ali walked up, recognizing the black cloak with the red lining as belonging to the Master. The other person he did not know, though he could see the man was a foreigner. His exposed palms were pale and white, and the wisps of hair peeping out under his furrowed hat were gold. When Ali drew nearer, the face seemed somehow familiar to him.

'Welcome, Rayiyas,' the Master said in Farsi upon spotting him. 'We were wondering if you were going to show up at all.'

'Who are *we?*' Ali stood facing the other man. Where had he seen him before? He could not place the face.

'Perhaps you know Father Ambrose from the Order of Friars Minor Capuchin?'

Ali observed the old man from head to toe. Now his attire made sense. He was wearing the customary robes which Christians of his Order usually wore on festive days. These monks had come to Surat years ago, and the previous Governor had given them a grant of land in the city to build a chapel. They had built a beautiful one, with wood from the finest trees, and stained glass windows, brought from their own country.

'I have seen him in the city,' Ali murmured. 'What is he doing here?'

'He is playing a part, just like you,' the Master replied tranquilly.

Ali nodded. If the Master thought it was safe for this monk to overhear their conversation, who was he to object?

'Are you sure no one followed you?'

Ali shook his head. 'No one did,' he said. He remembered the distracted guards at the gates. He had not even told his own men where he was going. He had left as soon as he had been summoned, not even going to get his horse from the stables.

'Are you sure no one suspects you in the events that happened on the road to Suwali a few months ago?' the Master enquired.

Ali did not move, looking at the monk.

'The Holy Father does not speak our language,' the Master assured him. 'You may speak without fear.'

'No one suspects me or my men.'

'Good.'

'So what is this plan you speak of?' Ali asked impatiently.

'What I tell you now, few are privy to,' the Master replied. 'The Qilladar, Muhabbat Khan, met you today in the city, did he not?'

Ali took a step back, shocked. The meeting had taken place less than a few hours ago. He had been taken by guards to the fort, dragged from his afternoon slumber. At first, Ali had thought he was being taken in. But the Qilladar had met him at the small chamber by the gates of the fort and the matter discussed had been something else entirely.

'Indeed he did,' admitted Ali. 'He wanted to hire me and my men to unload his cargo, which will be coming on the Angrez ships soon.'

'And what did you tell him?'

'I took the job,' he said. 'I need the pay.' Ali felt suddenly ashamed to have to admit it.

'Good,' the Master murmured. 'I was counting on you to take it.'

'It's just some personal cargo he has ordered,' Ali shrugged. 'He said he needed security because it was high value and he could not trust his own men with the task.'

'But he could trust you?' the Master asked politely, inspecting his hands.

'My reputation and lineage speak for me. He knows I can be trusted to complete tasks and I will not betray where I have given my word.'

'Good.' The Master looked at Ali. 'Now listen to me closely. His cargo contains gold bullion, equivalent to ten thousand mahmudis.'

Ali was taken aback by the revelation. He had never seen so much gold in his life. 'Are you sure?' he asked. The Qilladar had spoken of the cargo like it was small change.

'Yes, I am,' the Master nodded. 'And the important thing is that I have been sure right from the start. I promised you once that if you heeded me, you would one day be as rich as your ancestors. Today is the day I fulfill my promise.'

'You are proposing that we steal the cargo?' Ali moved back a step. Though the thought of betraying one whose money he had taken for a job was abhorrent, this was more gold than he could ever obtain taking street *thekas*.

'And I thought that a man of your reputation and lineage would not betray your purchasers. Perhaps I erred?' The Master moved away, staring at the waters of Gopi Talav. The waterbody appeared eerie in the starlight.

'Stealing it at the docks would be too risky,' he continued. 'The Qilladar would send a force to capture you as soon as he heard. And it would be almost impossible for you and your small band to outrun them.'

'Then what is it that you propose?'

The Master turned. 'You shall ferry the cargo from the docks to the fort. You shall fulfill your promise to Muhabbat Khan. You shall bow before him and take your pay. Muhabbat Khan will not transport the gold out of the city immediately. He'll wait for the summer, when he usually goes on his annual visit to his home *jagir*. Until then, he will keep it in the fort. We will steal it from there.'

'But how?' Ali asked, intrigued. Infiltrating the fort was impossible. He for one knew that very well.

The Master dismissed the question with a wave of his hand. 'When the time comes, I shall reveal how, as I reveal everything else.'

'But if we take it from the fort, what will stop the Qilladar from sending a force after us?' Ali asked, looking straight at the metal mask.

'Because he will never know who took it.'

'There will be guards at each of the city gates. We shall never be able to take it out of the city by road.'

'And we will not,' the Master nodded. 'We will take it out of the city the way it came, on boats, in small quantities, little by little, until all of it is gone.'

Ali rubbed his chin at the bold plan. 'But taking it out by boat in parts will mean that it will have to remain in the city for quite some time.'

'And it shall. Right under the noses of Muhabbat Khan and his father.'

'And where will *we* keep it?' Ali asked.

'That is exactly where the Friar comes in,' the Master said, turning to face Father Ambrose, who gazed back at them, a benevolent smile on his face.

Chapter Ten

The Audience

THREE MONTHS BEFORE

The audience chamber was up on the Balekilla, in a small building on the cliff Shashidhwaj had climbed to on his last foray. The Mavlas escorted him through the gates to the long, low building. It was cold and windy on top of the mound that morning and Shashidhwaj shivered as he stood outside, waiting.

Bahirji was already there, talking to some people. He nodded when their eyes met. Bahirji looked different from the last time Shashidhwaj had seen him. He had let his beard grow, but shaved off his moustache. He looked like one of the officers in Shaistekhan's Mughal army, whom Shashidhwaj had seen near Pune.

When Bahirji finished his conversation, he walked up to the boy who had grown muscular and tall in his absence. His hair hung below his shoulders, and his eyes were wary in his sunburnt face.

'What is happening here?' Shashidhwaj asked. The guards had suddenly appeared at Nanaji's hut and literally lifted him off his bed. He was still in his night clothes. Nanaji had not said a word when they took him, which meant he already knew.

'Did you not say you wanted to go on a mission?' Bahirji asked. 'Well, we are going on a mission, boy. You are coming with us. Raje personally talks to every person who goes on such missions, so he will talk to you as well.'

Shashidhwaj's eyes widened, and his mouth opened and shut soundlessly like a fish.

'Don't look so terrified,' Bahirji laughed, patting him on the shoulder. 'This is what you have wanted all along. Now you have it.'

Shashidhwaj looked around. There were a dozen others. 'These are your people?' he asked.

'My people are not coming on this mission. It is top secret. No one but we can know.'

'But I can?' Shashidhwaj felt his heart thudding in his chest. It was one thing to dream of an adventure, but now that he was faced with the reality of it, he wondered if he was ready for it.

'Indeed, you can, for you are coming with us. Look happy, you fool. It is your first step to joining our ranks.'

'Where are we going?' Shashidhwaj finally asked.

'Raje will tell you himself.'

The guard at the entrance signalled to them and opened the doors to the chamber. Bahirji walked in, Shashidhwaj at his heels. As they entered, the doors closed behind them.

'This is where the meetings with the Guptachars take place.' Bahirji's voice reverberated inside the chamber as he pointed to the windowless walls and dark interior. The only light came from the *samais*.

Bahirji opened another set of doors and walked through them to an inner chamber. Raje was seated at a desk in the middle of the chamber. A lamp burned to one side and a jumbled mess of papers lay spread before him. Beside him stood a mustachioed man in a hat that looked rather comical to Shashidhwaj's untutored eyes.

'He is just a boy,' the man was saying to Raje as they came in. 'Your Pramukh Guptachars have gone mad.'

'Raje.' Bahirji gave a quick bow. 'Punt,' he said, acknowledging the other man.

Moropunt smiled briefly. Shashidhwaj remembered Nanaji teaching him about the Swarajya's government, and about Moropunt Pingle, the *Peshwa*. Then, as all eyes turned to Shashidhwaj, still dressed in his crumbled night clothes, he quickly imitated Bahirji's bow.

'Come closer, boy,' Raje said.

It seemed to Shashidhwaj that each step took an eon, but he finally stood before the desk, the light from the burning *jyot* falling on him in golden waves.

'Bahirji has told me how he found you,' said Raje.

Shashidhwaj's eyes fell to the ground.

'Do not look down boy, be proud!' Raje said sternly.

Immediately, Shashidhwaj's head snapped up. He watched Raje rise from his chair and walk about the chamber, deep in thought.

'It is to rescue people from tyranny, like you saw in your village, that I took the oath of Swarajya,' he said. 'But now the Swarajya is in danger. Our enemies encircle us.'

'I will do anything to save the Swarajya!' The passionate words burst from Shashidhwaj's mouth before he could halt them.

Raje stopped and looked back at him. He gestured to Moropunt, who held up a long package. When the light fell upon it, Shashidhwaj realized it was a scabbard, with an iron hilt protruding boldly from it.

'I have no doubt Nanaji trained you well in the little time

he had,' Raje continued. 'It pains me to cut your training short but none of us in these troubled times have the luxury of extensive training. You too, will have to learn on the job as I did.'

He took the sword from Moropunt and presented it. Shashidhwaj extended both hands to take it from him.

'I have faith in you boy, just as Bahirji does. I am sure that the three of us together will bring fateh.'

Shashidhwaj pulled the steel blade from the scabbard. It shone in the lamplight. In that moment he was filled with an intense sense of jubilation at finally holding his own sword in his hands, and facing his Master. He knew he would remember this moment all the days of his life.

'Many *kos* north of here, inside the borders of our enemies, stands their richest town. A city made rich from the wealth looted from our brethren over many years,' said Raje, his every word spiked with anger. 'I want you to go to that city. I want you to find every source of coin and gold, every score you can find, and report back to me. Then I shall swoop down like a mountain eagle and make *batsurat* the great city they call Surat.'

***

They rode like the wind through the grasslands of Nasik, leaving the Trimbak Mountain many kos behind them. They rode by night, and remained hidden in the mountain passes by day. By the fifth day, they no longer passed any more villages, and the road disappeared into the forest.

'We have now entered Mughal territory,' Bahirji said, pointing to a piece of rock painted in the Mughal colours. 'Look at those tracks. They tell us the wheels that passed were narrow; probably a four-wheeled carriage. And look at the depth to which the marks have sunk into the ground. The carriage is certainly loaded to the brim.'

When they had passed Trimbak, Bahirji had mentioned that they had to follow a certain carriage. Speaking to a man at a temple in the foothills, they had learned the carriage had passed by in the early hours of the morning. Bahirji had soon discovered its tracks on the main road out of town. Now the tracks were clearer and more recent. They were getting closer.

Shashidhwaj looked at the faint lines in the mud, surprised. 'All I see is mud,' he complained.

'If you truly wish to become a spy, you must learn to see what others do not,' Bahirji said. 'I can merely teach you what to look at. But the looking, and more importantly the seeing, has to be done by you alone.'

Shashidhwaj nodded. 'So this means we are on the right track?'

'Indeed we are. And not so far behind.'

Bahirji's words proved to be true. Less than a kos ahead, as they climbed a steep incline, they saw the shape of a horse-drawn carriage below. It was as Bahirji had said, a four-wheeled vehicle, and it was filled with sacks.

'What are we going to do?' Shashidhwaj asked.

Bahirji pulled up his horse and rifled through his jacket, looking for something. He brought out a small tube which on being pulled, elongated into a looking glass. Bahirji pointed it towards the carriage and peered through it.

'We will do what spies need to do before a mission,' he said. 'Find a cover.'

Shashidhwaj looked at the tube with interest. He was sure by now that it was a magnifier of some sort. Whistling softly, Bahirji offered it to him. Holding it to his eye, Shashidhwaj looked through it. The scene was distorted in a curvy way, but the sacks in the carriage looked far closer than they actually were.

'You see the sacks?' Bahirji enquired. 'Do you see what's inside them?'

Shashidhwaj strained his eyes and finally noticed the pods showing through the little holes in the sacks. He recognized them at once, having seen these pods many times in the zamindar's storehouse. 'Cardamom,' he said, putting down the tube.

'Indeed.' Bahirji took the glass back and put it away.

Breaking into a trot, he said, 'Do you know from where the cardamom comes?'

Shashidhwaj shook his head. He knew it was not from anywhere near these parts.

'From deep down South,' Bahirji told him. 'From the Malabar – lands that neither you nor I have ever seen.'

Shashidhwaj was cheered by the thought that there was something the infinitely resourceful Bahirji had not done.

'Every week, these agents travel to Malabar from Surat, carrying opium and cotton in their carriages,' Bahirji explained. 'They always return with these spices. Finding them is not easy. First, we have to locate their tracks. They travel through hilly terrain and almost never carry any gold, so as not to attract bandits. Tracking this particular carriage was harder as the trader is one of the most experienced agents and always changes the path he takes, knowing there are always those on the lookout. But love is the end of any man. It is said this trader could not find love at home. But, to our good fortune, on the hills of Trimbak, where the road passes from Malabar to Surat, our agent found the love he sought.'

'Was the man you spoke to at the temple in the foothills one of your informers?'

'Yes, and he told me exactly what I wanted to hear. That this man, who has taken a woman in Trimbak, had just passed through Nasik. He often visits her, and will no doubt do so her on his way back as well.'

'Whose agent is he?' Shashidhwaj asked.

'He serves the slyest old man in all of the west country,' Bahirji replied. 'A merchant prince called Virji Vora, one of the richest men in Surat, where we're going.'

Shashidhwaj suddenly understood. 'So the agent will be our cover! Our way in. We will reach Vora through him?'

'No, he shall be *your* way in,' Bahirji said. 'So that *you* can reach Vora through him.'

Shashidhwaj was appalled. 'But how?' he stammered.

'Watch and learn, boy. From afar this time.'

Bahirji kicked his horse into a gallop. They had crossed the hill and were now on a straight track. Shashidhwaj turned his horse and disappeared into the trees. Bahirji crossed in front of the carriage and pulling on his reins, blocked the path. The carriage screeched to an abrupt halt.

The doors of the carriage were flung open and a gaunt man appeared, demanding angrily as he descended the three short steps to the ground. 'What is the meaning of this?' He was dressed in a fine *kurta* and had an embroidered hat on his head.

In answer, Bahirji mutely pulled out his sword. The horses neighed loudly, alarmed at the sudden commotion. The carriage rider jumped down from his seat and began running away, fearing to cast so much as a glance behind.

The gaunt man reached back for the door in fright but Bahirji placed his sword upon his neck.

'Please, I don't have any gold! I'm just a merchant,' he whimpered.

'And we are not brigands,' Bahirji retorted loudly. 'I am here for your life.'

'My life?' the man quavered. 'What have I done?'

'I am the brother of the woman you meet secretly in Trimbak.' Bahirji's anger seemed so intense that his words issued forth as undisputed truths. 'And I am here to teach you a lesson for defiling my sister.'

Shashidhwaj looked towards the figure of the fleeing cart rider. He had run to take cover in the bushes by the roadside. There he squatted, peering through the foliage at the spectacle on the road.

The trader joined his hands together in supplication. 'But she loves me,' he pleaded.

'Will you marry her then, in our village, and take the marriage vows with the sacred fire as witness?' Bahirji demanded.

'I cannot,' the man sighed. 'But I can pay you. You just need to give me some time.'

'Like I said, I am not here for your money.' Bahirji raised his sword. Shashidhwaj quickly closed his eyes. He heard the head fall to the ground with a thud and the sudden fluttering of birds in the trees above him, the neighing of the horses. He wondered how the birds and animals knew blood had been spilled. For a moment he did not dare open his eyes. Finally, he peeked sideways to where the carriage driver had been hiding. He was no longer there, having disappeared into the trees.

Shashidhwaj moved his head slowly, looking first at the carriage, and then at the body in the road. It did not look as gruesome as he had expected. The head was still rolling away like a ball. He noticed that Bahirji too, was looking towards the tree line, searching for the carriage driver. When he realised the rider had vanished, he looked in Shashidhwaj's direction and whistled. The youngster moved out from his hiding place and came towards the carriage. His horse was wary and took each step slowly, irrespective of Shashidhwaj's kicks.

Bahirji was wiping the blood from his sword carefully with a cloth. 'Don't want people to notice a bloody sword,' he said without looking up.

Shashidhwaj nodded meekly.

'Were you afraid when I beheaded him, boy?' Bahirji asked, checking the length of the sword.

Shashidhwaj shook his head.

'Do not lie.' Bahirji sheathed his sword. 'Everyone is afraid the first time they see a human killed.'

'I have seen men die before,' Shashidhwaj said. He remembered the hangman's noose in the village, where the zamindar hung those he wished to punish. He remembered the pleading cries to heaven and then the gurgling as the floorboard beneath their legs gave way. 'This was clean.'

'A spy should know when to be clean, and when to be rough.' Bahirji placed a hand on the lad's shoulder. 'The man was innocent of any crime, but he was a tool for us. He had to die so we could execute our plan.'

'I understand,' Shashidhwaj said, not wishing to be seen as weak.

'Do you also understand why I played the role of his paramour's enraged brother?' Bahirji asked.

Shashidhwaj nodded. 'The carriage driver was a witness. If he talks to someone and word gets to the merchant prince you speak of, our stories should match.'

'His name is Virji Vora,' Bahirji said. 'Learn to remember names. A spy must remember everything he hears, even in a passing moment.'

Shashidhwaj stared at the carriage and the goods in it. 'This is going to be our ticket in, isn't it?'

Bahirji nodded. 'We are going to take this carriage to Surat. You are going to tell its owner what happened along the way. How you hid in the bushes and continued the journey with the carriage and cargo of spices after the enraged 'brother' had departed, so that the goods would reach their rightful owner, unlike the cowardly driver who ran away.

You wished to make sure your father's death had not been in vain.

'My father?'

In answer, Bahirji got off his horse and bent down towards the headless man's body. He reached for a hand and held it up. On the finger shone a gemstone set in gold. He pulled the ring off and offered it to Shashidhwaj.

Shashidhwaj wiped the blood off and put it on his thumb. 'This will no doubt remind me of my 'father' every time I look at it,' he said.

Bahirji gazed at him for a moment. 'Tie your horse to the front,' he said. 'I'm not going to do everything for you.'

Shashidhwaj led his horse to the front of the carriage and carefully tied it to the harness, as the other two horses watched their new partner with sidelong glances.

'If animals could talk, we spies would have a hard life,' Bahirji commented, watching with arms crossed, having restored his cleaned sword to its scabbard.

Shashidhwaj walked to where the dead man lay and removed the man's jacket. He used it to carefully wipe the blood splatters from the woodwork of the carriage.

'Now, let's move before the scavengers from the jungle smell the blood and follow our trail.' Bahirji mounted his horse, clicking his tongue.

Shashidhwaj climbed into the driver's seat, collected the reins of all three horses and flapped them briskly. It was the same as driving the zamindar's bullock carts. The horses began to move forward in unison. Bahirji remained by his side as they moved into the setting sun.

Shashidhwaj's heart beat faster. His adventure had begun.

Chapter Eleven

Surat

THREE MONTHS BEFORE

The city appeared like a summer mirage in the light of the rising sun. As their horses galloped past the village of Udhna, the spires of the churches rose against the horizon first. Then came the massive bastions of the fort. As they rode further, houses and buildings stretched as far as the eye could see.

They stopped at a small hillock just past Udhna, to gaze at the city. Shashidhwaj gaped open-mouthed at what he saw. 'This is wondrous!' he muttered, his eyes never moving from the sight before him. He had never seen anything like it in all his life. When the zamindar's headman, in one of his foul moods, beat him, Shashidhwaj had climbed the hills of Katraj and stared down at the lights glimmering in the valley. But even the lights of Pune could not compare with what he saw now.

The city appeared colourful in the bright sunlight, but Shashidhwaj quickly noticed it did not have a protective wall. The stone gates stood high, towering over the road that passed below, but there was nothing else to separate the city from the surrounding farmlands.

'No walls,' he commented, glancing at Bahirji. It seemed strange. Even Pune, a city half this size, had a protective wall.

Bahirji nodded. 'Told you the Mughals are stupid.'

'But just look at all those buildings!' Shashidhwaj's eyes sparkled.

At his side, Bahirji looked unimpressed. 'We have to get rid of these horses before we enter the city, boy,' he said, reverting to the main order of business. 'And find a way to smuggle our swords in.'

He pointed to Shashidhwaj's waist, who quickly removed his scabbard and handed it over with both hands. Taking it, Bahirji fastened it to his saddle.

'I have never seen anything like this,' Shashidhwaj said, his eyes once again turned to the sight below.

'Nor will the city have seen anyone like us,' Bahirji responded lugubriously, kicking a heel into his horse's side. 'Let's go that way, past the trees.'

They stopped where the tree line opened onto the farmlands that stretched all the way to the edge of the city.

Shashidhwaj was the first to descend. 'Where should we take the horses?' he asked, looking around.

'I'll take them to the stables outside the gates, and cut a deal with the stable master there,' Bahirji said. 'I'll also look around how best to get our weapons in.'

'And what should I do?'

'Well, you wanted to marvel at the city, did you not?'

'Yes, but not alone,' Shashidhwaj protested.

'Afraid of being alone, boy?' Bahirji chuckled.

'Not afraid, just cautious, as Nanaji taught me to be,' Shashidhwaj mumbled, trying to convince himself as much as Bahirji. 'A spy should always be cautious after all.'

Bahirji burst into hearty laughter. 'You are not a spy. Not yet, at least.'

Leaving the carriage amidst the trees, they made their way down to the city, each riding one horse and leading another. They found the stables, where Bahirji had a quick chat with the headman and emerged holding a bag of coin.

'Sold the horses,' he said briefly. 'Now for the swords. That will surely take some time.'

'And what should I do?' Shashidhwaj asked, eager to play his part.

'Walk around the city and find our dear friend Naik.'

'Naik is here?'

'He is. He must have got here a week ago, to prepare for our arrival.'

Shashidhwaj looked at the scores of houses, lining every street and alley. To his country-bred eyes, it looked like a foreign land. 'But how shall I find him in there?' he asked, bemused.

'Oh, knowing Naik, you won't have to find him,' Bahirji chuckled. 'He will find you.'

***

Shashidhwaj walked in through the arching gates, jostled by the crowd making its way into the city markets. There were people everywhere; people to the right, people to the left, front and centre. Shashidhwaj crossed his arms in front of his chest to avoid bumping into someone. He could see people dressed in many kinds of clothing. There were merchants in exquisite long tunics and robes, ladies with black veils over their faces, fakirs wearing green turbans. One of the fakirs even collided head-on with him. Shashidhwaj cursed softly, rubbing his nose. It hurt from the impact. He attempted to walk on, but the fakir's hand held onto his *angarakha*. Shashidhwaj turned angrily, wondering what mischief this was. But the fakir began to pull him out of the crowd to the side of the road. Shashidhwaj looked around in fear. Bahirji had just left and here he was in trouble within minutes of entering the city. But when the fakir spoke his name, Shashidhwaj let out a sigh of relief. There was no mistaking the calm and composed voice of Naik.

As they came to a halt in a side street, Shashidhwaj turned to look at his companion. He looked nothing like Naik. He wore a green turban with a peacock feather nodding jauntily atop it. His beard was long and tied into a strange knot. Or was it a wig like the actors wore in the village theatricals during Navaratri? In his hand, he held a *kamandalu*. Shashidhwaj stared at him wide eyed.

But it seemed that Naik did not have time to waste. 'Come with me,' he said, pulling Shashidhwaj by the arm. 'We must get to the market area.'

Shashidhwaj let himself be pulled back into the crowd.

The market was thronged with people. Shashidhwaj had to squeeze his shoulders together to squeeze past. He had never seen so many people, not even when he visited the weekly market in Pune.

'Today seems to be market day here!' he exclaimed as they struggled forward.

Naik laughed on hearing this. 'Every day is market day in Surat,' he said, his voice was almost lost in the hubbub around them.

Shashidhwaj was astonished. He remembered how long it took the farmers in Pune to raise the *pendals* before market day and then take them down again. Now he understood why the pendals here were more permanent structures of brick, supported with metal girders.

'We have to go there.' Naik pointed to a relatively less crowded platform ahead, on a height, along a flight of stairs that climbed to an upper level of the city. 'Come on now, don't get lost!'

Shashidhwaj did his best to follow dutifully through the crowd. But people crossing diagonally often collided into him, causing him to lose his sense of direction. But Naik's green turban, atop his tall figure, helped locate him in the crowd again. Shashidhwaj worried when the gap between them increased. It was his first day in the city and he did not want to get lost. He wondered how long Bahirji would tease him about it if he did. But the platform was visible enough and finally he stopped tracking Naik's turban and began looking at the platform.

When he reached there, Shashidhwaj realized that his arms hurt from bumping into people. Naik, however, seemed completely at home. He leaned over the cast iron railing and gestured for Shashidhwaj to do the same. From their perch, they could see over the entire market area.

'Today is an auspicious day,' Naik remarked as Shashidhwaj marvelled at the sight below. 'Today, the important people of the city are here. I brought you so you can catch a glimpse of them.'

Shashidhwaj stared wide-eyed at the crowd below. All these people looked the same to him. But Naik, whose eyes were moving over the crowd, suddenly said, 'There! Look by the stall with the purple fabric. Look, don't point. Do you see the two men on horseback?'

Shashidhwaj strained his eyes to see which stall Naik wished him to notice. There were cloths in many different colours everywhere and it was hard to know. But then his eyes settled on the two figures. They were the only ones mounted on that side of the market. One wore a high hat and was chatting to the man in the stall, while the other, who seemed younger, waited.

'They are the most devious father-son duo in the Mughal Empire,' Naik whispered, leaning in. 'The fat one is Inayat Khan, Subhedar of this city. And the other is his son, Muhabbat Khan. He is the Qilladar.'

Their manner and the way their shoulders hung about their

ears, appeared mean enough. Shashidhwaj did not want to have anything to do with them. 'Does that mean they are in charge of the city?' he asked.

'Usually, the Mughal administrative system ensures a division of power. The Subhedar is Head of the commercial establishments in the city, while the Qilladar, who is in charge of the fort, oversees military and security matters. However, by greasing the right palms in Agra, this father-son duo now occupy both positions,' Naik said.

Shashidhwaj did not need to be told that this was an abuse of power. Back at Rajgad, Nanaji had explained the way Raje's administrative system worked. They did not have a division of power yet, but then the Swarajya did not have any cities in its domain.

'Surat is home to a large number of *topiwalas* as well.' Naik pointed to the other corner of the market.

Shashidhwaj turned his head and immediately noticed a group of soldiers walking in a column past the market entrance. They were easily distinguishable by their red and blue uniforms.

'See the man on the horse?' Naik said. 'He is President of the Angrez Factory in Surat. He goes by the name Sir George Oxenden.'

Shashidhwaj tried to say the unfamiliar name but it got stuck around his tongue. The man himself was easily seen, his white hair, tied in a ponytail, flowed down his back.

'Is that his real hair?' Shashidhwaj asked, amazed. He wondered how long it took to wash and comb each day.

'It is a wig,' Naik laughed. 'A ceremonial wig he wears when he appears in public, like today. You see the man leading his horse?'

Shashidhwaj looked at the man holding the horse's reins.

'Anthony Smith,' Naik whispered in Shashidhwaj's ear.

'Oxenden's right hand man. A vile creature.'

Shashidhwaj made a note of the names in his head, hoping he could remember them. If Naik was telling them to him on his first day, they had to be important.

'Surat is home to other firangs as well,' Naik said, pointing the other way. An orange, blue and white flag fluttered over a carriage crossing the road. 'They are the *Valandej,* fierce competitors of the Angrez. The two are always at loggerheads.'

By now Shashidhwaj was feeling overwhelmed by the information. 'What about the man whose house I have to go to?' he asked. 'The one Bahirji spoke of.'

'Virji Vora does not make an appearance here today,' Naik replied. 'I have been tracking him for a few days and he had gone to Ahmedabad to meet the Subhedar there, no doubt to broker a deal of some kind. He returned this morning and must be in his offices, going over the work he missed when he was away.'

'I should go to his house then,' Shashidhwaj said.

'Focused on the task at hand are you? I like that.' Naik showed him how to climb from where they were to the street above without having to enter the market crowd again. Shashidhwaj was delighted with this for he did not wish to enter the suffocating mass of people below.

'I hope Bahirji has told you what to say to Vora and how to say it?' Naik said as they walked.

Shashidhwaj nodded. On their way to Surat after the incident at Trimbak, Bahirji had told him how to create a good back story. They had rehearsed the facts they had decided on about his origins.

Naik tugged at Shashidhwaj's scanty new beard. As Bahirji had advised, Shashidhwaj had let it grow out, not touching it even in the face of Nanaji's disapproving glares. His hair had also reached his shoulders.

'You will fit in as a Musalmaan in anyone's gaze,' Naik approved, 'even Vora's. Prepared for what is to come are you?'

Shashidhwaj nodded, knowing well that he was not, but he had made up his mind that he was.

'Good. I will leave you to it then.'

Naik had stopped at the corner of a main street. Shashidhwaj looked ahead and saw a large building with wooden columns, a sloping roof, and brick walls.

'That is the house of the merchant prince Virji Vora,' Naik said. 'Look sharp boy, for you are about to do something serious for the first time in your life.'

Shashidhwaj rubbed his hands uneasily. A part of him wanted to turn and run away back into the crowd at the market. But a sterner side told him not to be a coward.

'Be careful,' Naik cautioned. 'At night, come to the hutments by the riverside, along the east bank. Finding our hut will be easy. It will be the only one with a lamp burning even in the dead of night.'

'I'll be careful,' Shashidhwaj said.

'Good,' Naik nodded. 'When you go in, look for a man dressed in long rich robes, wearing a turban. He will be the *Munshi*, in charge of the house. Talk to him. Tell him why you have come. It is the quickest way to reach Virji Vora.'

They went their separate ways. Naik turned and walked back, disappearing into a side street. When he was gone, Shashidhwaj took a deep breath. Lifted his foot, he took the first step towards the big house.

***

The doors to Virji Vora's house stood wide open. There were no guards anywhere. But Shashidhwaj hardly noticed this as he walked in, because the foyer was full of people. Some stood in groups, chatting, others were bent over a desk, occupied in writing out documents, yet others simply stood around waiting. The corridor that led to the reception room was also crowded with people. For a moment Shashidhwaj felt he was back in the market.

There appeared to be all kinds of people in the house. Some were well-dressed, in embroidered suits, others were dark-skinned, wearing simple, flowing robes. He even saw a man with white skin and blue eyes, who stood in a corner, alone, looking patently irritated. Shashidhwaj was still looking around, wondering where to go, when he stumbled into a tall man who towered over him.

The individual stared down at the youngster who had so rudely bumped into him, his brows lifted. 'Now who are you?' he asked, loftily.

Judging by his clothes, Shashidhwaj decided the man was possibly the Munshi of the house Naik had mentioned.

'I am here to see the Shethji,' he said, using the same form of address Naik had.

'Indeed. Well, look around you,' the man said. 'So are all these people. The question is whether the Shethji wishes to see you.'

Bahirji had warned him Vora would prove elusive and he would have to find a way in.

'I am the one who saved his Malabar caravan from being robbed,' Shashidhwaj said boldly. 'And if the Shethji wishes to know what happened, he will want to see me.'

'The Malabar convoy, you say.' The man rubbed his chin. 'We have been waiting for it to arrive for some days now. Come with me, boy.'

Shashidhwaj followed the tall man. When they saw who passed, the crowd immediately made way. The man opened a door that gave onto a stairway, leading upward. As Shashidhwaj made to enter, the man swung round and looked at him sternly, indicating his muddy footwear. Shashidhwaj quickly slipped out of his roughed up boots and then set foot in the carpeted interior. His feet were still dusty but there was nothing he could do about that.

The man sighed and closed the door behind them. They climbed the stairs in silence. Having entered the lion's den, Shashidhwaj knew there was no turning back. Upstairs, another corridor led to large ornate doors. Porcelain vases, as tall as a man, stood on either side of the entrance.

'Wait here while I inform the Shethji,' the man said. 'And try to remain in one place.'

Raising his hand, he knocked thrice on the lacquered wooden door with the back of his wrist. The door was opened by another man in similar garb, but with less embellishment. The two spoke in whispered tones and then the tall one turned. 'Come inside,' he said.

Shashidhwaj walked into the room. It was a study of some sort, with a large desk. The man who had opened the door went to stand beside a man dressed in the same dark robes and red turban as he. Members of Vora's administrative staff, Shashidhwaj realized. The two men hovered over the man seated at the desk, wearing an embroidered cylindrical hat on his almost bald head. He was studying some papers through a round glass he held in his hand. His bloodshot eyes suggested he had not slept for many hours. He was presently struggling to control his anger.

'I go out of town for one week,' he said in a harsh voice, pointing a finger to the ceiling, 'one week… and you make a mess of the bafta trade, forcing me to lose my bet to that vile creature, Haji Kasim!'

Shashidhwaj realized it was Vora, the man he had come to see. The merchant prince himself.

The two clerks eyed each other, unsure how to respond. Finally, one of them said, his voice jumping up and down like the Adam's apple in his throat, 'We apologize, Shethji. But the day was rightfully Kasim's.'

'When Kasim made the bet, I knew that to compensate for the shortage of yarn created by the Angrez, he would flood the market with yarn from China. If you had given a higher price to the Chinese merchants, they would have sold their yarn to you instead of to him. We could have disposed of the yarn to the English later, at lower prices.'

'But we would have lost money, Shethji,' the other clerk responded, dismayed by the thought.

'Yes, but I would have won the bet!' Vora declaimed, waving a hand in the air. 'But now I have lost.' His fist suddenly slammed down upon the table. 'You knew what the bet was, did you not?'

'Yes, Shethji.' The clerks looked down at their feet.

'Now I shall have to give him one of my servants. Perhaps I should give him one of you, considering the good work you have done.'

There was silence. The men addressed kept their gaze on their feet.

'By the gods, why do I have to work with fools!' Vora exclaimed. He put down the magnifying glass and looked at the two men. 'You know what Kasim will do with the man I give him?'

'He will use him to extract information, Shethji,' one of the clerks murmured meekly. 'He might even torture him.'

'Yes, and that leaked information will damage us far more than the small loss from the yarn, which you saved.'

The last three words were spoken with such venom that Shashidhwaj felt his heart begin to thud in his chest as the blood rushed through his veins.

'You can still hoodwink him, Shethji. Hire someone new, who knows nothing, and give that person to him,' the second clerk suggested.

'No, that would be deception.' Vora shook his head. 'I will not stoop to Kasim's level.'

'But all your people know a great deal about the ships that will be coming and going from Surat,' the second clerk protested in horror.

Vora grunted thoughtfully. 'All my men know my ships. What I need is a man in my service whom I can trust, who is not seen as a new recruit.'

At this precise moment, the Munshi, standing in discreet silence by Shashidhwaj's side, cleared his throat. This caught Vora's attention and he looked up in irritation.

'Pray what do you want, Munshi?' he asked. 'And who is this lad with you?'

'This young fellow says he has brought the Malabar carriage to the city, Shethji,' the Munshi explained quickly before Vora's temper could flare up again. 'The missing cargo of spices, Shethji.'

'Did he now?' Vora's hard eyes swung to look at Shashidhwaj, who quickly reached into his pocket and drew out the bill of lading. He handed it over to the Munshi, who took it and handed it to Vora.

Virji Vora's eyes once again moved over Shashidhwaj, from head to toe, in one swift glance, before falling to the document in his hand. 'What happened to my courier?' he asked without looking up.

'He was my father, Shethji.' Shashidhwaj was surprised at his own ability to bring tears to his eyes. 'While passing the village of Trimbak, unknown assailants attacked us. They ran him through with a sword.' He raised his hand and turned the signet ring for everyone to see.

Virji Vora rose, moved by the young lad's courage. He dug into his own pocket and found a silken handkerchief, which he handed to Shashidhwaj.

'And the goods?' he asked, as Shashidhwaj wiped his phony tears.

'They did not want the goods, Shethji. They seemed to have some personal beef with him. They left him to die on the road and fled.'

'And you brought the goods to the city on your own?'

'Yes, after burying him. With his dying words my father told me to come here, Shethji,' Shashidhwaj said, his voice trembling a little. 'He told me you would reward me. The goods are with the stable master, awaiting your acceptance.'

Vora's eyes twinkled. 'I am impressed by the courage and resilience you have shown, boy.' He placed a hand on Shashidhwaj's shoulder before turning away and going back to his seat at the desk.

'I have a small request, Shethji,' Shashidhwaj said nervously. 'I have nothing to go back home to. My mother died when I was a baby. My father was all I had in the world. Please let me work for you here in the city. I will work hard for you.'

'Incredible!' Vora mouthed. 'I was going to suggest the same thing. You have nothing to worry about, boy. The moment you made the decision to bring the cargo here and not loot the contents like some rabid dog, you came into my service. May I enquire what day that was?'

Shashidhwaj narrowed his eyes. 'A week ago,' he replied.

Vora looked at the Munshi. 'So, if he came into my employ a week ago, he fits the bill,' he murmured.

The Munshi nodded, pleased to have been the one to bring the boy to his master's attention.

'You boy, tell me your name.' Vora drew a paper from the stack in front of him. Picking up a quill, he dipped it in the inkstand.

'My father called me Aslam, Shethji.'

'You have done a good job, Aslam.'

Vora quickly reached for the paper and scratched something on it with bold strokes. Then he wrote carefully and stared down at it. Satisfied, he rolled the paper into a scroll. One of the clerks quickly lit a lamp and wet the lac stick, dropping a large blob where the edge of the paper closed on itself. Vora pressed his signet onto it.

'Here,' he said to Shashidhwaj, 'take your reward.'

Shashidhwaj took it with one hand, unsure what it was.

'Deliver this letter to the third house by the river,' Vora told him. 'You will specifically ask to give it into the hands of Haji Kasim directly, and to no one else. After reading this letter, Haji Kasim will take you into his service, and you shall get what you want.'

'But I wish to work for you, Shethji,' Shashidhwaj said.

'Consider it like this.' Vora tapped a fingernail on the desk. 'You will be working for me by working for him.'

The words made no sense to him, but Shashidhwaj did not wish to displease the man, so he merely bowed and said timidly, 'I thank you.'

'No, it is I who should thank you, Aslam.' Vora smiled and waved a hand, dismissing him.

Chapter Twelve

The Bullion Arrives

THREE MONTHS BEFORE

From the western bastion of the fort, Muhabbat Khan stared in the direction of Suwali, as the sounds of shouting filled the air. Behind him, in a long *aaram* chair, lounged his father, Inayat Khan.

'Hear that?' Muhabbat Khan's eyes flashed with excitement. 'The Angrez are docking their ship.'

Inayat Khan nodded. He was too old to get excited by baubles and gold. It was only power that mattered. 'Are our men ready?' he asked.

'Yes, indeed.' Muhabbat Khan nodded. 'At nightfall, the mercenary I hired will have his men load carts with the gold and enter the city in a convoy. His guards will protect it from curious onlookers or adventurers. The gates of the fort will be opened to let the convoy of carts in. To anyone watching, it will seem like a normal supply of gun powder or fort rations.'

'What of the payment?'

'Oxenden will visit us tomorrow. In the presence of our

men, we shall jointly count the gold. Our treasury will hand over the sum to him without further ado.'

'And does Oxenden trust us so much that he will give the goods to us before getting his payment?'

Muhabbat Khan shrugged. 'He can always go to Agra and tell them of our doings if we do not keep to our part of the bargain. I think the white man is laughing today, thinking of the power he holds over us.'

'We cannot keep the gold in the fort for long,' Inayat Khan warned.

'I have seen to that as well. We will not make the movement immediately, lest it raise suspicions. When the time is right, we will move the gold in small quantities to our *jagir* in Gwalior. It will be safe in the treasury there. And I ask that you allow me to return to Gwalior too, to ensure its safekeeping.'

'You only wish to be away from my watchful eye so you can fuck the peasant women and perform decadent acts,' Inayat Khan mocked.

'What is the use of all this gold if we cannot have a little fun?' Muhabbat Khan retorted.

Father and son joined in hearty laughter.

'I hope you have not made a grave error in trusting the firang,' Inayat Khan mused.

'Vora has him tied to a leash.' Muhabbat Khan leaned on the battlements. 'Anyway, the ship is here now.'

Inayat Khan raised himself. 'It is not the ship I am worried about. And Oxenden is not the firang I speak of.'

At this, Muhabbat Khan turned in surprise. 'Then who?'

'The Turk. This mercenary you have hired, the one they call Rayiyas. Can he be trusted?'

The question made Muhabbat Khan play with his beard. 'The Turk has an honest reputation,' he murmured. 'He is known for his resourcefulness and honesty. Anyway, he does not know about the gold.'

'Don't be a fool! When so much wealth moves around, word gets around too,' Inayat Khan said. 'We can never know who will say what, where, to whom.'

'The gold is camouflaged,' Muhabbat Khan said. 'The Angrez has confirmed this. He was as concerned about hiding it from pirates at sea as we are to save it from theft.'

'Pirates?' Inayat Khan laughed derisively. 'Pirates and the high seas are much safer than Surat, where every corner and alleyway is filled with brigands. Merchants, traders, artisans, whatever their occupation, everyone here lusts after money like a man in a whorehouse.'

The corners of Muhabbat Khan's mouth swooped downward. 'You say this to the finest Qilladar this city has seen?' he asked. 'I have put hundreds of men behind bars since I took office.'

'For each dacoit you put away, two more are created,' Inayat Khan said with a weary sigh. 'Two more who wish you harm. And what better way to harm you than stealing from you?'

'I will kill any man who dares.' Muhabbat Khan slammed his fist angrily on the parapet wall but such violence only served to bruise his hand, which he then rubbed gingerly.

'In any case, we could not have let our own men handle the gold. No one can know the gold is for us. They must think we are merely holding it in safekeeping for some higher authority. Even a hint leaking onto the street that it is ours, and it won't be long before word reaches Agra.'

'Something certainly to be guarded against,' Inayat Khan agreed. 'But we will be worse off if the gold is stolen before it even reaches us. I would be far happier with the gold intact, and Agra hearing of it, than having a clean slate with Agra, but no gold.'

'Relax, father. We can trust the Turk.'

'So you will not come running to me tomorrow to say the Turk, whom you so deeply trust today, has made off with our gold instead of delivering it to us?'

Muhabbat Khan laughed, his massive frame shaking in mirth. 'Samsher Ali will never leave this city,' he said. 'He *is* this city. They call him Rayiyas for a reason. He will never leave Surat, not for anything, even this much gold.'

Inayat Khan leaned back again. 'Your confidence in the man is reassuring,' he said. 'But I would feel more reassured if I knew the reason behind such confidence.'

'So you really do not know who he is?'

Inayat Khan shook his head.

'Then let me tell you.' Muhabbat Khan sat down in the empty armchair by his father's side.

***

The wind blew through the stone archways into the dome above, causing a whistling sound. Ali stood below, the eerie sound not disturbing him at all. He had on leather boots and a black cloak that also covered his head, leaving only his face exposed. He stared at the stone wall in front of him for some time, at the intricately carved *jalis* through which the wind also whistled. Ali did not notice. His gaze went to the carvings beside the blue doors that led downwards. Various shapes had been carved into the stone - a flower, a wheel, a strange four-sided animal.

Ali walked through the doors, calmly pushing back the hood of his cloak to expose his black hair. He stood in the empty hall, alone. The Imam was not there; probably gone for the night. He stood at the tomb with his eyes closed. The *chadar* on the *dargah* fluttered in the wind gusting in through the stone fretwork.

'Bless me respected ancestor, for today marks my path to greatness,' Ali besought silently, his eyes fixed on the tomb of his great-great-grandfather, Khudwand Khan. He often came here before embarking on a new mission, but not to pray. Praying to any other than Allah was *haram* in Islam. He came to seek reassurance. Now, he sank to his knees.

'You were a great *hasti*. Like you, I too, will rise to be one. You built the great fort here, but the minions of Agra now defile it with their corruptions. I will put a stop to it.'

As always, he felt the presence of someone watching him. He turned quickly, silently, but there was no one there. Ali breathed in deeply. 'I am bound for greatness,' he murmured. 'Like you, I will lead this city away from corruption and chaos.'

The only sound he heard was the wind.

Ali walked out, pulling the hood back over his head. Outside in the street, he found his horse had strayed a little, having freed itself from the pole to which Ali had tethered the beast. He hit the animal on the rump with a firm hand for its mischief. The horse whimpered, and Ali rubbed its mane. Mounting, he looked up the starry sky for a moment, and then trotted away from the tomb. Picking up pace, he rode through the empty streets, guiding his mount deftly down alleyways and blind turns.

When he rode out of the city gate, the air became cooler and the path narrower. He wended his way through the trees until the lights of Suwali became visible through the foliage. In the moonlight, he could see the mast of the English ship rising into the sky. He slowed when the palisades wall became visible.

Hatim was waiting for him at the opening. 'The men are ready, Rayiyas,' he said as Ali dismounted.

'And the carts?' Ali hitched his horse and pulled the reins into a tight knot, not wanting it to wander off again.

'A dozen carts, hitched to two dozen of the best horses

we could find,' Hatim replied, gesturing for Ali to follow.

As they walked along, Ali heard the sound of waves crashing against the wooden boardwalk. The white-skinned dockhands watched them go, but did not move closer. The man in charge of the carts wore a hat and stood with one leg propped negligently against the wheel of a cart. Between two fingers, he held a cigar, the burning tip of which sent lines of dancing smoke into the air. Ali stopped before him and folded his arms.

'This is your master?' the Angrez asked Hatim lazily.

When Hatim nodded, the man smiled and offered his hand. 'I am Smith,' he said.

Ali did not take the outstretched hand. 'Do you have it?' he asked briefly.

Smith looked sideways at Hatim, then stared at Ali. 'Do you have the papers?' he queried in return.

Ali reached inside his cloak and brought out the scroll Muhabbat Khan had given him. He offered it to Smith, who held it up to read in the meagre light of the torches burning on the walls of the Quartermaster's office.

'All seems to be in order,' the Englishman said, handing the paper back to Ali, who put it away. 'Follow me please.'

Smith made his way past the line of soldiers standing near the carts. Ali followed him. They walked towards the berth where the ship had been docked. It rose and fell with every undulation of the sea. Wooden planks had been laid to climb across to the deck. Two redcoats stood holding muskets. Smith gestured to them and they moved away.

'Through here.' Smith led them up onto the deck. The door into the hold was small, cramped between two rung ladders, one of which led to the bridge. Smith reached into his pocket and brought out a key. Inserting it into the lock, he opened it and then pushed aside the bolt that barred the door. He stood aside, gesturing his visitors forward.

Ali went in first, bending his head to enter the space, followed by Hatim. At first he could see nothing in the darkness. Then, as his eyes adjusted, he saw the place was filled with cylindrical shapes, from the door to the far end, with nothing but a few pillars between, that supported the bridge above. The lettering on the barrels was clear: British Standard Oil Company.

'Which of them has the gold?' Ali asked.

Smith chuckled. 'There's the catch,' he said. 'We do not know! This bullion came straight from the Royal Bank of England, delivered to us in these barrels.'

'So some have gold, and some have oil?' Ali asked.

'Classic sailor's trick,' Smith replied, looking pleased with himself. 'Even if a pirate raid hit, they would waste a lot of time deciding which ones to take and which to discard.'

Ali had to agree it was a good ploy. 'So we have to take them all?' he asked.

Smith nodded.

Ali nodded to Hatim, who went out and waved to the soldiers waiting near the carts. 'In a line!' he yelled. 'And drop your spears into the carts.'

There was a clanging of metal as the soldiers did as they were told. Then they moved in line towards the ship.

'Can I tempt you with some whisky?' Smith offered, pointing towards the Captain's compartment.

Ali stared at him, brows raised.

Smith shrugged. 'Some ale, perhaps?'

Ali did not reply.

'Very well, I'll leave you to it then.' Shaking his head at

such boorish behaviour, Smith walked away.

From the stern, Ali watched the men pick up the barrels in groups of two and move towards the carts. He watched them load the carts one by one. He smiled to himself. Since childhood he had wanted to be a rich man, lording it over this city like his great-great-grandfather, the famous Khudwand Khan had done. Now it was just a matter of time before his dream finally turned into reality.

***

Standing at the lone window of the room on the third level of the Surat Fort, Oxenden stared bemused at the flowing waters of the Tapi. The river flowed at full force, frothing on the surface. He leaned forward, placing his elbows on the sill and breathed in the cool air.

Behind him, Smith grunted as he opened the cover of yet another barrel, using the crowbar in his hands. 'That seems to be the last of them,' he said, heaving a sigh, for the effort had taken the breath from him. Fifty opened oil barrels stood against the walls, leaving little space to move between them.

Oxenden turned, pitying the man's evident exhaustion, but he could not take a chance on bringing any others in here to count the gold, and risk word getting out. He glanced at Muhabbat Khan, smiling in delight at all the gold.

'Twenty-five barrels filled to the brim with gold bars, a hundred in each, making twenty-five hundred in all. Bullion, as I promised. Now counted and displayed before your eyes for your verification.'

'And twenty-five barrels of whale oil,' Muhabbat Khan muttered. 'I wish you had marked them on the ship. The men who carried them up three stories charged me double for each barrel. I could have saved on the payment for those twenty-five worthless ones.'

'I never imagined you would want them carried to the highest level of the fort.' Oxenden closed the window and turned back into the room. 'Even loading them onto the ship was a great effort for our men back home, I'm told.'

'I reckon no one would dare move them from a room this high.' Muhabbat Khan turned away. 'You are going to have to seal all those lids again,' he told Smith haughtily.

Smith's shoulders drooped dispiritedly, distraught at the prospect of sealing each lid again with hammer and nails. 'It will take some time,' he finally muttered.

'Time we can utilize in counting the mahmudis you are going to give us in exchange,' Oxenden said, looking up.

Muhabbat Khan nodded. 'We can do that in the chambers below. This fellow is hardly likely to carry any barrels away.' He chuckled at his own joke.

Oxenden shook his head briefly, silencing the angry retort that rose to Smith's lips.

Leading the way out of the chamber, Muhabbat Khan looked carefully at the two guards who stood outside. 'Frisk the firang as he walks out,' he instructed in Farsi.

Oxenden realized the last words referred to him when the guards crossed spears and quickly went over his person.

'Smith is a trustworthy man, as am I,' he told Muhabbat Khan as they reached the stairs that descended to the lower levels of the fort.

'There is a saying here in Surat,' Muhabbat Khan told him. 'Never trust the most trustworthy man in the room.'

'Ah yes. That is why I plan to count every coin in the chest of mahmudis you give me,' Oxenden said, smiling.

CHAPTER THIRTEEN

HOUSE OF KASIM

THREE MONTHS BEFORE

The house before him was majestic. The walls seemed far too pristine and white to be surrounded by the mud and filth of the streets. Wooden beams held up the roof in an elegant curve. The colours of the painted metallic railings gleamed in the afternoon sun. The only ugly thing in the surrounding beauty was the sight of the two armed guards at the entrance, swords out, frowns on their faces.

'And what do you want, boy?' one of them growled when Shashidhwaj's unassuming figure appeared.

Shashidhwaj felt his throat constrict. He swallowed and said, 'I…I am here to hand the Master this.' He held out the sealed scroll given him by Virji Vora the day before.

The guards looked at each other, then laughed in derision. 'Do you know whose house this is? You better get lost, boy,' one of them said, gesturing towards the road.

'I am here to give this to the Master of the house,' Shashidhwaj insisted. 'It is important.'

The second guard took another look at him, more carefully this time. Perhaps the boy really had a message. 'Let me see what it says,' he said.

'Shethji Vora told me to hand it to Mir Kasim directly.'

'The tongue on this chap!' the first guard snapped. 'Do you want a beating, boy? 'He asked for the paper. You better hand it to him.'

'But…'

'Enough!' The guard raised a hand to slap the insolent boy.

'Still frightening away little boys are you?' a voice said from somewhere above.

The guard stopped. Shashidhwaj looked up and noticed a black figure standing on a balcony overlooking the street. It was a woman. Her eyes gleamed behind her black veil.

'Um...we...I…' Suddenly, the guard's tongue felt tied in knots, just as Shashidhwaj's had been moments ago.

'Let him in,' the woman ordered. 'I will see what the paper is and judge whether he speaks the truth.'

'At once, *Malika*.' The offending guard backed down while his companion quickly reached out and pushed open the massive doors.

Shashidhwaj did not waste any time. The further he was from these two guards, the better.

'Damn slut! Telling us what to do...' he heard one of the guards mutter angrily as the doors closed behind him.

Shashidhwaj walked in to discover white stone stairs, lined with an intricate railing, leading up to the higher level. Remembering the Munshi's lesson, he took off his shoes and carefully trod up the steps, trying not to make any noise. As he climbed, the main hall came into view, with a small water pool in its centre. The woman from the balcony stood beside the pool, staring at him. She had removed her veil and Shashidhwaj noticed that her eyes were blue, but of a shade he had never seen before. Her hair was jet black. He watched wide-eyed as she walked towards him, stepping into the ankle-deep water of the pool. When she came closer, he realized she was not a woman but a young girl. And there was a little mole beside her mouth.

'So, no boots,' she said, looking at his bare feet.

Shashidhwaj nodded, struck dumb by her beauty.

She smiled at him. 'Come.' She pointed to the other side of the pool. 'Just walk through this. The water is clean.'

Shashidhwaj followed her through the pool after dipping a foot hesitantly into the cool water. It felt wonderful after the rough, hot streets.

They emerged into a great hall with corridors leading away on four sides.

'I am Fatima,' she said.

'Aslam,' he managed to get out.

'As-la-m.' She struggled to pronounce it.

Unsure what to say, he held out the scroll. She took it from him and unrolled it, breaking Vora's seal. Her eyes moved over the page smoothly.

'So what you say is true,' she said. 'You do indeed come from the house of Virji Vora.'

He nodded. 'He writes for your master to take me into his service,' Shashidhwaj said.

'So you can read.' She lowered the paper, holding it in one hand.

Shashidhwaj merely nodded, not knowing what to say.

'Come with me,' she instructed.

Shashidhwaj followed her black-robed back along one of the corridors. The floor was made of some strange stone he had never seen. It felt cool, even chilly, in the heat of the summer day. At the end of the corridor, a man stood outside a door. She handed the scroll to him, saying, 'Show this to *Mia*.'

The man nodded and held the door open. As Shashidhwaj walked in, Fatima's face disappeared behind the closing door. He now stood in a large chamber. The walls were lined with shelves, filled with books. At the table that stood in the centre, a man sat, wearing a hat as high as his beard was long. He looked up, his brows lifted questioningly. The man with Shashidhwaj said nothing, merely handing over the scroll.

This must surely be the Mia, Shashidhwaj thought as Haji Kasim's eyes moved over the scroll and then settled upon him. Feeling awkward and uncomfortable, Shashidhwaj looked down at the floor.

'A damn boy he sends me!' Haji Kasim said in disgust. 'The *kafir* takes me for a fool.'

'He even looks straight from the village,' the man standing beside Shashidhwaj agreed. 'Where are you from, boy?' he asked loudly, as if talking to a deaf person.

'Aurangabad,' Shashidhwaj replied.

'How long have you worked for Vora?'

'I have not, Sir,' Shashidhwaj replied. 'My father worked for him, but he died. I went to Shethji so he would take me into his service in my father's stead. But he sent me to you.'

'See, he sends me an outsider, the sly fox,' Kasim retorted angrily. 'And here I had hoped he would send one of his city servants, from whom I could learn his secrets. What am I do with this boy who knows nothing?'

'You could torture him for pleasure,' the other suggested, giving a low chuckle.

'And have the housemaids denounce me as a demon? Fatima would kill me in my sleep if I did such a thing.' Kasim's forehead creased into lines as he stared at Shashidhwaj. 'He looks healthy enough,' he mused reflectively. What can you do boy?'

'Anything you tell me to, Mia.'

'See, just the answer a person with no skills gives,' Kasim sighed. 'Where do you live?'

'The hutments on the east bank.'

'Hmm...most of my house-help live there. Send him to the kitchens. The cook is always complaining how undermanned the *tandoors* are.'

'He looks Musalmaan. Are you Musalmaan, boy?' the other man asked.

'I am, Sir.'

'He can touch the food then.' The man turned towards the door. 'I will take him to the kitchens if it pleases you.'

Haji Kasim did not answer, staring at the paper in his hand. Abruptly, he tore it in two and threw the pieces onto the table. 'You keep this in your little mind, boy,' he said in a low voice, 'that you work for me now. You do whatever I tell you to do. When I tell you to shit, you shit. When I tell you to eat, you eat. You have nothing to do with Virji Vora anymore.'

Shashidhwaj nodded, eyes fixed on the floor.

'Good.' Kasim smiled. 'Now take him away.'

***

The heat from the tandoors bathed him in rivulets of sweat, as did the cook's menacing looks.

'Have you ever touched a tandoor, boy?'

Shashidhwaj peered into the red hot oven. A sudden wave of heat hit his face. He shook his head miserably.

'What use you are to me then?' the cook grumbled, slapping a ball of dough onto the table. 'Go sort the *barfis.*

That is the easiest job in this kitchen.'

The cook's assistant showed Shashidhwaj the huge stack of barfis on one side. 'Red ones go into this,' he explained, pointing to a red tray. 'The white ones into this, and the yellow ones into this.' He gestured at two more trays.

Shashidhwaj nodded and extended his hand towards the trays to start work.

The man slapped him hard on the wrist. 'Wash your hands first, boy! Do you know nothing?' he snapped, delighted to finally be the one barking out orders.

Shashidhwaj dipped his hands in the water bowl and wiped them on the cloth kept on the side. The assistant watched him work for some time, then left when he was satisfied the barfis were being put into the right trays.

'Psst…' Startled, Shashidhwaj looked towards the small aperture in the wall behind him, set with stone fretwork. She was wearing the veil again, but the eyes were the same.

'So Kasim Mia sent you here,' she remarked from her perch on a stone outside.

Shashidhwaj glanced quickly to both sides to ensure none watched. But even the rude assistant was at the far end, barking at a dark-skinned man peeling potatoes. He nodded at her.

'I'll take some of the red ones,' she said from behind the veil. 'Make it quick! At least half a dozen.'

Shashidhwaj looked at the red *mithais* in his hands. 'But I'm supposed to put them in that tray,' he whispered.

'I let you into the house, didn't I?' Fatima snapped. 'Else you'd still be out there in the hands of those guards.'

She had a point. Shashidhwaj counted six red barfis in a hurry. Placing them on a muslin cloth he found in the racks below, used for making *paneer*, he pushed the little hoard through the gap between the sill and the fretwork. She picked them up one by one, counting, but left the last one on the cloth.

'Take it quick!' Shashidhwaj hissed. 'Someone is coming.'

'That one is for you, fool,' she scoffed. 'Eat it now.'

Shashidhwaj could see her eyes gleaming behind the veil. He took back the cloth with the last mithai and held it in his hands. The assistant was done with the man with the potatoes and was walking back towards him.

'Eat it, you fool!' Fatima hissed.

The assistant stopped at the hanging pieces of meat. Shashidhwaj opened his mouth wide and devoured the barfi. He swallowed it in one go as the assistant turned, looking in his direction. He felt the weight move down his throat slowly. He heard Fatima's muffled laughter from behind the wall, move away. He looked up at the window, but it was empty. She was gone.

'You! No resting, finish the job!' the assistant barked.

Shashidhwaj nodded and went back to work. He could still taste the barfi on his tongue.

***

That night, in one of the huts by the river, Bahirji listened, intrigued by the tale. 'This is great work!' he exclaimed. 'You have as good as got the keys to Kasim's house.'

Shashidhwaj smiled, feeling pleased with himself. 'And what did you two manage to do today?' he asked his mentors, gazing at the blackened thatch above them.

Naik put the cooking pot on the *chullah* and blew into the coals. 'Should we tell him?' he wondered. 'Or will he soil his trousers hearing it?'

'You see, boy, Surat is a port city.' Bahirji breathed in the enticing aroma as Naik poured oil into the pot. 'Of all the wealth that flows through here, much comes in from the sea.'

'We must find where the money in Surat is. All we have to do is find who is bringing in the most wealth,' Naik said, throwing in some spices and stirring.

'Agra has levied taxes on everything that comes in by sea,' explained Bahirji. 'The *Shah Bunder*, Chief of the Docks, is appointed by charter of the Subhedar. He inspects all the cargo that comes in, and under whose name, letting Agra know how much tax is owed by whom.'

'And the Shah Bunder has his office just a few kos from here, by the docks,' added Naik.

'So how do we infiltrate this office?' Shashidhwaj asked, sneezing as the pungent smell of mustard filled his nostrils.

'The question is not how we are going to do it, but why we have not done it till now.' Naik said, adding millet to the dish he was preparing.

CHAPTER FOURTEEN

THE OFFICE OF THE SHAH BUNDER

THREE MONTHS BEFORE

The guard on the dock marched along quickly, knowing it would soon rain. The signs were all there, the grey sky, the cackling of the seagulls, and the violent waves which shook the boardwalk with each crashing of the waves before retreating to launch another attack. The hundred strides along the wharf to the Quartermaster's office felt much too far to the guard as the heavens threatened to burst. At his waist, the keys to the office jiggled jauntily against his scabbard with each hurried step, assuring him he was another step closer to refuge.

As he neared the building, he noticed a beggar sitting by the flag pole in front. He had never seen this one before. The fellow had on a ragtag mix of clothing, and his beard hung down to his chest. His face was grimy and his teeth yellow. The guard strode past the Quartermaster's office towards the beggar, his anger apparent in his gait. These fellows were not allowed in this restricted area.

The beggar, seeing him approach, raised his cup, babbling. Asking for alms, no doubt, thought the guard in irritation, raising his stick. The beggar shrank away fearfully, clutching the cup close to his chest.

'You cannot sit here!' the guard shouted angrily, holding the stick firmly over his head.

The beggar said something in reply, that the guard did not understand, but he did not move.

'Did you not hear what I said, fellow?' the guard yelled again. 'You cannot sit here! Get lost!'

The beggar seemed to understand and got to his feet. He looked around, confused. The guard bent and picked up a stone. He threw it towards a wall some distance away. It hit the wall and fell. 'Sit there,' he instructed, pointing with his stick.

The beggar seemed to understand, for he moved towards the wall. Cursing, the guard walked to the Quartermaster's office. He quickly turned the key in the lock and then pulled at the lock to make sure it was secure. Then, stick in one hand, he hurried towards the end of his beat, unaware that in the time he had spent frightening off the beggar, two shadows had slipped into the Quartermaster's premises, and were now locked safely within.

***

'Ummm...' murmured Bahirji, studying the scrolls thoughtfully in the meagre light of the lantern hanging from a nail hammered into the wall. 'Look at this. I see certain names repeated again and again.'

He had managed to look through as many scrolls as he could find in the Quartermaster's cabin, which contained everything from bills of lading to lists of goods, and volumes of trade.

'Won't they miss these papers?' Shashidhwaj asked as Bahirji riffled through the sectioned wooden shelves.

'Just look at the stacks of paper here,' Bahirji grumbled, selecting a few to put in the *jholi* that hung at his side. 'If anyone does indeed miss these, they would assume they are buried somewhere in this great stack on the table, or blown about by the wind.'

'There is no wind here,' Shashidhwaj remarked, looking through the papers. As he had been told to do, whenever he saw numbers, he put the paper into his *jholi*.

Bahirji looked up, then pushed open a window. 'Here comes your wind,' he said smirking, as a mild current entered the stuffy room.

Shashidhwaj went to the window and peered out. The streets were silent and dark. Suddenly, out of the dark shadows, three guards appeared. 'There goes our escape route,' he cursed.

Bahirji quickly blew out the lantern and gestured for silence, closing the shutters till only a crack remained. The guards had settled just below the window, talking desultorily, showing no sign of moving on.

'By the gods,' Bahirji cursed in a low whisper, 'another obstacle Naik will have to negotiate.'

'But he has already used the beggar tactic on the other one,' Shashidhwaj hissed back. 'It won't work again.'

Bahirji had by now finished filling his *jholi*. 'Watch and learn, boy,' he growled.

Through the crack, Shashidhwaj watched Naik emerge from the shadowy corner again. But this time he was not holding a begging bowl, but a broom. The three guards watched him sweep the street, moving the dust to the sides.

'A *fakir*!' Shashidhwaj breathed. He had seen such men in the city. They cleaned the streets and asked for alms, chanting strange words. Everyone appeared to treat them with great respect. He watched the three guards greet Naik.

'*Alakh Niranjan.*' Naik's voice and figure were unrecognizable as he responded to their greetings by touching his broom to their heads. They stood in respectful silence, their heads bowed, to receive his dusty blessing.

'Which of you wants to know your future?'

The guard in the centre looked up and nodded, his eyes widening with anticipation.

'Come into the dark, my son, for the light hurts my old eyes. They have perhaps seen too much.' Naik gestured to the guard to precede him into the shadows. The eyes of the other two remained glued on the duo.

By the window, Bahirji nudged Shashidhwaj. 'This is our chance,' he whispered. 'We go out together.'

Shashidhwaj nodded, his heart thumping hard in his chest. He watched as Bahirji let his feet dangle out of the window, then turned and lowered himself down slowly and silently, his arms carrying the weight of his descent to the ground. Imitating him, Sashidwaj followed.

'Your face says much about you,' Naik was telling the guard. 'It attracts love. You will soon meet a lovely maiden.'

As the other guards moved closer to their colleague, listening to this speech in awe, Bahirji and Shashidhwaj landed soundlessly on the soft earth together.

Bahirji was instantly alert, looking in the direction of the guards. But they were engrossed in what Naik had to say. 'Let's go,' he murmured to Shashidhwaj.

They scurried away into the darkness in the same way they had come.

'What about Naik?' Shashidhwaj asked, looking back.

Bahirji chuckled. 'I daresay the guards will keep him occupied the whole night. There is nothing so fascinating as knowing the future.'

Bahirji's words seemed to be true indeed, for the *prahars* passed after they had safely reached their hut by the river, yet there was still no sign of Naik.

Settling into a corner, Bahirji poured over the papers in the firelight, going over every detail. 'I see a few names repeated multiple times,' he finally said.

'Which names?' Shashidhwaj asked from his supine position on the *chatai*.

'Names of merchants bringing in the most valuable goods into harbour. Two of the names we are already familiar with – Virji Vora, thanks to our adventure near Trimbak, and Haji Kasim, thanks to your new vocation.'

'And the other names?'

Bahirji read on with interest, 'Merchant Haji Sayyid Beg is also bringing in vast quantities of goods. There are also the markings of the Dutch factories, and the Angrez topiwalas. They appear to do a vast amount of trade in Surat.'

'What are we to do with these names?' Shashidhwaj asked sleepily.

'There are two ways to rob a city,' Bahirji told him. 'Either you can knock on each house demanding booty, or target the ones with the most wealth. I think, after our adventure today in the Shah Bunder's Office, we already know who those with the most wealth are.'

'How many cities have you robbed?' Shashidhwaj asked mockingly.

'Oh none,' Bahirji smiled. 'But that's what makes me so good at it.'

'I am already working in the house of Haji Kasim,' Shashidhwaj said. 'I will find where he keeps his treasure. That leaves the houses of Shethji Vora and this Haji Beg you speak of.'

'It appears Naik and I are going to have to find new vocations soon.' Bahirji curled his moustache. 'Would not want a young boy like you to beat us now, would we?'

Shashidhwaj laughed, rolling over to his side. 'We can't get caught,' he said seriously.

'Look at you, afraid even before the real game has begun,' scoffed Bahirji. 'As long as you are very careful in what you do, the chances of getting caught are slim.'

At that moment the door opened and the figure of a *fakir* entered, his long grey beard blowing in the wind.

'What are you two up to?' Naik asked, taking off the beard and hanging it on a nail in the wall. 'Seems like I have to do all the work around here.'

'It appears I will have to find my own disguise soon, Naik,' Bahirji said, 'for we have found exactly what we have to do in this dammed city.'

Chapter Fifteen
Acquaintances at an Inn

TWO MONTHS BEFORE

"You boy! Pick up those scrolls and come with me.' The loud words echoed in the lofty hallway of the house.

Shashidhwaj picked up the bunch of scrolls, tied with the red thread the locals considered auspicious, and followed Kasim's heavy tread out the door. He knew better than to hesitate when the Mir's voice assumed that high pitch.

It had been three weeks since he had begun working in the Kasim household. He did whatever tasks he was called upon to perform, in the kitchen and in the house, often dusting the books in the library, or cleaning the precious and delicate objects that dotted the many public chambers. And by now he was familiar with the various pitches and tones of Kasim's voice. When he was happy, he spoke in a gentle, low tone. When he was discussing business, his voice would be excited, and slightly high pitched. When his voice was shrill, as now, Shashidhwaj knew he was very angry and it was best to hasten to do what he said.

Kasim's face did indeed look sullen as he stepped out through the big doors. The open carriage stood waiting for him. Shashidhwaj hurried forward, diligently holding the door open with his free hand. Kasim appeared pleased with the action for he nodded as he climbed in and took his seat. Shashidhwaj was about to take his place beside the carriage driver when Kasim loudly ordered him to come and sit behind.

'I must go over these scrolls at once.' The voice was lower now.

Shashidhwaj immediately stepped up into the carriage and shut the half door, sitting down gingerly on the seat opposite the great man. The vehicle began to roll forward.

Kasim was muttering angrily to himself as he cast a glance about. 'Report immediately, he says! Do I look like an Abyssinian slave?'

Shashidhwaj kept his eyes on the floor.

'Do I, boy?' The question was hurled at Shashidhwaj.

'No, Mia,' Shashidhwaj was quick to answer, extending one of the scrolls.

'Give a man a helping hand and he devours you whole,' Kasim complained, taking the scroll. 'Damn foreigners!'

Kasim brought out a magnifying glass and began moving it over the letters. His eye looked grotesquely large through the lens and made Shashidhwaj want to laugh. He quickly looked out at the passing scenery, biting his lip. He saw that they had left the market area behind and wondered where they were going. The three weeks at Kasim's house had been most useful.

'You have a contact inside the house,' Bahirji had remarked that first night, when Shashidhwaj had told him about Fatima. 'Now you must win her trust.'

Shashidhwaj had followed this instruction, attempting to encounter Fatima as often as he could. It had turned out to be easier than he had expected, for it was often she who found him in the kitchens. She wanted treats from the sweetmeats section, and he provided them to her silently, with cautious hands that grew ever more deft.

The head cook had noticed the disappearing sweetmeats by now, but his suspicions fell on the assistant cook, who was getting fatter by the day. No one suspected the skinny new boy. Shashidhwaj had also learned by now how to manage the tandoor. He had mastered the trick of slapping the breads against the hot sides of the oven and placing the skewered meats onto the coals to get exactly the right char. The hot tempered head cook had even spoken a word of rare praise, usually as hard to extract as an old tooth.

Fatima, on her part, was happy with her new sweetmeat supplier. It had not taken more than three days for her to ask if he wanted to see one of her secret places in exchange for some of the biggest *jalebis*. She had told him to meet her at the bottom of the central stairway. So, at the end of the day, Shashidhwaj had carefully wrapped the requested jalebis in a clean muslin cloth, and though she had not asked for them, he also put in a few *mawa* barfis. By now he knew what she was partial to.

Fatima passed him, going up the stairs, without once looking at him. Only when she had made sure there was no one watching did she gesture for him to follow her up. Shashidhwaj did so on silent feet, knowing this area of the house was off limits to him. But Fatima had never intended to take him to the first floor. She continued up the stairs, circling the central stairwell till they reached the door that opened onto the roof.

Shashidhwaj looked back to check no one had witnessed their foray up the stairs, then followed her onto the terrace. The view from there was unlike anything he had ever seen. The other buildings around them seemed dwarfed in size. In the distance, directly ahead, stood the Surat Fort, its bastions looming tall over the city like some primeval monster.

Fatima, however, did not seem interested in the view. 'Give them to me,' she said, pulling the little bundle from his hands.

In the orange light of the setting sun, Shashidhwaj watched her relish the jalebis, the sweet juice smearing her lips and chin. He found her girlish delight engaging. He smiled at the way her eyes twinkled on seeing the mawa barfis hidden in the pile of jalebis.

When the sweets were finished, they sat on, talking about their lives. Shashidhwaj learned that Fatima was not from this land, but had been born beyond the sea. She told him she had come to the house of Kasim with her mother, having travelled from Iran, and had been here ever since. And Fatima learned from him the same story Vora had. Bahirji had impressed upon him the importance of telling everyone the same story once an alias was established. Together, they watched the red ball of the sun disappear and darkness fall.

That night, Bahirji was all praise for his young protegé. 'You take sweet talking your way into someone's life quite literally, boy,' he said admiringly as the two of them ate their simple fare.

Naik had not yet returned from his daily role of a blind beggar. Bahirji and Naik had indeed found their individual vocations as promised. Naik had become a blind beggar, who sat outside the factories of the Angrez and the Valandej. Little did those he watched know that his bloodshot eyes were the result of two drops of a certain homemade solution he dropped into his eyes every morning. And so he sat, a blind man seeking alms, keenly observing the movements in and out of the factories, from dawn to dusk.

Bahirji, on the other hand, had made friends with a group of donkey keepers in the city. He worked as their deliveryman, carrying goods to the houses of all the rich merchants of the city, including Vora and Haji Sayyid Beg.

At night, the three of them met in the hut to update each other on the happenings of the day before eating a simple meal and falling asleep. The chalked chart on the mud wall was full of scribbled names, numbers, and cryptic information. However, neither Bahirji nor Naik had managed to develop connections to anyone inside the houses of their targets, as

Shashidhwaj had. Though the two men often praised him for this, Shashidhwaj merely grinned, knowing the chagrin they must feel.

'Yes, she seems like a beautiful angel,' he had told them dreamily.

'Careful boy! Spies are not supposed to fall in love,' Bahirji had been quick to caution. He knew it to be the deadliest blunder anyone could make in their line of work, for it made one blind. 'Only think of her as an asset you are developing.'

'Am I also just an asset you are developing?' Shashidhwaj asked, showing a long face.

Bahirji had merely laughed and put him in his place, commenting drily, 'You haven't been of enough use to qualify as an asset yet.'

Naik returned late that night, taking his own time to change out of his attire. But he too, was intrigued to hear Shashidhwaj's tale. 'Who would have thought the young apprentice would make progress faster than us?' he had muttered.

'What have you learned so far?' Shashidhwaj asked him with interest. He was sure the streets were far more interesting than being inside the walls of Kasim's house.

'Nothing yet that we can use,' Naik had said, going to the wall and working carefully on it.

On the wall, they had drawn a rough map of Surat, where they marked the prime centres of wealth. Shashidhwaj had already had the honour of marking Kasim's house. As Naik drew on the wall, the other two had watched with deep interest.

'You donkeys!'

Shashidhwaj was jolted from his reverie as the carriage plunged to a standstill and Kasim cursed. He was staring off to one side, shouting at whoever was blocking their way. Shashidhwaj heard a shuffling movement.

'Damn these beggars! Like litter in the streets!' Kasim grumbled as they began to move again. 'Now look here, boy,' he raised a finger at Shashidhwaj. 'We will be reaching soon. You must carry these papers like a good servant and stand where I tell you to, and hand me a paper when I ask you to,' he instructed. 'You will not open your mouth, and you will stand still like a statue.' Kasim's voice had turned shrill again.

Shashidhwaj nodded. His throat felt dry at Kasim's anger. In his short time in the household, he had seen how enraged Kasim could get. He had invited some of his friends to dine over the weekend, and all the servants, including Shashidhwaj, had stayed up late into the night till dinner was served and the dishes cleared. Kasim had been in a foul mood the entire evening, shouting at the servants. The air was so tense that even Fatima had not dared show her face at the window, even though delicious aromas had wafted through the house from the kitchens all through the day and into the night.

The disaster had happened at the men's table. One of the servants had made the mistake of filling the silver and copper water pitcher to the brim. All had been well until he had slipped a little on a greasy bone thrown by a guest and emptied the whole pitcher onto the floor. The male guests had cursed while the ladies had lifted the skirts of their *hijabs* with shrill cries of dismay. Kasim had been profusely apologetic and gentlemanly in front of his guests, and the mess had been quickly cleaned up. But once the last visitor had left, he had turned into a ball of fury. He had attacked the erring servant with menacing words. The crack of Kasim's whip and the man's screams had filled the Surat night as the others cowered in terrified silence.

Now, sitting at such close quarters to the man, Shashidhwaj tried to ensure he did not displease the wealthy merchant in any way. He knew Kasim had not brought him along without some reason. He wondered if he would have another interesting story to tell Bahirji and Naik that night.

The carriage finally stopped before an old, stone building. Kasim grunted and Shashidhwaj quickly got out to hold the door open for him. As Kasim climbed down, Shashidhwaj observed the area. It was a section of the city he was unfamiliar with. In fact, it did not appear to be part of the city at all. The fort seemed far away, and beyond the building they had stopped at, there was only farmland. Shashidhwaj realized they had reached the city boundary.

The doorway into the building was large, but no guards stood beside it. Kasim walked in and Shashidhwaj quickly followed, carrying the bundle of scrolls in both arms. The place appeared to be an inn of some sort, with tables and chairs, and a wooden staircase leading upwards. Kasim seemed to know where he was going for he took the stairs without hesitation. Shashidhwaj kept close on his heels. On the upper floor, Kasim walked to a closed door and knocked on it; three knocks in quick succession. Certainly some sort of signal.

The door opened a crack and Kasim pushed his way in, gesturing to Shashidhwaj to guard the door outside. This was getting interesting. Shashidhwaj handed Kasim the bundle of scrolls and remained outside. The door shut. Looking quickly up and down the corridor, Shashidhwaj put his ear against the door. The men were speaking so loudly that he had no difficulty hearing what was being said. Fortunately the language was familiar to him. Who would have thought those long hours studying Farsi under Nanaji's punishing stick would have led to this?

'You came here with someone,' a deep voice said. 'Are you mad? Can he be trusted?'

'Oh relax,' Kasim replied in an off-hand manner. 'He is just a boy. He is a new servant in my household, which is why I brought him; unlike the other snakes in my house who just want to rat out information to the highest bidder. He wouldn't know who to rat to even if he understood what we were saying, which he doesn't, being just a lad from the villages. Besides, did you want me to carry all these scrolls myself?'

Shashidhwaj heard the scrolls being dumped onto a desk.

'You should be more careful,' the deep voiced man insisted.

'It is you who should have been more careful, my friend,' Kasim retorted harshly. 'Sending a letter with a street urchin, asking me to come immediately!'

'I have been patient,' the man replied, 'but it has been weeks since we last met. Each day I grow more anxious than the last.'

'I would have been even more anxious than you, had I been in your place,' Kasim remarked. 'Carrying so much coin and jewellery in this bandit infested town.'

'It would help if you arranged the meeting quickly.'

'Believe me, if it was that simple, you would be sitting on your ass in Agra right now,' Kasim replied waspishly. 'It takes time to reach the Badshah. Trust me, I have lived in Agra long enough to know.'

'Well it has certainly taken more time than it took me to sail here from Abyssinia,' the other said.

'If the delay irritates you so much,' Kasim snapped, 'you are more than welcome to try your luck with the Subhedar. But you should know that he would probably take your gold and not even write to the Badshah, before finding some pretext to take all your coin for himself.'

'I worry, I worry…' the man mumbled morosely. 'The food here does not suit my guards. Most have fallen ill. How will they even guard me if something untoward were to happen?'

'Relax, my friend,' Kasim advised. 'I can always send

some of my own men to protect you. But you must learn the art of patience if you wish to meet the *Tanasahah* of this subcontinent.'

'Sometimes I wonder if you are actually capable of delivering what you have promised.'

'Yes, I am well aware of the lack of faith in you foreigners,' Kasim replied scornfully. 'Which is why I brought along this pile of letters received in reply to my own missives to Delhi. You can spend your idle moments reading them. Then you will understand I am trying to get your audience fixed to the best of my ability.'

'How many more days is all I want to know!'

'Just a few more months,' Kasim promised. 'My letters have now struck the right chord. All that remains is a few more knocks and the doors will open.'

'My people at home are dying,' the man said. 'The Christian rebels are closing in on our cities. If your Badshah does not help us soon, Islam will be finished in Abyssinia. One does not bring so much gold if one is not desperate. You must help me!'

'Speak a little more loudly and you shall be dead where you stand,' Kasim warned. 'This *sarai* has had its share of murders and robberies.'

'Your visit unnerves more than it soothes,' the man complained.

'Perhaps I can do something to pacify you. I will send you one of my best dancing girls. It will make you less anxious,' Kasim offered.

'The only thing that can make me less anxious is an audience with the Badshah.'

'But your face says that a nice girl would not hurt either,' Kasim laughed. 'I am going now. Stay put and do not send me any more messages.'

Shashidhwaj quickly retreated from the door. It creaked open and Kasim walked out. Through the opening, Shashidhwaj caught sight of the man inside. He was bald and was dressed in flowing embroidered robes. The colour of his skin was as black as ebony.

As the door closed, he heard Kasim say authoritatively, 'We must be on our way, boy.'

***

That night, Bahirji and Naik listened to Shashidhwaj's tale.

'So the man you saw inside the chamber has a great deal of gold and coins,' Bahirji mused. 'And he is stuck here for months.' A crooked smile appeared on his lips. 'Now that is just perfect.'

'But I don't know where the coins are,' Shashidhwaj protested. 'I never stepped inside. In that split second I only saw his face and robes.'

'But that can be rectified,' Naik said. 'You know where the man's room is. And how to get there.'

'It's a large sarai near one of the gates,' Shashidhwaj told the others. 'When I was there I didn't hear the sea, so it has to be the Burhanpur Gate.'

'A conjecture that can be confirmed in a day by one of us,' said Bahirji.

'But the man protects his chamber. No one goes in or out without his permission,' Shashidhwaj related. 'If the *najrana* he has brought to present to the Badshah in Agra is there, he certainly won't let anyone he does not know in.'

'Didn't you just tell us that Kasim is to send one of his dancing girls to him?' Naik asked, eyebrows raised.

'Yes, but he did not say which one. He is a *rangel insaan*. He has more than a dozen dancing girls.'

'Why would you need to know that from Kasim? You

have already befriended one of his girls have you not?'

'He will never send Fatima.' Shashidhwaj shook his head. 'She is too young, and the Mir is too fond of her himself. He will surely send someone else.'

'You may know this,' Bahirji tapped a finger on the wooden table, 'but the foreigner does not.'

'What will I tell Fatima?'

'If I have read this girl correctly from everything you have told us,' Bahirji replied, 'she seems to be an adventurous sort.'

Naik tapped Shashidhwaj on the shoulder. 'Tell her you have scouted out a good lay. Or rather, that you and your associates have. Tell her there is a good amount of money to be had, and she can collect her share if she plays a part.'

'No way!' Shashidhwaj shook his head vehemently. 'I'm not sending her alone into a room with that foreigner. He looked horrible!'

'But you would be there to protect her,' Naik said, rather amused by the boy's chivalry. 'You will climb up the back wall of the sarai and wait until she gains entry to his room and succeeds in distracting him. I don't doubt Nanaji taught you the blunt hit to the back of a man's head. I wonder if he is still making new recruits practice on that old dummy we use to practice on? And I have already seen how well you climb.'

Shashidhwaj looked at them wide-eyed. 'That would be spy-like wouldn't it?' His eyes gleamed. 'A true adventure!'

'A true adventure indeed,' Naik agreed gravely. 'And you will find the money if it's there in his room.'

'Also, you will get to spend some alone time with this girl you fancy,' Bahirji winked.

Shashidhwaj's face flushed red but no one noticed it in the lamplight. 'What if something goes wrong?' he muttered.

'If a spy thought of what could go wrong before a job, he would shit his pants before even beginning,' Naik chuckled. 'Besides, you will drug the man. He won't remember a thing later.'

Naik reached into a trunk and rifled through the contents. Finally, he brought out a vial. It contained a small dose of a crystal clear liquid. 'One of Nanaji's oldest formulas,' he said. 'Pour it on a cloth and hold it against the man's nose for a few moments. That should do the trick.'

'But he will surely raise hell with Kasim when he finds the money gone,' Shashidhwaj protested.

'Only, you will not take the money,' Bahirji told him. 'You will only mark where it is. The rest we will do when we sack the city.'

'It will be hard to drag Fatima away, leaving all that money without letting her take some,' Shashidhwaj mused.

'And that would present you with a legitimate reason to touch her,' Naik said with a nudge.

Shashidhwaj looked from one to the other, realizing he was being made a fool of. 'The two of you are making fun of me,' he grumbled.

'Indeed we are.' Bahirji chuckled in delight. 'But it does not lessen the effectiveness of the plan.'

Shashidhwaj nodded in silence before drinking his share of the buttermilk. His heart was already beating fast thinking about it, his first dangerous mission. Or was it beating because he would be sharing it with Fatima?

When he fell asleep that night on the rough floor, Shashidhwaj's dreams were all about the sarai. He saw Fatima and himself gaining stealthy entry, like adventurers, hearts high with courage. His dreams were dispelled only by the cold light of dawn.

Chapter Sixteen

Deception at the Sarai

ONE MONTH BEFORE THE RAID

As always, the meeting place was a dark field outside the city. Only this time the darkness was not that of night, but dense early morning fog. Ali stood by his hitched horse, pulling his shawl tighter in an effort to stay warm in the cold wind that blew around him. A carriage arrived soon enough, the lanterns dangling on its sides providing some illumination through the mist. Ali did not see it until it was almost upon him. A window opened to reveal the metallic face he had seen so many times in his sleep.

'I do not have much time,' the Master said without getting down. Only the mask and his shoulders were visible through the short window. A hand was extended, holding a rolled piece of paper.

Ali took it from him and unrolled it. All it took was one glance. 'A map of the fort!' he exclaimed.

'With the location of the gold marked.' The Master's gloved hand pointed to a hastily marked cross. The layout of the fort however, was neatly drawn, showing the structures within, as well as the various chambers.

'Listen now. The location is perfect. It is a chamber on the western side, overlooking the sea, on the top level.'

'Khan took the barrels to the top of the fort?' Ali rolled his eyes in disbelief. He remembered how heavy they had been and how difficult to offload from the ship.

'Creating a deterrent for anyone who wished to steal, I'm sure,' the Master remarked drily. 'But it has worked to our advantage. A window overlooks the western battlements, beyond which lies nothing but the river.'

'So the barrels could be lowered directly from this window,' Ali murmured reflectively. 'We could load them onto a waiting boat and move them in lots of ten. Fifty barrels would require five trips.'

'Or one trip with five boats,' the Master said.

'But what of the barrels with the oil?' Ali asked.

'You will move them all for now. There aren't that many. You could shift them all in one night. Once you have got them to the safe house, you can open them to see which have the gold and which the oil.'

Ali nodded. Looking up, he waved the paper, saying, 'But the fort is impregnable. Reaching the chamber will be the hardest part. Stealing the barrels once there will be easy.'

'That is the fun part,' the Master said. Ali could almost hear the smile behind the metal mask. 'You shall not infiltrate the fort from inside.'

Ali was astonished. 'Then how?' he asked. 'Surely there is no other way into the fort?'

A drain pipe runs down beside the window of the chamber in question, carrying water from the roof down to the ground below. The top of it is fashioned in the shape of a pig's face, made of cast iron.

Ali's face was tense. He remembered this was a common feature in every Musalmaan two-storied house.

'A rope, long enough to reach the river and strong enough to lower a barrel, has been fastened to the pig's head,' said the Master.

'But surely the guards will notice such a long rope during their patrols and take it down?' observed Ali.

'Not if it is rolled up in a loop.'

'But then we cannot use it to climb up the wall.'

'You can, if you infiltrate one of your men into the fort grounds,' the Master said. 'The man must be of short stature, however, and slim, for the window into the room is small. He should also be a good climber. I have devised a way to get him in, but he will have to climb up using the ledges.'

'Difficult and fraught with peril, but not impossible,' murmured Ali after a moment of deliberation.

'Good. Then know this. On the next new moon, a cart will drive into the fort. It will not be checked because it will be a gift for the Subhedar. The driver will stop at the river road and go to take a piss. Your man, hidden in the cart, must slip out at that moment. Once inside the fort grounds, he will be on his own.'

'I can be in a boat on the river,' Ali mused. 'When my man throws down the rope, we will scale the walls, force the window, and empty the chamber.'

'You already know where to take the barrels,' the Master said.

'I know how to take them from the fort and where to take them to,' Ali agreed, 'but what I do not know is how to take it from there out of the city.'

'One thing at a time, Rayiyas,' the Master replied as if restraining an impatient child. 'Move the barrels. Then we shall speak.' The window shut and the carriage moved forward, disappearing into the fog.

Ali looked at the map in his hand. He folded it carefully and tucked it into his jacket, under his shawl. The path of his ascendance had surely begun.

***

The sarai rose above the narrow alley, some way beyond the main street intersection. Shashidhwaj lingered near the stall of a jalebi maker, knowing he was early. The light was fading. The flames of the stall's chullah seemed to burn brighter, casting the area beyond their reach into shadow.

'You're early!' He recognized her only by her voice as her face and form were shrouded in a *burkha*. Her eyes gleamed through the veil.

Shashidhwaj picked up a jalebi from the stall and offered it to her, tossing a coin to the stall owner.

Fatima raised her veil to just above her nose to eat the offering. 'What are you staring at?' she asked.

Shashidhwaj, who was staring at her red lips, mesmerized, took a hasty step backwards and lost his footing, falling into the dust on his behind. Fatima bit back a smile.

Feeling foolish, he quickly rose to his feet and dusted himself off. 'It's nothing,' he muttered nonchalantly. 'Let's go in.'

They walked along the wall of the sarai and entered through the main door. The room inside was crowded and dimly lit. They sat down where they could see the stairway leading to the upper floor. Shashidhwaj glanced around to see if anyone had noticed them. Discreetly, he nodded towards the stairs, holding up one finger to indicate to Fatima that the foreigner was staying in the first room.

A serving boy appeared beside them. 'We have good strong toddy tonight,' he said in a disinterested voice, looking past them to the next table.

'Two glasses *chaas*,' Shashidhwaj said quickly.

When the boy went to fetch it, Shashidhwaj looked at Fatima. 'You know what to do?'

Behind her veil, she nodded. The serving boy returned with a tray and put down two clay mugs filled to the brim with frothy white buttermilk, with spices sprinkled on top. Shashidhwaj picked up his mug and drank thirstily. As he licked the last trace off his lips, he noticed that Fatima had not touched hers. It was obvious she did not like the place.

'Let's do what we came to do and get out of this place,' she hissed.

Shashidhwaj tried to see through the veil. 'You don't have to be afraid,' he told her. 'You know I will not let that man do anything to you. Even before he can touch you, I will have him unconscious.'

'I am not afraid,' Fatima scoffed. 'But I do not like this place. So let us do what we have to and leave.'

Shashidhwaj nodded and put two coins on the table to pay for the chaas. He got to his feet and they quickly walked towards the stairs. In the crowd, no one noticed them go. The doors to the rooms, including the one the foreigner was in, were closed, but lamplight flickered under several of the doors.

'Let me take position first,' Shashidhwaj whispered.

She nodded and went to stand against the wall beside the first door as he walked quickly towards a balcony. For a moment Shashidhwaj looked down at the dark street below. Turning sideways, he swung his legs over the wooden railing and found his footing on the ledge. He paused, glancing around to see if anyone had noticed his movements, but the street was too dark to discern anything. Where he stood was also in deep shadow, difficult to see from street level. The window of the foreigner's room was three openings away. Shashidhwaj moved along the narrow ledge expertly, ducking at the openings and dangling below the ledge, moving across using his fingers. When the first window had been crossed, he climbed back onto the ledge. When he came to the second one, he ducked down again, crossing in the same manner he had done the first.

As he approached the third window, he hesitated. The ledge was broken here; he would have to jump across. Taking a deep breath, he judged the distance and leapt, arms outstretched. He caught hold of the ledge below the window, his fingers gripping the rough edge. He hung there, swinging for a moment, wondering if some passerby had seen or heard. But the silence below remained undisturbed. He crawled up and took position by the window. Arms against the wall, he leaned sideways and peering into the room.

The dark-skinned foreigner was sitting on his bed, drinking from a silver cup. The familiar smell told Shashidhwaj it was the same toddy that was served below. With one hand he reached into his pocket and felt for the handkerchief he had carefully doused with Nanaji's potent potion, given to him by Naik. He waited for Fatima to make her entrance.

He did not have to linger long as almost immediately there were three soft knocks on the door. The foreigner got to his feet with a grunt. It was apparent he was not expecting anyone. Going to the door, he opened it a crack. Fatima stood outside, the veil still over her face.

'What is it?' the man asked, his speech a little slurred from the toddy he had consumed in generous quantities.

'I come from the house of Kasim Mia,' Fatima said softly. 'He sent me to dance for you.'

'Did he now?' the foreigner said, staring at her.

Fatima raised a fair, slim hand and placed it on the door. 'Pray let me in Sir, and close the door,' she said in a teasing voice, 'so we can be private.'

Shashidhwaj readied himself to jump in and press the handkerchief to the man's face if he tried to take Fatima towards the bed. But the man stood firm, rooted like a tree.

'Did Haji Kasim send you?' he asked again.

'Yes indeed. He asked me to entertain and cheer you.' Fatima now moved her hand to his cheek, but he quickly brushed it away as he would an irritating fly.

'You cannot cheer me,' he said heavily.

Fatima raised her veil to expose her face. 'Am I not beautiful enough?' she asked.

'It's not your beauty that is the problem, my dear, but who you are,' the man murmured.

Fatima stood still at the door, confused and unsure what to do. Shashidhwaj cursed to himself outside the window. He realized what was happening. Their plan had banked on Fatima seducing the foreigner, so he could enter and knock the man out. Now it was apparent the foreigner could not be seduced by a girl!

Shashidhwaj let himself hang down from the ledge again and began to make his way back towards the balcony. He had heard about such men in the lewd gossip of the markets and alleys of Surat, as he went to and from the riverside hutments to Kasim's house. Men who were attracted to other men. Some called it a disease, others a curse. Right now, all Shashidhwaj knew was that it was a hindrance to their plan. He had to find a solution, quickly.

He climbed back up to the balcony and hurriedly entered the corridor outside the rooms. Fatima was still standing at the door to the foreigner's room.

'So, unless Haji Kasim has sent someone else with you,' he was saying to her, 'you should go.'

Shashidhwaj did not waste a second in making his entrance, coming to stand behind Fatima. 'He sent me with her,' he said pleasantly.

The foreigner stared at him from under drowsy lids. Even if this sudden appearance was suspicious, the man was too drunk to notice. He studied Shashidhwaj's slim form from head to feet and nodded. 'You'll do,' he finally said.

Fatima glanced at Shashidhwaj strangely, but he brushed past her into the room. 'Wait for me outside,' he told her with a reassuring smile, and shut the door on her worried face. Now there was no one in the room but him and the dark-skinned man.

The man put down his mug and turned to stare. Shashidhwaj bit his lip, suddenly realizing he had not exactly thought this through. Fatima was now behind the door; no one would come to his rescue through the window if the man really took him to bed. He clutched the handkerchief, wondering if he could press it against the man's nose when he got near.

'You're a handsome lad,' the foreigner said, passing a red tongue over his dry lips. He sat down on the bed and folded his arms. 'Remove your clothes,' he said.

'What?' Shashidhwaj stared at him, wide eyed.

'Haji Kasim sent you here to please me, did he not?' the man barked. 'So take off your clothes and please me.'

Shashidhwaj looked around desperately but there was no aid to be found in the lamp-lit room. Taking hold of his *angarakha* with both hands, he pulled it over his head and stood before the man, shirtless, shivering in the cool breeze that blew in through the open window.

The man got to his feet and moved towards him. Shashidhwaj could smell the toddy on his breath.

'Remove everything,' he said.

Shashidhwaj looked down at his pyjamas. He sighed and bent down, rolling them down his legs, managing to hide the balled handkerchief in his fist as he did so. He stood there naked, except for his *langot*.

'Everything.' The man jerked a thumb downwards.

Shashidhwaj could not protest. He reached behind with his hand and loosened the cotton folds. His *langot* sank to his feet. Now he was completely naked, at the mercy of the foreigner. He curled his hand tightly around the handkerchief, ready to strike when the foreigner made his move. But the man did not move at all. Instead, he gazed down at the lad's exposed manhood, his brows lifted in surprise. This caused Shashidhwaj to look down too. For a moment he thought the foreigner was merely enjoying the sight. Then it hit him. He had been a fool! How had he not realized that being naked would expose his secret?

He was about to grab his clothes and run out of the room when the foreigner took hold of his cheek and pulled him forward, staring into his eyes. 'You are not a Musalmaan, are you?' he said, cold rage in his voice.

Shashidhwaj shook his head. He tried to think of a way to press the handkerchief onto the foreigner's face, but the drunk man's grip was too strong.

'And you wanted me to make love to you? Defiling me?' The man slapped Shashidhwaj hard across the face.

Shashidhwaj took a step back, rubbing his cheek, wondering what to do. The whole plan had gone awry.

'Fool!' the man shoved hard and Shashidhwaj fell back against the door. But the man did not stop. He picked up a carved stick from his desk and raised it.

Shashidhwaj scrambled to his feet and quickly opened the door and scampered out, stark naked. He looked around but Fatima was nowhere to be seen. There was no time to look for her. He ran towards the stairs, the foreigner rushing behind him, the stick raised to beat him with. Shashidhwaj leapt for the stairs, slipping down to the first landing. He did not look back to see if the man followed. He ran down the last flight and jumped down the last three steps. Landing with a thud, he made a dash for the door.

The foreigner arrived at the top of the stairs. '*Kafir*!' he shouted, throwing the stick after Shashidhwaj's retreating form. It narrowly missed him, landing near the door with a great clatter.

Shashidhwaj hurried into the darkness of the alley, ready to run, when he felt a strong hand on his shoulder. Had his attacker caught up with him even in the dark? His heart hammering in his chest, Shashidhwaj turned, but it was not the foreigner. It was a man in a black cloak, just like his own, that now lay in a heap on the floor of the foreigner's room in the sarai. The stranger quickly took off his cloak, revealing a white shirt and a leather jacket fastened with straps, black trousers in the Western style, and boots. He held out the cloak and Shashidhwaj, extending one hand, gratefully took it from him, using the other hand to cover his genitals. He could not recall where or when he had lost the handkerchief with Nanaji's potion.

'What were you doing in there?' the stranger asked.

'I just wanted to earn some money,' Shashidhwaj replied in a low voice.

The man gazed at him for a long moment, then said, 'There's enough work for a young boy like you on the docks. Why this way?'

'I do work in the day,' Shashidhwaj muttered, covering himself with the cloak, 'but the coin is never enough.'

'You misunderstand me,' the man said. 'There is enough work in this city for a young boy, even at night.'

Shashidhwaj looked at him. Was he another like the man he had run from? The stranger held out a coin. It gleamed in the pale moonlight. Shashidhwaj reached out and took it, wishing to appear hungry and desperate.

'I saw how you climbed across the wall of the sarai,' the man said. 'Can you climb like that anywhere?'

Shashidhwaj nodded, wondering where this was leading.

'Meet me near the river tomorrow night,' the man said. 'Work with me for one night and you will never have to do filthy things like this again.'

'Who should I ask for?'

'Samsher Ali,' the man replied briefly. Turning, he disappeared into the darkness.

As Shashidhwaj looked after the vanishing figure, he felt a tug on his cloak. Shashidhwaj whipped around, gripping the cloak around him. It was Fatima. There was a silver coin in her hand. She tossed it up. Shashidhwaj's hand shot out and caught it.

'How did you get this?' he asked, thankful for the cloak that hid his nakedness.

'I hid in an alcove. When that man ran after you, he left the door open and the room empty,' Fatima whispered.

'You looked inside?'

'There are three chests below his bed, all filled with coins like these,' Fatima disclosed. 'I did not have time to see if there was anything else. I was afraid that horrible man would return any moment.' She paused, suddenly noticing Shashidhwaj in his cloak. 'What exactly happened in there?' she asked.

'Let's just say I was saved from a fate worse than death.'

'Well, I shall keep the coin as my reward.' Fatima took it back from him. 'I hope you found what you wanted.'

'Indeed.' Shashidhwaj grinned as they walked down the alley. 'You will get your share after we hit the place.'

'For now, just take me home.' Fatima slipped her hand into his.

This caused Shashidhwaj's heart to skip a beat. And as he walked with Fatima towards the house of Haji Kasim, he thought of all the jokes Bahirji would crack at his expense when he related the story of this night's happenings. But feeling Fatima's warm hand in his, it seemed like the happiest night of his life.

***

To Shashidhwaj's surprise, Bahirji had no jokes to make, showing only concern when he heard the story. 'Are you sure you are alright?' he asked. 'You are not hurt, boy?'

'I am unharmed,' Shashidhwaj assured him.

'And you got rewarded with a walk in the moonlight with the beautiful girl you are so fond of,' Naik offered from the side, scribbling on a piece of paper.

'We discovered three chests of silver coins we can loot,' Shashidhwaj bragged. 'What have you two found in the city so far?'

'Well, I for one am more interested in this cloaked man you met, who asked you to meet him at the docks,' Bahirji said. 'I think we will discover interesting things through that lead. Let me look at that cloak he gave you, boy.'

Shashidhwaj rose and brought over the black cloak. It was finely made, and warm. It obviously belonged to a man of means. Tired from his adventures, Shashidhwaj lay down on the *chatai*. Naik was still scribbling frantically.

'What do you draw?' Shashidhwaj finally asked.

Naik held up the page. In the glimmering yellow light, Shashidhwaj saw criss-crossed lines that went up and down, covering the whole page, becoming circles, squares and arrows.

Shashidhwaj sat up. 'It is a map is it not?'

Naik nodded. He put a finger on the paper. 'The money moves into Surat through two pathways. One from the sea, the other by road. What the sea brings is huge, and we have already gathered information on this from our visit to the Shah Bunder's offices, but we cannot ignore what the roads bring too.'

At the very edges of the paper, Shashidhwaj saw that Naik had marked the four directions. 'Those are the three gates into the city,' he said, pointing.

'Indeed. The Burhanpur Gate to the East. The Navasari Gate to the South, and the Ahmedabad Gate to the North.' Naik traced a finger down from the top gate to the western boundary, where a flowing line ended the mesh of lines. It indicated the Tapi River.

'And what are these?' Shashidhwaj asked, reaching out to tap the big circles Naik had drawn near the gates.

'They are the places the money coming overland is accumulated,' Naik told him. 'Wealth comes to Surat in all forms - goods, spices, gold and coin. When we sack Surat, we will be able to carry back only the gold and coin. Wealth is heavy. All merchants bringing in goods or materials into Surat, have to pay at these circles.' He tapped them. 'These are the toll booths of the *Jakatdar*, and the revenue goes directly to the central Mughal treasury in Agra. Imagine the numerous merchants passing through these booths every day, depositing toll for the right to move goods to the city markets, or out to foreign ports. Bahirji here has done the important job of discovering the frequency with which this revenue is shifted to Agra.'

'It is most interesting, the way they shift it.' Bahirji peered at the paper. 'The revenue does not go to the Subhedar because it belongs to the Badshah. The *jakat naka* collectors gather the revenue each week and it goes directly to Agra in caravans. Thousands of coins go every week.'

'That means thousands of mahmudis will be sitting in these booths when the city is raided,' Naik nodded.

'How did you find out how they move the coins?' Shashidhwaj asked. It seemed much too complex a task.

'What do you think they need to move such heavy loads over such long distances every week?' Bahirji asked.

Shashidhwaj whistled. 'Carts.'

'And what pulls the carts?'

'While you have been warming the kitchens of Kasim's house all these days, Bahirji has befriended donkey keepers in the city outskirts,' Naik explained. 'These donkey keepers make a living by renting out their donkeys. They have a boasting match among themselves over whose donkeys pulled the most coin each week.'

Shashidhwaj suppressed a smile. 'Bahirji must have been quite at home in their vicinity.'

'I was, being used to living with you,' Bahirji retorted.

'So these toll booths are always overflowing with coin,' Shashidhwaj mused. 'I wonder if there are more places like that in the city? Maybe the sarais on the outskirts that are always full, or the city inns where traders stop?'

Naik shook his head. 'Those places have small change. During a raid, what we need is big money in a single place. That is more viable than looting several places for small amounts. Time will be short.'

'Have you raided a city before?' Shashidhwaj asked curiously.

'I have, boy, every night in my dreams.' Naik rose and put the paper away in his jholi.

'You ask too many questions, lad. Have you found out yet where Kasim keeps his treasure?' Bahirji asked.

Shashidhwaj shook his head. 'But I will,' he said. 'I have a plan.'

'And what about the mysterious man who has asked you to meet him at the docks?'

'I will meet him. But I don't yet know what he wants.'

'In that case, there is only one way to find out,' Bahirji opined, yawning. 'When you meet him tomorrow night at the docks, look him in the eye and ask.'

Chapter Seventeen

The Longest Night

ONE MONTHS BEFORE

Ali paced the alley alone. He felt more uneasy with each step he took. His visitor was late. Much too late! Instinctively, his right hand felt for his belt, his fingers closing on the hilt of the small dagger. He finished his round to the mouth of the alley and then turned back. They should have been here by now, he thought, if they cared for the life of their daughter. By the time he had completed two more rounds, he was not sure they did.

He had never liked the Angrez, much too fair in their hideous red jackets, who manned the docks at Suwali. He thought their pointed hats ludicrous and their polished boots unsuited to doing dock work. Sometimes, when he had nothing better to do, he would ride his horse to the coast and stop on the hill by the docks and just watch the Angrez go about their business. It was a sight to watch them helm a ship and unload the cargo. It was like some kind of bondage, the way they moved in lines, following every word that burst forth from the foreman's mouth. Ali would never be able to do something like that. He had the blood of the great Khudwand Khan in his veins.

He reached into his jacket and pulled out a gold pocket watch, the size of a walnut. He flicked the round cover open and stared at the dial, feeling every tick of the watch in the palm of his hand. He shut it again and put it back in his pocket. Arriving back at the mouth of the alley, he walked on a little further and looked left. Hatim was standing at the entrance to the next alley, his eyes sharp. He nodded when he saw Ali looking about. Ali nodded back. Behind Hatim, Ali knew there were a dozen men. If his visitors tried to ambush him here tonight, they would have to kill Hatim and his men first.

Ali turned and walked back to the other end of the alley. When he reached the wall, he suddenly stopped, sensing someone behind him. Ali did not panic. He turned slowly, deliberately, letting his visitor know he could not be intimidated by such common tactics.

But when he did turn around, he was not so sure. The man standing before him had on a black cloak which covered him from head to feet. Only the tips of his boots showed below its folds. His face was covered by an iron mask, like the war helmets used in sultanates of old. The breeze blew back the cloak a little to reveal a hand clad in a black glove. Ali's heart skipped a beat as he looked at the shining barrel of a small pistol pointed straight at his heart.

'Are you afraid?' the man asked in pure Farsi, the language of Ali's ancestors. He took a step forward and corked the pistol.

Ali stared at him as if transfixed by a vision. He knew a simple whistle with two fingers in his mouth would bring Hatim and his men running into the alley. But his hand felt frozen.

'I ask again,' the man repeated, 'are you afraid?'

Ali reached for his dagger, whipping it out of its leather sheath. He held the blade between thumb and forefinger, hand slightly raised, ready to throw. 'Do I look afraid?' he managed to utter.

'Good.' The cloaked man lowered his weapon. 'I wouldn't expect a descendant of the great Khudwand Khan to be afraid.'

Ali did not lower his arm. How did this man know his identity?

The man looked at the weapon in Ali's hand. 'Do not fidget, young Rayiyas, those you wait for will not be coming tonight. Instead, they have sent me.'

Ali caught sight of Hatim, standing behind the cloaked man, confused by what he saw. Ali nodded to him, signalling him to move back.

'Why will they not?' he asked his strange accoster. 'Do they not care for the life of their daughter?'

'Oh they care very much,' the man said, looking up. 'Which is exactly why they asked me to come tonight.'

'Do you bring the gold then?' Ali asked, lowering his dagger. As long as he got the gold promised in return for the girl, he didn't care about anything else.

'No, the only gold I bring is this.' The cloaked man raised the golden handle of his pistol, which gleamed in the meagre moonlight. 'Care to take it?'

The man tossed the gun with a flick of his wrist. It circled on its axis, travelling through the air as Ali raised his hand and caught it by the gold handle. It was an exquisite weapon. The handle was engraved and the corkscrew crafted in the shape of a sea lion.

Ali heard himself laugh as he raised the pistol, pointing it at his visitor. 'Then it is my turn to ask, are you afraid? You come here without the gold that was promised, and dare to threaten me on my own streets.'

The cloaked man did not flinch. He merely folded his arms and stood his ground. 'Do you know that the weapon you now hold in your hand once belonged to your great ancestor?'

Ali was taken aback but did not let it show on his face. 'And how do you know that?' he asked.

'Because he got it from me,' the man said.

'My great-great-grandfather Khudwand Khan died more than a century ago,' Ali said negligently. Nonetheless, he felt the hand holding the gun tremble.

'Some things you just can't kill,' the man said shrugging, the cool breeze ruffling his long cloak. 'Let the girl go. There is a buggy

waiting. It will take her to her parents.'

Clenching his teeth, Ali raised the gun, steadying it with both hands. 'They promised me gold. She goes nowhere without it.'

'But isn't it something far more valuable than gold that you are holding in your hands?' the man asked softly.

'Who in the world are you?' Ali asked angrily.

'I am a messenger, Rayiyas,' the man said. 'Sent to you by God himself. Just as God sent one to your great ancestor.'

'What message do you have for me?'

'To stop this petty thieving and kidnapping.' The man dropped his hands to his sides. 'Such pursuits do not become a descendant of Khudwand Khan.'

'They laugh at me behind my back!' Ali heard the tremor in his own voice. 'They say I am a fake descendant; that I was never born of his seed. They say I am a street urchin with a false claim.'

'And doing what you do will make them say otherwise?'

Ali felt his own breath choke his throat. 'My ancestor ruled this city,' he said. 'He built the great fort around which this city lives and thrives. I will not be a mere street urchin in its alleyways.'

'And so you ask for gold in return for an innocent child?'

'The Angrez I took her from has more than enough,' Ali said. 'I saw how he strutted about the market place, golden threads running through his doublet, a pocket watch the size of the full moon. The girl has not been harmed. She was treated well.'

'And that is your defense?' The man laughed. 'That is what you will tell the bards who write the story of this descendant of Khudwand Khan?'

'All of us are thieves,' Ali spat. 'My ancestor fought for the Mughals, and took this land from its earlier occupants. He built this fort to defend it from those trying to take it from him.'

'And he got a city as a reward. What will you get? A few gold coins, half of which you must share with your men as their price?'

'What would you have me do?'

'First, return the girl,' the man insisted.

'And then?'

'I will tell you that after you return the girl. You will have to trust me.'

Ali stared at the man for a moment. Then he put two fingers to his mouth, tasting the salt upon them as he whistled. He watched Hatim and his men appear at the mouth of the alley. In their wake came a girl in a ruffled blouse and calico skirt, blindfolded. Despite her youth, she neither wept nor struggled.

Ali pointed towards the carriage waiting in the distance. Hatim led the girl to it and opened the door. They helped her climb in. Ali heard the door shut, and then the neighing of horses and rolling of wheels. Hatim returned with his men. Ali raised his hand again and rotated it twice – the signal for dispersal. He watched the men disappear behind the wall. All except Hatim, who stared at Ali for a while longer. Then he too, left.

When they were gone, the cloaked man clapped softly. 'You command good men,' he said admiringly. 'They do your bidding; not a question asked. Do you know how rare that is these days?'

'The girl is gone,' Ali said. 'Now tell me what you came here to say.'

'What would you say if I was to tell you that you could be as rich as your ancestor, have as much gold as he had, and buy your own ship and sail the high seas like he once did?'

'I would say that you just caused a good amount of gold to slip from my grasp.'

'In life, as in war, we often have to take a step back so we can take two forward,' the man said.

'You say that I can be rich?'

'I do not say it. I know for sure that you will be, for you have already learnt to obey me.' The man walked towards Ali, one deliberate step at a time. When he was merely an arms length away, he stopped. 'There are secrets flowing through the streets of this city. Secrets which someone like me knows.'

'Why are you helping me?' Ali asked.

'I haven't helped you yet.' Behind his mask, Ali knew the man was smiling. 'Ask me this after I actually have. If you do as I say, and follow my every word, you will indeed be very rich, young Rayiyas.'

'What do I have to do?'

'The usual stuff you do anyway,' the man shrugged, 'thieving, looting, killing. Only this time, the stakes will be much higher, and so will the reward. And yes,' he said, touching the pistol's muzzle, 'now you have a lucky charm to carry you through all of that as well.'

'Ask and it shall be done,' Ali said. 'But betray me, and you will pay…

The cloaked man placed a gloved finger upon Ali's lips. 'Do not speak of things you know nothing about, young Rayiyas.' The hand dropped back to the man's side. 'I will send word soon. We will meet, and then I shall tell you what to do.'

Ali watched the man walk to the end of the street and disappear into the darkness beyond. He let out a long breath, gazing at the pistol in his hand. Then his eyes lifted to the sky, and he prayed.

Ali woke, his face and chest gleaming with droplets of sweat, his heart beating hard against his chest. It wasn't a dream but a memory, as vivid as when it had occurred, not so long ago. He sat up on his bed and thought about the Masked Master. On each occasion the Master had spoken, the words had proven to be true. If he was right about today as well, Ali knew it would be one of the most important days of his life.

He dressed silently. When he was finished, he stared at the night sky through the window. There was no moon. He closed the curtains and went out, walking down the single flight of stairs on silent feet. He pulled the hood of his cloak over his head. Tonight, he would not share his plan with his men. What they had to do was most secret. The men would only come to know what it was in the course of doing it. Except for the boy, none would know.

Had he made the right decision in trusting the boy? It was better to trust an unknown urchin than the regular thugs of the city, he thought. He had seen how the boy climbed the ledges of the sarai. The fort ledges were more spacious, and made of stone. They would pose no problem for the boy.

He wondered whether the lad would be afraid. But he had certainly shown no fear climbing the sarai wall. But what Ali had to discuss with him tonight, was no mere infiltration into a chamber at a sarai on the outskirts of the city. The boy could very well lose his life. Ali hoped the amount of coin he could promise would be enough to quell all else.

Little did he know that the mere opportunity to infiltrate the fort was more than enough for the boy to jump headlong into the mission! As Ali stood at the appointed meeting place on the docks, he unfurled the map of the fort which the Master had given him. He would explain it to the boy and tell him the plan. Then he would set it in motion, hoping to emerge as one of the richest men in the city built by his revered ancestor.

***

Shashidhwaj lay in silence, his arms wrapped around his body as the cart jolted forward over the uneven track. There was little to be seen between the chinks in the woodwork of the cart. He understood they had turned onto the main street when the illumination outside became brighter from all the lanterns that adorned it at night. The cart slowed and stopped. The driver shouted something in Urdu to an unseen person. Shashidhwaj felt his heart skip a beat when he heard the lowering of the drawbridge. He was passing beyond the point of no return. The cart rolled forward again, creaking over the wooden bridge. Shashidhwaj pressed his forehead against the side of the vehicle, trying to get a look at his surroundings.

The plan that the mysterious man had discussed with him had seemed most sinister. Shashidhwaj wondered if he was capable enough to execute it. But the knowledge that he was now inside the Surat Fort, which neither of his companions had managed to do yet, sent a rush of adrenaline flowing through his blood. Lying in the cart, covered by sacking, he imagined the chagrin on the faces of Bahirji and Naik when he told them what he had done and where he had been.

He was now passing through the main gate into the vast open courtyard the man called Ali had described to him from the map. The cart would turn left and stop near the stables. He would have to emerge from the coverings and drop off before the cart stopped and the driver began to unload.

Shashidhwaj peered out over the sideboard, quickly glancing around to make sure no wayward eyes were looking his way. As silent as a shadow, he rose up and jumped out, running on swift feet to hide in the shadow of a nearby building. The cart kept moving on, the driver oblivious to both his passenger and his disappearance. Shashidhwaj took a deep breath and gazed at the fort. The bastions appeared too high to climb.

Don't stay in one position for more than a minute. He remembered Naik's advice on infiltration, so he moved to the next wall. Suddenly, two large moving shadows appeared on the wall. Two guards carrying torches were patrolling the area. They saw the cart and walked towards it as it came to a stop near the stables.

Shashidhwaj waited till the guards had passed. He looked at the path ahead, trying to work out his next move. According to the map, he would have to cross the courtyard to get to the main building. He could see groups of soldiers patrolling the flat area as well as the battlements. He decided to stay close to the dark west wall, where the guards would not see him and the nooks would help him hide if a patrol suddenly showed up.

He looked towards the far end. A lone guard was walking away from the wall, and two others were moving on the battlements towards each other. *Look closely and you can predict anyone's patrol route,* Bahirji had told him when they had sneaked into the Shah Bunder's office. He had wondered then how to do that. Now, leaning flat against the western wall, Shashidhwaj realized how naturally he could tell the solitary guard would cross the whole compound to the other bastion and then return. It was a distance of more than five hundred paces. Once the guard was far enough away, he could slip along the wall to the other side before the man returned.

The air was filled with the sound of the river as he carefully made his way across. When he was halfway, he saw the guards atop the ramparts stop. Shashidhwaj froze against the shadowed wall, his heart thudding.

'Cold night!' one of the men said, blowing on his hands.

'And dark!' the other grumbled.

Shashidhwaj cursed under his breath. The guard on the ground would return all too soon, and he would lose the chance to dash to the safety of the far wall. The guards above continued to chat. From the corner of his eye, Shashidhwaj saw the patrolman on the ground had reached the other bastion and was turning. *When in trouble, improvise.* Nanaji's words suddenly sounded clear and strong in his mind. Shashidhwaj fell on all fours and moved forward. The darkness and cover from the calf high grass was enough. His hands and knees made some scrabbling sounds but he did not stop. He had to get to the other side.

As he scrambled forward, he heard one of the guards stop mid-sentence, look down, and say, 'I wonder how these street dogs make their way inside past all those gates?'

'It ain't a dog, but a cat,' the other one said. 'Dogs make much more noise.'

Shashidhwaj heaved a sigh of relief as he finally reached the other side. He was now directly between the riverside bastion and the wall of the main building. He waited, steadying his breathing and looking around to check if there were any more guards. There were none. It was here the guidance from the map ended. The man called Ali had told him he would have to climb up from somewhere around here. Shashidhwaj looked up at the plethora of windows. They all looked the same. Carefully moving his gaze along them, he noticed the metal pig-mouth drain Ali had described. Even in the surrounding darkness, it gleamed, reflecting the light of the courtyard torches.

Shashidhwaj looked around, seeking a way upward. There were gaps and rough patches in the stone wall of the fort and finding a footing would be easy. He began to move up slowly, getting a hold above his head with one hand before moving up with the support of the other. He found a wide ledge just above one of the windows of the first floor, and stayed perched on it for a while, looking down. There were no patrols on this side and the guards appeared far off. He tensed his legs again and moved off the relative safety of the ledge and climbed up again. Finally, he saw the bronze pig above his head. The looped rope around it was clearly visible.

Shashidhwaj carefully grabbed the sill and turned his head. He was above the fort walls and could see the river. He saw a light blinking in the darkness. He knew the light meant Ali had reached his position on the water, as he had said he would. Shashidhwaj clenched his teeth and reached up with one hand. He could now feel the rough hemp of the rope. He clawed his way up a little and grabbed the rope, holding on with both hands. He was now hanging against the side of the building, in mid-air.

His right hand moved expertly from the rope to the bronze drain as he shifted his weight, trying to keep his legs together. The sharp edges of the casting hurt his palm but he held on and brought his other hand round as well. He grunted as he lifted himself up using his arms, until his chest rested on the bronze head. Then he brought one leg over, and then the other. Shashidhwaj let out a deep breath. He was now sitting at the exact place he had to be. As he looked down at the light in the river and the patrol-less area below, he realized with a sudden thrill that he had succeeded in his task.

Ali had told him to make sure the room was the right one, and that there was no one inside, before letting down the rope. Expertly balancing on the bronze drain, Shashidhwaj slowly rose up and peered in. The room did indeed look deserted. As his eyes adjusted to the blackness within, small shapes began to emerge in his field of vision. Barrels, just like he had been told there would be. He could not read the Angrez letters on their sides, but they were just like the shapes Ali had drawn for him. Shashidhwaj turned his attention to the window itself. There was indeed a small gap between the panes as he had been told. Carefully, he inserted two fingers. He could feel the latch that held the panes together. One upward flick and a hard push was all it took for the panes to swing open.

Shashidhwaj did not waste any time. He carefully sat back down and searched for the loose end of the rope. He found it hanging by his lower leg. He tugged the other end, by which he had clambered onto the drain pipe, to make sure it was still secure. Then he carefully let the rope down. It unrolled as it fell and went straight over the wall, disappearing into the darkness. It was time to send the signal. Shashidhwaj dug into his pocket and searched for the small shard of mirror Ali had given him. Holding it wedged in his palm, he pointed it towards the light, moving it till the light was reflected back. Shashidhwaj knew that to those below, it would merely look like a shining speck, floating mid-air.

The signal had obviously been seen, for almost at once Shashihwaj felt the rope become taut as hands grabbed it from the ground. He rose to his feet again and, holding onto the ledge, pulled himself up and into the room. Leaning out of the window, he watched as the rope moved, twisted and turned, as the men climbed up in utter silence.

The first face appeared a few moments later. Samsher Ali

was the first man up. He grunted as he supported himself on the bronze drain and then climbed up to the window.

'You did well, kid,' he said.

Behind Ali, another man appeared at the window. Behind him came two more. They came into the chamber and bent over, gasping from the hard climb.

'You must leave,' Ali said. 'We take over now.' Pulling a bag from his belt, he tossed it to Shashidhwaj.

It clinked as he caught it. The coin he had been promised. Shashidhwaj nodded. He knew he had to get back down using the rope. He went to the window and hoisted himself onto the sill. Casting a last glance at the chamber, he grabbed the rope, and lowered himself, feet against the wall. Ali watched him disappear into the darkness below.

When he was on the battlements, Shashidhwaj saw the two guards were still patrolling on the wall, a hundred paces away, completely oblivious to what was happening right under their noses. He knew that one jump over the wall would take him into the river, to safety, but with adrenaline rushing through his veins, when adventure beckoned so temptingly, he did not wish to feel safe. He looked around for the stone steps that would take him down to the courtyard again. They were just a few steps ahead. With each step that led down, Shashidhwaj knew he was walking into the lion's den, but then, as Bahirji had said, who steps into the lion's den if not the hunters who are to kill it?

Once down, Shashidhwaj closed his eyes and tried to picture the map of the fort Ali had shown him, and which he had later drawn for Bahirji and Naik at the hideout before setting off on Ali's task. It had shown the military barracks as located in the eastern side of the fort. This meant he would have to cross the courtyard yet again, as he had when he came in.

Shashidhwaj decided against this, knowing it to be fraught with risk. The dark stretch along the fort wall next to the river seemed an alternative route. He waited till the patrolling guards had moved away and quickly ran to the fort building, where a staircase led up to the first floor. He wondered if he should go up, or just cross at ground level. He was still mulling the decision when a shadow appeared at the corner. It had to be a guard with a flaming torch. In that moment there was no longer a decision left to make, so Shashidhwaj scampered up the stairs, careful not to make any sound.

The top floor was dark and eerie. Shashidhwaj moved through a high vaulted corridor with open doors to his left, but they were empty. He found another stairwell at the end and peered down to see if anyone was about, then quickly scrambled down. He was now on the other side of the fort, but still had to cross the diagonal distance to reach the barracks. He looked around to ensure the guard who had surprised him at the last corner was not coming back. Once he was sure there was no one in sight, he darted across to the barrack building and squatted by some bushes.

The way up was guarded. Two guards stood with spears at the stairway. Shashidhwaj was still considering how to move past them when he noticed a tree at the far end, standing in relative darkness. Keeping to the grass and shadows, he carefully moved towards it.

Climbing the tree was child's play. The hard part was not to make any noise while doing so. He placed each foot carefully as he climbed up the trunk, testing each branch to ensure there was no creaking. Halfway up, a breeze began to flutter and ruffle the leaves; he used the sound of the rustling to climb to the very top. From where he sat, straddling a branch, the second level of the building was a couple of arms length away. He waited until the wind blew another gust and then made the jump.

Inside, he knew he had to look for the Qilladar's office. Bahirji had told him that Mughal officers usually decorated their offices with the colours of their flags. He found one such door straight ahead, the lamps inside still burning.

The door stood ajar. Shashidhwaj remained still as a rock, wondering if there was someone inside. But the room was empty. Candles burned in holders on the desk, and there were flaming torches on the walls. Taking a deep breath, Shashidhwaj entered, closing the door behind him.

Chapter Eighteen

Father and Son

ONE MONTHS BEFORE

In the Qilladar's chamber, papers littered the large desk. Shashidhwaj took a good look at them, rifling through the sheets for something of interest. As he leaned over the desk, he caught sight of a stack of papers in a box on the floor. Quickly, he lifted one of the candle holders so the light fell on the stack. The metal was hot in his hand but he did not feel it in the excitement of the moment.

Shashidhwaj studied the Urdu markings carefully, trying to remember what Nanaji had taught him. The papers seemed to be payment slips, marked with the seal of the Qilladar. The soldier's name appeared on top, with the amount paid below. Shashidhwaj's eyes moved over the stack. Fewer than he would have expected in a fort this size, with its large battalion. He moved his hands over the stack, remembering the technique Nanaji had taught him to count many pages at once. He saw there were about a hundred pages for the size of his palm. He moved his palm down, and then again, counting, till he reached the ground. Ten palms, which meant…

The sound of approaching footsteps disturbed his thoughts.

Shashidhwaj felt suddenly breathless as he stared at the door. Someone was in the corridor. He could hear voices. He looked around desperately for a place to hide. There were no dark corners in the room, nor a window he could slip out of. The only thing that offered safety was the cupboard located behind the desk. There was no time to think. Shashidhwaj prayed the cupboard was not locked as he reached for the handle. Praise Bhawani, it was not! It clicked open and he quickly slid inside, closing the door behind him. In the dark stuffy space, he waited, his heart thudding in his chest like a runaway horse. Perhaps the footsteps would pass by.

They did not. Instead, he heard the door of the chamber open and the footsteps come closer until they were merely an arms length away, separated by the cupboard door. Shashidhwaj peered through the small gap between the panels. There were two tall figures in the room. Both had long beards that fell to their waists, but one beard was white, the other jet black.Their clothing proclaimed they were no ordinary soldiers. The high hats on their heads proclaimed they had to be officials. Shashidhwaj held his breath as the younger man sat down at the desk. He prayed the man would not notice the candle on the desk had been moved. But the man did not appear to observe this.

The old man sat down opposite him. 'It is good we have finally reached the end of the circle,' he said. 'Gold prices are rising every day. I think a deal like this comes only once in a lifetime, if one is lucky.'

'We have indeed come a long way, Father,' the other replied. 'I remember well the stories of your youth, when you were just a soldier, living on meagre rations and pay.'

'Those days are far behind us now,' the old man smiled. 'Our efforts have been rewarded by Allah. Not only have we accumulated huge wealth, we have also managed to safeguard it right under the watchful eyes of Agra.'

'You can finally realize the bigger ambitions you have always dreamt of, Father. Of becoming the Mir Qazi, or perhaps, even the Wazir. With this much money, nothing is impossible.'

In the stark silence that followed, Shashidhwaj suddenly realized, with a missed beat of his heart, who these men were. He remembered the distant figures Naik had shown him from the bridge on his first day in the city. Instinctively, he leaned further back into the cupboard, as if they could see him through the small gap, as he saw them.

'And you could follow in my footsteps, my son,' Inayat Khan said. 'Muqtdar of the Delhi Imperial Guard, perhaps.'

'And when the time is right,' Muhabbat Khan replied haughtily, his voice sounding strangely hollow in the high-beamed, candlelit chamber, 'perhaps the *Taqht* itself.'

Inayat Khan held up a warning hand. 'Softly my son, for the walls too, have ears,' he cautioned.

'If they do, I shall cut them off with this.' Muhabbat Khan pulled his small sword from the scabbard at his belt and with a hard thrust, embedded the blade into the wooden desk.

'Well, it was all worth it in the end,' Inayat Khan said, his eyes closed. 'All the dirty things we had to do to get here, all those risky ploys.'

Muhabbat Khan pulled the dagger free and put it back in his belt. 'Even this!' He pointed to the papers in the box at his feet. Trembling, Shashidhwaj drew back, realizing it was the stack he had been looking at just a few moments before. 'I had sleepless nights you know, every time I made the payments to my thousand soldiers, knowing the grant we received from Agra each month was for five thousand men. I imagined *Sarkari Lokpals* dragging me from my bedchamber to answer for this. I felt relieved each time I opened my eyes to the morning light and found myself safe.'

'We fooled the Badshah in his own fort!' Inayat Khan laughed. 'Most of our wealth has come from this final deception. It would not have been possible to do without you, my son. The gold coins I paid the Qazi to make you

Qilladar of Surat, when I was appointed Subhedar, was worth it.'

Inside the cupboard, Shashidhwaj's heart resumed its mad gallop. He had just heard an admission of guilt straight from the horse's mouth. It explained the doubt that had crept into his mind when he had seen the shortfall in the stack of payment papers. He now realized what it meant. If only he could jump out of his hiding place and rush to Bahirji and Naik, waiting in the hut by the river, and reveal what he had just learnt!

Instead, Muhabbat Khan pushed his chair back and got to his feet. 'I have something to show you,' he said to his father.

Shashidhwaj froze as he realized the big man was coming towards him. He crouched down in the close confines of the cupboard, pressing himself into a corner, his arms around his knees. Muhabbat Khan opened the door a little and inserted a hand, looking for something on the shelves to the right. Shashidhwaj watched his hand move from one shelf to the other with bated breath.

'Pshaw! I know I put them here,' Muhabbat Khan muttered in growing irritation.

Shashidhwaj noticed some papers had fallen onto the tied bundles of scrolls, stacked below. Slowly, he pushed them towards Muhabbat Khan's groping fingers.

As his hand touched the papers, Muhabbat Khan's fingers clutched them. He turned away, slamming the half open door shut again. Shashidhwaj closed his eyes and let out a silent sigh. Luck had favoured him this time.

Muhabbat Khan went back to the desk. 'These are the bills of lading from Virji Vora's ship,' he said, sitting down again. 'We knew he had some hold over the redcoat, which he used to force him to do our bidding. But it seems he also did some bidding for himself.'

Inayat Khan lazily inspected the papers Muhabbat Khan

placed on the desk. 'Drums of oil,' he murmured.

'Why the hell would Vora take oil from the redcoat's ships into his store?' Muhabbat Khan asked. 'It has to be what I think it is – a facilitation fee!'

'We paid only for the gold we received,' Inayat Khan said, pushing the papers away. 'If Vora took something more for himself, then….'

'But, as you yourself have said, Father,' Muhabbat Khan interrupted, mid-sentence, 'the price of gold is rising.'

'Maybe you should send some of your men to investigate then.' There was a mirthless smile on Inayat Khan's face. 'Remind Vora who he really works for.'

His son gave a harsh laugh. 'I might do just that,' he said.

Shashidhwaj wondered how long the duo would sit there. If Muhabbat Khan returned to the cupboard to put the papers back, he felt sure he would be discovered. Of course, he could still run for it, using the moment of surprise. The door to the chamber stood ajar. A quick dash out of the cupboard, down the corridor to the window, and down the tree before either Khan could even realize what was happening, was possible. He could run for the walls before the guards were alerted, and dive headlong into the river. But he prayed he would not have to do so. Besides, he did not know if Ali had completed shifting all the barrels. And he now knew what those barrels contained.

'A few more years in this city and we shall be the richest Mughals in the entire subcontinent,' Inayat Khan boasted, pounding his diamond ring on the desk.

Suddenly, they heard hurried footsteps approaching. It sounded like a posse of guards running. Shashidhwaj rose carefully and touched his forehead to the cupboard door to see what was happening. A group of guards had appeared at the chamber door. Their Captain hesitated for a moment and then knocked urgently.

'What is it?' Muhabbat Khan asked, his voice sharp with

annoyance. He did not appreciate the disturbance.

'The third floor storehouse on the west wing, Lords,' the Captain said, panting from all the running. 'It has been burgled!'

'Burgled!' Muhabbat Khan shot to his feet like an arrow released from a taut bow. 'What do you mean burgled?'

'A guard on patrol heard sounds from inside, Lord. He reported it to me and I came running at once to you. We need to open the chamber to investigate. But the key is with you.'

Muhabbat Khan's hand went to the string around his neck, carrying the key. Viciously, he tugged it free and threw it at the Captain, who bent to catch it before it hit the ground.

'Let's go at once,' Muhabbat Khan commanded. 'Alert the guards! Surround the building!'

'At once, Lord.'

The Captain and his men disappeared at a run down the corridor.

Inayat Khan rose, his face clouded. 'Son?' was all he said.

'Let's go, Father,' Muhabbat Khan replied. 'It may be just a bird or rodent. Let's go and see for ourselves.'

The two men hurried out of the chamber.

Shashidhwaj did not waste a moment. Barely had the Khans disappeared through the door, than he pushed open the cupboard door and rushed through the now empty chamber into the corridor. He did not go to the tree, knowing the men who guarded the main stairwell would also have followed the posse towards the west wing, to surround the place. Quickly, he ran towards the stairs and peered down. His conjecture had been correct. The stairs were empty and unguarded. He slipped down into the courtyard easily and glanced towards the crowd gathering near the west wing. He turned in the opposite direction and ran across the courtyard.

Several guards were running to the west wing from the gate. They crossed right by him but paid no heed, taking him for a servant of the household. Shashidhwaj crossed to the walls. There was no one there. The guards who had been there earlier were no longer to be seen. Shashidhwaj quickly climbed onto the battlements and cast one last look at the west wing. The windows of the third level were now bright with light. Guards crowded everywhere. Orders and shouts rose into the night sky. Shashidwaj's eyes went to the window he had opened, that led into the chamber with the oil drums. The panes were no longer open, but shut tight. He caught sight of the pig face drain pointing out of the wall, and noticed there was no longer a rope dangling down. He wondered how Ali had done it - taken the rope off and shut the window while going down. But it was not a question he could spend time pondering on now.

Shashidhwaj turned to stare down at the water, far below, splashing up against the battlement wall. It was a steep drop. He wondered how cold the water would be. Then he heard a posse of guards running towards the west wing, and without another thought, jumped headlong. He hit the water like a stone and sank under. Quickly, he began kicking his legs and finally rose to the surface, gasping for breath.

The fort above had come alive in the middle of the night, one room after another lit with torches. Shashidhwaj looked around for Ali's boat, but it was nowhere to be seen. He began swimming towards the city side of the fort. There was no time to lose.

***

From the doorway Muhabbat Khan and Inayat Khan stared into the empty chamber, their faces etched in deep lines of disbelief.

'What in the name of...' Muhabbat Khan swore, his hands balled into fists.

The chamber was as empty as it had been before the barrels had come. Now there was no sign that anything had been stored there, even for a short time.

'Who could have done this?' Inayat Khan demanded, his voice shaking with suppressed rage.

'I have no idea, Father. I swear the security was tight.' Muhabbat Khan continued to stare into the empty chamber.

Suddenly, Inayat Khan grabbed his son by the collar, his grip unyielding. The onlookers hastily backed away. The old Subhedar apparently still had his iron strength. 'Did you steal it?' he shouted. 'Is this empty room just a farce while the truth is that you stole from me?'

Muhabbat Khan struggled to loosen his father's grip on his throat. 'Father, no!' he gasped.

'Do you lie to my face?' Inayat Khan asked angrily.

'I do not, Father…'

'That was our life security, you fool!'

'On the grave of my mother I swear I did not steal it,' Muhabbat Khan panted.

Inayat Khan stared into his son's eyes for a moment longer, then removed his hands. He knew Muhabbat spoke the truth. There was a chilly silence as Muhabbat Khan rubbed his bruised throat and pulled down his jacket.

'We must teach whosoever stole from us a lesson they will never forget,' Inayat Khan said in a voice from which all emotion has vanished.

'Without question,' Muhabbat Khan agreed, still rubbing his bruised throat.

Inayat Khan walked to the lone window at the far end and stared out. It was shut tight. 'Put the city under lockdown,' he instructed.

Muhabbat Khan went to stand by his side, nodding.

'Everyone who goes in or out of the city must be searched,' Inayat Khan said. 'They may have taken our gold, but transporting it out of the city will not be so easy. If we are vigilant, we can still catch them. Put up check posts at each of the gates, and patrol all the loading bunders on the river.'

'It shall be done, Father.'

'And send out *farmans* to every individual who knew of the gold – the Shethji, the Firang, the mercenary, all of them. I want to hear their accounts from their own lips first thing in the morning.'

'It shall be done.'

As Muhabbat Khan turned to go, Inayat Khan placed a hand on his son's shoulder. 'And do your best to find the gold,' he said in a low voice. 'Because if you do not, we will find ourselves in dire peril.'

Muhabbat Khan nodded. Letting out a sigh, he walked away.

***

Drenched from head to feet in the chilly water of the river, Shashidhwaj shivered in the gusty wind as he ran, not stopping even to catch his breath. The run from the boroughs outside the fort to the hut in the eastern quarter was a distance of over five hundred strides, but Shashidhwaj covered it quickly. The light in their hut glowed in the surrounding darkness. For sure both Bahirji and Naik were awake, waiting for news. Only Shashidhwaj knew what they did not, that the night had turned exciting beyond their wildest imagining.

Bahirji was the one to open the door. He held it wide, gazing at Shashidhwaj's soaked figure with interest as he walked in. 'You look like a fish that has been pulled from the sea,' he commented dryly.

Naik rose and handed the lad a cloth to dry off.

'This fish just learned one of the ocean's greatest secrets,'

Shashidhwaj said, his head buried in the cloth, rubbing vigorously.

'Did you find out what the looters took, and where they took it?' Bahirji asked.

'They stole oil barrels which actually contain gold. But no, I do not know where they took it. It has to be somewhere in the city. We can look for it tomorrow.'

'Then what is this great secret you speak of?' Naik asked, hand on hip.

'Khan has kept only one thousand men to guard Surat,' Shashidhwaj said.

'What!' Bahirji looked over his shoulder at Naik.

'The roster we found in the Shah Bunder's office mentioned five thousand men,' Naik recalled. 'It was written as clear as day. I never forget a word of what I see.'

'Nor do I,' Shashidhwaj said. 'Wages were only handed over to one thousand men this fortnight. I am certain of it.'

'But that is not possible,' Naik murmured, rubbing his chin in thought.

'It isn't,' Bahirji agreed, 'unless…'

'Unless what?'

'Unless Khan is not really keeping five thousand men in the city,' Bahirji replied reflectively. 'Unless he is taking the grant for five thousand men from Agra, but paying only the thousand he has.'

Naik stared at him in silence. 'Would he do that?' he asked. 'Would he really be that stupid?' Surely it would be the act of a treasonous fool?

'Papers don't lie,' Shashidhwaj insisted. 'Nor does the Qilladar Khan. I heard it straight from his mouth.'

Bahirji and Naik turned to stare at him, their brows lifted.

'How in the world did you hear that?' Bahirji asked.

Shashidhwaj pulled on a dry shirt and sat down on the *chatai* on the floor to tell his tale. As he related the events of the night, Bahirji and Naik heard him without interruption, their arms folded, their eyes steady on his face.

'The boy is right, Naik,' Bahirji finally said when Shashidhwaj had finished, 'papers do not lie.'

'But if it's true, it only means one thing.' Naik shuddered at the thought.

'We need to attack now.'

'There cannot be a more opportune moment,' Bahirji agreed. 'With this amount of gold inside the city, and the Qilladar not having an adequate force to defend the city, it is exactly the time for our army to come into the picture.'

Naik stared at the wall. 'Five days to reach Rajgad if I travel day and night,' he said thoughtfully. 'About fifteen more to bring back an army. Can you two fools survive a month without me?'

'Make the journey in fifteen days,' Bahirji said, placing a hand on Naik's shoulder. 'Send advance word through our couriers. We shall keep an eye here to ensure the gold does not move out of the city.'

Shashidhwaj knew Bahirji was talking about the courier network of their men placed in the villages along the route from Pune to Surat, for a situation just like this. A message given to the first courier would send him riding to the next village, where another courier, on a fresh horse, would take it to the next, carrying the message onwards until it reached Rajgad in the hills, and the ears of Raje.

Shashidhwaj watched as Naik, by the light of the single lamp, diligently copied every name and line from the wall chart onto a piece of paper. When his eyes closed in exhausted slumber, Naik was still scribbling by the wall, and Bahirji was talking to him in hushed tones. Shashidhwaj knew a storm was coming.

But what he was not to know was that the bustling merchant city of Surat would never be the same again. Nor would the Mughal Empire.

Chapter Nineteen

The Search

ONE WEEK BEFORE THE SACK OF SURAT

Ali stared at the stained glass windows with folded arms. A Capuchin monk inserted a key into the massive iron lock and turned it, securing the doors of the church and blocking out the light. Darkness fell within. Ali saw the flowing robes and wooden crosses hung around their necks as the monks passed him. He turned towards the masked Master, who stood some distance away, staring at the stained glass window as well. The luminous light fell in myriad shards into the dark interior.

'Are you satisfied now?' The Master's voice was dry, devoid of emotion.

Ali nodded. He had seen and silently counted the fifty barrels before the monks had closed the doors. The barrels now occupied the entire central aisle, from the entrance to the high altar, with the fresco of Christ on the cross behind it.

'The Qilladar and his men are leaving no stone unturned searching the city,' Ali remarked. 'It had me worried. I had to see with my own eyes.'

'The gold is safe here,' the Master replied. 'It shall remain so. No one will bring soldiers to check inside a holy church.'

'Not until they run out of other places to look,' Ali said with a laugh. 'We need to move it out of the city soon. But we cannot do so since the Qilladar's guards are guarding each of the gates.'

'Fear not, it will be moved soon,' the Master said, retreating from the window.

Ali too, turned away. 'You do not yet know how to move it, do you?' he stated calmly.

The Master stopped in his tracks. 'Do I hear doubt in your voice, Rayiyas?' he asked. 'Or is it worry?'

'Both perhaps.'

'I have brought you to here, have I not?' The Master's voice was as cold as ice. 'And I shall take you forward as well. When it is time to move the gold, I will find you.'

'But if you betray me in any way,' Ali said softly, 'I shall know where to find you too, masked or not.'

The two men stared at each other for a moment before walking out through a side door, leaving the gold, and glory of the stained glass window, to inhabit the silent church.

***

Shashidhwaj's plan to discover where Kasim had hidden his wealth involved asking Fatima to meet him at the stairs leading down to the lower level of the house. By now, he was sure Kasim kept his valuables somewhere in the basement. He had often heard the house help joke about how Mia Saheb never let anyone go down to the lower level to clean, so it must be filled with cobwebs and dust. But Bahirji had warned Shashidhwaj not to trust hearsay and see for himself.

Shashidhwaj had never been down the flight of stairs that led from a small corridor to the basement. But apparently Fatima had. After the incident at the sarai, when they had escaped danger together, she appeared to have grown fond of him. She would ask him to accompany her to the market in the evenings once his duties in the kitchens were done. Sometimes, she would slip her fingers into his on the way back, if it was sufficiently dark. It was during one such walk that she told him Kasim had a hall downstairs, where he entertained only very special guests, with dancing girls and intoxicants. It was at such sessions that she would be summoned to dance for the entertainment of his guests.

For days, Shashidhwaj had been making up his mind to ask Fatima to go down to the lower level with him. Bahirji had teased him on the matter when he had asked for his advice, saying, 'How will you fight the Mughals when you can't even get up the courage to ask a question of a girl?' Angrily, Shashidhwaj had declared he would ask her that very week and be done with it.

But he had waited another four days before doing so. On the day of Kasim's weekly fast, when the kitchens were slow and the tandoors cold, the cook did not mind giving him the afternoon off. Sashidhwaj usually spent such afternoons enjoying a nap on a chatai in the balcony by the kitchens. But not today.

He found her humming a tune to herself, watering the plants from an iron pitcher. He hissed through his teeth to get her attention. She turned, and seeing him, put the pitcher down.

'I was wondering whether you'd like to go to the basement with me,' he said to her, rubbing the back of his neck with one hand.

She stared into his eyes for a moment. 'What for?' she asked.

'Well, you did tell me no one is down there usually, didn't you?' He found himself tongue tied all of a sudden.

Fatima nodded, a hint of a smile appearing on her lips.

'Well, I thought we could go down there; be alone for a while.' There, he had said it. Now it remained to be seen how she would react.

'There are guards in the stairwell,' Fatima said thoughtfully, her cheeks flushed and rosy. 'But I know a window we can enter through.'

'You mean one of the windows from the garden?' Shashidhwaj asked.

She just raised a finger to her lips and motioned for him to follow. As Shashidhwaj did so, he could feel his heart beating quickly. She opened a side door and walked into the garden. He lingered a moment to make sure there were no guards before following her out.

To the left, alongside the garden, there was a skylight with glass panes, just by their ankles. Fatima stood in silence, looking at him. Shashidhwaj sank to his knees and carefully pushed it open.

'You go first,' Fatima whispered.

Shashidhwaj turned on his stomach and slipped his legs in, then inched downward. Holding the sill for support with both hands, he tried to locate the floor, but his legs swung in the air. Carefully, he lowered himself as far as he could, then jumped down, landing on all fours on the stone floor. Looking up, he saw that Fatima had already entered the skylight and was now hanging by the sill. He quickly wrapped his arms about her legs, telling her to let go. But, as she did so, her weight was too much for him and they both landed on the floor with a thud. Shashidhwaj's heart began to race as he felt Fatima's soft body on top of him, her face a breath away from his. They stared at each other for a moment and then burst into nervous laughter.

'Quite an entry,' she giggled, getting up and dusting off her clothes.'

Shashidhwaj nodded, getting to his feet. The room they were in was dark and smelt moist.

'Do you know where we are?' Fatima asked.

Shashidhwaj peered around in the darkness. There appeared to be floor cushions strewn around. He moved to his left and hit a tall metallic instrument. He grabbed it so it would not fall and make a clatter. It was a hookah stand, the long pipe coiled onto it.

'Is this where Kasim entertains his special guests?' he asked in a low voice.

Fatima nodded. She pointed to a discrete door in the opposite wall. 'And do you know what lies beyond that? The room where Kasim Mia keeps all his valuables.'

Shashidhwaj realized there was now only a wall separating him from what he had been trying to find all these days. He looked all around, making mental notes so he could draw a map of this level for Bahirji. Deep in thought, he never realized that Fatima was now standing very close to him. He first felt her moist breath touch his neck as she held onto his angarkha with both hands. Then she looked up at him, pulling his face down towards her's with a hand on his neck. He felt her other hand slip across his back and found himself doing the same as her lips touched his.

In that moment all thought left Shashidhwaj's mind as his entire body began to tingle with sensations he was powerless to resist. His lips gently moved over hers as she held him tight. Shashidhwaj tasted the sweetness of her skin. She moved, placing her head on his chest. He held her close, his heart hammering. He did not know how long they stood like that. All he knew was that time had stopped and the world had disappeared. The only reality was the two of them together, touching.

'This is why you asked me to come down here, was it not?' Fatima asked, smiling and retreating a step.

Shashidhwaj looked at her wide-eyed. Even in the darkness she appeared beautiful. 'I wanted to tell you…to say...' His tongue felt leaden as he struggled with the words, wondering if he should tell her what he had been feeling for her.

'What is it?' Fatima raised her eyebrows in arch enquiry.

'You are beautiful, Fatima!' he managed to say.

She smiled. 'And?' she prompted, revelling in his tongue-tied confusion.

'I wanted to tell you that I...dream...'

Before he could finish, there came the sound of heavy footsteps above them. Fatima's eyes flashed to the ceiling and the coquettish smile on her lips vanished. 'Someone is coming!' she whispered below her breath, clutching his hand.

Shashidhwaj let out a breath. How foolish to think such an enchanted moment could last. They heard footsteps on the stairs, coming down. There was only one person the guards above would allow to pass without question.

'We must go, now!' he urged, pushing Fatima towards the window.

He quickly crouched down and cupped his hands so she could step onto his clasped hands. He hoisted her up so she could reach the window sill and pull herself up. All the while he could hear the ominous tread of descending boots. He looked up and gave a final push. As Fatima's legs disappeared through the window, Shashidhwaj clenched his jaw and jumped towards the ledge. His fingers touched the sill but could not take hold. He fell back. The footsteps were now at the bottom of the stairs. Feverishly, he looked up and saw Fatima's face at the window. She stretched down a hand to him. Shashidhwaj jumped again and managed to grab hold of the sill with one hand and Fatima's hand with the other. He clung on desperately, pulling himself up.

In that instant, he heard the door open behind him. For a moment the footsteps halted as Kasim tried to make sense of the sight before him. Then he gave a loud shout and Shashidhwaj felt rather than saw him run towards the window. Grunting, he pulled himself up with all his strength, even as he felt Kasim's strong grip on his left foot.

'Thief!' Kasim shouted, as he pulled at Shashidhwaj's dangling foot.

Shashidhwaj clenched his teeth and pulled with all his strength. He felt his shoe loosen and fall back into the room even as he managed to squirm through the opening and emerge into the garden. He kicked the skylight shut.

Fatima was already on her feet. 'Are you alright? She whispered.

'Yes. It was Kasim. I don't think he saw my face, but I lost a shoe,' Shashidhwaj's voice was low, his eyes scanning the area for guards. In his mind he already knew that he could not take the risk of assuming Kasim had not recognized him. Besides, his work in this house was done

'I have to run from here,' he told Fatima.

Fatima pointed to a small iron gate which opened onto the street, used by the gardeners to bring in supplies. 'Do not open it, just jump over,' she said quickly.

Looking to right and left, Shashidhwaj scrambled to his feet and ran for the gate. He could hear Kasim's shouts echoing through the house and knew the place would soon be crawling with guards. Reaching the gate, he turned to look for Fatima, but she had already disappeared, having long perfected her own methods to reach her room without anyone seeing her. He regretted not having been able to bid her farewell. But there was no time for whimsy. Taking a deep breath, Shashidhwaj jumped over the gate and landed in the street. He fled from the house without once looking back.

***

Muhabbat Khan sat at his desk, his head bowed over his clasped hands. His head ached as if someone had hit him with a blunt instrument. Hearing footsteps, he looked up. It was one of his captains, come in to report. Khan had ordered his men to report to him every *prahar* on the progress made in searching for the gold in the city.

'Do you bring good news or bad?' he asked wearily.

The soldier's eyes fell to the floor. 'We have finished looking in all the bundar warehouses, *Sarkar*,' he said. 'The merchants made a hubbub when we cleared out their belongings and checked every nook and cranny. But there were no barrels.'

Muhabbat Khan slammed his fist on the desk. 'What do the guards at the gate report?' he asked.

'They are detaining every carriage going out of the city and checking thoroughly,' the soldier replied. 'We found some contraband being smuggled, but no sign of any barrels.'

'Bollocks!' Muhabbat Khan cursed. Of the men he had sent the farman to, none had reported back to him. The mercenary Rayiyas had disappeared into the alleys of the city, as if he had never existed at all. Virji Vora was on a tour of Bharuch, not scheduled to return for another week. Oxenden too, had taken a convoy South to visit the English territories in the Konkan. It would be some time before he was back. Khan felt his head buzzing like a disturbed hive of angry bees. Thoughts crowded his mind. He wondered which of the three had backstabbed him.

'We still have the other warehouses in the city to look into, Sarkar,' the captain said.

Muhabbat Khan got to his feet. 'You better find those barrels or I shall see to it that your bodies are chopped and put into barrels and thrown into the river!'

The captain bowed and turned away, his face grim. He did not doubt Muhabbat Khan would do as he said.

But even as the Qilladar stood at his desk, he knew with utter certainty that the threat he had just made would be the fate he and his father would suffer in Agra if they did not find the gold.

***

Oxenden sat atop a grassy knoll. A folding chair and table had been set up for him. A platter with a crusty loaf of bread and a dish with spats of freshly churned butter sat on the table before him. Around him, his men lounged on the grass. They were enjoying a peaceful breakfast in the morning sun. The horses had been left to their own devices, to graze.

Oxenden picked up one of delectable potted meat sandwiches the cook had made for him, and bit into it with relish. He did not see Smith approach until he stood directly before him.

'We have a problem!' Smith said, his face pale.

'What is it, man?' Oxenden asked genially, the food and open air having put him in an unusually convivial mood. He popped the last bite of sandwich into his mouth.

They were two days ride from Surat, on their journey towards the Islands of Bombay, further south. The matter with the Subhedar having been cleared up, Oxenden had found he could finally focus on the work to be done in Bombay again. The road through Mughal territory was thought to be safe, without any danger of brigands. The dangerous stretch under control of the Maratha rebels, would come later.

'You need to see this, Sir.' Smith gestured for Oxenden to follow.

With a heavy sigh, the large Englishman got to his feet. He looked around at the others, still busy eating, then followed Smith to a rise where a lone *jamun* tree stood.

'There!' Smith handed him a spyglass, pointing.

Oxenden peered through it in the direction Smith had indicated, and swore. On the horizon, he could see a line of raised spears, and a long column of men, some riding, some on foot. Almost all wore white garb, their heads covered by helmets. 'Who are they?' he asked.

'Look to the very front Sir, at the man leading them,' Smith said, standing beside Oxenden.

Oxenden moved his spyglass, peering at the blurred image till it settled and cleared on the man at the very front, seated on horseback. He had on a tall bent hat and sported a pointed beard. 'Why do I think I have seen him somewhere?' he mused aloud.

'You have not, Sir, but I have,' Smith said with a sigh. 'I could never forget that face. Years ago…at the warehouse in Rajapur…'

Oxenden drew in a sharp breath. He did not need to be told who the man was. 'What is Sevagee doing here?' he asked.

But the obvious answer hung in the air like the sword of Damocles. Oxenden spun about on his heel and went back to where the remaining sandwiches now lay forgotten.

'Rally the men!' he ordered. 'We do not have any time to lose. We must ride back to Surat immediately!'

Smith nodded in silence and walked off to give the necessary orders. The accompanying orderlies immediately rushed into frenzied activity, packing up the picnic and loading their chattels onto the horses.

Chapter Twenty

The Raiders Cometh

TWO DAYS PRIOR TO THE SACK OF SURAT

Muhabbat Khan paced the hallway uneasily as he waited to be summoned to the *Diwan-e-Aam*. The continuing rumble of voices from within grated on his nerves. Every morning, a session was convened for the *aam* population of the city to present any matters to Inayat Khan, in his position as Subhedar. With nothing better to do, Muhabbat Khan counted his steps as he paced about outside the hall. It annoyed him that he could do nothing but wait for the daily session to adjourn.

Suddenly, there was a commotion at the far end of the corridor leading to the hall. Muhabbat Khan halted and looked in the direction of the noise. He could hear the guards arguing with someone, and then there were footsteps. Men in red coats walked down the corridor. It was Oxenden, though it took Muhabbat Khan a moment to recognize him in the white wig.

'Qilladar!' he called imperatively as he hurried forward.

'What are you doing here?' Muhabbat Khan asked, surprised. A few days ago he had sent four consecutive farmans to the British warehouse, summoning Oxenden, only to be told he was on his way to Bombay and was not expected to return for a good long while. Now, suddenly, the man was here, arguing with the guards.

'Same as you, I suppose,' Oxenden muttered. 'We have a problem.'

'We have a problem indeed,' Muhabbat Khan said, stroking his beard. Taking a step closer to the Englishman, he lowered his voice. 'The gold is gone.'

Oxenden's face changed abruptly. 'What do you mean gone?'

'Stolen from the fort. No one knows how. That was why I sent you the farman to appear, to ask you personally if you knew anything.'

'I received no farman,' Oxenden said. 'I was out of the city and have only just returned, at full speed. I came to the fort immediately on entering the city gates.'

'If not in response to my farman, why *are* you here?'

Oxenden brows rose. 'Surely you know by now?'

At that moment, the doors opened and Inayat Khan walked out of the hall in his stately robes. He stopped when he saw the gathering.

'What a strange morning,' he remarked. 'First, people bring news of an army within a few miles of Udhna, and now I see the two of you here, with somber faces.'

'Father,' Muhabbat Khan said, stepping forward to speak into his ear. 'I have bad news! We have not found the gold.'

'Save your bad news for later,' Oxenden interjected harshly, 'because Sevagee himself is almost at the gates with a large force.'

'Who did you say is here?' Muhabbat Khan turned to look at Oxenden with narrowed eyes.

'I do not know if I pronounced his name correctly, but he is the same rebel who captured forts in the Sahyadris and gave your men a run for their money,' Oxenden smirked.

Inayat Khan gave a mirthless laugh. 'I spent this whole *baithak* with people telling me the same thing. I have been hearing this rumour since last night. Rest assured the rumours are false. The army belongs to a Mughal Subhedar riding from the Deccan to Ahmedabad.'

'Yes, one of my own men confirmed it,' Muhabbat Khan nodded. 'The *aam janta* like a bit of drama and heave the house upon their heads as soon as there is a gust of wind.'

Oxenden stared at the Qilladar as if he was seeing a ghost. 'You are wrong!' he finally said, breaking the silence. 'They rode by our camp when we were on our way to Bombay. On seeing their marching army, we abandoned the trip at once and returned to Surat post haste. My man recognised the man leading the army. He is no Subhedar. He is Sevagee!'

Oxenden looked towards the door where Smith stood, detained by the guards. He gestured for him to approach. The guards let him pass when Inayat Khan nodded in confirmation.

'My man Smith,' Oxenden said, indicating the pallid, slim man with one hand. 'He was posted in Rajapur, overseeing our warehouses there, before coming here to Surat. He saw this Sevagee with his own eyes when the Rajapur warehouse was raided by him and his men three years ago. Now, he has seen him again at their camp outside Udhna. There is no doubt the man is Sevagee himself.'

The faces of both Khans were now grave. 'How large a force was on the march? Did your man say?' Inayat Khan asked, looking at his son.

'About eight thousand men.' Muhabbat Khan felt beads of sweat form on his forehead. 'And twice as many horse.'

'Surely you can hold them off?' Oxenden asked, looking at each Khan in turn.

Muhabbat Khan glanced at his father, as if such a question

could only be answered by him. But Inayat Khan merely cleared his throat without saying a word.

'Because if you can't,' Oxenden continued, 'I am taking my men and all the goods we can carry, to Swally Hole. We will board our ships and stay on the water if need be, till Seevagee is gone.'

'There will be no need for that,' Inayat Khan assured him. 'We have a five thousand strong force here. We can hold them off.'

Muhabbat Khan shrugged. 'Certainly we can,' he said. 'The mountain rat is a fool to come here.'

'So there is no cause for worry then?' Oxenden tapped his cane on the floor. 'No reason to resort to any hasty action?'

'Indeed no,' Inayat Khan smiled.

'About the gold!' Muhabbat Khan burst out. 'Do you know anything about it?'

Oxenden looked at him strangely. 'The last I saw of it was when we counted it,' he replied. 'Whoever stole it from the third level of the fort has to be either a lunatic or entirely audacious.'

'It is still inside the city, that much is certain,' Muhabbat Khan said with unnecessary force. 'My guards have been checking every cart and vehicle. Every gate is guarded. The gold has not left the city.'

'Then I daresay you will have to continue your search as you can, in light of the latest news,' Oxenden said. Bowing, he walked away, with Smith following close behind.

When both men had disappeared down the corridor, a frown appeared on Inayat Khan's face. Deep lines ran from his nose to his thin mouth. 'We are ruined,' he said.

Muhabbat Khan turned to him, hands outstretched. 'The fort is strong, Father. No one can take it. Not even eight thousand mountain rats.'

'Idiot! What about the city?' Inayat Khan snapped. 'We do not have the men to protect the city! We have lost the gold. Men from Agra are sure to come here as soon as word of Sevagee's attack reaches there.'

'We still have time,' Muhabbat Khan said. 'The rich merchants will be panic stricken on hearing the news. We can give them shelter in the fort. They will pay us anything to be let in. We can recover some of our wealth before the Emperor's men come knocking on our door.'

'It will be nothing compared to the gold lost,' Inayat Khan lamented. 'But so be it. Order the best of your men to bring all the rich merchants of the city to us immediately. Tell your men to drag them off their chamber pots if need be. Meanwhile, I will send a courier to Agra, informing the court of this sudden threat.'

'I will ready the men and arm the fort.'

As his son turned to go, Inayat Khan held up a hand. 'You must find that gold,' he said. 'For if you do not, as soon as the Maratha army reaches the city, everything will be over.'

***

Shashidhwaj loitered uneasily in the street behind the white walls of Haji Kasim's house. He had been there for close to a prahar. Twice, Kasim's haughty face had appeared at the windows of the upper level, gazing out across the city. Each time, Shashidhwaj had quickly disappeared from sight behind a tree.

Following the events in the basement, he had made a point not to set foot in the Kasim house. He was sure Kasim had by now connected the intruder in the basement to his missing kitchen hand. It no longer mattered, for he had completed the task assigned to him. He had come today, at the risk of being spotted, to see Fatima one last time before the city was plunged into chaos. But she did not seem to be in her room on the first level. He had been waiting since early morning and had already thrown three stones to hit the exact spot above her window sill, with no response. Shashidhwaj leaned against the wall idly, whistling idly to himself as people passed by. Not that they had the time or inclination to observe his behaviour.

The entire city had gone mad after the news of the invading force had been announced in the markets. Word seemed to travel around Surat on the wind, and soon every last person had heard the Marathas were coming! The final axe had fallen when the fort gates were closed, instead of an army marching out to defend the city. Everybody knew then that the Subhedar and the Qilladar had abandoned them.

In the short distance from the hut to Kasim's house, Shashidhwaj had passed dozens of carts, pulled by bullocks or donkeys, and possessions piled high in crazy confusion, as the common people tried to flee the city. The carriages of the rich merchants, with their high bred horses, crawled through the crazed meleé. He had even seen a merchant load up his carriage and depart, even as his old parents ran after the carriage, begging him to take them with him. But he preferred to fill any available space with precious goods.

The whole city seemed to be caught up in a fever of activity that morning. Bahirji too, was nowhere to be seen. He was already gone when Shashidhwaj woke. No doubt he had gone to hang about Virji Vora's house, to see how the Shethji was taking the news of the invading force. Shashidhwaj had quietly had his breakfast and then rushed to Kasim's house.

His fourth stone hit the pane and caused enough noise to attract the attention of people in the courtyard behind the wall. Shashidhwaj quickly slipped behind the tree again, leaning out cautiously to see if he could spot Fatima's face, but the jalis of the windows remained tightly shut. He was about to take the desperate gamble of going over the wall and climbing up to her window, when he felt a tap on his shoulder. He spun around, heart thudding, ready to run.

Fatima stood behind him, her face entirely covered by a veil.

'Where have you been?' she asked. 'Mia has asked for you many times.'

'I know…it's hard to explain,' Shashidhwaj replied. He longed to reach out and hold her after the time apart, but her eyes looked forbidding.

'Perhaps it'll be easier once you tell me where you've been and what you have been doing,' she said, playing with the basket in her hands.

In that moment, all Shashidhwaj desired was to protect her. He reached out and held her wrist. 'Listen!' he said urgently. 'There is no time to explain anything. But you must escape from the city now! It is not safe here.'

She jerked her wrist free. 'Why? What do you mean?' she demanded.

'Have you not heard the news of what is happening?' Shashidhwaj waved his arms in the air. 'Can you not see people leaving the city?'

'Mia thinks it is false news,' Fatima said. 'He says it is just a Mughal General riding with his army to Ahmedabad. That the people are foolish to be frightened.'

'No Fatima! It is your Mia who is foolish not to take heed.' Shashidhwaj took hold of her shoulders and looked into her eyes. 'Listen to me now. You must get out of the city without delay!'

'But Mia is usually right about everything.' Fatima did not free herself from his hold this time, her eyes worried.

Shashidhwaj shook his head. 'Not this time. It is the Maratha army that comes. They are coming to raid the city.'

'What! But how do you know for sure?' Fear flickered in Fatima's eyes. She had heard of the Marathas and their atrocities.

Shashidhwaj let her go and retreated a step. He did not know how to break it to her. He had made up his mind to do so before coming here this morning, but all his resolve seemed to dissolve before her fixed gaze.

'Are you going to answer or not?' she demanded, her shoulders tense.

'I know for sure because I am one of them,' Shashidhwaj said, looking away. He did not dare look into her eyes.

'What!' she gasped, unbelieving. 'But you said…'

'I know. I lied.' Shashidhwaj finally looked at her. There, he had done it. He had told her the truth.

Fatima pursed her lips but said nothing.

'I am one of their spies, who came to Surat to prepare for their arrival,' Shashidhwaj went on.

Her eyes did not betray anger or disappointment, but she stepped back, suddenly afraid of him.

'Fatima, I am sorry.' He reached out to touch her but she shrank from his touch.

'Why are you telling me all this now?' she asked.

'So you can save yourself!' Shashidhwaj urged. 'There will be chaos once the army reaches the city. Houses like Kasim's will be looted.'

'So that's why you were in the house?' she finally said. 'The sarai too, was for this? You used me. You lied to me.'

Shashidhwaj could think of nothing to say. His gaze fell to the ground.

'Can you at least save me now?' she asked, her eyes glittering at him. There was no anger in her voice, only a strange desperation. 'Can you save me if I come with you?'

Shashidhwaj stared at her blankly. He had not expected this. He knew it to be impossible. He shuddered to think how

Bahirji would react if he took her to the hut. Where would they put her? And once the army reached the city, he knew he would have to go and be amongst them. He would even have to lead the men to Kasim's house.There was no place with him for her.

'Well, can you?' she asked again, grasping the basket to her chest.

'I cannot,' Shashidhwaj sighed. 'That is why I am here, to warn you to get out of the city. Get as far away as you can. When all of this is over, you can return.'

'Get out and do what?' Fatima snapped. 'All I have known my entire life is the house of Kasim Mia. Where do you expect me to go, what do you expect me to do?'

'Then stay,' Shashidhwaj said. 'But tell Kasim Mia what I have told you. He will protect you.'

Fatima stared at him as if she did not know him at all.

'I suppose this is farewell then,' Shashidhwaj said, his heart strangely heavy in his chest

She said nothing. She merely stood there holding her basket, looking at him. Shashidhwaj turned and walked away. Only when his slim form was lost amidst the milling crowds in the street did she allow the tears to fall from her eyes and trickle down her face.

***

Bahirji caught up with Shashidhwaj in the market place. He was in Naik's fakir disguise, looking like his companion in the waist length beard and flared moustache.

'It's chaos!' he said to Shashidhwaj. 'People are leaving the city in hordes. It appears that they prefer to flee than take their chances here. Soon there will be not a horse or donkey left in the city. The donkey stables have been busy since morning, helping their own folk get out.'

'But that does not affect our work, does it?' Shashidhwaj said. 'Our main targets are the houses of the rich merchants, and the toll booths. And they will be unable to move their wealth given the lack of donkeys.'

Bahirji nodded. 'True. And there will be fewer people left in the city to get in our way. You did what you had to at the house of Kasim?'

Shashidhwaj bit his lip. He had not exactly disclosed that he had gone to see Fatima that morning. But he should have known that Bahirji would discover it. 'Aye, I did,' he said. 'Kasim still thinks it's all a hoax.'

'Well, he won't think it for much longer because his friend Virji Vora just decided the news is true,' Bahirji scoffed. 'I sat outside his house this morning and he seemed to have produced two donkeys and a cart from somewhere, as well as his carriage and horses. His servants were busy loading them up all morning.'

'He is leaving the city too?' Shashidhwaj frowned in thought. No doubt the merchant was trying to move his wealth away from his house.

'Who would dare leave the city with such a mob rushing around, carrying valuables in a cart?' Bahirji laughed. 'No, the merchants have struck a deal with the Subhedar. They are going to the fort to hide before our army arrives. I am sure that what they can carry with them will be little compared to what they must leave behind in their houses.'

'So Mir Kasim is going to the fort…' Shashidhwaj felt comforted knowing Fatima would be safe as part of the merchant's household.

'Yes. And there will be none to resist the looting of these empty houses.'

'What about the toll booths?' Shashidhwaj asked.

'Complete chaos!' Bahirji commented pithily. 'The men on duty have long since left their posts to save their own homes. No one even tried to rob the storerooms, knowing no wealth would be safe. We should be able to meet our targets in one ride through the city.'

'We must keep an eye on the factories,' Shashidhwaj reminded him. They both knew the Angrez and Valandej factories had weapons, and were fortified.

'Our men are already on it,' Bahirji replied.

'Our men?'

'Now that the raid is upon us, the need for secrecy is over,' Bahirji explained quickly. 'Naik has sent a contingent ahead to us, while he himself rides with Raje. Those men arrived early this morning. I have been busy showing them their watch posts in the city.'

'So everything is in motion,' Shashidhwaj said. His throat suddenly felt dry.

'The city will be empty before the sun sets today, boy. You have my word. These fools running away think they are escaping, but they are not. They will run straight into our men on the march. Netoji will have much to do detaining each group he encounters, to search for valuables.'

'So what is left for us to do?' Shashidhwaj asked.

'We must keep our eyes and ears open, lad,' Bahirji said. 'There is still the matter of the missing gold.'

'Aye.' Shashidhwaj suddenly remembered they had still not found the gold, despite their best efforts. In the empty city, they now had another chance to look where they could not have done before. Bahirji had heard from his donkey cart friends that no large load had moved out of the city recently. That meant the gold was still here.

'Whoever has it will try to escape with it in the confusion. That is why I have placed two of our men at each of the gates, and two on the river,' Bahirji told him. 'While they check the exit points, we will look inside the city.'

Shashidhwaj nodded.

'You start with the warehouses on the docks. I'll go to the city *godams*,' Bahirji said. 'Look for any place big enough to house the barrels, then look inside.'

Shashidhwaj watched Bahirji disappear into the crowds, then he too, turned and hurried away.

***

Oxenden watched the gates of the factory open. He and his entourage rode in and hurriedly dismounted and went in.

His personal orderly met him at the door to his office. 'Have you heard the news, Sir?' he gabbled, his eyes as large as saucers.

'Son, I brought the news,' Oxenden replied, walking into his office with Smith close on his heels.

'I sent word to Swally Hole as you asked, Sir,' the man said, unsure what to do next. 'They have replied they can send only sixteen armed men to help us here at the factory.'

'Damn!' Oxenden muttered, sitting down at his desk. He had barely thirty people here. How was he to defend the factory if the need arose?

'I have sent all the women and children to Swally Hole,' the orderly hurried on. 'They will be safe on the ships there.'

'Quick thinking that.' Oxenden smiled at last. Relieved to have the women and children out of the way. 'Now if you will excuse us.'

The orderly went out, shutting the door. Oxenden stared through the window, lost in a dark reverie.

'What are we going to do, Sir?' Smith asked, clutching the back of a chair.

'We cannot leave…' Oxenden muttered, more to himself than to Smith. 'If we leave, the attackers will have open access to loot the factory. If we lose the factory, the loss will be too great to recover from. Gaining a foothold back in Surat will require years of repeated efforts.'

'But we do not have enough men, even with the meagre reinforcements,' Smith reminded him.

'I know.' Oxenden tapped a finger on the table, a thing he often did when he was nervous or stressed.

Smith cleared his throat. 'Everyone seems to be fleeing the city, Sir.'

Oxenden looked up angrily. 'I have already said that is not an option for us.'

'What are your orders then, Sir?'

'What are the Dutch doing?' Oxenden wanted to know. In times such as these, foreigners had to stick together.

'The men say the Dutch are fortifying their factory.'

'Then we shall do the same.' Oxenden tugged at his beard. 'Barricade the gates. Position shooters at vantage points. Take control of the church to the left of the gate, and the house of Haji Sayyid Beg on the right. Barricade their gates as well. The enemy can gain entry into our compound from there, so we need to hold them too.'

Smith went quickly through the door and Oxenden heard him barking out terse ordes to the men outside.

Once they were up and running, Smith returned. 'Morale appears to be very low, Sir,' he remarked.

'Then we must do something to uplift it,' Oxenden said, getting to his feet. 'Have the men from Swally arrived?'

'Aye, Sir!' Smith nodded, pointing to a line of redcoats outside the window.

'We will take them on a route march through the city, covering all the main streets. We will also march past the fort before returning here.'

'We are few in number,' Smith said. 'What advantage would such a march give us?'

'You do not understand the psyche of soldiers as I do,' Oxenden said, putting on his hat. Pulling open a drawer, he extracted his pistols and cocked them. 'Just give the damned order,' he snapped.

Smith hastily left the room. Oxenden placed the pistols in the holder he wore at his waist, one on either side. He went to the glass cabinet on the wall behind his desk. There, a matchlock musket hung, one of his most prized possessions. He opened the glass panel and retrieved it. Hearing the increasing sounds of chaos outside, Oxenden knew the time of reckoning had come. Till now his life had been uneventful. As the second son of a minor Lord, he had been knighted as a matter of tradition rather than reward for actions undertaken, and sent to this dusty hellhole, where the only thing that mattered was commerce. Now, God had thrust an opportunity into his hands. He knew he had to convert it into glory.

If he could save the factory in this attack, he knew the people would remember him for this incident alone. He had been granted a moment that came but once. It was the opportunity of a lifetime. He felt like Arthur Wellesley marching towards Waterloo, like Richard the Lion Heart laying siege to Jerusalem, like Henry V viewing the field of Agincourt atop a hill. As Oxenden slung the rifle strap across his chest, he had made up his mind to give to this defense everything he had.

***

Ali felt cramped in the small space he and his men were holed up. The roof was low and the thick wooden walls seemed to converge on them from all sides. All he had to judge what was happening outside were the sounds he heard. He longed to get out of this cramped place, but knew he could not, for it was where the Master's note had instructed him to be.

He heard the sound of marching feet, and peered through a narrow gap in the wooden slats. In the street, he saw the redcoats going past. These firangs were strange people he thought. While everyone else was running away, they were marching. At the very front of the small formation, he caught sight of President George Oxenden, in full uniform, weapons at his belt and a musket slung across his back. Ali watched the column move past where he and his men sat hidden, and halt at the next intersection. Someone barked an order and the men began to move into single file. The drummers began to beat their kettle drums, filling the air with their rhythmic drumming.

Ali was deafened by the sound, so he did not hear the door behind them open and someone enter.

'Rayiyas!' called a voice.

Ali spun around, instantly alert. It was the Master, enveloped in his black cloak, his face hidden as usual behind the eerie metal mask. But there was something different about his voice today, something Ali could not quite place.

'I am here as you asked,' Ali said, knowing there was little time to waste on conversation. 'The city is in chaos. It will be under attack at any moment. How do we retrieve the gold? We cannot do it while Khan's men are still looking all over the city. They will only return to the fort when the enemy is at the gates.'

'Then the gold will have to be retrieved when the enemy has thronged the city,' the Master replied calmly. 'A boat will come up river and stop at one of the bunders. It will ferry the gold out of the city.'

'Bullshit!' Ali swore. The Master's voice still sounded strange to him. 'The streets will be filled with ganim!'

'Yes, the streets will be, but not the rooftops.'

Ali sighed. Scaling the roofs would need sophisticated equipment. Metal claws they could attach to ropes, and clamping with holders to swing from. The Mughal army used such things, but their store was located inside the fort.

The Master suddenly clapped his hands. Two men in dark cloaks similar to his own, walked in carrying a box. They put it down on the floor and retreated.

'This box contains all you will need,' the Master said.

'How will I transport the barrels from the chapel to the river?' Ali asked, gazing at the box.

'The Friar has not moved the two carriages he has in the stable. Take them and the donkeys.'

'Two carriages will not hold all the barrels.'

'There will not need to,' the Master replied briefly. 'I have marked those containing the gold with large markings in chalk. Take only the marked ones and leave the rest.'

Ali nodded, taking a deep breath. The final stage of his ascendance was at hand.

'Gather your men in an alley away from the church, so suspicion is not aroused,' the Master instructed. 'Hide in the day when the enemy will throng the streets. Wait for nightfall. Do not move until it is safe to do so. Wait for a complete day if need be. The enemy will not touch the church. I have already made sure of that. '

'Why would they not?' Ali asked, surprised, trying to see past the slits in the metal mask.

'Have I ever failed you, Rayiyas? I will not do so now.'

Ali nodded. 'I trust you.'

'When night is upon you and the time is right, scale the buildings and reach the roof of the church. Enter from above. You know what to do after that.'

The Master's voice had a nasal sound that was strange to Ali, who once again narrowed his eyes, staring at the mask.

'Once you bring out the two carriages from the church, I will meet you in the street and let you know which bunder the boat is docked at.'

Ali bowed. 'It shall be done as you say.'

'Good.' The Master turned to walk away.

'One more thing!' Ali called after him. 'If we succeed, we shall make a fortune. But if I fail, I could die. I am not afraid of death. But I wish to know the face behind the mask before I go.'

The Master gave a short laugh. 'Very well, but there is one more thing I wish you to do first.'

The Master spoke in a low voice that reached only Ali's ears, drowned in the drumbeats of the redcoats outside.

The expression on Ali's face changed dramatically as the Master finished speaking. The drumming ceased and orders were barked out. The redcoats prepared to march on.

'I take my leave now,' the Master said, his voice loud in the sudden silence. 'May Allah grant you luck and victory, young Rayiyas.'

He turned and was gone in a whirl of his cloak, leaving Ali standing there with his mouth open. This thing had just been blown out of all proportion. And he would have to find a way to face the situation, as he had always done before.

***

They had made a small fire on the gentle slope that ran from the city to the edge of the forest. In the silence, Shashidhwaj could hear the waves crashing against the rocky coast to the west. Bahirji blew on the pile of sticks to make sure the flames did not go out. Then he slowly packed his chillum, as though he had no other care in the world.

'What is that stuff that you smoke?' Shashidhwaj asked, watching him blow small puffs of smoke into the night sky.

'You are welcome to try it,' Bahirji replied without looking up. 'But I should warn you it won't be the last time you will.'

Shashidhwaj hesitated. 'Nanaji frowns upon it,' he said.

'Nanaji frowns upon many things, boy.' Bahirji settled into a comfortable posture, satisfied the chillum was properly alight. 'Old people like him seldom do anything but frown. But then what would be the difference between them and us?'

Shashidhwaj lay back on the grass, taking in the starry sky. 'I've never been in a battle before,' he mused. 'Is it brutal?

'I reckon there isn't going to be much of a battle,' Bahirji replied calmly. 'The Subhedar will not dare face us with his meagre force of a thousand men.'

Shashidhwaj turned on his side and gazed at the lights of the city, glowing even at this late hour. 'We are going to take everything the people of Surat have earned through their labour,' he said thoughtfully. 'We are looters.'

'Given enough time, everyone is a looter, boy,' Bahirji said dreamily. 'Think of the time long ago when hordes of barbarians descended from the north-west upon these very lands, led by Musalmaan Sultans, ready to prey on the weak and puny, and snatch away any wealth. This land was rich once, but now it is being looted by foreigners. They lord over the natives as if the local people were merely born to do their bidding.'

'So we are just paying the Mughals back in their own coin?' Shashidhwaj asked.

'Aye, that we are! And some day, someone else will pay us back in the same way. It is a cycle, my boy. You take what you want from somewhere, and some day you will have it taken from you.'

'How strange,' Shashidhwaj murmured. 'We have lived among these men as fellow dwellers. We have had the adventures of a lifetime. Yet, when the sun rises tomorrow, we will fall upon them like a pack of wolves, taking from them all they hold dear.' He sighed despondently. 'I thought we were supposed to be different? That we were supposed to be better.'

'You knew the stakes when you came here, boy,' Bahirji reminded him without emotion.

'Yes, I did. But somehow I had hoped it would not be like this; that we would not be mere looters!' Shashidhwaj closed his eyes and Fatima's face appeared before him, floating in the blackness.

Bahirji smiled. 'Oh but we aren't. When their forefathers made their way to our lands, raping, pillaging and looting, when Ghouri defeated the great King Prithviraj Chauhan on the battlefield of Panipat, when they marched on Delhi and bathed the city streets in blood, they did not call themselves looters. They said they were raiders. And that is what we are too, boy. We are the raiders who will fall upon Surat when daylight comes, and we shall take whatever we can. And we shall take it so that our Swarajya can survive their deadly attacks. The only thing that matters in the end is to survive!'

Shashidhwaj nodded, acknowledging the truth of this. But in that moment, he longed to be with Fatima, standing on the roof of Kasim's house, staring at the sunset and then the first stars twinkling in the sky.

'How do you live with causing all this killing, destruction and change?' he asked Bahirji. 'Do you sometimes feel you did wrong?'

'Sometimes boy, sometimes.' Bahirji took a drag and lay back upon the grass.

'Then how do you cope?'

'I look at the night sky and ask myself whether a Mughal would think the same thoughts before he set off to burn my lands,' he said. 'And the answer I hear is no.'

'When people die here tomorrow, will their blood be on our hands?' Shashidhwaj said into the night.

'Indeed it will,' Bahirji muttered. 'But we do so knowing

the spoils of war will save the Swarajya from certain destruction, and rekindle hope in the huts of the mavals.'

'I think I am ready to try that thing now,' Shashidhwaj said, extending his hand.

Bahirji passed the chillum to him. The clay pipe felt warm as Shashidhwaj put it to his mouth. Formed a fist around it as he had seen Bahirji do, he sucked in. Immediately he burst into a fit of coughing as the smoke hit his throat and lungs.

'I told you, vile stuff,' Bahirji laughed.

'Then why do you smoke it?' asked Shashidhwaj, wiping the tears from his eyes with the back of his hand.

'To remind me of the vile things we sometimes have to do to ensure that our goal is achieved.'

Shashidhwaj felt heavy in the head and let the chillum fall onto the grass. Bahirji did not try to retrieve it. They both trailed off into slumber.

***

It was the sound of hooves that woke Shashidhwaj at the break of day. He sprang to his feet. He looked at Bahirji, who was still snoring. His gaze lifted towards the sound of trumpets. He ran up the slope. Horsemen, wearing triangular *fetas* on their heads, emerged from behind the trees, riding straight at them in formation. Shashidhwaj waved at them and the man leading the men lifted his hand to slow their pace.

Shashidhwaj ran back and shook Bahirji, who groaned, still half asleep. 'They are here!' Shashidhwaj told him, his voice breaking with excitement.

Rubbing his eyes, Bahirji got to his feet. 'About time,' he muttered.

Chapter Twenty-One

Blood and Fire

DAY ONE OF THE SACK OF SURAT

Shashidhwaj stared at the city from atop his horse. A few months before, he had stood at this same spot, gazing down at the same sight. Except now, his gaze dwelt on something different. 'Look at the bridges,' he said, pointing.

Bahirji and Naik, astride their own horses on either side of him, turned their heads to see what the lad was pointing towards. Mughal soldiers in uniform, looking like a swarm of ants, were striking at the wooden columns that held up the bridges across the river.

'Let them do all they can,' Naik said. 'A small river cannot stop the Maratha horses today.'

Netoji Palkar came up behind them, his face as grim as when Shashidhwaj had last seen him. He observed the spectacle for a while. 'We shall set up camp there,' he said, pointing to a banyan tree, next to a large well. 'It seems to be the water source for the city. It will serve us as well for a few days.'

Raje rode up to join the little group, calling, 'Moropunt!'

The Brahmin in his distinctive hat immediately brought his

horse forward, saying, 'Raje, you wished to speak to me?'

'I hope you have the scroll prepared?' Raje asked.

The diligent Punt smiled. 'Exactly as you desired.'

'Good.' Raje gestured towards the city. 'Send two of your best men into the city, to the fort, with the scroll. They should carry white flags. On any other campaign I would have sent you, but today, even I am not too keen on them accepting our exacting demands.'

'What does the scroll say?' Netoji asked, irritated that he had not been consulted.

Moropunt drew open the scroll and read aloud: *Subhedar Inayat Khan, accompanied by the merchants Virji Vora, Haji Kasim and Haji Sayyid Beg, should report immediately to us to discuss a ransom amount. Failure to do so will cause the entire city to be put to the sword.*

'That sounds dire enough,' Raje said.

'Why do we have to waste time in all this talk?' Netoji protested. 'Why not just commence the sack?'

'This communication will be delivered at the same time our camp is set up, Netoji,' Raje said. 'I do not expect the Subhedar to accept a single word of these terms. But ah, when people hear of this, they will know Shivaji tried to parley first.'

Netoji shook his head, unconvinced, but he offered nothing in opposition.

'So it is decided,' Raje said. 'We shall set up camp. Do not waste time putting up tents and shelters. The sky has been our roof for long enough, and it shall be the same here. Only one *shamiyana* to be erected, to receive those who surrender. Our men will camp in the open. The horsemen should be divided into groups of twelve. Netoji, you, Prataprao, and Tanaji, will each lead a group. The others will be led by their *mansabdars,* but will report to you. As soon as the camp is ready, we shall enter the city. Bahirji, Naik, and the boy… what was your name?'

'I am called Shashidhwaj, Raje.' Shashidhwaj sat straight up as straight an arrow on his horse, proud to be mentioned.

'Yes, Bahirji and Shashidhwaj will lead two groups into the city. We will target the larger loot first, which they have already scouted. Once found, send it back here to the camp. You must be the spearhead; do not attempt to carry anything yourselves or it will slow you down. Take prisoner all those who resist, and send them back here under guard. Only after the main loot is in our hands should we start knocking on other doors. I shall remain here in camp to oversee everything you send back from the city. Those who do not give up their wealth easily, I shall break them here. I will also oversee the packing and loading, so that by the time you get back, we shall be ready to depart.'

Every man nodded silently at this authoritative speech.

'Only accept valuables that can be carried by a single man,' Raje continued. 'We are not here to carry heavy artefacts back home. Stick to coins, ornaments, and anything small in size. Leave the larger goods in place.'

'What of the fort?' Netoji asked, gazing sideways towards the city. The fort looked like a giant black hill against the light blue morning sky.

'Let the fort be,' Raje instructed. 'But keep attacking the men on its walls with muskets. Do not force them to open the gates. Do not try to assault the fort. Our Guptachars have told us there is ample wealth outside the fort. We do not need to lose men in an attack on the walls.'

'So the Mughals are locked inside their own city!' Prataprao gave a hoarse laugh. 'I have long wished to see such a sight.'

'None of us will have time to see any sights,' Raje retorted curtly. 'We all have our allotted tasks to complete. There can be no failures. This is our one chance to save our Swarajya. I hope all of you understand that.'

Though they stood in silence, Shashidhwaj knew that every man there understood the grim reality only too well.

'As Bahirji and Naik have told us, their men have already spread out towards the northern villages,' Raje continued. 'We shall depart as soon as any of them brings news of an approaching Mughal force. Remember, we are not here to fight, only to loot. Cut down anything that stands in your path. Do not stop till you have stripped the city of valuables.'

The men raised their swords to the sky. Shashidhwaj wasted no time in pulling out his own and holding it aloft over his head. In that moment, his heart pounding as he sat on his horse among the men of the Swarajya, he barely felt the weight of it in his hands.

'*Har Har Mahadev!*' Raje cried, his sword glinting in the sunlight.

The war cry was taken up by thousands of Maratha voices, the sound filling the heavens. Those cowering inside the walls of Surat, heard them and trembled.

***

Muhabbat Khan walked towards the drawbridge, where the guards had stopped two carriages in the dawn light. It was not difficult to recognize the sullen face of Virji Vora. He appeared not to have slept at all. His robes were crumpled, and his hair and beard unkempt. The guards hurriedly made a note of the things in the two carriages, both filled so full that the vehicles appeared to sag.

'Carrying your entire house with you?' Muhabbat Khan asked, observing the guard desperately scribbling in his entry ledger.

'A quarter of which I will need to pay you for the privilege of being here,' Vora scoffed.

Muhabbat Khan's forehead furrowed. 'One thousand mahmudis do not occupy this much space,' he observed.

'That is because it is not just one thousand mahmudis.' Vora looked into the Qilladar's eyes. 'I will give you twice the amount you ask.'

'To let in yet another person from your house?' Muhabbat Khan asked, crossing his arms across his great chest.

Vora shook his head. 'I have already sent my entire household to Suwali on the Angrez ships,' he said.

'Then why pay me double?'

'To deny entry to one specific person,' Vora said curtly.

Muhabbat Khan began to laugh. 'As long as my father gets the amount, it won't matter who gets in and who is left out.'

Vora nodded. 'You will have the money. But see to it that my demand is met.'

Muhabbat Khan shrugged. 'Oh I will see to it.'

Vora began to walk away, but Muhabbat Khan placed a hand on his shoulder. Vora stopped in his tracks.

'I will see to it, but not for double the amount.'

Vora sighed. 'How much?' he asked wearily.

'If your friend, whom you are paying me to keep out, does not survive the Maratha attack on the city, I am sure you will profit immensely from his absence in the markets. Make the amount four times.'

'Four times! That is robbery,' Vora protested.

'Do I look like I am negotiating?'

'No, but I am,' Vora replied. 'Three times, paid at once. If not, I will take my chances against Kasim in the market.'

Muhabbat Khan looked at Vora, his eyes narrowed. He

quickly calculated how much had been collected till then. As expected, the merchants had poured into the fort, only too happy to pay for the refuge. But the real collection would come from Vora, Kasim and Beg. He smiled inwardly, thinking of the look on his father's face when he told him the collection had been tripled in a single shot.

'I am beginning to understand why you are such a successful merchant,' Muhabbat Khan said, rubbing his hands together.

Vora returned the Qilladar's gaze without emotion. 'And I am beginning to understand how you and your father came to be Mughal Subhedar and Qilladar of Surat.'

The gates of the fort closed behind them.

***

Haji Kasim hurriedly jumped off his horse. He knew he had no time to loose. He gestured to his sons to lift down the chest from the cart, and then turned towards the moat. Beyond it, the gates to the fort were firmly shut. As he crossed the over-bridge, it swayed with every step he took. The guards at the other end blocked his way, spears crossed.

'What is the meaning of this?' Kasim demanded angrily. He had not expected to be stopped. His sons, carrying the heavy chest behind him, stopped and put down their load. Kasim's wife, in her hijab, who was about to get down from the family carriage, froze.

'The gates are closed,' one of the guards said loudly. 'No one may enter.'

'Careful, fool! Do you know who you are addressing?' Haji Kasim growled. 'The Subhedar would kill you here and now if he came to know you refused to let me in.'

The guard shrugged. 'The orders are from the Subhedar himself. Perhaps you should scurry back into your carriage and leave.'

'But he agreed to let me in!' protested Kasim.

'Perhaps the Subhedar changed his mind,' the guard suggested as his companion snickered. The spears remained crossed, barring the way.

Haji Kasim's heart began to beat quickly. He looked back and saw the fear on the faces of his sons. 'Let me talk to the Subhedar!' he demanded angrily of the guard.

'The Subhedar has said he will not talk to anyone,' the guard declared with finality. 'The gates are shut.'

'What in the name of…' Haji Kasim's gaze flew upwards to the battlements. If only he could see a familiar face up there, who he could talk to, he thought desperately. This had to be a mistake. But his gaze fell upon a figure standing at a distance, staring down at him intently. In that instant Kasim knew the die had been cast. He did not need to be told who it was who stood looking down. Virji Vora.

The air came alive with the sound of *tutaris* being blown from beyond the walls, announcing the enemy was closing in on the city.

Kasim looked helplessly at the guard. He had to get inside the fort somehow! 'Let us through,' he begged. 'I will pay you anything you want!'

The guard grinned. 'We have already been paid,' he said.

'No!' Kasim lunged forward, struggling to get through between them, but they held him off. When Kasim tried to dash past again, the guard who had been silent thus far, punched him in the face. Kasim fell into the dirt. Crawling onto his knees, he looked at his sons. They had reached a dead end.

Kasim got to his feet and retreated, never looking back at the guards. His sons picked up the heavy chest and hurried after him as best they could. Reaching the cart, they once again hauled the chest into it, before scrambling in themselves.

'Let's go!' Kasim said to the carriage driver, getting in.

'Where to?' the man asked, snapping the reins.

Kasim knew there was no longer time to get out of the city. 'Back to the house,' he said quickly and pulled the door shut behind him.

The horses started moving forward. Kasim cast a look of irritation at his wife, muttering prayers in a panic stricken voice. He suddenly wished there was someone he could turn to for advice. But there was no one. He looked out at the eerily deserted streets. The tutaris sounded again, much closer now. Kasim's gaze fell on Fatima, sitting beside his wife, holding her hand and trying to comfort her. He could see the fear on her face as well.

Vora had beaten him with one quick move. It seemed that Allah had forsaken him. He wondered how much Vora had paid the Subhedar to keep him out. Whatever it was, he knew without doubt that he, Haji Kasim, the great and wealthy merchant, had been beaten. All his scheming, all his trade victories, all his negotiations, had come to naught. Vora had won the fight with one bold move. He wondered fleetingly if he could perhaps make a deal with the raiders, but he knew it would mean handing over every last coin of his wealth; all he had acquired in his life with sweat and toil.

The carriage came to an abrupt stop before the house and Kasim got down. His sons had already descended from the cart and stood staring at him, waiting for instructions, unsure what was to be done. Kasim reached into his pocket and extracted the house key. He tossed it to one of his sons, who immediately went to the door, hung with a large padlock.

Kasim turned to see Fatima helping his wife down from the carriage. 'Take her inside. See to her comfort and care,' he instructed. Fatima nodded in silence and complied.

The carriage driver flapped the reins, giving the horses the office to start, anxious to get to the safety of the stables behind the protection of the compound walls.

Kasim instructed his sons to carry the heavy chest into the house. When they had done so, he followed them in. In the shuttered silence of the great house, Kasim gained sudden clarity. He knew he could not go down without a fight. If the looters wanted his wealth, they would have to take it over his dead body, and over the dead bodies of his entire household. He would not permit them to take from him what was rightfully his, as people had tried to do all his life. As he had done before, he would fight again to keep what was his.

***

Shashidhwaj watched the men set up the bamboo poles to support the single shamiyana that was to be erected in the grounds of the kabaristan. When the poles were in place, they began to attach the colourful yards of fabric. All around, the Marathas were busy marking their spots with cotton cloths. On them they placed their saddlebags, before taking up weapons suited to the raid. They put down their spears and picked up their swords. From a distance it appeared that those buried in the kabaristan had suddenly leapt to life from their graves.

A small group of a dozen men gathered at the farthest end of the ground to set of up a kitchen. Shashidhwaj watched them light multiple cooking fires, unload the large bronze vessels from the horse-drawn carts, and place them on the flames. Some were already by the large well, drawing water. These were the men who had the task of ensuring the Maratha soldiers would be hungry only for loot that day.

As Shashidhwaj turned away, he noticed the twelve mansabdars who would lead the men, gathered around a wooden table. Bahirji stood with them, the tip of his sword indicating points on the cloth map on the table. Naik's map of the city had been meticulously recreated on a large cotton cloth. Netoji and Prataprao stood looking down at it, their attention focused on the criss-crossing lines. Bahirji pointed to various locations, explaining where they needed to go for the most loot. The mansabdars followed the movement of his sword, never looking away.

By the only banyan tree in the grounds, Shashidhwaj saw Naik talking softly to Raje and Moropunt. Two visitors had already arrived at the camp, asking to see Raje. Naik was updating him about them. Shashidhwaj looked with interest at the two firangi monks standing to one side, with guards on either side. They wore long flowing brown robes and dangling wooden crosses around their necks.

Raje listened attentively to Naik, then gestured to Moropunt to permit the monks to come forward.

Naik, in the meantime, strolled towards Shashidhwaj and playfully punched him in the arm. 'Are you ready?' he asked.

Shashidhwaj nodded. He had already donned the light breastplate and helmet one of the soldiers had handed him. 'Who are those men?' he asked curiously, jerking his chin towards the monks. He had never seen them in the city. But perhaps Naik had while loitering in the streets in one of his many disguises.

'The tall one is Father Ambrose,' Naik told him. 'The other is his assistant. They are priests of the Capuchin Church in the city. They have come to beg Raje to spare them and their church when we enter the city.'

Shashidhwaj could see fear clearly etched on the faces of the two men. 'Will Raje accept their demands?' he asked.

Naik nodded. 'Raje is always respectful to monks and priests of all religions. Besides, there is not much to loot in those Christian churches.'

'If these monks are so afraid, think of how fearful the Mughals in the city must be.'

Naik laughed. 'Give the Mughals hell from me, boy.'

'You're not coming with us?' Shashidhwaj asked, surprised.

'The Mughals aren't going to sit on their backsides while we loot their city,' Naik said with a shrug. 'Word must have already travelled north. An army will be dispatched to fight us. My men and I shall take up lookout posts in the hills around the city, to keep an eye out for an incoming force.'

Shashidhwaj gave a disappointed sigh. 'I was looking forward to the three of us riding into the city together.'

'Then you will not have much to look forward to,' Naik said, chuckling. 'The twelve mansabdars you see there will lead various groups. The city is vast, so different groups will target different areas. Bahirji and you will each lead a group, to two of the prime target areas. The other groups will venture out on their own. That is why he is explaining the lay of the land to them.'

'When will I see you again?' Shashidhwaj asked as Naik put on his helmet and prepared to mount his horse.

'That will depend on how fast the Mughal horses can march from their camps in the north to Surat,' Naik winked.

'Stay safe!' Shashidhwaj called. The man was always going somewhere.

'I'd rather tell that to the poor souls inside the city,' Naik called over his shoulder. Kicking his horse, he rode away, gesturing to a group of horsemen to follow.

In the cloud of dust the horses kicked up, Shashidhwaj almost did not notice Bahirji waving at him. He ran over immediately. Netoji smirked as Shashidhwaj took his place by the table beside everyone else.

'I have explained to everyone the places we must target,' Bahirji said. 'By the time night falls upon the city, our men will be ready. You and I will take two groups to the residences of the richest merchants. I shall go to the house of Virji Vora, with the group led by Prataprao. You will take the Sarnaubat and his men to the house of Haji Kasim. You know it well. The others will hit the toll booths and the house of Haji Sayyid Beg. We shall find whatever loot we can until the carts are full, then bring it back here to camp, where Raje will oversee the sorting and reloading, while we return to the city for more loot.'

Netoji cleared his throat and looked at the Mansabdars. 'This cycle will continue till we receive word from Naik that a Mughal force is approaching. None of you, or your men, shall sleep, shit or rest until this is over. We will eat whenever we get the chance, between ferrying the loot from the city to the camp. Piss in the houses and *jakatkhanas* you loot. Together, we shall bring Surat to its knees.'

'Aye, we shall!' the Mansabdars yelled in unison.

'I shall leave you men to prepare now.' Netoji raised his hand in dismissal, watching as the men returned to their own groups. He then looked down at Shashidhwaj with interest. 'I hope you have prepared this young boy well,' he said to Bahirji. 'I will get to see your training firsthand, will I not?'

'You may be surprised by what you see, Sarnaubat,' Bahirji grinned, placing a hand on Shashidhwaj's shoulder.

'We will see.' Netoji nodded curtly and walked off to where Raje stood in conversation. Still grinning, Bahirji followed.

Left alone at the table, Shashidhwaj took a deep breath. The height of his adventure was about to unfold. Now all that remained was for night to fall, so he could lead the Sarnaubat and his men through the streets of Surat, directly to the house of Haji Kasim. He hoped Fatima had gained the safety of the fort with Haji Kasim's family. He closed his eyes and said a short prayer, the only one he knew, learned in his childhood in the village. Then he squatted down on the ground as he had so often seen Naik do, his palms folded over the hilt of his upright sword, waiting for darkness to fall.

Chapter Twenty-Two

The Burning City

FIRST NIGHT OF THE SACK OF SURAT

Night fell quickly over the deserted houses, streets and markets of Surat, almost as if the setting sun hurried away before the Marathas could enter the city walls. Shashidhwaj mounted his horse and waited for Netoji and his men do the same. Netoji gestured to him to lead, so Shashidhwaj kicked his horse into a trot. Their's would be the first group to enter the city. As they moved off towards the city gates, Shashidhwaj stole a quick glance at Bahirji, mounting his own horse and preparing to lead his group. Taking a deep breath, he looked ahead, focused on the way forward.

They passed through the gates quickly, finding no guards to challenge them. The once bustling streets wore a deserted and forlorn aspect. Shashidhwaj led the men past the twists and turns in the road till the house of Haji Kasim towered over them at the corner of a main street.

Netoji was the first to dismount. He looked at the tall house with interest as the others got down and hitched their horses. Shashidhwaj calmed his nervous mount, patting its mane, then jumped down. He saw the firmly shut doors and hoped again that Fatima had taken his advice and made for the fort.

'Break open the doors!' Netoji ordered, moving forward.

Shashidhwaj watched him stride towards the front entrance, then quickly looked up. He had noticed a figure crouched behind the fretwork of the topmost balcony.

'Sarnaubat, stop!' he shouted. Netoji halted in his tracks. 'Take cover!' Shashidhwaj yelled, even as a musket shot embedded itself in the dust a few steps from Netoji.

Shashidhwaj ducked behind his horse. The others found shelter where they could. Netoji crouched behind a wall. Shashidhwaj looked for the attacker but could see no one. He dashed for the wall and found himself by Netoji's side.

'You said there was no one inside,' Netoji hissed angrily.

'I expected the house to be empty. Apparently it is not.'

'I almost lost my life, boy.'

'And you certainly would have lost if I had not seen the shadow on the upper level and warned you, so keep your angry voice to yourself.' As the blood rushed to his head, Shashidhwaj did not feel afraid anymore.

Netoji's eyes glittered angrily but he did not dwell further on the matter. There were more important tasks on hand. 'We need to know who is inside, and warn them to get out,' he said stringently.

Rising to his feet, he shouted imperatively, 'Lay down your weapons whoever you are, and come out of the front door! Or we shall kill you.'

A musket shot rang out, smashing a flower pot into a jumble of pottery shards, roots and foliage.

'To kill me, you have to get to me first!' said a loud voice.

Netoji glanced at Shashidhwaj, who nodded. 'It is Haji Kasim's voice,' he said. There was only one voice like it in the world. But why was he in the house and not in the fort? Did it mean Fatima was inside as well?

'What else can one expect from the Guptachars' pet?' Netoji muttered to himself, looking to right and left to see if there was anything they could anchor their ropes to. There was none. He gestured to two of his men. They made a run for the wall and settled by his side. 'Go around and see if there is any other way in,' Netoji instructed.

'Think again, Kasim!' Netoji yelled again. 'Your life or your money?'

'I will never part with my money to a gang of looters like you!' Kasim bellowed from inside.

Shashidhwaj wondered how they were going to break open the doors. He knew they were as thick as half a tree trunk, and were bolted with a crossbar from within. He glanced towards Netoji, who was deep in thought.

Finally, Netoji looked sideways at Shashidhwaj and said, 'You said the treasury is in the basement, did you not?'

Shashidhwaj nodded, pointing to the ground.

'Good.' Netoji stood up straight and began walking towards the house. 'I will forgive your words Kasim, but not your impudence,' he called out, stopping right in front of the main door.

Shashidhwaj watched, intrigued. There was something strange in Netoji's voice.

'Over my dead body!' Kasim retorted. 'And the bodies of all those inside my house.'

The words sent a chill down Shashidhwaj's spine. It meant Fatima could still be inside.

'Good, I prefer it that way.' Netoji turned towards the mansabdar behind him. 'Do you see the small shop by the side of the road, the *Tel Bhandar*?' he yelled. 'Break it open. Bring the oil and burn this house down!'

'No!' Shashidhwaj shouted, running forward, shocked by this sudden, merciless order. Fatima could still be inside.

She would have nowhere to run if fire consumed the place.

Netoji frowned and put a finger to his lips. He was playing a bluff, wanting to see if Kasim would surrender if they threatened to burn down the house.

For some moments there was no response, then Kasim shouted, 'Do what you please, you dacoit!'

'So be it.' Netoji nodded to the men.

Immediately, a dozen men ran to the Tel Bhandar and smashed its doors and windows. It did not take them long to roll out the wooden barrels containing the oil into the street. The men quickly formed a line and rolled the barrels from man to man till they reached the house, where they were broken open and the oil poured against the walls of the house. The oil would start the fire, the wood would do the rest.

Shashidhwaj looked on anxiously, his mind racing. How was he to stop them?

When the ground was drenched in oil, Netoji pointed to the mashaals beside the door. 'Hand me those torches,' he commanded one of his men. The captain tossed him one of the flaming mashaals. Netoji caught it in one hand.

'No!' Shashidhwaj shouted in protest.

Netoji turned to look at him in surprise, then laughed as if he found the boy's distress humorous. Abruptly, he stopped laughing and roared, 'Shut your beak and let me do my job!'

'Let me sneak inside,' Shashidhwaj pleaded. 'I can open the doors. I know the way.'

Netoji waved a hand as if to shoo away an irritating fly. 'Why waste so much time when the house is built of wood and flames are aplenty?'

Shashidhwaj stared into Netoji's eyes. 'There is a girl inside,' he said, his voice steady. 'A girl I love.'

'Aren't you a Guptachar now?' Netoji mocked. 'One of Bahirji's little spies? You aren't supposed to have girls.'

'I beg you…'

'What is this girl's name?'

'Fatima.'

'Look at you, boy, rooting around after a Musalmaan girl!' Netoji pshawed in derision.

'Please, I beg you.'

'Beg the gods, boy, this is war!' With that, Netoji turned away, holding high the mashaal.

'No!' Shashidhwaj shouted, but Netoji never turned back. Desperately, Shashidhwaj turned towards the house and shouted, 'Fatima! Fatima!'

'Aslam!' a voice answered from behind the jharokas of the upper level.

So she was inside! Shashidhwaj's heart began to hammer painfully in his chest. 'Run!' he shouted. If only she could get to the back of the house, perhaps she could jump into the street below.

Netoji took aim and threw the mashaal right at the wooden doors. In another instant fire enclosed the structure like hay burning on a summer night, lighting up the dark sky.

Har Har Mahadev! the soldiers yelled, as they too, threw flaming brands towards the house. The entire wooden structure was now in flames. There were terrified shouts and screams from inside; both men and women's voices. One of them had to be Fatima.

Shashidhwaj stared at the burning house like a madman. He had to do something. He began to run but an arm grabbed him from behind. 'It is fire, boy,' the Mavla said. 'You cannot jump in.'

'Let go of me!' Shashidhwaj fought the restraining arm, but the man did not release him. In desperation, Shashidhwaj bit into the arm with all his strength. Cursing, the Mavla let go. Shashidhwaj rushed forward, only to find his path blocked by the figure of Netoji, dark against the orange flames.

'What in god's name are you trying to do?' he yelled. 'Let the walls burn. The treasure is underground, you said. When the whole structure falls, we will walk in.'

'I must save Fatima!' Shashidhwaj said, his voice hoarse.

'There is no way you are saving anyone from this burning hellhole,' Netoji said. 'We warned Kasim. He should have listened and come out.'

'You can't stop me!' Shashidhwaj cried, hand resting on the hilt of his sword.

'You impudent peasant! Do you dare challenge your Sarnaubat?' Netoji growled. 'Your masters have made you as arrogant as themselves. Move back boy!'

'Or what?' Shashidhwaj's head throbbed with anger. He could no longer think; his hands moving automatically.

'I warn you!' Netoji raised a warning hand.

Shashidhwaj's sword moved out of his scabbard in a flash. But the soldier by Netoji's side moved first, his blade met Shashidhwaj's in the middle. Shashidhwaj moved back. The Mavla by his side tried to grab him, but Shashidhwaj hit out at him angrily. The blade hit something and Shashidhwaj bore down with all the power of his arm. The Mavla stared at him, holding up a bloodied left hand. It was only then that Shashidhwaj realized he had chopped off the man's thumb.

Suddenly, his sword went spinning from his grasp. Netoji had disarmed him. His face was grim, his eyes glittering with rage. 'Do you realize what you have just done?' he growled.

Fear rushed back into Shashidhwaj's heart like water from a broken dam. Netoji picked him up by his shoulders and lifted him off the ground. Shashidhwaj felt the blood rush to his head.

'You will die for this!' Netoji yelled. 'Loot the house, Tanaji!' he yelled to another soldier, 'while I carry this filth back to camp and give him the punishment he deserves.'

Shashidhwaj felt himself being thrown onto Netoji's horse. He struggled to free himself, but Netoji's arms came around him like iron.

'Fatima!' Shashidhwaj shouted as the horse began to move. He had failed her. He had left her to die in the flames.

The house continued to burn, a bright torch that lit up the sky, the massive front doors still resolutely barred against the leaping flames. The Mavlas stood by, waiting.

Netoji's horse galloped towards the city walls. Behind him, flames spread from other fires, bathing the streets in dancing light.

***

Shashidhwaj struggled to maintain his balance as Netoji tore through the streets with as much speed as the beast could muster. He sat hunched over the horse's mane, Netoji' arms his prison. When the towering city gates appeared, he knew they were leaving the doomed city.

Soon, they arrived at the kabaristan. Shashidhwaj could see they were riding towards the lone banyan tree in the grounds. Netoji was taking him directly to Raje.

Finally Netoji pulled on the reins and the horse reared to a halt. Shashidhwaj clung to its mane so as not to be thrown off. Netoji dismounted and then roughly hauled his captive from the horse. Shashidhwaj struggled, trying to free himself from the deadly grip. He felt the cold night air hit his face as Netoji remorselessly pushed him forward. Then he was thrown to the ground. Shashidhwaj felt the grass tickle his face, and tasted mud. He dug both arms into the ground trying to raise himself, but when he felt the cold sharp edge of Netoji's sword on his neck, he let himself fall back.

'Where is Raje?' Netoji demanded.

'In his shamiyana,' said Moropunt, who was sitting on the *chabutara* of the tree. 'Overseeing the counting of the first loot, and giving audience to those from the city who desire to see him.'

'Tell him I wish to see him urgently!' Netoji demanded.

'What is the meaning of this?' The voice belonged to Bahirji, who now stormed onto the scene. Word of what had transpired outside Kasim's house had doubtless reached him from one of his men who inhabited the shadows.

'The boy attacked one of my soldiers!' Netoji said angrily. 'He has to die.'

Moropunt looked at the two men staring aggressively at each other, the boy between them, and got to his feet. 'I shall bring Raje,' he said prudently and left.

'Get your sword off him!' Bahirji's words were followed by the drawing of steel.

Shashidhwaj felt Netoji's blade tip press into his neck.

'And why would I do that?' Netoji asked harshly. 'Why would you even ask me to do that?'

'He is my ward,' Bahirji said. 'If he is to be punished, I should be the one to do it.'

There was a pause, then Shashidhwaj feel the pressure lift.

'Very well,' said Netoji, withdrawing his blade.

Before he could rise, Shashidhwaj felt strong hands pull him to his feet and push him towards Bahirji. He stumbled and would have fallen again but for Bahirji's restraining hand on his arm. As he steadied, he heard Bahirji's low voice in his ear, 'What in god's name did you do, boy?'

'I wounded a guard,' Shashidhwaj whispered back, avoiding the unwavering gaze bent upon him. 'They killed

Fatima! She was in Kasim's house. They set it on fire.' Breathing heavily, Shashidhwaj looked up into Bahirji's eyes.

Suddenly, his head snapped back from the impact of an open-handed slap across his face. It was so forceful that Shashidhwaj staggered backwards. Rubbing his burning cheek, he looked up at Bahirji in wounded surprise.

Bahirji stared back at him, his eyes hard. 'Are you a fool?' he hissed. 'How could you wound one of your own comrades for the sake of a foreigner you have known for three months?'

Hand on cheek, Shashidhwaj knew Bahirji was right. 'It just happened. I am sorry,' he mumbled.

'This is war boy, people die. Even people we know. But we must get our priorities right,' Bahirji said sternly. 'If you cannot accept that, then maybe you should remain here in Surat and not return home with us.'

Angry tears filled Shashidhwaj's eyes but he refused to let them fall. Fatima was gone. There was no way she could have survived that fire. Nor would she have chosen to. Now, the time had come for him to make his own choice.

'I have told you that sometimes we have to do things we find repugnant, for the good of the Swarajya.' Bahirji lifted a finger. 'And you can only do that if you love our Swarajya, the ideal of it, more than anything else in life.'

'I do now,' Shashidhwaj said, raising his head and meeting Bahirji's eyes. 'I should not have done what I did. I will never do such a thing again. You can trust me.'

Bahirji glared at him for a moment. Then he turned to look at Netoji, who stood watching them, hands on hips. 'It is done, Sarnaubat,' Bahirji said quietly.

Netoji stared at him, then pulled out his sword again. 'It's not done until the boy pays with his life,' he said through clenched teeth.

'I will not let you spill more blood amongst our own than has already been spilt,' Bahirji said, raising his own blade.

The two men stared at each other like two wild tigers about to leap into combat. But before either could move, they heard footsteps approach and an imperative command rang out: 'Stop!'

Shashidhwaj did not need to look to know that Raje himself had appeared amongst them.

Raje stared at the angry scene and then turned towards Netoji. 'What is the meaning of this, Sarnaubat?' he asked.

'The boy attacked one of my men,' Netoji declared loudly. 'He sliced off his thumb. Blood was spilled.'

'It was an emotional reaction,' Bahirji intervened to say. 'No further harm was caused.'

'Due to my timely intervention.' Netoji crossed his arms.

As Raje's eyes turned to him, Shashidhwaj's own gaze fell to his feet. He felt as if strong sunrays were burning his skin. He waited in trepidation to hear the verdict Raje would pronounce for all to hear.

Raje tugged at his beard thoughtfully, his eyes still upon the youthful face before him. Deep lines were etched on his face. 'Enough!' he finally declared authoritatively. 'Are you fools not able to see that we are presently at war? Any differences between us will be resolved after the raid is over, not in the middle of operations, as you are doing. You of all people should understand this, Sarnaubat. And you too, Bahirji. I am surprised at you.'

Netoji shook his head. 'We must rip such bad flowers in the bud at once,' he objected. 'Give me the command and I shall rip his head off for all to see.'

At his words, Shashidhwaj's heart began to race. Was he to die this night, here under this tree?

Bahirji now spoke. 'Raje, he is my ward. I am the one you should blame. Punish me, not the boy.'

Raje flashed him an angry glance. 'If anybody is to decide

who is to be punished, and how, it shall be me. I am your Raje. It is my word that is law. And I have decided the boy is to come with me.'

None dared question his words. Raje gestured to Shashidhwaj, who meekly followed the striding figure away from the tree. Moropunt too, followed them in silence.

'I am sorry,' Shashidhwaj managed to utter when they were some distance from the others.

'It is evident that you are,' Raje said, walking on. 'Do you know why I extricated you from that stand-off?'

Shashidhwaj shook his head, unsure what to say.

'You were the cause two of my best men drew steel on each other. We must never fight amongst ourselves in times of war. Whatever differences we have, we must settle them in times of peace.'

They reached the lone shamiyana standing a hundred steps away. Raising the fabric, Raje walked in, followed by the other two.

'Stand over there,' Raje instructed, pointing to a corner.

Shashidhwaj did as he was told. He watched as Raje took his place upon the diwan, sitting sideways, one leg crossed horizontally over the other.

'Resume the audiences, Punt,' he said to Moropunt.

'In the presence of this boy?' Moropunt asked, surprised.

Raje nodded. 'The boy needs to cool his head,' he said. 'Better he do it under my eye than someone else's. Besides, given Netoji's temper, I am not sure the boy would be safe anywhere outside this tent. And give him another sword for he seems to have lost his."

Moropunt nodded. Raising the flap of the shamiyana, he gave orders to the men outside. Pulling a paper from the satchel he wore across his chest, he peered at it. 'The next is the Angrez captured wandering the streets,' he said. 'He has refused to divulge his name. Perhaps he will to you.'

Raje grunted. Two guards brought in the white man. His clothes were dishevelled and his face bore marks of injury. It was apparent the men had used him for their entertainment.

But Shashidhwaj recognized him at once as the man he had seen in the market on his first day in the city, accompanying President Oxenden. He looked at Raje, wondering if he should move closer and whisper the information to him. He wondered how such an action would be taken by the guards and the venerable Moropunt, standing on the other side of Raje. Finally, Shashidhwaj threw caution to the winds. It hardly mattered what happened to him after all. Outside, Netoji already hated him. As would others. Sidling towards the divan, he whispered, 'He is the right hand man of the President of the Angrez warehouse, one Mister Smith.'

Raje turned to look at him, wary at first. Then, as the words registered in his mind, he sat up straight and nodded. 'Do you speak the common tongue, Smith?' he asked.

The man gazed at him, a blank expression on his face. But his eyes blinked when he heard his name, and he shook his head.

'He *does* speak it,' Shashidhwaj whispered again. 'I have seen him speak to traders in the market.'

'*Shiledars*! Take this man and flog him on all fours like an animal in the street!' Raje spoke, suddenly angry.

The soldiers moved towards Smith, who began to shake. 'I speak it Lord, I do,' he blubbered as the guards laid their hands upon him.

Raje held up a hand and the guards let go. 'Why does your President barricade the factory?' he asked. 'Why does he not allow my men free access to the goods inside?'

'We are humble merchants, Lord,' Smith said. 'We have nothing to offer you. The President worries for the safety of the women and children.'

'Liar!' Shashidhwaj shouted, then bit down on his lower lip as everyone turned to stare at him. 'The women and the children were moved to the ships, out of the city two days ago,' he told Raje. He had seen the carriages taking them from the English factory in Surat the day before the Maratha army reached the city.

Raje glared at Smith. 'Do you dare lie to me in my own shamiyana?' he roared.

Anthony Smith looked down at his feet. He felt the cold steel of a guard's sword on his neck. 'I apologize, Lord,' he said.

'I sent one of the Greeks we captured in the city, who knows your language, to your factory,' Raje told him. 'But your President refused my request. He said I could attack if I wished, but he would not submit.'

'Let me go back into the city,' Smith said, looking up. 'Let me go to my President and tell him you will be true to your word. He will believe it if it comes from me.'

'How do I know you do not lie to me now as you lied before? Should I order your hands cut off for such insolence?'

Smith raised his hands. 'Why just my hands?' he said. 'Take my head if you think I lie.'

Raje shook his head. 'A head is too easy,' he said. 'I take off your head and you will feel nothing. It is done in a moment. Besides, I need the information in your head. So, hands it shall be if you tell me anything but the truth.'

Smith bowed. 'Anything I know I will tell you.'

'What is in the factory?' Raje asked, his brow furrowed.

'Just goods for trade,' Smith replied. 'Wares of all kinds. Textiles. All in bundles and sacks.'

'What about valuables?'

'There are no valuables,' Smith replied.

'Why do I hear the words of a liar?' Raje retorted angrily.

'I can show you,' Smith said. 'I can take one of your men into the factory to verify what I have said.'

'If any of my men enters your damned factory, he will not return without booty,' Raje declared. 'So you better think twice before saying another word.'

'I only seek to be on my way,' Smith said. 'I have no beef with you.'

'I will let you go if you pay a tribute of three thousand mahmudis,' Raje said.

'I am a humble clerk. How can I pay what you ask?' Smith beseeched.

'Then you shall remain here as my prisoner until your friends in the factory agree to pay.'

Raje's decision was final. They heard Smith pleading and protesting even as he was led away by the guards.

Raje turned to look at Shashidhwaj. 'Does this man speak the truth?' he asked.

Shashidhwaj gazed back at Raje. They both knew Smith was lying.

'How was he captured?' Shashidhwaj asked, looking towards Moropunt.

'The soldiers found him walking the streets in the eastern part of the city,' Moropunt said from where he stood.

'But the Angrez factory is in the western section,' Shashidhwaj recalled. There was something suspicious about Smith's actions.

'Well, while you sit here clearing your head, maybe you can deduce what exactly is wrong,' Raje remarked, gesturing to Moropunt to let in the next visitor.

***

The sky was still dark but he knew it would soon be morning. From where they stood on the bastions of the fort, they could see the fires that still raged through the city, bathing it in a deceptively warm glow. Muhabbat Khan walked along the ramparts towards the lone figure leaning on the battlements, gazing at the burning city.

'You shouldn't stand there too long, Shethji,' he said, clearing his throat to get the man's attention. 'One stray arrow would render in vain all the mahmudis you have paid my esteemed father for your safety.'

Virji Vora turned slowly. His body looked frail and old in the meagre light, yet his face remained that of a younger man. 'No, we shouldn't be standing here at all,' he agreed. 'We should be out in the streets, teaching those dacoits a lesson. Even an old fool like me.'

'Anger does not become the freckles on your face, Shethji.' Muhabbat Khan strode forward and placed both his heavy arms on the battlements. But the sight of the city burning made the fury rise in him as well.

'Yes, anger does not become me, as inaction does not become the valorous robes you wear,' Vora said, turning.

Muhabbat Khan did not reply. Standing there, both men knew there were more things at stake that night than soldierly valour. They still had not found the gold. Muhabbat Khan said a silent prayer the enemy had not found it either.

'Look around. There is no way out. Ganim surround us. Look at our burning city. How in the god's name are we to do what we must?'

Vora turned back to stare at the beleaguered city. Placing a hand on his hip, he said reflectively, 'What we need is a distraction.'

'What distraction is big enough to start the wheels of our plan?' Muhabbat Khan asked, looking up at the sky.

Vora did not speak; he merely stood looking on in silence.

Muhabbat Khan cast him an angry glance. 'Do you have something to discuss or did you summon me here just to stare at this horrible mess?'

Vora stood up straight and cleared his throat. 'As I said, we need a distraction. And what better way to create one than to strike right at the heart of the enemy?'

'I would land such a blow myself if there was a way to do it,' Muhabbat Khan assured him, his hands curling into fists.

Vora stared at Muhabbat's face in the meagre light. 'Leave the strike to me,' he said. 'You better start putting on your armour, for we strike this evening, as darkness falls. In the ensuing chaos, as the Marathas withdraw to their camp, you will go out and find the gold.'

***

The shouts and cries from outside haunted the corridors of the fort like ghosts from some hoary past, even as faint morning light began peering through the jharokas. Muhabbat Khan felt the weight of those cries with each step he took. The conversation he had just had with Shethji had made his head spin. He knew he had to find his father at once. The Subhedar had disappeared into his personal chambers as soon as the gates of the fort had been closed and the drawbridge raised. He did not desire to face either those who had taken refuge inside the fort, or those left outside its walls to fend for themselves in the turmoil.

Muhabbat Khan climbed the stairs to the far side of the fort, overlooking the river, where the Subhedar's personal chambers were located. He pushed open the door and cleared his throat to announce his presence.

Inayat Khan sat in the dark chamber. Smoke rose from the hookah at his side, and from the last guttering remnants of the wicks in the lamps. In the darkness, it was hard to tell whether the Subhedar's eyes were open.

'What do you want?' Inayat Khan asked, annoyed to be

disturbed, even by his son.

'We must do something, Father!' Muhabbat Khan pleaded. 'Outside, a whole night has passed with the Maratha rats looting the city.'

'You are right,' Inayat Khan replied dreamily. 'We have to do something. But the question is, what?'

'The Shethji has a plan,' Muhabbat Khan told him, rubbing his wrists. 'Or rather, I have a plan.'

'The fact that you hesitate, tells me it is not something I wish to hear.'

'We need a distraction,' Muhabbat Khan declared, echoing Vora's words. 'Or rather, we must create one.'

'We are prisoners within the walls of this fort,' Inayat Khan said, his voice hard. 'How in the seven hells are we to do anything?'

'We are surrounded, but we are not dead. Nor is our manhood taken from us.'

'No, not yet,' Inayat Khan sighed. 'That shall be done later, when we stand before the Badshah, carried to Agra by his army, which is doubtless on its way to rescue our city from this plight.'

In the darkness of the chamber, Muhabbat Khan felt a fire begin to burn within him. 'How can you be so afraid, Father? You are the Subhedar of the largest city outside Agra itself. How can you admit defeat thus easily?'

'The man who errs is a man who fears. We have erred,' Inayat Khan said. 'We did not keep the army of five thousand we should have. Now we don't stand a chance.'

'We have money. The merchants paid us heaps of mahmudis to gain entry within these walls. Once the Marathas leave, we can take a ship and disappear from here.'

'You are much too naïve, my son,' Inayat Khan said. 'The

money is not enough for us to disappear. We will need much much more to do that.'

'But that is precisely what I am getting at,' Muhabbat Khan declared. 'The gold!'

'Assuming the Marathas still have not found it...'

'They have not,' Muhabbat Khan assured him. 'I am certain of it. Allah guides me and tells me I am right.'

'But the gold is outside these walls.'

'We can look for it,' Muhabbat Khan insisted. 'I can!'

'My son...' Inayat Khan replied wearily, 'there is a battle raging outside.'

'And that is why we need a distraction.'

The fading coals glowed intermittently atop the hookah, struggling to survive the dawn light. 'You said the Shethji had a plan,' Inayat Khan finally said.

'We need a distraction that will cause the Marathas to leave the city,' Muhabbat Khan said.

'Why on earth would they turn away from the loot and wealth?'

'The Shethji has a plan about how it can be done. First, we rain fire upon the Maratha troops.'

'But the Maratha camp is outside the range of our cannon,' Inayat Khan reminded him. 'It is as if they knew the Kabaristan would be out of range of our guns.'

'Who said anything about their camp?' Muhabbat Khan replied. 'There are Marathas inside the city. We turn our guns on them, letting the wicks burn and the cannons boom.'

'It would destroy the city.'

'Is it not already destroyed?' Muhabbat Khan banged a fist angrily against the wall. 'Yes, more buildings will fall. So what? Many have fallen already. There will be more fires. But the city is burning already. It will make the Marathas think we are retaliating. At present they are moving through the city as free as birds in the sky.'

Inayat Khan considered this. 'The canon fire may deter them, but it will not make them leave.'

'No,' his son agreed. 'But what we do next will. We will kill that mountain rat Siva, their leader. We will plunge a dagger straight through his heart.'

For a moment a flicker of amusement flitted across Inayat Khan's face. How impetuous and foolish the young were! 'And how shall we do that?' he asked.

'I have men who will lay down their lives for me,' Muhabbat Khan replied. 'I shall send one of them, disguised as a messenger, to carry an official message with your seal, to the Maratha camp. He shall also carry a dagger hidden in his clothes. He will seek audience with the mountain rat himself. I am told he refuses none who wish to see him on legitimate business.'

Inayat Khan leaned forward. 'If your man succeeds, the Badshah will reward us for having killed an arch enemy.'

'However that turns out,' Muhabbat Khan said, 'I shall leave the fort with a few of my trusted men. We will scale down the fort wall on the river side. That way we will not be observed.'

Inayat Khan sat suddenly upright. 'What for?' he asked.

'I shall look for the gold in the city,' Muhabbat Khan said, twisting his moustache. 'If my man does manage to assassinate Siva, there will be turmoil in the Maratha ranks. They will run out of the city to discover who killed their leader. The ensuing chaos will give me an opportunity to hunt for the gold. And as Allah is my guide, I shall find it and bring it back to you.'

'Why does it have to be you, my son?' Inayat Khan

asked, rising and placing a hand on his son's shoulder. 'You can send the soldiers.'

'And trust them to return with the gold?' Muhabbat Khan laughed derisively. 'You yourself have said that gold is enough to pollute even the most honest of men. But if I am there, they must obey.'

'It is a dangerous plan.'

Muhabbat Khan moved away from his father's hand. 'What choice do we have?' he asked. 'The gold is our future.'

'We can still disappear,' Inayat Khan said. 'We can go across the seas.'

'And live as paupers?' Muhabbat Khan burst out. 'The men who once ruled Surat turned into beggars, living on the charity of others?'

'Nothing is more valuable than life itself.'

Muhabbat Khan looked into his father's face. 'For me, there is,' he said. 'Your blood flows through my veins. And Allah willing, I will find the gold.'

Inayat Khan hesitated for a moment, then nodded. 'Bring the messenger to me,' he said, 'I shall seal the letter myself.'

'Yes, Father.'

As Muhabbat Khan turned to leave, Inayat Khan held out a trembling hand. 'I want you to know that you are worth more to me than all the gold in the world, my son.'

Muhabbat Khan stopped in his tracks, fighting back tears, unsure what to say. 'Then let me prove worthy of the value you place upon my humble head,' he finally said.

Turning, he hurried from the chamber.

Chapter Twenty-Three

The Shamiyana

SECOND DAY AND NIGHT OF THE SACK OF SURAT

Shashidhwaj noticed a tall Mughal fiddling with his belt as he waited in the line of visitors outside the shamiyana. He quickly identified the man as Mughal by the *mutsaddis* robes that all Mughal officials in Surat wore. But there was something strange about him. He was restive and nervous. Shashidhwaj wondered who he was and what he was doing here in the Maratha encampment. The others in line were common Baniyas, rounded up by the raiding Marathas and sent back to the shamiyana under guard, where Moropunt had bodyguards frisk them and then wait in line for audience with Raje.

Once inside, Raje asked them to offer their valuables on the rug at his feet. Then, depending on the response, his manner either softened or hardened. Sometimes he nodded or smiled encouragingly. Shashidhwaj was amazed to see how his manner changed with each person, depending on what would make him give up his wealth most easily. Once the mat was filled with the coins, ornaments, gem stones and items of value offered, the soldiers would pick it up and take it outside and Moropunt would have the mat replaced with another.

The raiders inside the city walls kept sending more and more people back to the camp. The line of those waiting to appear before Raje was now so long that even though an entire night and day had passed, and the setting sun had once again turned the sky red, the procession of men continued.

But the Mughal Shashidhwaj had noticed did not fit in with the merchants and traders in line. He nervously rubbed his palms against his sides as the man before him fell to his knees at Raje's feet. Clearly visible now, Shashidhwaj noticed there was a scroll pushed into the man's belt. So he was an envoy. Had the Subhedar decided to surrender after all?

When it was his turn, the Mughal took two long strides and stood before Raje. He did not bow, but performed a cursory *adaab* before pulling the scroll from his belt and offering it.

Moropunt cleared his throat. 'Raje, this man claims to be an envoy sent by the Subhedar of Surat.'

Raje's eyes gauged the man from head to toe. 'You mean the Subhedar who has hidden himself in the fort?' he asked.

'The very same,' Moropunt replied.

The taunt did not seem to affect the envoy. He continued to extend the scroll, saying, 'The Subhedar sends this communication to be read out to you in person, Lord.'

Raje clapped his hands. 'Certainly! Let us hear what the most timid Mughal I have ever met has to say.'

The bearded messenger bowed slightly. He turned the scroll to display the unbroken seal on the letter. Moropunt nodded. The man broke the seal and unrolled the paper. Clearing his throat, he read: *Subhedar Inayat Khan, from his glorious seat of power in Surat, desires to discuss the terms by which you may carry the wealth you have gathered from his city.*

For a moment there was complete silence in the shamiyana. Then the guards began to snigger. Raje smiled, but raised his hand. The amusement subsided.

'Your Subhedar hides in his fort like a woman,' he said, his voice like a whiplash, 'yet he dares to send me terms?' Raje's eyes glittered dangerously.

The envoy met the blazing gaze. 'You have not heard the terms yet, Lord,' he said.

Raje lifted one foot onto a small stool; the other rested on the ground where the mat lay. 'Very well,' he said amicably, 'let us hear what your Subhedar has to say.'

Still holding the Subhedar's message in one hand, the envoy quickly pulled something from his sleeve with his free hand. No one was prepared for what happened next. As the last light of the setting sun hit the small knife, making the metal gleam like some living thing, it seemed to Shashidhwaj the entire scene before him slowed, taking place in slow motion. The envoy raised the dagger and rushed across the tribute mat on the ground, to attack Raje, sitting a few paces away. Shashidhwaj did not know when his own hand reached for his sword, which he pulled out in one swift motion. Clenching his teeth, he swung it with all the power of his arms and shoulders, without waiting to take aim. Warm blood spurted as the attacker's hand was sliced off. Blood splattered Shashidhwaj's face and chest in a mottled web of red. He closed his eyes and turned his head. When he looked back, the attacker was lying over Raje, on the divan, his arms outflung. Raje's clothes were bloody.

For a moment, Shashidhwaj's heart missed a beat as he rushed in and grabbed the attacker by the shoulders. The man groaned as Shashidhwaj and two soldiers pulled him back, his legs dragging across the ground, roiling the mat on the ground. The man screamed in agony, holding the stump of his right hand with the other. As they dumped him on the ground, Shashidhwaj lifted his sword and plunged it into the man's heart. Instantly, the agonized cries ceased.

Raje looked down at his blood-soaked clothes and then at the Mughal on the ground, the sword still embedded in his chest.

'Guards! The Mughals have attacked Raje!' Moropunt yelled, rushing out of the tent.

Instantly, there was confusion. Shouts and curses rose into the air as men rushed forward to witness what had happened. Shashidhwaj saw one of the Maratha guards draw his sword and run it through one of the traders waiting in line. The man fell to the ground with a thud, his mouth open in helpless surprise. Instantly, other guards followed suit, attacking the helpless line of men. Senseless mayhem and death ensued.

Shashidhwaj felt a hand tug at his tunic. Raje.

'Quick, help me up! I am unharmed.'

Shashidhwaj bent to help him to his feet. Outside, yells and shrieks filled the air. Suddenly, there came a familiar voice, shouting commands. Netoji rushed in, sword drawn. His gaze fell on Shashidhwaj's blood splattered visage beside Raje's blood-soaked form.

'You bastard!' he yelled. 'I knew it was you!'

Before Netoji could move, Raje, looking like an apparition from some bloody hell, stepped in front of Shashidhwaj. 'Calm down, Netoji,' he said, his voice loud and firm. 'The assassin is dead. This boy killed him.'

Looking down, Netoji noticed the body on the ground, lying in a spreading pool of blood, the sword still embedded in his chest. His eyes swung back to Raje. 'Are you hurt?' he asked anxiously.

Raje shook his head impatiently. 'It is just the assassin's blood you see. The boy sliced his hand off before he could touch me. Come, I must get out of here.' He took the cloth a guard offered him and cleaned himself as best he could.

As they walked out, Shashidhwaj saw Netoji look back at him, his eyes hard and inscrutable. Still stunned by what had transpired, Shashidhwaj followed the men out. Raje stopped outside and looked around. Everywhere there was confusion and an orgy of bloodletting.

'Stay your swords!' Raje shouted into the gathering darkness. 'Do not harm these men who have done us no harm! The one who attacked me is dead. An assassin sent by the Subhedar of this city!'

The Marathas, hearing his voice, paused. As the men saw he was indeed alive and unharmed, the chaos gradually subsided. The killing halted, leaving the survivors shaken and trembling. Bodies lay heaped one upon the other. The cloth of the shamiyana was splattered with blood in a macabre festival of colour.

As everyone turned to stare at Raje, still fearing to believe he had not been hurt or killed, he raised an arm into the air. 'What is done is done!' he declared. 'Every man is to get back to his post immediately.'

As the crowd thinned and cleared under the directions of the captains, Shashidhwaj reached Raje's side. 'Raje, this had to be a distraction!' His voice hoarse with urgency.

'How can you be so sure?'

'Look at what has happened around us,' Shashidhwaj implored. 'Our soldiers are running out of the city as the news has spread. Netoji will lead back those who have run here, but the city has three gates. Everyone will want to see you alive with their own eyes now that the news has broken. They will all want to come back to camp. Someone wanted this to happen.'

Raje stared at the young face for a moment, then nodded. 'The gold,' he said. 'They must be moving the gold.' He said over his shoulder, 'Netoji, take a party and ride back to the city. Make sure to give a patient hearing to any groups of our men you encounter running out. This is not the way we have drilled them to react.'

Netoji nodded and turned away, shouting for his horse to be fetched immediately.

'Raje,' Shashidhwaj said when Netoji had disappeared into the dusk, 'the topiwala…we must make him speak. He is connected to this in some way.'

Raje played with his beard thoughtfully. 'Why do you think so?' he asked, looking down at the eager young face.

'When all the topiwalas had barricaded themselves inside the factory, what was he doing walking around the streets?'

Raje said nothing.

'And why is he so anxious to go back now? Why does he not want to wait it out here? He'll be safer here, he knows that. If we were to let him go and then storm the factory, he would be a dead man.'

Raje nodded, his eyes searching for Moropunt in the crowd. He beckoned and the old man came quickly, clearly still shaken by what had transpired.

'Punt, let us assemble in my shamiyana. Bring Anthony Smith to me.'

Moropunt nodded and disappeared back into the milling crowd of men.

'Walk with me, lad,' Raje said, so Shashidhwaj followed a step behind. 'You saw what kind of man the topiwala is. He will not give away his secrets even if we torture him.'

'No, not easily,' Shashidhwaj murmured, as they walked back towards the shamiyana. He longed in that moment for Bahirji and Naik's reassuring presence.

'It is your job to make him talk, boy, whether willingly or not,' Raje replied, walking into the tent. 'I was almost killed. Now I will not rest until we get that damned gold in return.'

'I have an idea.' Shashidhwaj hesitated, not knowing how to disclose what was in his mind.

'Speak freely,' Raje said, glancing at Shashidhwaj.

'What if we let the man go?'

Raje's eyebrows lifted in surprise. 'What do you mean, boy?'

'The man was ready to have his head cut off, but he wanted to get back to the city first. It means there is some place he has to go.'

'And once we release him, he will run there,' Raje mused.

'And when he does, I will follow him,' Shashidhwaj said.

Raje nodded. 'So be it.'

***

Anthony Smith's face was bloodless as he knelt before Raje in the shamiyana. No trace remained inside of the bloody incident that had taken place. Moropunt and a few of the other Sardars stood on both sides of the divan. Shashidhwaj remained unobtrusively at the back, against the cloth wall.

'I have decided to give you another chance,' Raje said deliberately. 'The other traders have surrendered their wealth. But I am told that you are a poor man without many possessions. So I have decided to let you go if you offer everything in your purse to me.'

Smith quickly reached into his coat and drew out a small leather pouch and placed it upon the mat at Raje's feet.

Moropunt picked it up and emptied out its contents. Bronze coins clinked onto the mat. Crouching, Moropunt counted them one by one. 'Three hundred and fifty mahmudis,' he finally declared, looking up.

'Then that shall be the price of your ransom,' Raje said, his eyes fixed on Smith's pale face.

The Englishman appeared wary at first as the guards lifted him to his feet, and led him out. He wondered whether the Maratha was playing with him. But when the guards released him outside, he hesitated but a moment before taking off at a run towards the city gates as fast as his legs would carry him.

Back in the shamiyana, Raje looked at Shashidhwaj. 'He is all yours now,' he said.

Chapter Twenty-Four

The Master Unmasked

SECOND NIGHT OF THE SACK OF SURAT

As night fell and an almost full moon gleamed bright in the sky, Muhabbat Khan walked calmly through the streets with a dozen men behind him. Wearing chainmail armour and his helmet, he held his bare blade in his hand. The men with him were dressed in similar fashion. When Maratha patrols approached, they blended into the shadows and alleyways, waiting for them to pass. This night was not about battle.

In the last prahar, the patrols had reduced noticeably, while the hubbub outside the walls had increased. Vora had been right. Most of the Maratha raiders seemed to have rushed madly out of the city to see what had happened back in camp. Muhabbat Khan suppressed a smile. They would arrive to find their beloved leader dead.

'We shall search every building large enough to hold those oil barrels,' he had told his father before climbing down the riverside battlements. 'I shall find the gold and bring it to you. Then we shall leave, before the Emperor's henchmen come to find us.'

But now, out in the streets, he did not feel as confident. They had already searched the warehouses along the river, as well as in the *jakat ghar*. Where could the gold be? Then, as they passed the Church of St Jude, enveloped in smoke, a sudden thought crossed his mind. Fool! he berated himself. He had been the worst of fools for not having thought of it before.

'Break open the church doors!' he ordered.

The men rushed towards the barred doors with its rickety sign, 'Under Repair', held up by two hastily hammered nails. They attacked the doors as Muhabbat Khan looked around. The place appeared to be deserted; not a single Maratha patrol to be seen. One by one, the planks across the door were dislodged. The church had been closed for repairs just before the gold had reached the city. Was this mere happenstance? He cursed himself for his folly.

As the last plank came down and the doors were pushed open, Muhabbat Khan stepped forward. They were carrying no torches in order to conceal their presence, so he had to wait for his eyes to adjust to the blackness within. Then he saw the entire space was bare. The pews had been pushed against the walls. He cursed under his breath. But then it occurred to him that this was not the only church in the city.

'Let's move!' he shouted to his men.

Outside, he instructed them to keep to the alleyways again, away from the main streets. But there was a change of plan. They were to look inside every church.

***

On silent feet, Shashidhwaj and his two companions followed Anthony Smith at about a hundred paces, careful to ensure he did not notice them. The men with him were two of Bahirji-Naik's Guptachars. Moropunt had sent them to help track the Angrez Smith, who had fled the Maratha camp as fast as the wind, had slowed his pace when his lungs and legs began to protest. He was gasping for breath by the time he reached the gates of the city, but he did not stop till he was within the walls. Then he sank down on the ground, exhausted, waiting for his chest to stop heaving.

It was certain that Smith was in a great hurry to get somewhere. 'It is not the Angrez factory he is going towards,' Shashidhwaj whispered to the other two as they sidled round the market square that had once bustled with people and echoed to the cries of vendors. Now it was awash in fiery light and rang to the shouts of desperate people fleeing the flames. Nevertheless, he was certain his conjecture was correct. All he had to do was follow Smith to where he led.

It did not take Smith long to reach his destination. He crossed the market square, leading them eventually to the open gardens that adjoined the Capuchin Church in the northern section of the city. The gardens housed the Capuchin monks seminary, and to the north, beside the main street, stood the church with its high spire. Shashidhwaj looked up and saw the flames reaching avaricious hands towards the soaring spire. It would not survive the night. He sighed, knowing Raje had given his word to the Christian monks that their properties would not be touched. There were no raiders within the compound of the monastery. But the fire spreading through the city had no such promise to keep.

Smith ran across the grass and emerged onto the gravel on which the church stood. He stared at it for a moment and then walked on, eventually reaching the long, muddy road beside the river. Shashidhwaj knew there were several bunders along here, where smaller sailing vessels came. They watched Smith turn a corner and stop at a dark building. He peered about, as if expecting to see something or someone.'

'We will have to get closer to see what he's looking for,' Shashidhwaj said.

One of his companions pointed to a deserted house a few paces from them. They had halted in its shadow. The open doorway revealed the ghostly outline of a staircase. Shashidhwaj nodded, and the two men followed him through the door and up the stairway, silent as shadows. Having reached the top, they ran towards the side of the building that faced the river. Now they were above Smith, clearly visible below. As Shashidhwaj's eyes followed Smith's gaze, he let out a hiss of surprise.

Where the ground met the flowing waters of the river, a man was restlessly pacing about, apparently waiting for someone. Shashidhwaj stared intently. The man stopped to pull out a pocket watch, peering at it, visibly anxious. As the flickering light of the flames fell upon his face, Shashidhwaj's heart skipped a beat. There was something eerie about him. A black cloak covered him from head to feet. Black leather gloves shone in the meagre light, covering his hands. Suddenly a gust of wind blew back his hood. Shashidhwaj swore at what he saw. The man's face was covered with a black metallic mask, leaving small slits for his eyes and nose. Having noticed something, the man walked anxiously to the side of the road.

Shashidhwaj turned his head to see a group of men coming along the river road towards them. Armed with swords and spears, they were guarding two horse-drawn carts. As they drew near, Shashidhwaj saw they were carrying wooden barrels. That was all he needed to see. He turned to the men with him. 'Bahirji!' he said, his voice hoarse with urgency. 'Find Bahirji and bring him and his group here. We have found the gold!'

He knew Bahirji was somewhere in the city, probably near the house of Virji Vora. He also knew the Guptachars would be able to find him. They nodded, and ran for the stairs, not speaking a word in enquiry or surprise. Shashidhwaj peered down again and saw that Smith still stood hidden at the corner, observing the scene as he had since he arrived.

The armed convoy came to a halt about ten paces from the masked man. Their leader them came forward. Shashidhwaj recognized him immediately. Ali. The same man who had paid him to infiltrate the fort. He breathed in deeply and prayed Bahirji would come soon.

***

Ali faced the masked Master. He suddenly felt consumed by a towering rage he had never experienced before. But his face remained composed.

'Have you brought it?' the Master asked, walking forward to meet him.

Ali pointed to the carriages behind him. 'All of it,' he said.

'Good!' The Master turned. 'We must go. We do not have much time.'

Walking forward, Ali placed a hand on the Master's shoulder. 'Not so fast. There is something to do first.'

The Master's eyes glittered through the slits of his mask. 'You wish to see my face; know who I am? Surely it can wait till we reach the ship?'

Ali's hand remained on the Master's shoulder. 'That will not be necessary, for I already know who you are.'

The masked man struggled to free himself from Ali's grasp but could not. Rage burned in Ali. This man had deceived him all these days. Now it was his turn to land the final blow.

Suddenly, Smith walked forward from where he had been lurking in the shadows beside the house on the corner.

'You!' The Master stared at him as if he had seen a ghost.

'Yes, it is I!' Smith ran forward and quickly dislodged the contraption that held the Master's mask in place. In the scuffle, the mask fell to the ground. Blue eyes, dilated with fear, stared back at them.

Ali pulled out his sword and placed it against the Master's throat. He no longer felt shock as he stared into the blue eyes, only rage. Shock had enveloped him in the wooden cabin as he had watched the Angrez march through the city, Oxenden at their head. What a fool he had been! But the deception was finally over. Now he, Ali, would fulfill the destiny thrust upon him by his great ancestor, Khudwand Khan.

***

Shashidhwaj felt a hand creep onto his shoulder. He recoiled, grabbing at his sword. It was Bahirji, with a dozen men behind him. Shashidhwaj withdrew his hand from his sword and pointed downward, out of the window. 'The gold…' he whispered.

Bahirji's eyes rested on the cloaked man and the others below. He saw the cargo as well, but did not move. 'There are too many of them' he murmured in a low voice.

'But we must attack now!' Shashidhwaj exclaimed, trying to move.

Bahirji's hand pushed him back. 'I have sent a message to the Sarnaubat to bring his men here. Once they come, we will have the numbers. That is when we atack.'

Shashidhwaj sighed. 'And what until then?'

'Until then we observe,' Bahirji said.

***

Below them, Ali stared at Smith, holding the now maskless George Oxenden at gunpoint.

'How did you get here?' Oxenden looked from Smith to Ali. 'I do not understand.'

'That is because you thought yourself so smart and me too stupid.' Ali felt his anger go to his head. 'How very wise of you to learn my lineage and use it to gain my trust, handing me that fake heirloom!' He flung aside his cloak.The flintlock pistol was pointed straight at Oxenden's heart.

'But I helped you,' Oxenden pleaded. 'I showed you the way to the gold.'

'You merely planned to use me,' Ali said. 'When you told me to kill Parekh, you knew I would kill everyone there with the carriage. You wanted the Dutch killed all along. It served to disrupt their trade for a few months. All you have told me was to facilitate your own gains. I was to steal the gold and bring it to you. You were going to use me to have it loaded onto the getaway vessel, and then kill me and my men. That was the whole plan was it not?'

'No, I swear...' Oxenden protested. For the first time there was a quiver in his voice.

Ali held up a warning finger. 'The last time we were to meet, about instructions on moving the gold out of the city in the midst of the Maratha raid, you could not come personally as you had to march your men through the streets in a show of defiance.' Ali's finger dropped to his side. 'So you lent your cloak and mask to the man you trusted most.'

Ali turned to look at Smith. 'Well, your trusted man told me more that day than just how to get the gold out.'

Smith shrugged. 'You always planned to send the bullion back to England,' he told Oxenden. 'You wanted England to benefit in double measure, by accepting the tainted mahmudis from the Subhedar, as well as by retrieving the gold bullion from these corrupt bastards. You are a patriot, Sir, but it so happens I am not.'

'Your man brokered a deal with me in exchange for a stake in the gold.' Ali stared into Oxenden's eyes. 'This morning, you told him to sneak out of the city to Suwali, and instruct the men on the docks to send a small boat upriver at nightfall. The vessel was to carry half a dozen men armed with flintlock muskets. You were going to lead us to it and once we had loaded the gold, your men would have shot us all. Your man Smith here, delivered your message all right, but he also changed it. He told them to send a vessel, anchor at one of the bunders, and use a smaller boat to return to the Suwali. The vessel you look for is here alright, but empty.'

Smith looked at Oxenden's flushed face. 'I am sorry Sir, but I simply could not resist. When so much gold is offered, which man can be trusted not to be blinded by avarice?'

'Yes, when so much gold is offered, which man can be trusted?' Ali agreed. He gestured to his men, who grabbed Smith from behind, separating him from Oxenden.

'No!' shouted Smith, his face convulsed in fear, 'You promised!'

'You white men all think you are superior to us. Let me tell you that you are not.' He spat on the ground. 'You betrayed your own for gold,' Ali looked at Smith disdainfully. 'You would think nothing of doing the same to me. I do not wish to have anything to do with the likes of you. We retrieved the gold; we put our lives on the line for it; and to us it shall belong.'

'What will you do to us?' Oxenden asked.

Ali laughed. 'With the Marathas in the city and you two unarmed, I do not have to do anything. Unhand them!'

The last words were to his men, who kicked both the white men to the ground. Oxenden fell to his knees. Smith struggled, but they made him eat dust.

Ali looked at the two pitiful men lying in the mud by the river. He threw back his head and laughed. He had come a long way from being a street urchin in this filthiest of cities. This was finally his night, as it had once been his ancestor's when he had defeated a massive army at the very spot where Surat now stood. 'Onwards men!' he called. 'We do not have much time.'

The convoy of men and carts moved forward, raising dust. The men kicked and poked at the two Englishmen kneeling in the mud, as they went past. Oxenden could only watch the carts with the gold, his gold, rumble past.

Ali did not look back. Now all that kept him from his destiny were the hundred paces to the designated bunder on the river.

***

When Ali and his men had disappeared into the darkness, Shashidhwaj turned to Bahirji. 'Seize those Angrez!' he said. 'They will tell us about the gold.'

Bahirji nodded and gestured to his men. Below, Oxenden and Smith, getting to their feet, never heard or saw the Marathas descend upon them. They looked up to find themselves surrounded, the tall figure of Bahirji emerging from one of the dark houses nearby. Both men knew it was pointless to resist and slowly raised their hands, their cloaks fluttering like sails in the wind.

'Bind them,' Bahirji ordered.

Shashidhwaj stood watching as the men were frisked for weapons and their hands bound behind them. One of the Marathas pulled the two flintlocks from Oxenden's belt, while another tore the hood from his head.

***

Oxenden watched the men surround him on all sides, their swords held menacingly. Then his gaze fell on the man emerging from the dark. He breathed in sharply. Surely it was the donkey runner he had seen on the docks not three days ago? Only, the man was now wearing Maratha colours.

'Where is the gold?' the young boy with the donkey runner demanded, drawing his sword.

Oxenden cursed. How did they know about the gold? The boy brandishing the sword looked familiar as well, just as the older man had.

The donkey runner walked forward, amused by his silence. 'You better tell us about the gold, or it will be your head,' he said in plain English.

'Why not cut off his nose, then march him back to his factory and let him watch us burn it to the ground?' a tall Maratha by his side suggested.

A deep chill ran down Oxenden's spine. He knew from all the fires burning around him that the threat was real.

'Do they speak a different tongue back on your island?'

the donkey runner asked. 'Tell us where the gold is, or you heard what my friend here wants to do to you.'

Oxenden sighed. He knew he had a choice to make; only it was not really a choice. It was either the gold bullion he could have recovered for the home country, or the factory that was the commercial centre of their enterprise on these shores. Suddenly, he felt enraged by these heathens. 'I am not afraid of you!' he declared angrily.

'You should be.' The donkey runner took a step closer, barely a breath away now. He grabbed Oxenden by his cloak. In that instant, Oxenden felt his anger dissolve into fear.

'The gold or the factory, you decide.'

Oxenden looked into the man's eyes. Drawing on a deep well of resolve he hardly knew he possessed, he said, 'You must give me your word that if you take the gold, you will leave the English factory alone.'

'I give you my word,' the donkey runner agreed.

Suddenly, there was a great commotion. More Marathas had arrived on the scene, this time on horseback. The man leading them flung away the reins and jumped off his horse. 'Who do you have here, Bahirji?' he yelled.

'I have here the keys to the vault of Surat's Subhedar, Sarnaubat' the donkey runner replied. He looked back at Oxenden, his grip tightening.

'The river bank,' Oxenden said, looking sideways at Smith. 'The third bunder; the smallest along this stretch of the river. It is difficult to see a small vessel from the street there because the river is low. You will have to hurry. The man who took the gold will have reached it by now.'

The donkey runner let go. 'Horses!' he shouted to his men. 'Let this white man go!'

The men released Oxenden, but not Smith. 'What do you want done with this traitor?' the donkey runner asked, pointing his sword at Smith.

Oxenden turned to the man he had trusted so implicitly. He saw fear writ large on his sallow face. The man had betrayed him. He half wished he could see Smith's inert body lying in the dust at his feet. But he also knew judgment was not his to make. The man would be tried in Her Majesty's courts in London, and punished according to the law.

'Release him,' Oxenden said. 'I shall take him back with me to the factory.'

'So be it.' The donkey runner shrugged and gestured for the men to release Smith. 'Now run!' he said.

Smith took off like a child told that goblins were after him. Oxenden too, did not look back. He ran into the first alley he saw, away from their captors, swallowed by the night.

***

'Let me come with you!' Shashidhwaj pleaded as Bahirji mounted his horse. 'I found the gold and I should play a part in capturing it.'

Bahirji nodded. 'Give the boy a horse,' he ordered.

A soldier brought him one. The saddle was high but Shashidhwaj mounted into it without struggling.

'Let's ride,' Netoji said, giving his horse the office to start.

They rode forward together, the men behind them, raising a cloud of dust as they went.

Chapter Twenty-Five

Chasing Ali

SECOND NIGHT OF THE SACK OF SURAT

Muhabbat Khan watched the narrow building of the Capuchin Church from across the street. Dancing flames approached from both ends, threatening to engulf it. Finally, he raised his sword. 'Break open the doors!' he shouted.

The guards looked at each other, fear in their eyes. Their Captain said in a placating voice, 'The building will be on fire at any moment, Lord.'

'So do it before it is!' Muhabbat Khan burst forth. 'That door must be broken down now!'

The guards did not move.

'It is most inadvisable, Lord,' the Captain said again.

Muhabbat Khan stared at the fool angrily. Was anything around them that night advisable? They were walking through a city on fire, with enemies all around. 'Break the door open now!' he repeated imperatively.

The guards still stood looking at each other. Muhabbat

Khan felt consumed by anger. His mind was like a bubbling cauldron he could no longer control. A red haze coloured his vision. Picking up his sword, he set off, striding across the street. *They will follow when they see me breaking down the door,* he thought.

But when he glanced back, the mouth of the alley was empty. The soldiers had fled. '*Fools!*' Muhabbat Khan spat. In all the chaos, even one brick of gold a soldier might have hidden away would have made him a rich man. Nor would he have prevented them from doing it. Fools! Perhaps they were destined to remain bonded to soldiery and death.

The church doors were shut tight with a lock the size of a coconut. Muhabbat Khan did not bother with it. There was a stained glass window to the right, its vibrant colours almost alive in the firelight. He raised his blade and brought it down on the glass. It did not shatter at the first blow, bound together by its leaded panes. He raised his arm again and this time brought it down with considerable force. The glass shattered into a flying cascade of colourful fragments. Darkness loomed inside. Khan kicked aside the broken glass and climbed through, careful not to touch the shards that protruded around the edges like the teeth of some wide-jawed sea monster.

As his eyes adjusted to the darkness, he swore. Barrels filled the space from door to altar. He did not need to look twice to know that these were the same barrels that contained the gold. He cursed the men who had run for being frightened fools. He would now have to go back and tell them he had finally found what they had been looking for.

With heart beating hard against his ribs, Muhabbat Khan touched the first barrel. It felt moist in the hot air all around. He reached for the crowbar hanging at his waist and forced the cover open. He dipped his hand in and grimaced. His fingers were coated with sticky oil. He quickly moved to the next barrel and opened the cover. Oil again! Cursing under his breath, Khan moved from barrel to barrel, the air around him getting hotter and hotter. He noticed there were gaps between the barrels. Some were missing. He opened one right in the centre. Oil again. Burning with anger, Khan kicked it viciously. The liquid spilled over the stone floor in a reluctant, viscous flood.

Muhabbat Khan realized that whoever had brought the barrels here had moved the ones with the gold, leaving only the ones containing the oil. But he had to be sure before he could leave. Even if he found one barrel with gold, that the thieves had overlooked, it would be worth the effort. Like a man possessed, Khan opened barrel after barrel. It was futile. The same black liquid gleamed up at him each time. Possessed by a strange madness that would not let him stop, he kept moving towards the altar. Panting with exhaustion, he hooked his crowbar into the lid of another barrel and pried it open. When he saw the oil, he kicked the barrel angrily, spilling its contents. It had been a fool's errand.

Khan took a deep breath to calm himself. He counted the remaining unopened barrels around him. If only he could find just one with gold! He smashed his crowbar against the one nearest him. The wood splintered and a slimy puddle formed at his feet. Oil again. In that moment he thought that those who had left had been the wiser ones; it was he who was the fool. He wiped the sweat dripping from his brow into his eyes. It was hot and suffocating now, as the fire outside devoured the oxygen in the air like a ravenous creature with tongues of flame.

The stained windows along the wall shattered as the fire reached the church. Muhabbat Khan stared at the flames creeping in with wide-eyed horror. Looking up, he noticed the sloping roof was aflame as well. He dashed towards the door, but his feet slithered and slipped on the oily floor. He fell with a thud. He tried to rise, pushing with his hands, but could find no purchase as they too, slipped in the thick oil around him. The air kept getting hotter as the flames spread. Muhabbat Khan watched in helpless horror as a beam above him erupted in flames. His shouts were drowned in the crackling blaze. He gazed in horror at his oil-covered body and rolled over the floor, barrel to barrel, in a desperate effort to flee. It was in vain.

Muhabbat Khan was still moving when a burning spark torched the oil around him. The last thing he saw was the huge burning beam above him, and the stained glass window above the altar shining with unearthly light, as if beckoning him to the doors of heaven. Then the flames engulfed him in a blazing hell.

***

Ali stopped his horse at the designated bunder. He looked back as the carts lurched to a halt like overweight ladies grateful for a reprieve. 'Hurry!' he called. 'We do not have much time.'

Hatim jumped down from one of the carts, sweat running down his face. 'Look sharp men!' he ordered, as they began to haul the oil barrels down from the carts.

Ali ran down the stone steps to the wooden boardwalk. The large-sized boat was there, tied to the anchorage with a thick rope; rising and falling with the current. He pulled on the rope with both hands. There was no time to lose. Over his shoulder he saw the men rolling the first barrel down the slope to the wooden pier. Ali helped load it into the boat. The water splashed as the boat swung from the sudden load. Ali did not stop. He helped lift the second barrel in. As if in protest, the boat sank a finger deeper into the sloshing water.

***

Shashidhwaj rode along the river with Bahirji and Netoji. The air felt cool in his face, the fires being left behind. His eyes scanned the river continuously.

'There!' Bahirji said, pointing.

Oxenden had spoken the truth. It was the third bunder on the river where dark figures were moving. Shashidhwaj saw the toiling figures carrying barrels from the carts to the boat, and immediately kicked his horse into a gallop.

***

They had loaded a dozen barrels when Ali saw the horsemen flying towards them. He cursed under his breath. They had been so close!

'Rayiyas!' Hatim called from the shore, fear ringing in his voice. 'They come!'

'Let them.' Ali reached for the flintlock pistol that hung at his belt. He cocked it and pointed it at the riders, taking aim. He waited till he could not miss, then pulled the trigger.

***

Shashidhwaj felt a sudden blast of hot air hit him even as he watched in horror Bahirji's horse stagger to the ground, a bloody mess. He saw Netoji pull on his reins and look towards Bahirji as well.

'Go! I'm fine,' Bahirji shouted even as he struggled to free himself from under the horse. The dry earth sucked thirstily at the warm blood.

***

A hand-to-hand skirmish erupted on the river bank as the Marathas fell upon Ali and his men. Gripping his sword, Shashidhwaj, joined in the fray. Until then, he had always wondered how it was that soldiers ran headlong into battle, unafraid. Now, his blood rushing through his veins like a wild horse galloping free, he understood. He hacked and slashed his way into the fray, never feeling the cuts he received from the swords of the enemy.

Somewhere to the left, Netoji was fighting too. He pierced his sword into a man's heart and then, as the man fell like a felled tree, placed his foot upon his chest and pulled out his blade, the dead man's blood splattering his face. '*Har Har Mahadev!*' he yelled at the top of his lungs, looking like some *asura* of legend.

As he fought on, Shashidhwaj kept an eye on the man at the very back of the fray. He knew they were here to get the gold, not just win a fight. And Ali knew that too.

***

From where he stood near the boat, Ali watched his men fight off the Maratha attack. He saw Hatim and another man load the last of the barrels onto the boat and then look towards him for instructions.

Ali took a deep breath. He had a decision to make. He wondered how his ancestor, the great Khudwand Khan would have behaved at such a moment. Just then, a Maratha arrow flew past and embedded itself in quivering fury into the side of the boat, narrowly missing him. Ali knew the time for cogitation was over. 'Get on board!' he called to Hatim.

'Rayiyas?' Hatim gazed at him wide-eyed. 'We must fight with our men.'

Ali shook his head. 'We cannot win this.' The Marathas were too numerous. 'Board now! We sail with the gold, just the two of us.'

But Hatim stood frozen. 'I cannot do that, Rayiyas,' he said.

'Are you a fool?' Ali yelled angrily. There was no time for fruitless argument. He saw another of their men fall. Grabbing Hatim's shoulder, he pulled him towards the ship. But Hatim jerked away.

'Are you insane, Hatim?' Ali yelled. 'We must go now!'

'You go.' Hatim looked him in the eye.

In those eyes, Ali saw only a deep dark void; all trace of friendship and respect had disappeared. 'If my men, *your* men, die here today, then we must die with them. We got this gold together. We risked our lives for it. And we shall reap its benefits together, or not. I will fight with my brothers. You should do the same.'

Ali watched wide-eyed as Hatim turned and ran towards the

fight, his sword held high. But before he could reach the thick of the action, an arrow swooped through the air, piercing his neck from side to side like a trussed fowl on a spit. Hatim fell sideways, the momentum of his run going into the fall.

Ali let out a hissing breath. But there was no time to mourn the dead. He turned and ran for the boat. Behind him, his men fought on, to the last man.

***

As Shashidhwaj sliced his sword through another enemy, a hand pulled him back. It was Bahirji. 'He is escaping,' he said, pointing.

Shashidhwaj saw that Ali had already climbed into the boat and was savagely hacking at the rope holding the craft to the bunder with his sword.

'We must stop him,' Bahirji said.

With one accord, they moved out of the thick of the fighting to where they could approach the boat. Two of Ali's men lashed out at them, but Bahirji made short work of them with his sword. 'Come!' he yelled to Shashidhwaj.

They crossed into the enemy's rear. The boat was now less than ten strides away. Ali saw them coming and hacked harder at the ropes.

'You bastard!' Netoji yelled from the centre of the melée, having noticed Ali as well. He raised his sword and directed the archers to release their arrows towards the fleeing man. But Ali held his ground, ducking below the hull as the arrows pierced it in shivering quivers. When he raised his head, he was holding his flintlock pistol.

'Look out!' Shashidhwaj yelled even as the gun fired,

Bahirji ducked behind one of the poles that stood along the boardwalk like silent sentinels. Dropping the gun, Ali began hacking at the ropes again. A last rope remained.

By now, Netoji had also crossed over to the rear. 'Board the vessel!' he yelled.

The Marathas gained ground as Ali's men fell, yet many remained, prepared to fight to the death.

'Ready?' Bahirji shouted, looking towards Shashidhwaj, who nodded.

They made a run for the boat together. From the corner of his eye, Shashidhwaj saw Netoji do the same. They reached the vessel together and ran across the wooden gangplank in a line. At the same instant, Ali finally managed to free the vessel from its moorings and it began to move away from the bunder. The river current pulled it away, the laden craft creaking and swaying. Netoji, the last of the three on the gangplank, leapt across the watery divide as the boat moved down-river.

'Duck!' Bahirji yelled as Ali picked up his flintlock again, having refilled the powder and aimed it.

The blast erupted near them, splintering wood, as Shashidhwaj hid behind one of the wooden barrels containing the gold. The ship moved sluggishly forward, and then more quickly as it caught the current. The fighting on the bunder disappeared into the darkness behind them. The glow of the city fires reflected on the water as the three Marathas converged on Ali. Seeing this, Ali threw down his cumbersome flintlock and pulled out his sword.

Netoji was the first to charge, but Ali deflected his blow with his blade and moved quickly to one side. Bahirji moved in to corner him from the other side. But before either could make a move, Ali sprinted between them, straight at Shashidhwaj.

Shashidhwaj raised his sword to defend himself, but Ali's momentum threw him back, and he fell with a thud onto the wooden deck. He quickly composed himself, hanging onto his sword with a white-knuckled grip. Netoji and Bahirji had rushed after Ali by then and Ali turned to face them. Shashidhwaj used the moment to spring to his feet. He grabbed Ali from behind with all his strength and placed his sword across the back of his neck. Netoji quickly disarmed Ali and then punched him squarely in the gut. Ali moaned in pain as the sword fell from his hand.

'Don't move!' The tip of Netoji's sword touched Ali's chest.

Shashidhwaj's blade still sat across the back of Ali's neck. He stood still, giving up his efforts to pick up the weapon. The boat moved on, waddling from side to side like an obese matron.

'We have to stop the boat.' Bahirji leaned over the railing, watching the river push them in the direction of the open sea.

Netoji nodded. 'Let's drop anchor.' With his free hand, he pointed to the front of the vessel, where the heavy iron anchor and rope lay on the deck, a reminder of many a voyage in deep waters.

Bahirji ran towards it shouting, 'Help me!'

Netoji hesitated for a moment, then dropped his sword arm and ran to help push the heavy anchor over the side. The weight of the anchor pulled the rope taut as it disappeared into the water. Shashidhwaj continued to stand guard, his sword firmly against the back of Ali's neck, waiting for the vessel to slow and stop.

They felt the anchor hit the river bottom and the large boat jerk to a halt. Netoji and Bahirji looked at each other and began to laugh. Just then, they felt another jerk and Shashidhwaj was thrown off-balance. The boat began to move again as the anchor slipped along the riverbed.

The fall shifted Shashidhwaj's sword from Ali's neck and as he hit the deck, he saw Ali grasp his flintlock and run. 'Look out!' he yelled.

But it was too late. Ali had reached the railing, his flintlock raised. Bahirji and Netoji halted in their tracks, looking at the gleaming barrel of the weapon pointed straight at them.

'Prepare to meet your Maker!' Ali shouted, even as the boat once again plunged into an uneven roll from side to side.

In that instant, Shashidhwaj did not care about his own life. All he saw was the flintlock pointing straight at Bahirji. Springing to his feet, he dashed towards the railing. Ali never knew what hit him as Shashidhwaj rammed into him. The flintlock fell from his hand. He turned to grapple with his assailant, and in the skirmish, both fell overboard, their arms interlocked.

As he let go of Ali, Shashidhwaj felt the water rise over his head, pulling him down. He kicked his legs hard. As he surfaced, he felt Ali's arm grip him tight. His other hand held the anchor rope, and they were both dragged along in the water. Shashidhwaj struggled to free himself, but Ali's grip tightened around his neck.

Shashidhwaj struggled to breathe as he desperately thrashed with his legs. Ali's grip on his throat was still strong. Shashidhwaj jerked his elbow backwards, hitting Ali in the ribs, still Ali did not release him. He looked up in horror at Netoji on the stern of the boat, as the rope dragged them along. He felt himself sinking into the water.

Suddenly, a loud crack rang out and he felt Ali's grip loosen. Finally, he broke free. Kicking hard, he rose to the surface and sucked in the night air like a greedy infant at his mother's breast. Looking back, he saw Ali hands move away as he slowly disappeared into the turbulent waters.

Shashidhwaj looked towards the boat and saw Netoji standing in the stern in the light from the lanterns abooard, his outstretched hand holding Ali's flintlock, its muzzle still smoking. He had blown away Ali's head.

'We are even now, boy!' he yelled.

Bahirji leaned over the railing, shouting, 'Let go of the rope, boy!'

Shashidhwaj, who had grabbed the rope instinctively, loosened his grip. He felt the rough hemp slide over his palm as the force of the water carried him away. Shashidhwaj managed to drag himself onto one of the rocks that dotted the riverside and lay there panting like a grounded platypus. Turning his head, he saw the boat drifting some distance away. He got to his feet shakily.

'The current is too strong!' he heard Bahirji shout across the water. 'We will have to navigate back to the coast once we reach the open sea. Ride to camp, boy! Tell Raje to send riders along the coast to get us!'

Shashidhwaj waved his arm to communicate he had understood. Carefully, he made his way back to land and then started running down the road towards the bunder. He caught sight of a horse, cantering riderless along the road, no doubt fleeing the fight at the bunder. Shashidhwaj ran towards it, clucking through his teeth. Seeing an unfamiliar figure, the horse reared back on its hind legs, neighing in panic. But Shashidhwaj quickly caught its reins and patted its mane, calming the frightened animal as best he could. In one swift motion, he mounted into the saddle and pulled the horse around. It was evidently a trained animal for it obeyed the hand on its bridle. Leaving the river, Shashidhwaj guided it in the direction of Navasari Gate.

***

The fabric of the shamiyana fluttered, and Moropunt's turban with it, as a gusty morning wind blew over the Kabaristan. It travelled over the city, nudging the flames gently, making them rise higher in some places, extinguishing them in others, before losing itself in the sea. It was only in the light of day that the horror of the raid became apparent. To Shashidhwaj, it no longer looked like the city he knew so well. Houses were still burning and smoke colluded in the sky. There was more rubble than rooftops. An eerie silence defied the senses. He took a deep breath and kept moving, heading beyond the walls to the Maratha camp.

As the shamiyana drew closer, exhaustion began to overtake Shashidhwaj. Moropunt saw him approach and reported it to Raje, who came out and stood at the entrance of the tent.

It took Shashidhwaj all the strength he possessed to pull on the reins and stop his horse. He got off, his limbs shaking. 'We found the gold,' he panted.

'Where is it?' Raje asked, walking forward.

'On a boat on the river.' Shashidhwaj tried to remain upright, but his head was spinning. Utter exhaustion from two nights without sleep, and all that had happened, rushed upon him like a tidal wave. 'Bahirji is on board. He asked me to bring you word to send men down the coast.'

Raje nodded, his face serious. He said to Moropunt, 'Give the command to Tanaji of the Malusare clan. I shall talk to him myself before he leaves. We must send men, horses and carriages down the coast at once.'

Moropunt nodded and hurried away. Raje's gaze returned to Shashidhwaj, desperately holding onto his mount's saddle for support. As exhaustion overcame him, he toppled forward muttering, 'Tired…so tired…'

Raje rushed forward to catch him. 'Summon a vaidya immediately,' he called over his shoulder.

Shashidhwaj could not tell who Raje spoke to but he felt hands lifting and placing him flat on the ground. Heavy weights seemed to force his eyelids closed. 'Bahirji…' he murmured, 'he is still there.'

'Yes, and he will bring back the gold. You did well, boy.'

Raje's smiling face and the blue sky were the only things Shashidhwaj could see. 'I did it for the Swarajya,' he managed to say.

'Didn't we all,' Raje replied, smiling down at him. 'Rest now, boy. Let me take care of the rest.'

The words seemed to have a magical power for Shashidhwaj felt all the cares of the world vanish. He no longer felt the burning sensation in his arms, nor cared about the dirt and blood coating his skin, nor smelt the thick smoke in the air.

The noise around him seemed to fade away. The last thing he heard was Raje instructing someone to attend to him, probably the vaidya. Then there was only silence.

Chapter Twenty-Six

The Departure

FINAL DAY OF THE SACK OF SURAT

When he opened his eyes, Shashidhwaj was still lying under the open sky. He moved his head and saw Naik. Grunting, he propped himself up on one elbow.

Seeing this, Naik's lips bent in a crooked smile. 'I hope you had a good sleep,' he said.

Shashidhwaj sat up. His head spun. He looked around, feeling disoriented. He was still in the Kabaristan, but was lying away from the shamiyana, on a hastily made hay-bed. Naik was sitting to one side, his clothes dusty, his face blackened with soot.

'What are you doing here?' Shashidhwaj asked. 'What happened to your face?'

'Whatever you did in the city caused the smoke to rise up towards our hill lookout points.' Naik wiped his face with his arm. 'It was the blackest smoke I have ever seen.'

'But you are not on the lookout now, which means…'

Naik nodded. 'The Mughal army is fifty kos from the city.

Our men are packing as we speak. I rode and delivered the news to Raje some time ago. Moropunt brought me to you.'

'So I have been asleep?'

'For a full day and an entire night. Moropunt was worried about you. But I for one know how much you love to sleep,' Naik said matter-of-factly.

'Where is Bahirji?' Shashidhwaj asked. *And what became of the gold?*

'Relax, boy.' Naik placed a hand on his shoulder. 'Bahirji piloted the boat to the coast, just beyond the city. The gold is now in our custody. The caravan there is already loaded up and will join us as we depart.'

Shashidhwaj let out a deep breath and fell back upon the prickly hay. 'We did it,' he murmured, looking at the sky.

'Indeed we did, boy.'

Shashidhwaj's heart felt full. A lump rose in his throat. There were so many things he wanted to tell Naik, about what had happened to Fatima, the Englishmen, the chase through the burning streets, being dragged through the water… but he had a feeling Naik already knew. Instead, he said, 'The city is gone.'

Naik stared in the direction of the city walls. 'It is still burning,' he agreed. 'And it will continue to burn long after we are gone.'

Shashidhwaj got to his feet. Following Naik's gaze, he saw once again the destruction the raiders had left in their wake. He felt suffocated by his emotions. In the silence of that moment, a thousand feelings fought for space within him.

Neither of them saw Moropunt scurrying towards them until he stood directly in front, blocking their view. 'I see that you are awake,' he said to Shashidhwaj. 'Raje asked me to take you to him once you were. He is worried about you.'

Shashidhwaj turned and looked at the shamiyana. The extra supports protecting it from the wind were gone, and it stood ready to be dismantled as quickly as it had been put up.

'Come, we do not have much time.' Naik patted him on the back, and they began walking towards the tent.

'I wonder what Nanaji would say if he was here,' Shashidhwaj said, a boyish grin on his face.

The question brought a smile to Naik's lips. 'He would say there is too much smoke in the air. What is Bahirji smoking?' he chuckled.

Shashidhwaj looked up, laughing. He suddenly remembered something. 'Do you know how they caught the black Abyssinian from the sarai?' he asked.

'How?' Naik asked, curious. He had missed that story.

'We didn't have to do anything. He came here himself and handed over his treasure at Raje's feet.'

'Did he now?' Naik appeared amused.

'He said that if Aurangzeb liked to keep him waiting for an audience, he too would have to wait for his *nazrana*.'

'Never thought he had such a sense of humour,' Naik said.

'Not only that, he fell at Raje's feet and asked to be taken into the ranks of our army! He said he had nothing left back home. Raje agreed, so he is now one of our comrades.'

Naik suppressed a chuckle. 'We will have to be careful sleepers if he now rests among us.'

They were now at the shamiyana entrance. Shashidhwaj looked up at Naik. 'What will he say to me?' he asked. It had somehow been easy to converse with Raje in the heat of battle, but now it was awkward and strange.

'Let's go in and find out,' was all Naik said.

They walked into the tent together.

***

Inside, it felt strangely calm, as if the chaos and noise outside was magically filtered out by the tent cloth. There were others there too – Netoji, Prataprao, and the other mansabdars who had led the raid on the city. Moropunt stood in front, waiting for Raje's arrival. The only missing person appeared to be Bahirji, who was still out with the carts carrying the gold to join the main convoy.

Shashidhwaj stared at the leather scabbard that hung on a wooden stand. The golden hilt shone in the soft light that penetrated the pale tent fabric.

'The *Bhavani Talvar!*' he whispered to Naik, awed at how close he was to the revered weapon, claimed to have been bestowed on Raje by the Goddess herself.

'It's just an ornament,' Naik murmured. 'He never uses it in battle.'

'How do you know so much about him?' Shashidhwaj asked curiously.

Naik merely smiled.

'Raje approaches!' a sentry announced outside.

Everyone straightened as Raje entered the tent nonchalantly. He stared at Shashidhwaj silently for a few moments, then approached Naik. Reaching out, he placed a hand on his shoulder. 'This raid could not have succeeded without the guptachars.'

'We did what we had to, Sarkar, as always,' Naik replied.

'As always,' Raje agreed.

Shashidhwaj's heart started beating fast as Raje turned back to him. 'I do not know how to express my gratitude to one so young and fearless,' he said, placing a hand on Shashidhwaj's head. 'You saved my life. The men have also told me what you did to capture the gold.'

Shashidhwaj looked down at his feet, unaccustomed tears blurring his vision. 'For the Swarajya, Raje,' he managed to say. He felt a reassuring hand on his shoulder. Naik.

'You were right when you said this boy would be gold,' Raje remarked, glancing at Naik.

'It is said I am a good judge of men,' Naik replied.

'Not better than me, I suppose?' Raje smiled, lifting an eyebrow. From his hand, he pulled a ring from his little finger. 'Take this,' he said, extending it to Shashidhwaj.

Shashidhwaj shrank back hastily. 'I cannot…' he protested.

'Do you refuse a gift from your Raje?'

Shashidhwaj did not dare. Silently, eyes lowered, he stepped forward and held out his cupped palms. But his gaze was dragged upwards as Raje lifted one of his hands and slipped the ring onto his index finger. Shashidhwaj knew the ring would never leave his finger all the days of his life. He could not forbear glancing at Netoji, standing stiffly to one side.

'Now, there is one more thing left to do.' Raje looked towards Moropunt.

Punt gestured to the guards at the entrance. They went out and almost immediately the tent flap lifted and a soldier was escorted in. Shashidhwaj stared at him wide-eyed. He looked strangely familiar. Then his eyes fell to the man's bandaged left hand and he knew. It was the Mavla he had attacked outside Haji Kasim's house.

'It is a code amongst us Marathas, that no crime is left unpunished,' Raje said, addressing everyone in the tent. 'This boy has shown remarkable valour in capturing the gold for our Swarajya. But as Netoji himself witnessed, he also, in a fit of blind rage, attacked one of his own brothers-in-arms.'

Shashidhwaj's mind began to buzz like a swarm of bees, until he felt Naik's hand drop onto his shoulder. At that he composed himself.

'We bless the boy for his service,' Raje continued, 'but he must also be punished for his crime.'

Shashidhwaj saw the malicious gleam in Netoji's eyes, even as he his own respect for Raje increased a hundredfold at these portentous words.

'A thumb for a thumb,' Raje declared, raising his hand, 'taken by the man he hurt. That is justice in a just Rajya. We cannot ever be blind to what is just.'

Shashidhwaj felt his heart beat hard against his ribs. Naik bent and grasped him by both shoulders. 'Face it like a man,' he said, his face hard.

Shashidhwaj nodded. He felt no fear. Instead, a strange sense of calm enveloped his senses. He walked towards the table where the Mavla stood, holding the knife, and placed his left palm, face down, on the wooden surface.

'Clench your teeth,' Naik rumbled in his ear, standing close behind him.

Shashidhwaj closed his eyes and obeyed. The soldier brought down the knife in one swift motion. Shashidhwaj felt warm blood spurt from where his thumb had been. Hot, searing pain hit his body in seething waves. The vaidya moved in and took his hand, applying pressure. He rubbed on a potion and then tied a wet cloth around his hand. Immediately, the cloth was soaked scarlet. Shashidhwaj stood in silence, his eyes closed, his mind far away.

When he opened his eyes, the face before him was that of Raje, who nodded and patted Shashidhwaj on the shoulder before turning away.

'You did well,' Naik murmured in Shashidhwaj's ear.

Raje looked around him. 'I hereby grant you liberty to enjoy this shamiyana till we are ready to depart.' So saying, he walked away.

Shashidhwaj took Raje at his word and sank down on the calico-covered ground, lying back with eyes closed, giving in to blessed oblivion. When he opened his eyes again, it was evening. It was time to depart.

The Marathas moved as the sun disappeared behind the horizon, leaving red splendour in its wake. The horses pulled the heavy carts up the slope that led away from the city. From the top of the hill, it appeared like a massive exodus.

'It's finally over,' Shashidhwaj said, knowing he would never forget this sight. Bahirji was a dot at the very front, leading the way.

'It isn't done until we are safely back on Rajgad,' Naik reminded him. 'Though I am sure it is just a matter of time.'

'So the Swarajya is saved.'

'Indeed it is, boy,' Naik nodded, his face grave.

A smile spread over Shashidhwaj's face like an incoming tide.

***

From the eastern bastion of the fort, Inayat Khan watched the Marathas break camp. There were tears in his eyes and his hands were clenched into fists. His son Muhabbat Khan had gone into the city the previous night and not returned. Nor had any of those who had accompanied him. But it was not grief over his son that distressed his mind just then. He knew the departure of the Marathas meant only one thing. The news had reached Agra and another Mughal Subhedar was now on the march towards Surat, with a large army. He knew that in the investigation that would inevitably follow this raid, it would be impossible to hide his actions from the Emperor. In the little time he had, Inayat Khan had ordered all official records that could incriminate him destroyed and fresh ones created, to safeguard his position as well as he could. Documents were burned and clerks sat endlessly, making hasty entries.

When he received word that Muhabbat Khan could not be found anywhere in the smouldering, smoking city, he had stopped his efforts. He had known the truth in that moment. His son was dead. Now, as he watched the enemy load their carts and depart, a long line of ants going over the hill into the dusk, a well of despair flooded Inayat Khan's being. He wondered what the future would be, how Agra would treat him once it was known what he had done.

For a few moments his mind urged him to jump off the ramparts. Surely it would be a quicker, more merciful end than all the cruel torture he had heard about. Hell was better than what happened to traitors in Agra. But somehow he could not muster the courage to jump. He stood there for a long time, resigned to his fate. He watched the last of the Maratha horde depart into the dusk, leaving behind only chaos and destruction.

***

Virji Vora watched, lost in the crowd gathered in the courtyard, as the massive gates of the fort finally opened. He watched as the drawbridge was lowered slowly. When it hit the ground with a thud, the crowd swarmed forth over it like a dam that had burst its banks. He watched his servants bring forward his own palkhi and put it down. Resting a hand on the shoulder of one of the palkhi-bearers, he climbed into it. Sitting down on the cushioned seat, he breathed a weary sigh of relief.

'Where to, Shethji?' his superintendent asked, knowing that most of the city had been reduced to rubble.

'To the river,' Vora said.

The superintendent stepped back without comment. The bearers lifted the palkhi and moved forward. They were obliged to wait for the crowd at the drawbridge to clear, but finally they moved out of the shadow of the fort walls.

Vora left the curtains open as they moved along the streets. Everywhere, he saw disorder, buildings burnt to the ground, exposing columns that looked like forlorn sentinels frozen in time. The stench of rotting garbage, dead animals, human blood and excreta, stifled the senses. The very air was full of soot; he could feel it in every breath he took. As they passed through the main market, he saw the wide square completely vacant. On a regular day there would have been no place for a man to stand. Now it was deserted, not a figure in sight. Burnt bamboos lay strewn everywhere, remnants of the burnt down stalls.

As they turned alongside the river, he saw the carcasses of horses, and corpses of men, fallen no doubt in a bid to resist the raiders. Finally, he came to where Haji Kasim's magnificent white house had once stood. He could not recognize the place. Only the exposed skeleton of the house remained, a ghostly presence.

'Stop!' he ordered, and the palkhi came to a halt.

He stared at the burnt shell of the house of a man he had hated and feared, and often wished dead. But, at that moment, Vora felt nothing but pathos and pity. He knew the markets would be easier to control without a man like Kasim there to check his every move. And certainly some other would claw his way up from the bottom to take Kasim's place, but Vora did not want to think of that now. He would cross the bridge when he came to it, in the same way he had crossed over Kasim. He knew he would recoup whatever had been seized in the raid by the Marathas. Without Kasim's opposition in the markets, it would be quickly achieved.

'Take me home,' he ordered.

As the palkhi moved forward, Vora jerked the curtains to and sat back. Like the other inhabitants of the city, he prepared himself to look upon what remained of his house and possessions after the raid.

***

Sir George Oxenden, hand on hip, observed the damage to the factory gate. It would need to be strengthened and repainted, but did not require total replacement. He let out a deep breath, knowing he had successfully negotiated past the fearsome danger to the factory, the men, and to himself. Certainly, he had lost the gold, but it had long since been exchanged for mahmudis. So all he had lost was a bonus profit for the Company.

He had already started thinking of how he could use the sack of the city to his advantage. Perhaps he could ask Agra for a tax relief, citing damages caused by the raid. He was sure the Badshah would grant it, already worried over the prospect of traders leaving Surat, and fearing another raid.

But Oxenden was not afraid. In fact, he was intrigued. Here, in this foreign land, there was no stability, just infighting. Each man concerned only with carving out his own fiefdom. Oxenden wondered whether he had strayed into another age, like that of the Germanic tribes and ancient Rome. The stories his nanny had often related to him in childhood, to warn against bad behaviour, now came back to him. He suddenly smiled, realizing he could use the same tactics against the natives here, that the Romans had used in Gaul. Oxenden knew his people had a great future here. They were just getting started.

***

Shashidhwaj rode with Bahirji in front and Naik behind, part of the long Maratha march back to the shadow of the Sahyadri Hills. They separated a little from the others to look back upon the city from the hillock on which they stood; the burnt houses, the smoke rising up into the sky.

'We have destroyed the city,' Shashidhwaj said as realization dawned upon him. 'The life of these people will never be the same again.'

'You are wrong, boy. They will be back to normal in a year,' Bahirji replied. 'Baniyas always get back on their feet. The streets will be flooded with goods, coin and corruption soon enough. Perhaps we should pay another visit here. The people may change a little, but trade will not.'

'They will build a stronger wall,' Shashidhwaj mused.

'It will be all the more challenging then,' Bahirji smiled.

Gazing at the destruction, a sudden feeling of sorrow overcame Shashidhwaj. 'How are we different from the Mughals?' he asked. 'They loot our lands, we loot theirs. They destroy the lives of our people, we do the same. How are we different? How is the Swarajya different?'

Bahirji smiled. 'In truth,' he said, 'we are not so different. Nor is our Swarajya. Except that we belong to the Swarajya. It is our's. We belong to its soil. It is who we are. The Mughals came here to our lands and became overlords. They did for their people what we are now doing for ours. It is just the clashing of two Swarajyas, one old, and one new.'

'Except that our's does not yet have the corruption, strife and guile we see in theirs,' Shashidhwaj reflected.

'Not yet, boy, not yet…' Naik pulled on the reins to calm his mount. 'We do not know what will happen in the future.'

'But that is why we are here, is it not?' Shashidhwaj said. 'To keep a watchful eye? To tell Raje when someone does not abide by the rules; to warn him when an enemy threatens; to safeguard our borders and save the Swarajya from danger?'

Naik nodded, amused by the idealism that underlay the lad's words. 'That will be our job when the Swarajya is at peace, established and settled,' he said. 'For now, our job is to win Raje's victories before they are even fought, and lay waste our enemies. Now you are one of us. Hell, after all you have seen and done, even I must accept it!'

Shashidhwaj looked at him. Joy flooded his being. What he had yearned for had finally come to pass. Yet, looking at the death and destruction of the desolate city below them, his face remained grave.

They heard a sentry call out, 'Bahirji! Naik! Raje wishes to see you now.'

Bahirji smiled. 'And here we go again.' His mouth curved in a crooked smile. He and Naik heeled their horses and moved past the long column to where Raje's pennant flew.

Shashidhwaj watched them go, knowing in his heart and mind that he too, was one of them now - the people who did what had to be done, sometimes even kill, for the good of their Swarajya. He was now one of its silent guardians, the watchers on the walls, the ears in dark corners, and the eyes in the heavens.

He was a Guptachar.

THE STORY CONTINUES IN BOOK II: SIEGE OF PANHALA

Epilogue

RECORDS OF THE TIME SUGGEST that Surat burned for three more days after the departure of the Maratha raiders. About three thousand buildings were destroyed. The entire city was brought to its knees.

Mughal forces reached Surat after the Marathas had departed with their loot. They were too late to chase the escaping Maratha army to the South, or attempt to recover the loot. Inayat Khan was removed from the post of Subhedar and taken to Delhi under arrest, to answer for his failures.

On the request of George Oxenden, Badshah Alamgir waived the *Jakat* tax for a year to give relief to the trader community for the staggering losses they had suffered in the sack. Also, taxes on all English imports were reduced by a half per cent for one year, to reward the courage shown by the English in defending their factory and surrounding areas, none of which were touched in the raid. A mere ninety years later, the English had made themselves political masters of Surat.

Virji Vora's net worth rose immensely in the years following the sack. By 1670, he was one of the richest men in the Indian subcontinent.

Anthony Smith was deported to England after the sack of Surat. In one letter written during that time, an Englishman described Smith as, 'A more athiestical wretch than Anthony Smith never was Suffer'd to live on the earth.' The exact reasons given for the hasty departure remain unknown, as does his eventual fate.

The Marathas managed to obtain a huge booty from Surat, thereby saving the Swarajya from imminent collapse.

To avoid the same kind of situation in Surat again, the new Subhedar, Ghayasdin Khan, oversaw the construction of a massive fortified wall to surround the city, to safeguard it against future invaders.

Despite all the precautions taken by the Mughals, the Marathas sacked Surat again in 1670, crossing the hundreds of miles to Surat as stealthily as shadows in the night. The raid once again came as a complete surprise to the Mughals.

Both sackings are taught to this day as supreme examples of well-executed covert operations, in training programmes of intelligence agencies around the world, from the CIA to the Mossad. And the events live on in history and folklore alike.

SHIVAJI RAJE'S PERSONAL SEAL

Pratipachhandralekheva Vardhishnurvishwawandita.
Shahsunoh Shivsyaisha Mudra Bhadraya Rajate

The seal of Shahaji's son Shivaji glows for the people's benefit.
Like the new moon, the power of this seal will keep growing.
And like the new moon worshipped by the people,
this seal too, will be revered by the people.

Glossary

Vernacular Words used in the Book,
With approximate meanings in English

Barfi	Sweetmeat
Batsurat	Ugly
Bunder	Port or dock
Fateh	Victory
Guptachar	Spy
Ganim	Enemy
Kos	A unit of distance
Kamandalu	A vessel used by ascetics
Kafir	Non-believer
Kabaristan	Cemetery or burial ground
Mithai	Sweetmeat
Mashaal	Flaming torch
Peshwa	A title
Paneer	A soft cheese
Palkhi	Palanquin
Sarai	Inn
Shamiyana	Tent
Tel Bhandar	Oil storehouse
Theka	Contract

Acknowledgements

JUST AS COUNTLESS MAVLAS HELPED Shivaji Raje build his Swarajya, many people helped me in the writing of this book.

First and foremost, I thank my parents Rajeev and Swati, who instilled a love of history in me from childhood, and who were excited participants in my brainstorming sessions for this book as well.

I thank the many Marathi writers who have written extensively on Shivaji, works I grew up reading. Without their influence, this book could not have been written.

I thank Khushboo Joshi of KJoBlogs, who is always one of the first beta-readers of my books. Her inputs are invaluable.

I thank my Commissioning Editor, Chandralekha Maitra, who has always believed in me from the start, helping me to take my works from amateurish drafts to published books.

I thank Malini Nair, for being my first introduction to Leadstart Publishing, which started a life-long journey of writing. I also thank Swarup Nanda and the entire Leadstart Publishing team, for supporting me and helping me bring my writing to a wider audience. I thank the designer for the wonderful cover done for the book, and my dear friend Sheshagoni Tejoguna, for the Maps & Illustrations.

Finally, I thank you, my readers, for your interest in the history of our great country and its hidden treasure troves of stories. With your blessings, I shall remain committed to writing about our country's historical past, and the people who shaped it.

THE LEGEND OF BAHIRJI-NAIK

BOOK II

SEIGE OF PANHALA

MARATHA SWARAJYA, 1665

Surrounded by the Mughals, Raje Shivaji debates his next move. Fort Purandar is under siege by the ruthless Dilerkhan, and the equally devious Mirza Raje Jaysingh. All seems lost.

But such a situation has occurred once before, when Mughal and Adilshahi forces under Siddhi Jauhar surrounded the Swarajya, trapping Raje himself on Fort Panhala. A dangerous plan was concocted but escape could only be attempted under the cover of darkness, right under the noses of the enemy. Discover what happened in that famous escape to Vishalgad, and the ensuing Battle of Umberkhind, that destroyed the Mughal army in one of the greatest examples of guerilla warfare in the world.

Yet again, the *Guptachars* seek to outmaneuver the Mughal Army. But all battles are not fought on the battlefield, and a temporary peace is achieved through shrewd diplomacy in the Treaty of Purandar. By its terms, Raje must travel to Agra to meet Badshah Alamgir Aurangzeb himself. The *Guptachars* have the unenviable task of ensuring his safety to and from the lion's den. Book 2 of *The Legend of Bahirji-Naik* is the story of their greatest achievements and sacrifice.

THE LEGEND OF BAHIRJI-NAIK

BOOK III

ESCAPE FROM AGRA

MARATHA SWARAJYA, 1666

Raje has stepped foot in Agra, accompanied by his firstborn son, to accept the employment offer of Badshah Alamgir Aurangzeb, to fight his enemies in Kandahar. However, seeds of treachery have already been sown. As Raje is put under house arrest in Agra, the wheels begin to move preparing for his escape. It is one of the greatest challenges his *Guptachars* ever face. Operating on enemy soil, devising a way to rescue the most famous prisoner in the city is no easy task. In a place where walls have ears and no one can be trusted, they must find a way to extricate Raje from the clutches of the Mughal Lion. But with thousands of *kos* of enemy territory between Agra and their homeland, the *Guptachars* know that escaping Agra itself will be but the beginning of a long and treacherous journey that will test their skills to their very core and call for great sacrifice.

Book III of *The Legend of Bahirji-Naik* narrates the most famous event of Raje's life, and the most difficult task the *Guptachars* will ever face. If they succeed it will be the highpoint of their lives. If they fail, they will fail not only their King, but the entire populace of the Maratha Swarajya.

Wish To Publish With Us?

We are always keen to look at interesting content across genres. Please email your submission to:
submissions@leadstartcorp.com
and include the following:

1. **Synopsis**

   A summary of the book in 500 - 1000 words.
   Please mention the word count of the manuscript.

2. **Sample chapters / Poetry**

   A couple of chapters from the book; these need not be in order, just send the best two chapters of the book. Or a few poems if the same is a collection of poetry.

3. **A Note About The Author**

   An interesting note about yourself (about 200 words).

4. **Additional Information**

   - Target audience
   - Unique selling proposition
   - List of illustrative content (if any)
   - Other comparative titles
   - Your thoughts on marketing the book